TRUTH TO POWER

by

J. S. Matlin

J & S Publishing Ltd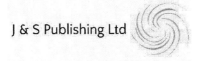

www.jspublishing.biz

ISBN: 978-0-244-19527-4

To Linda
My best friend and critic

To Phil,

Happy reading.

John Matlin is a former City of London solicitor who changed his career in his 50s. He attended Brunel University and Birmingham University, where he earned a Ph.D. in American political history. He taught at Birmingham for a while, and he now gives talks and lectures to numerous groups.

Truth to Power contains an amalgam of the characters and incidents which emerged in John's research for the doctoral thesis. His interest in American politics was aroused in 1960 with the Kennedy campaign. He has remained enthused by American politics and publishes a weekly blog on the American political scene.

John was a founding member of Teenage Cancer Trust, where he was a trustee for more than thirty years. He is married to Linda and they have two married daughters. He is an enthusiastic Tottenham Hotspurs fan, thus enured to disappointment.

Prologue

It was early winter, 1944. The nave of the Church of the Holy Mother, a St. Luke's Catholic Church, was freezing. I was one of the few attendees at Michael Doyle's funeral. Doyle was my contemporary and far too young to die. No Doyle family member was present; just me, my wife and a small scattering of people from the old days.

Where were Doyle's people? The politicians and the judges he championed, controlled and corrupted. Where were the businessmen he assisted and corrupted too. What about the poor and destitute he befriended and helped? Where were the great and good of St. Luke and the rest of our state, not to mention members of the St. Luke Democratic Party, who he had ruled for so long? Where was the public of St. Luke who had doffed their caps and bent a knee to a man whose word was law for so long in this city?

It has been said that politics is a rough trade. Perhaps none came rougher than Michael Doyle, but in all his years at the top, Doyle never forgot a friend and never abandoned anyone in need. Neither did he forget an enemy. He manipulated the levers of political power like no other in our city, before or since. Did he deserve such a barren, lonely end?

I could understand why a man would end his life prematurely when he knew his death was imminent. Doyle drank himself into a lonely, miserable demise. The man had always been a paradox. He could be generous to a fault, yet a more mean-minded man was almost impossible to find. He was an astute, manipulative politician, linking himself to the most corrupt of men. He had wealth a-plenty, more than he could spend in ten lifetimes, yet he squandered it all. He was a man the ladies loved to love, yet in all the years I knew him, he was unable to manage a long-term relationship with any member of the opposite sex.

I watched as the pallbearers from the funeral home carried Doyle's coffin from the church. I followed them to the graveside, where Doyle was lowered into the gray brown earth, next to his mother. I heard the final words uttered by the Catholic priest. Cemetery workers shovelled brown shards of mud onto the pine box. No one cried. There was to be no wake. For Doyle, it was over.

Why did I feel so conflicted? Doyle had done terrible things, both to the city I loved and to my family and me. He'd lied, cheated, stolen and left wreckage wherever he went. But he would have argued that I repaid him in kind. He would have pointed the finger at me and accused me of both damaging his loved ones and ruining him. And he would have reminded me that at the most anguished, terrifying moment of my life, he had helped me, no questions asked, no payment sought.

So, were we even? I didn't know. The few mourners left the graveside. My wife linked her arm in mine and we walked away.

Book One: 1924

The St. Luke Bugle
Established: 1875. 11ᵗʰ April, 1922. Circulation: 274,369.

NEW DEMOCRATS WIN CITY HALL IN A LANDSLIDE
SARGENT MIKE DOYLE AND HIS TEAM
ARE VICTORIOUS

Ed Hanrahan has ruled this city for ten years but today his machine has been destroyed at the polls. After a battle lasting many months, one where no quarter was asked or given, The New Democratic Party, led by Sargent Michael Doyle, won sixteen of the city's twenty-two wards in yesterday's three-party election. As expected, The Republican Party held the Twelfth and Fourteenth Wards. However, the Democrats suffered defeat in all but the Ninth, Tenth, Thirteenth and Sixteenth Wards. Surprisingly, Hanrahan himself, the leader of the Democratic Party, lost the Eighth Ward to the New Democratic candidate, Sargent John Santino.

Mr. Hanrahan refused to grant an interview last night. Instead, a spokesman said that Mr. Hanrahan was dismayed by the outcome of the election and felt sure there had been a massive fraud perpetrated on the Democratic Party and on the electorate by the New Democrats. When asked for details of the allegations, nothing was forthcoming. The election judges said they had neither seen nor heard anything untoward at any of the voting stations.

Large crowds gathered in front of City Hall last night to greet Sargent Doyle and his colleagues. Now the New Democrats hold a large majority of seats on the City Council, it remains to be seen whether the promises they made will be kept. Sargent Doyle made the following statement from the steps of City Hall:

"The people of St. Luke have spoken. They have entrusted the city government to a group of men who are apparently untried and untested in government. However, these same men have been tried and tested, time after time, in Great War battles and were never found wanting. We are both proud and humbled to have been empowered to direct the future of St. Luke by the very people we fought for. We will not let you down.

"Tomorrow, there will be announcements about detailed duties which Councilmen will undertake. Also, we hope soon to announce some new policies, including a revision of property tax and appointment to public office on merit. We want to be a government which restores the city to the people."

Chapter One

At 7:54am on New Year's Day, 1924, *Hiawatha* puffed into St Luke's Union Station. On its own, this was an unremarkable event. However, the train arrived more than fourteen hours late. If you travel in the American Midwest in winter, delays are unavoidable. Well, that was the line taken by the railroad managers. I alighted, found a porter to help me with my two suitcases, which held all my worldly possessions, hopped into a cab and gave the driver the address of the B and B. On arrival, I asked the driver to wait. I ran inside, found my landlady and explained my predicament. Within minutes, my cases were placed in my room. I had a quick wash, changed my clothes and got back into the cab. Looking somewhat disheveled, I arrived at my new workplace with three minutes to spare. I was a new junior reporter at *The St. Luke Bugle.* It would not go down well with the bosses if I arrived late on my first day. I was under sufficient of a cloud as it was.

My name is David Driscoll. I spent the first eighteen years of my life growing up in small towns in the northern Midwest. I was just eighteen when the Great War ended, so I did not serve in the armed forces. In 1919, I entered state college to study journalism and in the fall of 1921, I was accepted as a postgraduate at the Columbia School of Journalism, University of Missouri, where I graduated with a master's degree. I had hopes of joining *The Chicago Herald Tribune* or even the holy of holies, *The New York Times,* but competition was fierce and I failed to "get the gig". Instead, I landed a job with *The St. Louis Star,* where cub reporters cover the law courts and the society news as they learn their trade. In less than a year, I had progressed to report on politics at the state and federal level, not that there was that much of it in those days. This was the era of political bosses who took any public criticism badly.

My time in St. Louis was spent in a way that neither my mother nor Mr. Sam Perkins, my mentor, would have approved. After years of concentrating hard on my studies, I was let loose in a big city with no one to supervise my leisure time. On the law court beat, I became acquainted with a thirty-something court stenographer who took me under her wing, and into her bed. Soon after, I met a middle-aged widow who took a fancy to me. For a while, I juggled my relationship with these two women until I was found out by both of them. What did I care? "Onto the next" was my motto.

The "next" proved to be a secretary of my own age, working at *The Star*. She had illusions of monogamy and marriage. It took her a while to figure out that her dreams had no appeal to me whatsoever. After more brief dalliances with the fairer sex, I met Clarisse Edwards, the wife of *The Star's* editor-in-chief. I knew I was on dangerous ground but the triumph of cuckolding the most powerful man in the building was too hard to resist. Clarisse was probably in her early fifties, but she disguised any wrinkles with make-up and money. Maybe her muscles were not as firm and toned as one would wish but her perfumes and potions were intoxicating and my relative inexperience in bed, not to mention my stamina, was a huge attraction to Clarisse. As her willing pupil, I was educated in her considerable repertoire. What knowledge Clarisse lacked about sex was probably worthless.

One of *The Star's* major advertisers, a manufacturer of household goods, sought me out. He asked me to write some stories about his corporation that would put it and its products in a good light. Taking on such a project was entirely unethical, but as the request came from an advertiser who was also a member of the newspaper's board of directors, and as the offer was spiced with a personal financial incentive, I fell victim to temptation. Everything came to light soon after, when the corporation ran into financial difficulties. *The Star's* editor, John Edwards, demanded the resignation of my corruptor from the newspaper's board. I awaited my fate. I was certain my conduct would not go unpunished.

The same morning, I received a telephone call from Clarisse. "David, my dear," she said in that way of hers that I adored, "I have had the most awful altercation with John. Tempers were not controlled and I'm afraid I let slip our little affair. Much to my disappointment, I regret that our arrangement cannot continue. I fear, too, that you will soon be forced to leave St. Louis. I am sorry for the inconvenience. Dear David, you were scrumptious."

Clarisse put the phone down before I could say a word. Within minutes, I was summoned to the editor's office. Mr. Edwards did not just want to dismiss me, but put me before a firing squad. He ranted, I remonstrated and we negotiated. As the story of his wife's infidelity with almost a juvenile might have become public, making him look a complete fool, he and I reached an agreement. I would keep my ill-gotten gains so long as I left St. Louis immediately without any contact with Clarisse. Mr. Edwards would find suitable employment for me elsewhere.

So it was that in January, 1924, I became a junior reporter with *The St. Luke Bugle,* a newspaper with a Republican leaning and one that enjoyed a nationwide reputation for fair and balanced reporting – the litmus test for all good newspaper titles.

In a way, I suppose I got the job under false pretenses, but I realized that I had behaved stupidly as well as badly and that if I wanted a career in journalism, I needed to mend my ways, at least professionally. So, I agreed to take up the post.

When I left St. Louis, I said goodbye to only a few colleagues. My departure needed to be kept quiet. I consulted Kelly's Directory for St. Luke and reserved a room in an inexpensive B and B, some ten minutes' walk from *The Bugle* building. I packed my few belongings, removed my cash from the bank and headed to Culpepper to spend Christmas with my mother and sister Jane.

The holidays passed without fuss, except for my meetings with Sam Perkins. He did not greet me with his usual effusiveness. Lily Perkins was unwell and this may have been the cause of his distance from me, but I had the distinct impression he was disappointed in me. Perhaps John Edwards had contacted him. The newspaper world was a village in those days. Sam's low-key approach was enough to put me on my guard when I met Henry Brady, the renowned editor of *The Bugle.*

The Bugle building occupied a prominent site in St. Luke's commercial district. In fact, it took up the whole block on the corner of Washington Avenue and Main Street. The six-story City Hall was directly opposite *The Bugle* building. The basement, sub-basement and first floors of *The Bugle* building were used for storage, printing and distribution. Blue collar employees, printers, setters and truck drivers were not permitted access through the main entrance. Their route was to the rear of the building, past the loading bays. White collar employees and members of the public entered the building through its large, impressive double doors and wide marble staircase, up one flight to Reception on the second floor. Behind Reception, the advertising department occupied the remainder of the second floor and all of the third floor. The fourth and fifth floors were for the journalists and editorial teams. Management occupied the top floor. All in all, *The Bugle* employed some 1,500 people in January, 1924.

I arrived at *The Bugle* at 8:57 am. I was told to go to the sixth floor. When I alighted from the elevator, a woman in her later middle age, wearing a smart navy blue suit with a lilywhite blouse, told me in imperious tones that, 'Mr. Brady will see you shortly.' I waited ten minutes or so. The woman reappeared to tell me, 'Mr. Brady will see you now.'

I entered Mr. Brady's office, which was cluttered with books. Papers were strewn everywhere. On his desk were a number of photographs, including one of a glamorous woman whom I took to be Mrs. Brady. Another was of Mr. Brady shaking hands with Calvin Coolidge.

Henry Brady was well preserved for a man in his late fifties. He was handsome, just six feet tall, and he had a full head of silver-gray hair. He cut a splendid figure, made all the more so by his prominent position in St. Luke society. Everyone knew Henry Brady.

"Sit down, Driscoll."

I sat. No good morning, no handshake.

Brady fixed me with a stare. "You're here because I'm doing a friend a favor. I know all about your shenanigans in St. Louis. John Edwards needed you out of town without a fuss, so I've taken you on. I also know Sam Perkins. If it wasn't for Sam, I'd have buried you in the advertising department or in obituaries. And I still might do this anyway. You'll be on the Metro section for now. Sam tells me you have promise, so I'm giving you a chance. But let's be clear, you have one chance only. Don't screw it up."

He pressed a buzzer on his desk; the navy blue-suited woman appeared and escorted me out. "Go down to the fourth floor and ask for Ted Page," she ordered. I looked at her quizzically. "He's the editor of the Metro section," she explained.

8

I needed a minute to catch a breath. How badly was Sam Perkins hurt when he found out about me? What must he think of his protégé? I'd have to work this out another time. Mr. Page was expecting me.

I took the stairs down to the fourth floor. Most of the floor was open plan and noisy. I went to the first desk where a man was hammering on a typewriter.

"Where will I find Mr. Page, please?"

He pointed to a room at the rear of the floor. I walked through the rows of desks where people were typing, talking on the phone and calling for "copy." It was the usual hum and pandemonium of a busy newspaper floor. I felt at home.

I reached Page's room, but the door was closed. Through a glass panel, I could see several people inside, sitting round a large rectangular table. I knocked on the door. Everyone looked up. I felt my face redden. A short, balding man, chewing on the rag end of a cigar, beckoned me in.

"I'm looking for Mr. Page," I said as I opened the door.

"You've found him. Who are you?"

"David Driscoll, sir."

"Ah, you're the new politico writer. This is Mr. Driscoll, formerly of *The St. Louis Star.*" He looked at his colleagues. "This young man comes to us from the big city and he's going to teach us a thing or two about city politics and the like." It was said in a friendly way, and Page's audience laughed. "Okay, David, you might as well sit in on this meeting and listen to what we do here on Metro. There's lots of local news. We'll talk after."

After the meeting ended, Mr. Page took me to his private office. It was cramped, but it had a splendid view of City Hall.

"Welcome to St. Luke," said Ted Page, offering his hand.

I shook it. "Thank you, sir."

"I'm not 'sir', I'm Ted."

"Okay, sir, Ted."

"Now, I'll be open with you," said Page. "Henry has told me about you. I know what's happened in St. Louis. But I have read some of your work and I see promise. Keep your nose clean and we'll get along just fine."

I blushed for the second time that morning. "I don't know what to say, Ted. I made mistakes. I'm really embarrassed. But I am what I

9

am. From now on, I'll just steer away from editors' wives and pushy advertisers."

"I'm not your mother, David. You're a grown man and you have to take responsibility for what you do, just like everyone else. I'm more interested in what you can add to the Metro section of this newspaper. We cover everything in the life of St. Luke. Now, what do you know about St. Luke politics?"

"Not much. Between being told I was coming here and now was just two days. I had no time to learn. I gather there was a change of administration in 1922 but I don't know anything about the people involved. At *The Star,* I was being grounded in state and federal politics and their effect on St. Louis. St. Luke didn't appear on the horizon."

"So, what do you know?"

"I know this state is one of those oddities in America. The capital city, Cameron, is small and has a migrant political population. It's in the center of the state and its business is government and pretty well nothing else. There are two large cities in this state. At the western boundary is Paxton. Its economy is based on ranching and farming. According to the 1920 census, its population is some 270,000. Here in the East, St. Luke is becoming an industrial base of considerable importance nationwide. It embraces new technologies and its population has doubled to 400,000 over the past twenty years and shows no sign of stopping. I also know there will be city elections this year."

"That's splendid, young man." This was said with irony. "Now, apart from reading out entries from a guide book, what else do you know about St. Luke's politics? Do you know the city has a new charter? You do know what a charter is?"

"Sure, it's the rules of government for a city, a bit like the Constitution."

"That's right. The Founding Fathers sorted out the federal rules but nothing for the States or cities and towns, so cities and large towns now have rights of self-rule under charters. You could call it democracy in action. And while we're talking, what do you know about muckrakers?"

"Muckrakers? Only what I learned in my time with the *Culpepper Post* and at college, Mr. Page. I used to read M*cClure's.*"

10

"It's Ted. So you'll know that the art of digging up the dirt is dying if not dead but we at *The Bugle* are not averse to a little muckraking. Who was your favorite muckraker?"

"I guess most people would go for Lincoln Steffens but I thought Marie Van Vorst was amazing. She was so brave, especially writing that story exposing the dangerous lives of working women. She took a job in a shoe shop, risking her life by working with poison in the shoe dye, just so she could get a story."

"Let me get to the point, David. There's something odd going on in St. Luke city politics right now, and it seems you don't know anything about it. We're used to machine government here, and the corruption that goes with it. Two years ago, Ed Hanrahan's Democratic machine got kicked out of City Hall. A bunch of youngsters, all veterans of the Great War and calling themselves New Democrats, won the 1922 election. Amazingly, they're doing a proper job of city government. There is not a whiff of corruption. The thing is, we don't know how they are doing it. In politics, so much is done behind closed doors and *The Bugle* is not exactly a friend of the Democrats, old or new."

"Sorry. What do you mean by a proper job?"

"The City is hiring people on merit, reducing property taxes, providing good services, balancing the books and not taking any vig."

"Vig?"

"Vigorish. You know the expression?"

A memory from my childhood came flooding back. "You mean a special payment?"

"Yeah, you could call it that. Actually, it's an illegal payment. You'd know about stuff like that." He winked at me.

I looked down. "Ted, just how many people here know about my past in St. Louis?"

"Only Henry and me and if you do your job properly and keep out of mischief, nobody else will find out. Now, I think a good way of getting yourself immersed in St. Luke politics would be for you to research the political goings-on for the past three years, look at how Mike Doyle's New Democrats beat the Hanrahan outfit. See what you can make of the new city charter business. I'll give you a week. I want five hundred words on my desk next Tuesday."

The name "Mike Doyle" rang in my head.

11

Ted looked at me closely. "Doyle, do you know him? You seemed interested in the name. Here's his picture."

Ted showed me the morning paper. On the front page, Doyle was pictured on the steps of City Hall, welcoming the New Year. It had been fourteen years since we last met, but I immediately recognized my boyhood friend. I gave Ted a non-committal shrug.

"Never reveal anything until you are certain of your facts" had been drummed into me as a journalism student.

I stuttered, "The assignment, I'll do my best."

"Here at *The Bugle*, doing your best is not optional. You always do your best. Now, let's find you a desk and get you started. I've got a few minutes. I'll give you the ten cent tour of the building."

The tour was pure brevity. Ted would say, "Here is the fifth floor, we do such and such here." I asked where I could do research. "Back issues are on the third floor, so is the library."

We finished the tour in just over twenty minutes. I was shown to a desk some twenty yards from Ted's office. I dealt with the boilerplate paperwork for my new employment, then headed straight for the back issues, where I spent the rest of the day. I decided to start with 1918, and quickly learned that the Democrats had been in charge of St. Luke and its politics for decades. Their leader, Ed Hanrahan, took power in 1912. He started well, as many leaders do, but his regime became corrupt all too quickly. However, there were insufficient numbers of Republican voters in St. Luke to unseat the Democrats.

In early 1922, the back issues became fascinating. Over the space of a few weeks, a group of disaffected voters, all war veterans and calling themselves the New Democrats, published their proposals for clean city government. Their leader, Michael Doyle, was a war hero. His uncle, Joe Doyle, was a well-known character in St. Luke politics but Joe's power had waned as Hanrahan's had soared.

I saw photographs of the New Democrat leadership. Michael Doyle was unmistakable. Small features, heavy eyebrows and narrow eyes. This was undoubtedly the older version of the boy who I met at morning recess on my first day at grade school.

I was playing marbles on my own when a boy, two heads taller than me and several pounds heavier, scooped up my marbles in his large hands and walked away.

"Hey," I yelled at him, "give them back."

"Make me," was his response.

Before I could reply, a scrawny boy, shorter than me and of smaller frame placed himself front and center before the bully with clenched fists.

"They're not yours and I'm givin' you one chance to give 'em back," he told the bully.

The bully laughed at him and uttered his standard, "Make me," reply.

The small boy said, "Your funeral," and, without hesitation, feigned a left hook. The bully laughed as he leant to his left to miss the punch. I didn't see what happened next clearly, it was too quick, but the expression on the bully's face told me that a hard kick was causing him to suffer excruciating pain. He lowered his hands towards his privates and flopped onto his knees on the concrete ground, moaning loudly.

The scrawny boy rifled the bully's pockets and extracted the marbles along with some coins. He placed the coins in his trouser pocket. He put the marbles on the floor and removed the two best, my favorites, for himself, returning the rest to me.

"Okay," he stated. It wasn't a question.

I nodded, too dumbfounded to say anything else. He saw me looking at his pocket where he had placed the coins.

"Vigorish. You understand," he said. Again, it wasn't a question.

I nodded for the second time, but didn't understand at all. My six years of life had already taught me that I lived in an unequal world and that the biggest and the strongest were not always the winners. Whoever the scrawny boy was, he had a code to live by, one where smart thinking received reward and profit.

He offered me his right hand. "Michael Doyle." I shook the hand and muttered, "David Driscoll." We heard a harrumph from behind. Without a pause, Doyle turned and kicked the bully hard in the stomach, saying, "Stay there till we're gone, if you know what's good for you." In the near distance a bell rang.

"Time for Addin'," Doyle smiled, pleased with his morning's activity and off he trotted, the spoils of the playground in his pocket.

I made myself concentrate on *The Bugle* back issues. Ed Hanrahan was an old-style, crooked boss. Since 1922, the new Boss, Mike Doyle, changed things and his administration appeared to be squeaky clean. Hanrahan had done some bad things, but he never got close to organized crime. He got involved in insider dealing but that wasn't a crime, at least not in this state. He taxed people pretty high but tax-payers got the services. I got the impression that Hanrahan became lazy and over-confident. He didn't think he could be challenged at the polls, let alone be beaten and he forgot to look after people enough, especially poor people, who loved the appeal of a war hero.

The St. Luke Bugle
Established: 1875. 10th April, 1922. Circulation: 286,342

WAR HERO WINS ELECTION

After decades of Democratic Party rule, St. Luke now has a new council leader from a new party – Michael Doyle's New Democratic Party was only established last year with the support of a number of St. Luke's brave war veterans, of whom we are all very proud. These men want to see changes made in the way our city is run. As Doyle himself said, "The political leaders of this city have grown lazy and sloppy. The fat cats in City Hall and the businessmen who support Hanrahan and his cronies have lost touch with the man on the street, as well as the men who fought in the Great War. Something needs to be done for a fairer society for all of us."

Mr. Doyle has promised great things for the poor including improved housing and assistance in finding work. This seems something close to his heart as he was brought up in The Trench, one of the poorest wards of St Luke, by his widowed mother. His uncle, Alderman Joe Doyle, encouraged Michael Doyle to care for the worst off in our society and Michael Doyle clearly has not forgotten his roots. He has offered a lifeline to many who are starting life much like he did: poor and in The Trench.

But where the money for all these new and impressive sounding services is going to come from remains to be seen. This newspaper will be vigilant and will closely watch Mr. Doyle and his administration.

Doyle's administration was off to a successful start, but something looked too good to be true; politicians could not be trusted. Taxes were down and services were up, but I wanted to know how he had balanced the books. I wondered what the new charter said about scrutinizing public accounts. I was also curious to find out what had happened to Doyle in the past fourteen years. After all, for four years, we had been the closest of friends. I had to accomplish two things: to complete a complicated assignment in one week and to make contact with Michael Doyle.

Chapter Two

Early morning, one week after joining *The Bugle,* I sat outside Ted Page's office. He arrived, tore off his overcoat and jacket and stared at me.

"What?"

"Here's the assignment you asked for," I said.

"Never see me before I've had coffee," he growled. "Let me look at it while someone gets me a hot drink," he shouted. "There are two things I dislike: freezing cold mornings and cub reporters. Come in."

A secretary delivered coffee as Page started to read.

The New City Charter
By David Driscoll

Next month, we will experience the first test of our new city charter. St. Luke is not the first city in America to experiment with local democracy, nor will it be the last. It is refreshing that the citizens of St. Luke are willing to try new, modern government methods and find out what works best for them.

The old charter was fit for purpose when our city was smaller. Currently, the charter appoints its representatives ward by ward. There are no aldermen who look at the problems of St. Luke as a whole. There is no individual who has responsibility for the day-to-day management of the city's business. This, say the New Democrats, needs to be changed.

However, it has been said with good reason that political change is the slow boring of hard boards.

Changes to citizens' political rights need deep thought and thorough questioning. Without wanting to criticize the St. Luke administration for its innovative methods, has the new charter has been introduced too quickly? Have the voters of St. Luke been offered a proper chance to consider and deliberate the pros and cons of its terms?

For example, take the case of the councilmen at-large, the men who will soon sit on the City Council and rule our city. These candidates will be revealed later this week. Councilmen were voted for ward by ward and were well-known by local voters. This will no longer be the case. The election of each councilman-at-large will be citywide. How will the voters know these men?

Bugle reporters have spoken to several registered New Democratic Party supporters, who seemed troubled when the point was put to them. One, who wished to remain anonymous, said, "*I want to know who I'm voting for. I want to know who the man is that I can turn to for help when I have trouble. Under the new system, I won't know my local guy, so I might as well go straight to City Hall. What use is that? That wasn't the way it was meant to be.*"

Although streamlining the management of the city could be beneficial, there are other potential problems with the new charter: who will be the City Manager and how will he be accountable to voters if things go wrong? If city accounts aren't to be published on a timely basis, how will the voters know what the books look like?

Interestingly, none of the senior employees at City Hall were willing to be interviewed about the new charter and one of them hinted that there was a gag order imposed by the executive. What is the executive worried about? Is there a hidden agenda?

We also interviewed members of the council. We asked why our charter is so much more complicated than that of other cities. We were told that these matters are under consideration. There is only so much change the voters will accept.

Ed Hanrahan of the Democratic Party said, "We are standing in this election to return St. Luke to the people. We want the people to know that *we*, not those impostors sitting in City Hall, are the real Democratic Party. We were opposed to the new charter because it has taken power away from the people and when we get back in, we'll seek to reverse these changes."

Michael Doyle, the leader of the New Democratic Party, was asked to comment, but he declined to add any further details to the plans. He said, "The New Democrats will do their talking at the appropriate time and in the right manner. We'll be running on our record of the past two years: taxes down, jobs up, patronage used in the right way to assist deserving people; not even a hint of corruption. Compare this to Hanrahan's record."

St. Luke will have a three-way fight this April. The Republicans, the Democrats and the New Democrats must resolve who will stand for election. This will be decided in the primaries. Afterwards, the candidates will come out slugging.

This newspaper will be at ringside. One thing is certain: without strong refereeing, expect some low blows.

Page finished reading, looked up and said, "Sit there, I'm going to read this again." After a few minutes, he stared at me. "First, I asked for 500 words, you've given me more than 750. Second, you need to make the writing snappier. Third, you've mixed up editorial and reporting. I don't want your views on the new charter and the elections. I want to know what the people and the politicians are saying and thinking. Is this a direct quote from Doyle?"

"Sort of," I replied. "It came in a cable. I didn't interview him."

"You need to make this clear. And you need to think some more about what happens in a three-way fight. Sorry, I can't use this piece as it is."

I couldn't help showing my disappointment. I had worked really hard on the article. I stared back into Page's eyes, not knowing what to say.

"However," continued Page, "I'll work on it with you. It has the makings of an interesting story. David, you got yourself up to speed very quickly. I gave you a tough brief. I wanted to see how you would cope. Now, I want you to work out how you think the February primaries and April elections should be reported. Try to give the coverage a new angle. Maybe we'll include you in the team to cover the whole story. No promises, but it would be good experience for you. You'll have time to interview the politicians and get some new stories. Get back to me by the end of the week."

Outside, I breathed a sigh of relief. Back at my desk, I picked up the telephone and asked the operator to get me City Hall. When I was connected, I asked for Mr. Doyle's office. A woman answered. "Is Mr. Doyle in today?" I asked.

"May I enquire who is calling?" she replied.

"Sure, tell him Books from Rawlings wants to talk to Irish about the Marbles Maulin'."

In the unimaginative way of boys, my nickname was "Books" for my love of reading and he was "Irish". Irish told me he wanted to be called Doyle by all except for his closest friends who were allowed to call him Irish or Mike. The only people who called him Michael back then were Mary, his mother, Father Graham, the Catholic priest, and our teacher, Miss King.

"Pardon?" was the response.

I repeated my message. Within seconds, a voice I didn't recognize came on the phone.

"That's never scrawny Books Driscoll?"

"The very same," I replied. "And I assume this is Irish Mike Doyle."

"Good grief, how are you and where are you?"

"I'm fine, thank you and I'm only over the road. Want to meet?"

"Yeah, get over here. I'll free myself up."

19

Doyle and I had history. We were both of immigrant stock. His family had made it from Ireland, mine from England. We all ended up in Rawlings, a mining town owned by the Allied Tin and Metal Corporation. Thankfully, my grandfather had scraped together sufficient money to put my father through grade school and high school. Then my father worked his way through community college to qualify as an accountant, so while my father was manager of the accounts department, Doyle's was working down in the mine.

I was the eldest child in my family; Doyle was the youngest in his. I had book learning, whereas he had native cunning. Doyle knew the dives of Rawlings and its more enticing and dangerous countryside. What we had in common was a sense that boys needed to have adventures. We became firm friends and soon the bully and everyone else in the class regarded us as worthy of respect.

For four years, Doyle and I enjoyed a childhood in a harsh land. Then, when Doyle was ten, his father died in a mining accident. In my time in Rawlings, the mine had enjoyed an almost perfect safety record. There had been the occasional broken bone, but nothing major and certainly nowhere near as serious as a major tunnel collapse. So the haunting moan of the mine's siren, announcing to the town that something was amiss, was new to me. By the time I arrived at the mine head, I saw many faces I knew, but they looked different – those faces were now screwed up, skin gray with anxiety. Some had tears running down their cheeks and all looked worried to death. The rescue took almost two days. By the time the rescuers had cleared their way to the scene of the accident, thirty-two men had died and fifteen more were mortally injured.

William Doyle was one of those injured beyond hope. He held onto life for ten days. I spent much of that time with Doyle. The school was closed, so we stayed by the makeshift hospital where Doyle's father lay stricken. I don't remember much conversation. Doyle sat silent most of the time. I had known him to be serious on occasion but never uncommunicative. He did not complain, let alone wail, like others around us. He refused solace from Father Graham. He even shrugged off Miss King's efforts to comfort him.

On the sixth day after the accident, Doyle said, "I wish he would just die." I looked at him aghast. He continued with a shrug of his shoulders. "It's no use, he's going to die. Why drag it out? He's in such pain." Later he said, "I must look after my mother."

I replied, "Of course, I'll walk home with you."

He sighed. "I don't mean now, afterwards, when it's over. My brothers won't be up to it."

Later, I discovered he had taken it on himself to write to relatives in St. Luke and secure accommodation there for the family. For a month after the accident, the mine was closed. It seemed like we attended one or two funerals every day. I have never known anything like it in my life, before or since.

Two weeks after William Doyle's funeral, the Doyle family left Rawlings. Doyle gave me no forwarding address. He promised he would write when he got settled in St. Luke. But he never did and, like most ten year olds, I soon found other friends and forgot about Doyle. Now, more than a decade later, we were to meet again.

I was shown into Doyle's office in City Hall. "Nice work if you can get it," I grinned as I walked over to Doyle and shook his hand. His handshake was firm. He stared into my eyes.

"Take the weight off, Books. Sit here. I can't believe it. How many years has it been?"

"Thirteen, maybe fourteen, Irish."

"The Marbles Maulin'. That was somethin'. Bet you didn't know how scared I was. If my kick had missed, I was mincemeat."

We laughed.

"Let me look at you, Mike. You look good. I've been reading lots about you. You've done really well."

"I've done okay. Sorry, I don't know anythin' about you. Why are you here? What are you doin' these days? Fill me in."

I needed to gloss over my current employment. If I told Doyle I was a reporter, the meeting might end very quickly. "I'm in the newspaper business. I got to town a few days ago and saw your picture and name in the paper. You've changed a bit but haven't we all."

"Newspapers, eh? Should I be on my guard? You guys in the press ain't always kind to politicians, tellin' untrue stories about us and all that." I could tell he was being serious, but there was no menace in his tone.

"That's pots and kettles, Mike. Are you saying that politicians always tell the truth?"

21

"You've got me there," he smiled. "Hey, let's talk over old times."

We seemed to shrug off the missing years and resume our friendship as if the time had merely been days. Interestingly, Doyle also glossed over his past, omitting any mention of his bravery in the Great War. I knew from the stories in the St. Luke papers he had been highly decorated.

But I couldn't kid myself. Mike was now an important city politician and growing into a successful head of a city administration. Who was I, just a fledgling reporter trying to recover from disgrace?

As we talked, I got the impression that Mike was older than his years. True, he looked like a version of the boy I knew and still spoke staccato fashion, using short declamatory sentences as he used to do in the old days. When we were boys, he was usually the leader. I was often the follower as we got into all kinds of scrapes. However, it wasn't all one way.

"What are you smiling at?" Mike asked.

"I was thinking of Halloween in Rawlings. I seem to recall we earned quite a lot of notoriety for the tricks we got up to."

"Your tricks, you mean. You had a veritable armory. What you did with soapy water and raw eggs had to be seen to be believed. And who was it that often refused a treat in order to inflict a trick? You got me into a lot of trouble, Mr. Driscoll. Do you remember those little devil costumes your mother made for us? They fitted to perfection in more ways than one. Good job we could both run. I lost count of people chasing me, wielding a broom. And it was always your fault!"

Doyle laughed and checked his watch. "Like some lunch?" he asked. "They do great corn beef sandwiches over the road. I can order in. Or shall we go over there? Whatever you like?"

I decided that I didn't want to be seen in public just yet with St. Luke's political leader. I didn't want anyone from *The Bugle* to realize that we knew each other, at least not for a while. And with what I had in mind, a conversation in a public place might not prove a sensible idea.

"Let's order in. Corn beef is fine with me. Pity we can't have a beer with it."

"I don't keep any booze here. Even this room is public in a way. Prohibition is a pain. Next time, let's meet at my place on Main Street. You'll get a beer there."

He called an aide on his intercom, "Would you order some corn beef sandwiches, mustard, pickles and all the trimmin's? And cancel anythin' I've got for the afternoon."

"Okay, boss," came the answer.

Doyle moved to the drinks cabinet where he fixed us both a soft drink. "What about your family news, David? How is everyone?"

"My father died a few years after the mining accident. Mom went back to teaching and she lives in Culpepper with my sister. They are both doing well. Janey's at college now and is quite the musician. She's a pianist."

"I'm sorry to hear about your dad. What happened?"

I told Mike about my father's death, deciding to hide nothing. "My father was badly affected by the mining accident. A taciturn man at the best of times, I hardly heard him utter a word for weeks and if he did, it was to reproach my mother, my sister or me for some trivial indiscretion. My mother, Elizabeth, remained stoic. Her Protestant English ancestry gave her this characteristic. My father took to the bottle when he came home, a new departure for him. I suppose he felt himself in some way to blame for what had happened."

"If anyone was to blame, it was Allied. They refused to invest in safety. What more could your father have done?"

"Well, the accident and his assumption of blame set him off. I thought I should tell you. He felt guilty for not insisting on more safety checks. Eventually, he asked Allied for a new position within the company, somewhere away from Rawlings. He persuaded the bosses it would help the town's healing process if there were new executives at the Rawlings mine. With the knowledge I now have about business, I doubt that Allied would have cared. However, there was an opening in an Allied mine in the adjoining state, so I said goodbye to Miss King and my classmates and took a three hundred and fifty mile car trip north east with my family in our Ford motor car on barely made up roads. Such a pleasure!"

"I had no idea about this. What was it like in Culpepper?"

"One thing you can say about the northern Midwest, it is consistent in both weather and countryside. I settled okay in my new school and got a job as a delivery boy for the local newspaper. I realized even then that the newspaper world would be the one for me."

Mike returned with drinks. "How did you get started in newspapers?"

"In a word, Sam Perkins, well two words."

Doyle laughed. "Explain."

So I brought Doyle up to date. *The Culpepper Post* was published twice weekly in those days. Typical for local papers, it was usually four pages long. The front page covered important events in the town and the state. Page two was a diary of federal and international news, coupled with society goings-on and the like. The third page contained editorials either written by the editor or syndicated from other newspapers within the state and around the country. The back page was for advertisements and the funny papers.

Sam Perkins was the editor, but he was also the publisher, setter, printer and even the office and delivery boy if I was not around. Mr. Perkins was a newspaper man through and through. He didn't stand on ceremony. He had spent his formative years on the West Coast, learning his trade in San Francisco but he met a Culpepper girl, Lily, married her and moved east. Culpepper then had no newspaper and Sam's father-in-law helped finance *The Post* to get it on its feet. Thirty-five years later, the newspaper was going strong with a circulation of some 5,000.

Mr. Perkins – I still cannot refer to him as "Sam" – was a fervent believer in the independence of a free press. He was short, maybe five feet four, chunky build, with a mustache and a large bald spot atop his head. If you had cut him open, I believe you would have found the First Amendment to the Constitution printed on his heart. He would often quote Thomas Jefferson to me. "David", he would say, "never forget the words of Mr. Jefferson: 'Our liberty cannot be guarded but by the freedom of the press, nor be limited without danger of losing it.'"

"So, Mr. Perkins was a kind of mentor, a bit like my Uncle Joe. Mind you, Joe taught me the harsh realities of life in this city: how to cope, how to relate to people, that kind of thing.

"I guess there is a comparison. Anyway, within weeks of starting as a paper boy, Mr. Perkins began to teach me the rudiments of the business. He showed me the fiddly task of setting the characters for the press. My mother looked so shocked the first time I came home after setting the print. Black ink was everywhere, all over my clothes

24

and me. Gradually, I became more proficient and took the precaution of cleaning myself up before I arrived home, with the help of Lily Perkins. She and Sam wanted children but Lily was barren, so over the years, I guess they looked on me as the son they didn't have.

"On the days when *The Post* was not published, Mr. Perkins would consider what he would publish. He taught me the journalist's mantra: 'Who, what, when, where, why and how is what you have to write,' he would impress on me. 'The cat sat on the mat.' is fine as an English sentence, he said, 'but it ain't news. Readers want to know when the cat was sitting, where the mat was, who the cat was sitting with and why the cat sat there'. Mr. Perkins also taught me about writing editorials, to be honest and fair, and to write both sides."

"So, you're a reporter. Now I'm worried." This was not said in jest.

"Don't be. Anything you tell me here is off the record. I wouldn't use it. This right here is just two old friends meeting up after a long time."

Doyle still looked a little uncomfortable, so I ploughed on. "Time at school and *The Post* was sweet. Time at home was bitter. My father, an introvert at the best of times, grew further into his shell. His habit of consuming a bottle of gin over several days moved to a bottle a day. Quite how he kept his drinking habit from his colleagues, I don't know. He was neither a violent drunk, nor a happy drunk, nor an emotional drunk, just a drunk. My mother remained stoic. Nowadays, she would probably have taken her children and left the marriage but she just did her best to protect Jane and me from the unhappiness.

"Finally, when I was fourteen, my father died. The doctor said it was a heart attack, but I knew better. My mother needed to earn some dollars to supplement what little my father had left her. He had drunk so much of our money away. So she started teaching young ones and slowly, smiles appeared again on her lovely face. She was hardly all sweetness and light. She had suffered too much from a bad marriage, but she found a kind of happiness in the molding of young minds and the achievements of her own children. She encouraged my ambitions for journalism."

"So while I was out fighting in the Great War, you were writing for a paper?"

"When I was twenty-one, I left for Columbia, Missouri and graduate school. I had been too young, officially, to join up for the

Great War and, anyway, I was determined to follow my dreams of a career in journalism, fighting for good over evil, for right against wrong, to expose the ills of society and to keep the public informed." Doyle gave me a wry smile. "Well, I was very young and if you cannot have ideals then, when can you?" I asked.

"So here you are, a reporter, right here in St. Luke?"

"Yes, and now you know everything. But what about you Mike? What happened to your family after you left? I often wondered about you. People used to ask if I had any news."

"Well my Ma was in a state after my Da's death. Uncle Joe, put us up and looked after us – thank God. He had already done quite well for himself by the time we came, he owned The Donegal Tavern in The Trench. It's St. Luke's home to the poor Irish and Italian communities of the city, as well as migrant workers, gamblers and prostitutes."

"Sounds lovely?"

"Yeah that's what Ma thought, but he helped us out when we were in trouble, what could she say?"

"But Joseph Doyle wasn't just an Irish publican?"

"Well, aside from his pub he had a nice thing going supplying liquor to a number of saloons in The Trench and elsewhere in St. Luke. He also ran a courier service for businessmen, both within the city and the county. And he owned a number of buildings in The Trench and downtown St. Luke."

"But what about politics?"

"He was a popular Democratic politician and a six -term alderman for St. Luke's First Ward, which included The Trench."

"Can you tell me stories about how he used his position as First Ward Alderman to great advantage, securing all manner of city contracts and jobs?"

At this Doyle gave me a wry smile.

"Why not? It's what politicians do and he didn't just help the rich. A lot of poor people benefited from his actions. Anyway, Uncle Joe had no children so he saw the potential for a successor in me and my brothers. Only it didn't take long for him to realize my brothers were no-hopers – they're just the same by the way, forever causing me trouble. I hardly see them anymore. Joe did find low-level jobs for them, but they couldn't stick the jobs –you know what they're like. Ma didn't work so it was left to me to bring the money in."

I didn't want say anything, but I had noticed Doyle's brother's names cropping up in the back issues for minor thefts and disturbances.

"So, how old were you when you started learning the ropes?"

"I started pretty much as soon as I got here, but I left school at thirteen."

"And what did your Ma have to say about that?"

"God, you know her too well. You can imagine! But when Joe spun her a line about getting me a job at his courier company, she softened."

I laughed, "But what were you really doing?"

"Well I did actually deliver a package or two."

"Quit fooling me, I'm not your Ma." We were laughing like we had done as children.

"Okay, I know when I'm beat. Joe spent about a year teaching me the rudiments of life as a businessman and a politician. I was a fast learner. I was soon persuading saloon owners to choose Joe to supply the hooch, indicating that things would go well for them with Alderman Joe Doyle if more business were put his way and implying that things could go ill if the overture was ignored. It was also my job to collect unpaid debts."

"Jesus, I can't imagine a scrawny teenager going in and speaking to men like that?"

"Yeah, I know it sounds strange, but I did it, and it worked – every time. One time I went round to a tavern called Molloy's. Poor Molloy owed around $450. Ryan Molloy stood five feet eight inches tall and pretty well the same size wide. I think I'll always remember him. He was unshaven, surly and uncommunicative. He sold booze to the men of the Trench, didn't welcome women in his place, whether serving or drinking, and provided no entertainment whatsoever. For him and his customers, life was something to get through. So when I stroll in, all four-foot nothing, asking for $450 he refuses to pay up, complaining that Doyle'd been watering down his liquor. I left him in no doubt what could happen to him if Joe cut off his supply and revoked his license. He gave it all the talk, but a few days later he stopped me in the street with a bag full of cash, $500 in five and one dollar bills. Joe

27

just put the money in his safe. He said nothin' about the extra fifty bucks."

"What a powerful little tyke you were."

"I wasn't just running errands, I also learned the local politicians' trade from precinct captains and ward heelers alike. We would find out which families needed help the most desperately and then Joe would hand out everything – from jobs to food. He's a great man and he taught me never to forget where you come from."

"A valuable lesson," I agreed. "How's your Ma doing?"

"She's not aged well. She's got religion in a serious way and doesn't really approve of my political career but Adele, thinks I'm the bee's knees. She's in town at the moment. And she will be so pleased to hear you're around. Did you know, all those years ago she had a crush on you?"

"You're kidding," I answered, hardly remembering Doyle's twin sister.

There was a knock on the door. The aide appeared with a tray of sandwiches, pickles, potato salad and a pot of coffee. "Anything else you want, boss?" he asked.

"No, that's fine, Gerry, thanks."

Over sandwiches, we started to talk politics but Doyle returned to the topic of his father's death. "Maybe one of these days, the guys at Cameron, or even in DC, will look at corporate responsibility. Well DC certainly won't, not with the present Congress. And Coolidge is a real do-nothin'."

"Forget federal at the moment," I replied. "The state's a better bet but sadly not until there are more big accidents. Corporations can move profits and factories from state to state as well as closing mines and the guys at Cameron, as you call them, won't want to lose taxes or jobs."

"My, my, Books, what makes you so politically savvy?"

Suddenly, butterflies started to fly in my stomach. 'Hold your nerve,' I told myself.

"Irish, I need to explain something. I started at *The Bugle* last week. I'm working in the Metro section and my brief is city politics."

Doyle gave me an old fashioned look. "So, this isn't a social call? At least you work for the best title in the state. Okay, what do you want from me?"

28

"I was really pleased to see you had made it here, big time," I replied quickly. "I can see an opportunity for both of us. This is my chance for some vigorish!"

Doyle chortled. "Good to know I taught you somethin'. I'd have preferred it if you came clean about your job at the outset. Let's finish lunch and then we'll talk your newspaper business. If I've learned anythin' in politics, it's always be willin' to listen."

"Mike, maybe I should have told you about my job when we first said hello but I was so pleased to see you were here. I remembered the old days. I wanted to find out about you and what happened in those fourteen years. We were close friends way back. I repeat my promise: everything you've told me and tell me will be off the record."

Doyle seemed to relax a bit. For a while we talked business and sports. He referred to, "the goings-on in Wall Street," a subject on which I confessed virtual ignorance, while he seemed particularly knowledgeable. Gerry, the aide, entered and cleared away the lunch things.

Doyle said, "Let's not talk your business here. I'd like to show you my town."

"Gerry," he called through the intercom, "Get the car ready. I'm drivin'."

We left the building a few minutes later. I half expected a Cadillac to be waiting for us but a Buick was parked outside City Hall, guarded by Gerry. "Will you want me later, boss?" he asked.

"I'll call you. Get in Books."

I was a stranger in town but Doyle wanted to show me the places that mattered to him. We headed south, away from the center of town. Very quickly, commercial buildings gave way to residential, the poorer variety. Soon, I was in the boondocks.

We drove past the school Doyle attended when he first came to St. Luke.

"I didn't stay there long," he pointed out. "I wasn't suited to school life and my uncle Joe knew this. By the time I was thirteen, formal school was over for me."

I looked out the window. I saw nothing but old tenements, shabby stores and saloons and dirty and dusty streets.

"Welcome to The Trench," said Doyle. "This is where I started in St. Luke. It's where the poor live. We have saloons and places of the night here to take the skin off your eyes." He pointed to a rundown tenement block. "That's where the family lived when we came here. We stayed there until I left for the army. My uncle Joe moved my family into better housin' soon after."

Doyle drove further out of the city into tree-lined streets and attractive suburban homes. After some fifteen minutes, he stopped. I looked at a clapboard house, painted a creamy yellow. "This is our hacienda now. I live here with my mother and Adele, when she's home. Let's go in."

Doyle led the way through the front door into a large room that served as the hall, parlor and dining room. "This is called open plan. I like it. No secrets. Hi, Ma, I'm home. And I have a visitor."

A flustered Mrs. Doyle came out of the kitchen. "Michael, you're home so early. Is anything wrong?" I was shocked by her appearance. She was now an old woman, her face crumpled inward, not the sweet, pretty person I remembered from all those years ago.

"Hello, Mrs. Doyle," I said, "how nice to see you."

She looked at her son as if to say, "Who is this?"

Mike said softly, "Do you remember my friend from Rawlings? Way back. It's David Driscoll."

"David Driscoll," she murmured, then again, "David Driscoll." Slowly her memory returned and a broad smile crossed her face. Suddenly, there was a semblance of the Mrs. Doyle I remembered. "David," she said, "let me look at you! I'd never have recognized you. How are you and how are your parents?"

The three of us sat in the parlor and I gave Mrs. Doyle the edited version of the past fourteen years. After a few minutes, Mrs. Doyle looked at her son. "Where are our manners? David, would you like some coffee?"

Mrs. Doyle went into the kitchen and soon emerged with a tray, cups, saucers and plates, a pot of coffee, creamer, sugar and cookies. She handed a cup to me and then to Doyle. After we chatted for a while, I noticed that Mrs. Doyle became quiet and remote.

"I'll take her up for a nap," Doyle said glancing at his mother. He lifted her gently from her chair and carried her upstairs.

When he came down, he took the coffee things into the kitchen and left them. "Let's get out of here. I could do with a drink. You?"

Back in the car, it was dark. Doyle looked at me. "Thank you. It's good to see Ma as her old self, if only for a few minutes. She won't remember today, you know. Somethin' has happened to her mind. The doctors don't know what it is. She just forgets. She's not a danger to herself, thank heavens, but it won't be long before I'll have to move her into a home."

"Don't your brothers and Adele help?"

"I don't talk about my brothers. I have nothin' to do with them. I avoid them when they're in town. Adele helps but she has her own life on the West Coast. She lives in Los Angeles most of the time. I try gettin' help in but Ma terrorizes them! You got the good side today. I'd have a drink at home but Ma won't allow hooch in the house."

"Okay, where to now?"

"I think a bit more sight-seeing, and we'll get a proper drink. I assume you're a wet? Prohibition! What a ridiculous law."

"Prohibition is a hopeless failure. The trouble is the Republicans who introduced it are still in power. It would take a different government to make the changes the voters want."

Doyle talked more about growing up in St. Luke. "I won't forget my thirteenth birthday. Ma had baked a cake specially but my brothers were nowhere to be seen and Adele was in one of her moods. So I took off and went to work."

"Doesn't sound like much of a birthday."

"Well, it wasn't until Nora and Judy, two of the Tavern waitresses, came over to my table. Neither woman was in the first flush of youth, nor the second for that matter, but each was attractive in her own way. Nora was a buxom blonde, Judy a slim brunette with a smile that revealed two lost teeth, courtesy of a dissatisfied customer. They were ladies of the night as well as waitresses, you see."

"I think I see where you are going with this," I laughed.

"Nora told me that they had a birthday present for me and that I should follow them. So I did, right into a dingy room at the rear of the tavern. Jesus, I can still remember that room: just a couch, a bed, one crimson lamp and red curtains. Judy turned on the lamp, which gave a dim, reddish light and locked the door."

I stayed quiet.

"I was terrified, I had no idea what to do. So Nora announces 'For your birthday, we thought you would like to stop being a boy and become a man.' Then they pushed me on the bed and undressed me. My fear must have been obvious. But get this, Nora murmured, 'Doyle, don't look so scared. You'll enjoy this,' as she felt inside my underpants.'

"That's pretty wild for a thirteen-year-old."

"I know. Guess what happened next? Nora put my thirteen year old cock in her mouth."

At this we both burst out laughing, "God I almost feel sorry for her."

"Don't. She didn't do it for more than a minute or two before I came. When I recovered I was determined to fuck them both."

"For at least two minutes?" I joked.

"It made me a bit woman-crazy for a while. You can imagine all the waitresses I met in my line of work."

"Must be why waitresses always like you."

"Well, not always, you see I was a little bit of a heart-breaker and my uncle was not impressed. Thought it was bad for business, so I tried to keep what I was doing away from his prying eyes."

"Jesus, I can just imagine what he said and I bet you deserved every word. My dad had a terrible temper, rest his soul. Only after a drink."

"It's a familiar story, but to be fair to Joe, whenever he shouted at me I always deserved it."

"I bet you did, womanizing on company time – you scallywag."

"If only it was just that."

"What do you mean?"

"I started working for the competition."

"Christ, have you ever heard the saying 'don't bite the hand that feeds you?'"

"I know. I was terrible. But I was the only one working – remember ma and the boys didn't earn anything, so it was up to me to provide for the four of us."

"With your uncle's help, don't play the martyr."

"We were short of cash. That's all there was to it, so I got involved in a numbers racket with an outfit headed by a man called O'Neill."

"Is that like a lottery?"

"Kind of. Each punter chooses 3 numbers between 1 and 50, and if they match the numbers drawn, they get a thousand dollars. The odds were over a million to one, you know. I got five per cent of the vig.

Anyhow Joe gave me an ultimatum, so I had to stop working for O'Neil's operation, but you know what these guys are like – you can't just quit. O'Neill said I owed him fourteen hundred dollars – a ridiculous figure from even more ridiculous calculations."

"How did they work that out?"

"You know what gangster math is like. I refused to pay and bluffed that Joe had instructed the St. Luke PD to raid O'Neil's place in fifteen minutes, unless I came back in once piece."

"And it worked?"

"You bet. He packed up and left town the next day, and Joe gave me a raise."

I could easily see how the young entrepreneurial street kid had become the city politician in front of me today.

"But Uncle Joe still thought I had something to learn about discipline and authority, so he packed me off to the war."

"Ha – he couldn't control you so thought he'd give the army a go, more like."

"Something like that, although he always planned ahead. It was Joe who saw the potential in my sorry teenage ass. He told me straight, 'If you wanna be a politician in this town, some day you'll find yourself running against another guy who fought for our country in the war. If you didn't you'll lose.'"

"So the Michael Doyle master plan had begun." I wondered how he got in when we were both the same age. "I was too young to join, but you weren't?"

"Well, what Joe wants, he gets. But let's talk business Mr. Newspaperman."

Mike pulled up outside a nondescript doorway. He knocked on the door, a flap opened, a man inside grunted "okay" and we entered a speakeasy. Mike was welcomed by a man wearing a tux and shown to a quiet table at the rear. Soon after a waitress provided cups, saucers and a coffee pot with whisky inside and a jug of water. I sipped the whisky. Not bad.

I poured myself a glass of water. I needed to keep my head. I had no idea what Doyle the politician would think of what I had to say.

"Mike, there's going to have to be a level of trust between us. I'm the new man in St. Luke. I want to make my mark quickly at *The Bugle*. You are in power, but the spring election is no foregone conclusion and the New Democrats could use as much good publicity as they can get. Are we agreed so far?" Doyle nodded his head.

"So," I continued, "what if I can persuade the editor of *The Bugle* to endorse the New Democrats?"

Doyle's head extended backwards as he guffawed loudly. "Looks like the booze has already gone to your brain," he told me. "There's a bigger chance of our baseball team, The St. Luke Angels, winning the Pennant this year. And they are shockin'. Nice try, Books, but you'll have to do better."

"Look, *The Bugle* always endorses the Republicans, but this time round they may not pick up even one seat on the council. At best, they'll get two, or so I'm told. That means *The Bugle's* endorsement of the Republicans is a complete waste of time."

Doyle sat up in his armchair. "Keep talking."

"Would you give *Bugle* reporters unfettered access to you and your key people during the campaign? You would have to agree to be interviewed by the editor or someone nominated by him to get the ball rolling."

"I don't see a problem with this," said Doyle, relaxing back into his armchair.

"I know you've refused interviews before, but we'd want to ask a lot of questions about things like your policies and the new charter and how it will operate, as well as the role of the City Manager?"

"Would it be you raisin' these issues?"

"I don't know. I might get the editor to agree to let me kick off with an interview with you. Why?"

Doyle sat in thought. Then he answered, "I'd need to see your questions beforehand."

"Let me take this idea to my bosses. I can't see any point in you and I taking this further if I can't get them to even consider having *The Bugle* endorse the New Democrats. Can I get back to you in a few days? And there is no way I'll let you see our questions beforehand. That's not the way it works."

Doyle grinned at me. "Okay. Can't blame me for tryin'. You've come a long way, too, Books. Who'd have thought? One for the road?"

I looked at my watch. It was 10:45 p.m. "Irish, next time. I have a date." It was a believable lie. I needed to get away and marshal my thoughts.

"Books, I'm goin' to stay here awhile. Talk with you tomorrow. I'll get someone to call a cab for you. I'm pleased you looked me up."

We talked for a few minutes until I was told my cab was waiting. We shook hands and I left. What a day! As I left, I saw Doyle talking with the cigarette girl, making her giggle. She was fascinated by him. I couldn't help wondering whether Mr. Doyle would spend the night with company.

Chapter Three

Next morning, I waited for Ted Page outside his office. When he arrived, he grumbled as usual. "Haven't you learned anything? I told you about cub reporters and cold mornings. What on earth do you want this time?"

"Ted," I said, "I have a proposal which you will find incredible but please hear me out. It won't take long."

"Come back in ten minutes," Page growled. "Let me get in and have a coffee. Then I'll give you five minutes. I have a busy morning."

Ten minutes later, I sat in Page's office. I began. "When I was a boy, Mike Doyle and I were best friends." Ted's eyebrows rose. "So, you do know him."

"Until yesterday, I hadn't seen Doyle for a long time, not since I was ten. He knows I work here at *The Bugle*. He has an interesting election ahead. I suggested a deal to him." I paused, took a deep breath and continued. "If *The Bugle* is satisfied about the New Democrats' intentions for St. Luke and its proposed actions under the new charter, it should endorse the New Democrats."

Ted Page looked at me square in the eyes. He started to reply but I ploughed on, speaking rapidly. "I have an agreement from Doyle that he will submit himself to an unscripted interview at the outset with you or Mr. Brady. You can ask him whatever you like. You can even ask about the charter, future plans. We'll have an exclusive."

Ted stared at me for what felt like an hour, but was probably just seconds while he digested what I had said. "This is preposterous. Do you think I'm stupid?"

I wanted to leave, but my head told me to stand my ground. Finally, Ted spoke. "Just take me through the thinking and the details again."

This time, I went through things slowly, setting out my argument why *The Bugle* should abandon the city Republicans and support the

New Democrats. As I spoke, I saw a grin forming at the corners of Ted's mouth.

"Don't leave the office," he told me. Thirty minutes later, I was given a message. "Mr. Brady and Mr. Page want you upstairs, now."

I took the stairs to the sixth floor and waited outside Mr. Brady's office. There have been moments in my life when I was worried or even scared, but on this occasion, I was terrified. Had I taken things too far? Would I be fired on the spot?

I knocked on the door and heard Brady's voice bark, "Come in." Mr. Brady and Ted Page were sitting at the conference table. "Sit down," Brady said. "Young man, you really are full of surprises." I still didn't relax. "How did you come up with the notion that *The Bugle* would endorse the New Democratic Party?"

I explained my reasoning, using the same logic offered to Doyle and Ted. I also went through the terms that Doyle would agree to. I must have spoken for five minutes. Neither Brady nor Ted interrupted. When I finished, Brady sat in thought.

"Have you told me absolutely everything?"

I nodded. "Yes, so far as I can think. I had a long talk with Mr. Doyle. Much of it covered our boyhoods and family stuff. I've told you pretty well everything we discussed about the endorsement idea."

"I have to say," said Brady, "your suggestion is anathema to me personally, but it might be good for the newspaper. We can show our readership that we keep an open mind. Leave this with Mr. Page and me. It will take a while. You can use the time to get more information on this fellow Doyle. If we're going to endorse him and his party, I need to know all there is to know."

That seemed fair. I would have off-the-record conversations with Doyle, his colleagues and people who knew him from the old days.

I left, mumbling, "Thank you," more than once.

I called Doyle. "They haven't thrown the idea out but it's going to take a few days and my bosses want to know more about you and your people. Can we meet and talk. I need time with people who know your story?"

"Okay, but my private life is private. You can have anything that's to do with my public service."

"So when can I get started?"

"Well I was thinking of dropping in at the place we talked last night if you care to join me. Say 7.30."

"See you there."

I spent the rest of the afternoon reading all I could on Doyle's war years. There were all sorts of patriotic articles, which were full of praise for the town's veterans. I came across one:

The St. Luke Bugle
Established: 1875. 14th May, 1920. Circulation: 253,927.

OUR HERO RETURNS

Today, one of St. Luke's heroes, Michael Doyle, the boy from rural Rawlings who made St. Luke his home, and the nephew of Alderman Joe Doyle, was given a warm St Luke welcome. Hundreds of people turned out to cheer our returning veteran. Mayor Bolen welcomed Mr. Doyle to the stage to personally congratulate him on receiving America's highest military honor for gallantry. "Michael, St. Luke salutes you and is delighted you are back safe with us. Here in the Midwest, we don't normally go in for big shows and the like, we don't award keys of the city or other such honors but I can say this: Tonight, the town is yours. For you, beverages and eats are on the house. Now, will you say a few words for us?"

Doyle approached the microphone, coughed twice and spoke. "I have been waitin' for this day for a long time. I am so pleased to be home with my family and friends. I owe everythin' to this community. In the dark times over there in France, I had your letters and everythin' you taught me to keep me goin'. Now I'm back, I'm hopin' my Uncle Joe will put me to work so I can serve the community as best I can. Now, if you'll excuse me,

I'd like to spend time with my Ma and my brothers and sister, but I'll see you all soon."

The crowd cheered and the music started up once more. Once the celebrations are over, we may see Michael Doyle in the same political light as his uncle. However, there must be concern that Ed Hanrahan holds the reins of power in City Hall and Joseph Doyle's fortunes may be waning. The city election this April could leave Mr. Doyle badly exposed. Will the return of his nephew help? Time will tell.

Having spent the afternoon in preparation, I had a list of questions I wanted to put to Doyle, but I was happy to be led by Doyle himself. I thought about his rise from the gutter as I made my way to the speakeasy.

Doyle was at the same table as yesterday and stood up to wave me over. Before I could even sit down, he poured me a drink from the coffee pot on the table. It was bourbon this time.

"Books, good to see you so soon. I've got some business to attend to tonight," he said giving a knowing wink and glancing in the direction of a very curvy brunette at the bar. "So I'd appreciate it if we could keep this short."

"Of course. Let's keep to the point. Do you want to start with your war years? Our readers sure love hearing about our brave and valiant veterans." I wanted him to feel like he was on safe ground.

"Okay, in 1917, I joined the St. Luke Eagle Regiment, Company C. We were shipped out to a camp in Tennessee for basic training and, weeks later, were on board the SS. Shooting Star on route for France."

"And no one suspected your age?"

"Fortunately, I had the wisdom to start shaving as soon as Joe had warned me I would be joinin' the army and even though my cheeks were like a baby's bottom. By the time I joined up, there was somethin' of a shadow of a beard to boast about.

"What a picture."

"In France, I was soon promoted as attrition hit the ranks of our non-commissioned officers. I took to the camaraderie of army life. The

39

first time I came under fire at the Battle of Cantigny, I realized that Joe was wrong – that it was not every man for himself."

In my research I had uncovered a great story about Joe O'Hare, who had been hit and called for Doyle's help. It sounded like an act of bravery and I asked Doyle for the full story.

"Well I couldn't see him, but hearin' O'Hare wasn't a problem, he was screamin' in pain and panic – sure he was going to die. We were both in no man's land. I crawled to where I heard O'Hare and found him. I checked him over in the moonlight, and could see blood gushing from O'Hare's leg but it was just a scratch. We couldn't stay there. The Germans would see us eventually, but O'Hare just would not move or even crawl. I fixed a tourniquet and ordered O'Hare to get on my back.

"Twenty minutes later, with O'Hare still on my back, I found the Eagle Regiment's trench. Medics lifted O'Hare off me – he was treated and back in the line the next day. The incident didn't go unnoticed. I was mentioned in dispatches."

"That must have been quite a big deal."

"It was. Shortly after, my new officer – he sent me a message to go to the officers' tent, where all the important stuff happens. I was introduced to Jeremy Pressman, who told me that my lieutenant had been killed by sniper fire earlier that afternoon. We'd already lost quite a few men and Pressman could see the concern on my face. He invited me to sit down. He opened a bottle of bourbon and poured me a shot. 'Here's to mud and crime,' he toasted. Then he showed me a phonograph."

"In an officer's tent?"

"Yes, I'd never seen one before. I heard Mozart for the first time."

"And how the hell did he get the liquor?"

"Well, I soon thought there could be a market to exploit, so I wrote to Uncle Joe, asking him to send cigarettes and spirits to get a business going. Joe cabled back refusing help, stating it wasn't worth losing a clean army record. Instead, he said he would wire me an allowance of $100 a month. By all army standards, I was rich."

"Sounds like Joe really did want you to keep your nose clean."

"Yeah, and I did – by and large. Well, there wasn't much in the way of entertainment. The sergeants' mess was hardly well-appointed, but it was a haven in the trenches. Here I met Sargent Alexei Gann and

Sargent John Santino, who was very ambitious and fond of saying, 'When I get back to St. Luke, I'll be making my mark'."

I eyed Doyle. "Looks to me like you're all making a mark."

Doyle cast a glance at brunette sitting at the bar and said, "I'll give you one more story, then I need to see to that lady."

"Just one?"

"I'll make it a really good one."

"Okay, let's have it."

"In June, 1918, the Eagle regiment was based in Reims. I spotted a man, white as a sheet, holding a bayonet pointed towards his own throat. I approached him asked him his name. The soldier whispered, 'Berman'. 'I'm Sargent Doyle,' I said. 'Let me help you.' I placed my right hand underneath the man's wrist and gently pushing the bayonet outwards and away from the man's head. Then, with a swift jerk, I twisted the man's wrist, forcing the man to let go the bayonet and said, 'Okay, private, talk to me. Let me know why I shouldn't put you on a charge.'"

"What did he say?"

"Berman whispered, 'I wish you would,' and started to cry. I told him that if I did that he'd be court martialed and probably shot, but the poor boy was ready for death. He'd been in France for nine months, seen a lot of action and, in my view, was suffering from nothing less than fear and exhaustion, not cowardice. I made a quick decision. I told him that it was goin' to hurt a bit but it would get him away from the front for a while. Then I grabbed Berman's arm and, with a swift jerking movement, broke it.

"I bet he didn't know what had hit him."

"I told him to remember, that he tripped and fell then took him to a treatment area. He was given a desk job until he was ready to return to duty."

"Amazing. I'm sure he thanked you for it in the end."

Doyle pushed back his chair as if to leave, but I was determined to conclude his war years. "Were you ever injured?" I asked to stall him.

"Sure, quite a serious shoulder wound when we were fighting close by a French village, Chateau Thierry, but I couldn't leave my men to get it cleaned up."

"So you were a good leader."

"Strangely, although I was barely more than a kid myself, it came naturally. I always took time to talk with the troops. I helped the weaker ones and straightened those who thought they knew best. But I didn't want to be an officer."

"Were you asked?"

"Sure, but I knew I was best off in the ranks."

"Not anymore, you're the leader of the New Democrats."

"That may be, but I have a date," he said as he made his way over to the brunette whose giggles carried to my table. It was time to leave.

Chapter Four

A few days later, I sat with Ted. I chose the afternoon to meet with him. I needed to show I had understood something about his work habits.

"Okay, Mr. Driscoll, what have you got for me?"

I took out a legal pad. "What do you need that for?" asked Ted.

"I have a pretty good memory, but I have spoken with quite a few people over the past week, so I put down what I was told in chronological order. May I remind you that I agreed with Doyle that all this is off-the-record, unless it relates directly to his public service?"

Ted nodded. "Shoot. Start with the background. I want to know where this guy came from."

I filled him in as best I could, starting with his arrival in St Luke, his apprenticeship with Joe Doyle and then his bravery in the war. What I liked about Ted was his listening skills. He did not pepper me with questions, but let me talk. Finally, he asked, "What happened when Doyle returned to St. Luke? I remember there was a big do in town: bunting, bands playing, the whole shebang. The hero had returned, and it wasn't long after that he formed the New Democrats was it?"

I looked at my legal pad and started to talk again. I relayed what Alexei Gann, one of the St. Luke veterans who served with Doyle, had told me.

"After the fanfare, Mike Doyle spent the rest of his first day with his family. Mike told Gann what happened on his first evening home. Doyle had sat with Uncle Joe and the two men talked late into the night. Joe soon realized that the Mike Doyle he had known was gone forever. He now saw a young man, strong, fit, confident, articulate and ready for business. Luckily, Gann has a great memory, and set the scene well:

'I did what you told me, uncle,' said Mike. 'I had a good war, kept my nose clean and survived. So, what are we goin' to do about Hanrahan?'

'Michael, I'm sorry. When ye left, I had hopes that when ye came back, I would be able to get ye on your way in the local Party. Hanrahan will block ye. He will do anything to secure his hold on St. Luke. And every day, my position gets weaker. The next election may see me on my own, no support from elsewhere and what good is it to ye to be a cog in the wheel of a one-ward boss?'

'Uncle, the war was really good for me. I learned a lot about all sorts of things, not just fightin' and drinkin'. So, let's enjoy this evenin' together, talkin' about old times, sipping some booze and tellin' sad tales. Tomorrow we'll start plannin'. What I know is that everyone has a weakness. Hanrahan's an old time boss and my guess is that he's got greedy and lazy. There'll be gaps in his fences. Now, where's the bourbon? I assume Prohibition hasn't reached this room!'

"So this is when the scheming started?" Page asked, nodding and processing the information.

"Yes, I got to talk with Doyle myself about his rise to power."

"What did he have to say?"

"Doyle told me how he put his strategy into play. Four weeks after arriving back in St. Luke, he paid a visit to Ed Hanrahan without an appointment. Doyle waited in Hanrahan's outer office for most of the morning. Shortly before noon, one of Hanrahan's aides appeared and said, 'Mr. Doyle, Mr. Hanrahan apologizes for keeping you waiting. Unfortunately, he has a lunch engagement. May I fix an appointment for you for another time?'

"Sure. When shall I come back?" Doyle replied

"Shall we say ten o'clock on Friday?"

"At the appointed time on Friday morning, Doyle arrived at Hanrahan's office. After waiting for almost an hour, the same aide appeared. 'Mr. Doyle, Mr. Hanrahan's apologies. He has been caught up in other things. There's no chance he can get to you today. Can we re-schedule?"

Doyle remained calm but said, 'I get the message. Please tell Mr. Hanrahan that I only came to pay my respects.'

Doyle left and went to his uncle's office in The Trench where he relayed the outcome of the past days. 'Hanrahan's message is that he dismisses me. I don't signify. I'm not worth talking to.'

Joe Doyle's face went crimson with rage. 'I'll fix this. I'll talk with him. He can't disrespect ye like this. I've had it with that bastard.'

"Before Joe could say another word, Doyle interrupted. 'All to the good, uncle, all to the good. If he doesn't regard me, he won't have me watched. As far as I'm concerned, it couldn't have gone better.'

"Three weeks later, a full page advertisement appeared in *The St. Luke Post*, as well as other newspapers in the city and Monroe County. Let me show you," I said pulling the ad out of my file.

To all Veterans of the St. Luke Regiment

There will be a reunion dinner for all St. Luke veterans of the Great War at The Independence Room, The Warwick House, 4th Street, St. Luke on the 10th October, 1920.

All refreshments provided free of charge. Come one, come all for good company and times remembered.

"Doyle told me what happened. On the night of 10th October, some 600 war veterans arrived at The Warwick House, sporting uniforms and medals, all determined to have a good night out. At the entrance to The Great Room, Doyle had placed attractive women, seated behind desks, who registered each entrant, noting their name, address, regiment and rank. Once registered, the men entered to find tables groaning with food and beverages. A band played songs the men recognized from their war days. Flags of the regiments, the city and the state were placed around the room. The atmosphere was both military and triumphal.

"Some thirty minutes into the reunion, a number of waiters entered bearing coffee pots. As they went around the room, they offered to provide or top-up coffee cups with what he described as 'an interesting potion', which was quickly recognized as bourbon. Soon, the hum in the room went up by several decibels as coffee cups were refilled. It was not Doyle's intention to get six hundred veterans drunk, merely to loosen them up.

"At 8:45pm, the band stopped playing. There was a drum roll. Over a public address system, a voice announced, 'St. Luke veterans, attention!' Almost to a man, everyone stood up, ramrod stiff. 'Gentlemen, please welcome your host this evening, one of St. Luke's favorite sons and a Great War hero, Sargent Michael Doyle.'

"Doyle mounted the stage to polite applause and approached the microphone. He let the applause continue for a short time and then held his hands up, asking for quiet.

"Men,' he started, "veterans of the Great War, it is me who should applaud you. I know many of you standin' here. Please, either stand easy or sit. You're making me nervous." Laughter ensued as the audience made themselves comfortable. Doyle continued: "You are the bravest of the brave. You fought a war that was not of your makin', you traveled thousands of miles to help people you never knew or met. You did it because it was the right thing to do. You won the war to end wars. And no one ever thanked you. Well, tonight, on behalf of everyone who should say so, I'm sayin' thank you." This received shouts of approval.

"So, what sort of world do we find now? How is life for us in America, in the Midwest, in St. Luke? I think some of you know I've been takin' my time gettin' back home. I've been visitin' friends and talkin' to people in the East and around the country and findin' out what's going on.

"We seem to have a difficult choice comin' up in November. We have a President in Washington, but I don't know who's runnin' the White House now. Is it Mr. Wilson or Mrs. Wilson? All I know is President Wilson got elected on keepin' us out of a foreign war, then he put us in it.

"There'll be an election soon and everyone says the Republicans will win. There's a Republican fellow, Mr. Hardin', goin' all over the States, talkin' about a car in every garage and a chicken in every pot. And he's promisin' the good life for all of us and spoutin' about returnin' to 'normalcy'. One day, someone's going to have to tell me what 'normalcy' means. Seems to me Hardin' wants a return to the old ways before the Great War, you know with those rich folks tellin' us

46

what to do and when to do it, while they are the only ones who get to drive a car and eat a chicken.'

Doyle received a huge cheer as he took a breath.

"Now, I'm no politician. But I've been lookin' around St. Luke since I got back. How many of you have got a job? Let's have a show of hands.' Most of the men put up their hands. 'That's great,' Doyle continued. 'How many of you have got good wages and a job with good prospects?' Far fewer hands were raised.

"Okay. Now, let me ask, how many of you think there have been improvements the past few years in the way things are done here in St. Luke?" No hands were raised. "Do you think while you were fightin' a war on foreign shores, those remainin' here feathered their nests at your expense?" There was a lot of mumbling in the crowd.

"Listen, it's just human nature for this to happen. I'm not pointin' a finger at or complainin' about anyone. It's just the way the world is. But if we, the men of St. Luke who fought the war, want to make a change, we have to do it ourselves. So, maybe a few of you boys might want to throw your hats in the ring and run for office in the next city election. I know it's a long way off, but if you do, let's talk about it. Let's see what kind of deal we can put together to shake things up a bit in 1922.'

"The room had quietened and there was a low hum as men talked with each other about the suggestion. Doyle tapped the microphone. 'Oh, let me ask somethin' else? Is there anyone here for Ed Hanrahan? Come on, don't be shy.'

"This produced a laugh.

"Well, if you're too scared to say anythin', just tell Ed this from me. What we're doin' here ain't no challenge to you, Ed, but maybe you should give those of us who put our lives on the line a fairer share of the good things that you have.'

"At this, the veterans stood roaring Doyle's name. Doyle raised his arms up high with fingers pointed towards the ceiling, palms outward, a gesture that would become familiar to the St. Luke voters over the years.

"Boys, let's be nice. Hanrahan has done good for this town. Well, at least for those close to him.' This got a big laugh. 'Please enjoy the rest of your evenin'.'

47

"Doyle climbed off the stage to thunderous applause. He mingled with the crowd for an hour or so, talking with men he knew from his army days. He spent time with old friends from C Company and was delighted to see a ruddy-complexioned Tom Berman."

"So this was the start of Doyle the public figure?" Page said with a wry smile.

"You could say that," I agreed. "Doyle told me how sore his uncle was the next day over the bill, but Doyle assured him it was 'money well spent, an investment'. Joe was having none of it and harrumphed himself out of the office.

"Later that day, Ed Hanrahan's secretary telephoned Doyle. 'Mr. Doyle, Mr. Hanrahan would appreciate seeing you this afternoon. Will you come to his office at 3:30pm?"

"Certainly,' Doyle answered, 'I'll be there.'

"At 3:30pm prompt, Doyle presented himself at Hanrahan's downtown office. He was kept waiting twenty minutes, then ushered into Hanrahan's room. Hanrahan stared at him.

"So, you're what the fuss is all about. I gather you were shooting your mouth off about me last night. What's your beef?'

"Doyle remained calm. He selected a chair angled away from Hanrahan's direct line of sight so that Hanrahan would have to move his position to continue the discussion. This would make Hanrahan angrier.

"I have no beef. I decided to have a party for my old friends from the Eagle. We all fought in the Great War while you warmed your backside here. What gives you the right to say I can't hold a reunion?"

"I'm not saying that,' replied Hanrahan angrily. 'I know you told the crowd I was no good for St. Luke. So, you're going to take me on, are you? Joe Doyle will regret it. I'll see to that. Good luck with your political career, son, you're going to need it.'"

"Listen, Mr. Hanrahan, you've got the wrong end of the stick. Maybe I shouted my mouth off a bit, but we were juiced up and the boys love this kind of stuff. I'm not political. And my uncle knew nothin' about this. I'm sorry if I offended you."

"Hanrahan's color slowly changed from red to normal. 'Okay, we both got a bit heated. Just don't let me hear things like this anymore. Now, git.'

"After Doyle left, Hanrahan turned to an aide. 'I think that's the last we'll hear from that whipper-snapper.'

"Doyle left Hanrahan's offices with a contrite look on his face. When he was back on the street, he stopped, looked back to make sure he wasn't followed and started to laugh. 'So, that's the great Ed Hanrahan,' he said to himself. 'Well, well. What a blowhard.'

"Doyle returned to his uncle's office and related the interview. 'Uncle, we're going to take Hanrahan in '22. What we do now is lie low. I've got a plan that will give Hanrahan a real run for his money.' He explained what he intended in broad terms. Joe couldn't stop grinning.

"Over the next few months, Doyle visited many of the men, like Alexei Gann and John Santino, who had attended the reunion. I talked with them. Both were pretty forthcoming about Doyle. He recruited veterans who would relate well to voters, not only in The Trench but also the more affluent wards of St. Luke. Some men agreed they would stand for election in 1922. Some would act as ward lieutenants and precinct captains, in turn engaging ward heelers, the local workers who made sure to get the voters out. Others would act as security guards, making sure Hanrahan's men didn't strong-arm anyone. Several would apply for jobs at City Hall to get information on what Hanrahan demanded from employees in exchange for his patronage.

"Doyle conducted the task like a military operation, with a strict hierarchy and allocated tasks. By the autumn of 1921, Doyle's political army was ready. Doyle himself told me he is very proud of the way he handled things. On the 1st November, 1921, another announcement appeared in *The St. Luke Post* and all other newspapers serving St Luke and Monroe County."

"Do you have the article?" Page interrupted. I placed the short clipping on the table.

To the People of St. Luke

The New Democratic Party of St. Luke will rally at Fellway Park, St Luke on 4th November, 1921 at 5:30pm. A Marching Band will leave City Hall at 5:00pm. Join us in our fight to change life in St. Luke for the better.

The New Democratic Party of St. Luke stands for good quality housing for all citizens, good quality education for all children, law and order, an equal chance for city employment, properly run services at a price all can afford and fair play for all citizens.

In the February 1922 primary elections and in the April, 1922 city-wide election, New Democratic Party candidates will stand in all wards of St. Luke. All our candidates served their country in The Great War and now want to serve the people of St. Luke in peacetime. Come meet our candidates, ask your questions and support the New Democratic Party in a fairer and better deal for St. Luke. Come rally with us. All welcome.

"Underneath the script were pictures of twenty-two candidates and their names. This was an innovation. Candidates for city elections in St. Luke had never advertised themselves before using photographs."

"So then what happened?" Page asked.

"Well, from looking through the newspaper reports it seems that three days later at five o'clock in the afternoon, to the fascination of office workers, retailers and shoppers downtown, a huge marching band, mostly college students, started to play ragtime music outside City Hall on Main Street. Soon after, they began marching through downtown to Fellway Park, gathering crowds along the way. Large banners proclaimed: ***"The New Democratic Party has arrived."***

I explained how people had marched enthusiastically behind the band. Eventually, thousands followed the band to the Fellway Park bandstand. Of course, many in the crowd, veterans of the Great War, had been primed to come and bring people from their wards with them.

"At 5:30pm, an unseen announcer was heard over a public address system: 'Ladies and Gentlemen, the New Democratic Party is proud to introduce a son of St. Luke and a great servant of the people for many years, Alderman Joseph Doyle.'"

Joe Doyle climbed the stairs to the bandstand. He gave the appearance of an elder citizen, dressed formally in a black tailcoat and pinstripe trousers. A handsome-looking Mike Doyle, who wore no hat, no coat and was dressed in a jacket and shirt without a tie, accompanied him. Young Doyle looked the picture of a working

-class, blue-collar man. He had grown his hair and his fringe almost covered his right eye. He was clean-shaven but there was a five o'clock shadow.

Joe Doyle took the microphone. "Ladies and gentlemen, I am proud to have served the First Ward as a Democrat and to have devoted many years to the people of St. Luke. However, I will not be a candidate in the 1922 election." The crowd reacted with "noes".

"I'm retiring from politics. I'm getting too old. Now is the time for young men to play their part and take the reins of power. But the main reason for my retiring is that the Party that I have served, and that made me so proud to be a member, no longer exists in this city.

"The Democratic Party run by Ed Hanrahan serves special interests. It panders to well-heeled friends, the rich of this city. It gives jobs to people who are wholly unqualified. It turns a blind eye to crime. And it rejects calls for change. The Democrats of St Luke are no longer the party of the people. They are in power for themselves and God help anyone who gets in their way. For sure, Hanrahan's machine won't help any of ye.

"Fortunately, there is a new generation of Democrats who have been forged in battle in the greatest war the world has ever seen and who are ready to take up the baton of service for ye. Ladies and gentlemen, the leader of the New Democrats is a young man I've known since he was a child. He fought with distinction in the Great War, he was awarded the Congressional Medal of Gallantry and he has decided to dedicate himself to improve yer lives in St. Luke. I give ye my nephew, Mr. Michael Doyle and the other New Democrat candidates who will fight the April election."

Joe Doyle stepped forward and waved to his colleagues to join him. He grinned at Mike and shared a private moment. Mike had written Joe's speech. Mike strode confidently to the microphone, adjusting its height. The crowd erupted in wild applause and cheering, prompted by the veterans amongst them.

"Ladies and gentlemen, it is my great honor to announce the formation of the New Democratic Party of St. Luke. Now, there is much we respect in the old democratic values: we uphold the beliefs of the Founding Fathers. We want life, liberty and the pursuit of happiness, but we want them for all the people, not the few! We seek freedom and prosperity for all the people, not the few! We want everyone to have a sound roof over their heads, food on their tables and good schools for all our children. Now, there's nothin' new in this.

"If only the Democrats, led by Ed Hanrahan, held to the same principles, there would be no need for a New Democratic Party. My colleagues and I stand before you, wishin' we could support Hanrahan's Democrats. But we can no longer offer to give our support to Hanrahan and his buddies. Just look at Hanrahan's record for the past two years. Has crime reduced in this city? Has the police force, influenced by Hanrahan's henchmen, made the streets safer for our citizens? Has Hanrahan created jobs? Are you better off now than you were at the end of the Great War? Have there been improvements in your children's schoolin'? Has Hanrahan helped meet your medical bills when you get sick?"

After each question, Doyle paused, giving the crowd time to answer, "No". Each "No" was louder than its predecessor.

At the last "No," there was a commotion at the rear of the crowd. A fight broke out. Armed city police appeared, ostensibly to stop the fight, but in reality bent on breaking up the rally. To the amazement of the police and the crowd, a number of men wearing New Democratic Party armbands and sashes quickly made their way to the center of the commotion, removed the perpetrators and handed them over to the police. The interruption took no more than a minute. Hanrahan's attempt to disrupt and end the rally proved futile.

Doyle saluted the city police. "We are delighted to see our city's finest keepin' the peace. Thank you. We can now get back to our rally, knowing we are protected from those who would seek to prevent a lawful meetin' from taking place."

The crowd appreciated Doyle's irony. They applauded loudly.

"Now, as I was sayin'," continued Doyle, "the old Democrats have let you down. But why is this? I'll tell you why. They have gotten too rich, too fat and too used to luxury in City Hall. They don't have anyone to challenge them. They sit in their comfortable offices and homes, lining their pockets and fillin' their bellies at our expense. I say enough!"

This last statement was acclaimed by a roar of approval.

"I say we unite as a new force in St. Luke and we give Hanrahan and his people a run for their money in next year's election. I say we register every voter we can between now and February 11th next year, primary election day. Then we'll turn out the vote on Election Day in April. We, the real people of St. Luke, will take back City Hall!

"Now, the New Democrats can't do this alone. We need your support. And, frankly, we need your money to fight the campaign. But if – no, not if – when we win, we will return St. Luke to you. As New Democrats, we will bring back democracy to the people of St. Luke. Look at me and the people standin' by me. All of us fought in the Great War. We didn't risk our lives to live under Hanrahan's yolk. We've survived to come back and do what is right in this city. We won't let you down. We love this city too much to do that. So, we ask you to join us. Join us today in our fight. Let's take this city back."

At this, there was rapturous applause.

"There are people yonder," at which Doyle pointed to a row of desks and chairs by a nest of trees, "who want to take your details. We want to talk to all of you soon. We want you to register and vote for us. Please read your newspapers, watch for notices and listen to the radio. The New Democrats are here for you. Join us and let us together get rid of this diseased, useless Hanrahan administration once and for all."

"The day after the rally, Doyle himself told me how a group of fifty men gathered with him in a private room at The Warwick. Each knew the others, although in some cases only as nodding acquaintances. Coffee and cookies were served. There were five tables, ten chairs round each table and Doyle invited the men to sit.

"Gentlemen," he began, "welcome. Among us are the New Democratic candidates for the February primary and the April '22 elections, but we are in no shape to govern. I am hoping that by the end of this meeting, we will have agreed a way forward. I have spoken with each of you individually. Here's the plan. There are twenty two of us who will stand for the council and six of us who will stand for election as judges and county judges. Ten of us will stand for other offices. That leaves twelve people for whom there will be no elected office, but I want to suggest that those twelve act as deputies for those standing for the council."

The throng mumbled but no one openly objected. They waited.

"We need to elect officers for our Party," continued Doyle. We are a democracy, so all positions are up for grabs. I would like to make one nomination. Tom Berman has served my uncle as his accountant

53

since the end of the Great War. Tom is a financial wizard and I want to propose him for Party Treasurer. Is this agreed?"

Alexei Gann – the man of interesting parentage and prospective alderman for the 3rd Ward – chimed in, as he had been primed by Doyle to do. "'Financial wizard, you're not kidding. We can't do better than Tom.'"

Doyle continued: "The other offices to be filled are Chairman and Secretary. Are there any proposers?"

John Santino, candidate for the 7th Ward, called out. "Doyle, who else would lead us? You be the chairman."

"Whoa! Slow down. Let's have a little discussion here." People turned to see who was speaking out. A man, well over six feet tall, stood up. "My name is Billy Walters. I fought with Sargent Doyle in Company C. He is a great guy, but shouldn't we see who else is out there? This is too important to be rushed."

"Good to see you, Billy," said Doyle. "Billy was with me at the Marne and other battles. I trusted him with my life and I have nothing against what he is sayin', but the point about the New Democrats is that we have to be new. We can't bring in someone like my Uncle Joe to lead. We have to be the new broom."

Billy Walters slowly nodded his head. "Just wanted to air the issue. This is a democracy, after all," he grinned. "Also, why don't we make the decisions today temporary? Let's see how things pan out and we can vote again in four weeks."

Doyle frowned. "I don't think that's too clever. If we make public our choice of officers, only to change them in a month, we'll be called flip-floppers. What do you others think?"

There was an uncomfortable silence, which was broken by John Santino. "Okay, let's have a show of hands. Do we make today's decisions firm? All in favor?" Most hands were raised. "Fine, do we elect Michael Doyle as chairman?"

"Don't freeze me out," called Billy.

"Santino looked threatening as he walked towards Billy. "It's too important to be spoiled by you. Billy Walters, you were an annoying little rat when we served and you're doing the same now. Maybe we should take this outside?"

"Alexei Gann stepped between Santino and Billy. "Cool off, both of you. Billy, do you seriously believe Mike isn't the best choice?"

"No," replied Billy hesitantly.

"Well, let's go with it. Everyone else here is happy." Alexei turned his head looking for support, which he received with many heads nodding.

"Billy put his hands up in surrender. Doyle was elected unanimously and the business continued. After the election of officers, Doyle allocated separate tasks to each table. He posed a number of questions to the groups. How should the April election be fought? What was needed to defend the New Democrats against Hanrahan's machine? How would the New Democrats be financed? How should the press be handled? What policies should be followed if the New Democrats were elected in April?

"By the close of the day, courses of action were agreed upon, especially the policies to be put to the St. Luke electors. Clean government, public offices filled on merit, improper patronage to end and caring for the poor. The New Democrats were ready to go public.

"After the meeting, Doyle indicated to Santino and Berman that he wanted a word. 'What did you two think of Billy Walters?'

"Not much," replied Berman. "Troublemaker," was Santino's conclusion.

"I agree," said Doyle. "We need to get rid of him. Tom, you know what to do?"

"Sure," said Berman, "consider it done."

"Two days later, a story appeared in some local papers about Corporal Billy Walters, one of the New Democrats, who had been tried for cowardice in a court martial convened just after the end of the Great War. He had been convicted but, as the war was over, the death sentence had not been imposed. Instead, he was ordered to serve one year in the stockade and be dishonorably discharged. He had been released from army jail nine months after the war ended.

"Billy tried to have his denials published but most newspapers refused to do so without proof. He was told to resign from the New Democrats. By the time Billy had documentary evidence to prove his innocence, a month had passed and the story was cold.

"Mike laughed when he told me how over the coming weeks, Joe Doyle went white as a sheet when he saw the bills coming in. It was all very well to be reassured by his nephew that the cost would be recovered ten-fold if the New Democrats won the spring 1922 election. Young Michael wasn't footing the bill.

"Time sped on and The Warwick Policies, as they came to be called, were soon well known through frequent announcements in the press. In the February, primaries, all the New Democratic candidates stood unopposed and were elected to fight against the Democrat and Republican nominees in the April election. However, there was an Achilles heel within the New Democrats, namely lack of governing experience. When Doyle or any of his colleagues were challenged, their reply was: "What do you mean lack of experience? I learned what I need to know in the trenches in France and Belgium, going over the top and making sure my men were safe."

"If still challenged, the reply was: "And what experience does Hanrahan's machine have which they actually use for the public benefit? We will govern for the benefit of all in St. Luke, not the few. If you don't think we can do this, then don't vote for us."

"Hanrahan did not stand idly by. He arranged newspaper coverage for himself, although *The Bugle* refused to support him at all. He had made too many enemies over the years. Hanrahan tried bullyboy tactics, using the St. Luke Police Department to break up New Democrat meetings. Hanrahan's ward heelers threatened small businessmen who supported Doyle. But Hanrahan was simply ill-prepared for the Doyle onslaught. Almost every day, stories and pictures of the "slate", all the men running for office as New Democrats in the election, appeared in the newspapers. New Democrat men were interviewed in the press and on popular radio programs, spreading the simple New Democrat message of taking back City Hall for the people.

"The press loved the New Democrats. They were reportable, as young veterans returned from The Great War to fight again for their fellow citizens. Their attitude to city politics was also new, different and refreshing, so much so that newspapers from as far away as New York and San Francisco covered the race.

"*The Chicago Sun Times* ran an article in March, 1922, which was syndicated throughout the St. Luke press. I have a copy here," I said, passing the article to Page.

A New Democratic Party for St. Luke

There is a wind of change in the Mid-west city of St. Luke. The Democratic Party, under boss Ed Hanrahan, has run the show for many years without any serious challenge from the local Republican Party. But in what must be a shock to his system, Hanrahan has a serious challenge from a group of World War veterans, calling themselves the New Democratic Party.

The New Democrats have published a manifesto that appeals to all sections of the electorate. They stand for clean government, public offices filled on merit, an end to improper patronage and for the proper care of the poor. However, no details have been forthcoming about the funding of the proposals. Hanrahan's Democrats are challenging the policies on grounds that they cannot be afforded.

The St. Luke Republican Party has been strangely quiet, when there is an opportunity for them to divide and rule. Republican supporters have to be disappointed with their leadership.

City elections in America rarely produce much interest except for locals. However, in St. Luke this is not the case. A three-cornered fight is a rarity. We shall be watching.

"At the end of the day, there was not much of an election race. Joe Doyle, in a manner reminiscent of his heydays as a city politico, had made sure that the vote would be got out, although Mike ordered him not to use some of the more unorthodox methods. "The last thing we need, Uncle, is to be caught out usin' methods that the Hanrahan machine uses. No ghosts, no ballot box stuffin'. We'd be branded as no better than them."

"In April 1922, Doyle and his men swept to power, taking sixteen out of the twenty two St. Luke wards. Hanrahan was beaten almost everywhere he ran. He won only four wards. The Republicans held two wards. The New Democrats' landslide in the ward elections was repeated in the elections for City offices. All New Democrat candidates for judge and county judge won. In the history of St. Luke city elections, there had not been such a comprehensive defeat of a party in power.

"The day after Doyle took power, he announced a reduction in property taxes, endearing himself to Republican voters and the property owning class of St. Luke alike. The local newspapers ran stories about the proposals to streamline services for citizens and make them more efficient, with commensurate savings in expense. Within a week, all Hanrahan hangers-on, hundreds of them, were summarily removed from their jobs in City Hall, creating substantial savings, which paid for the property tax reduction. Also, only those city employees who Doyle's people regarded as able, regardless of political affiliation, were re-engaged. A new program for selection of all city employees was publicized at City Hall and in the local press. Those best equipped to carry out tasks for the city would receive jobs. Those who were unqualified would be replaced.

"I have another clipping for you," I pulled the small square of paper out of my files and handed it to Page.

He seemed impatient with me, which he confirmed when he told me, "You're good but you're not that good. I've seen plenty like Doyle in my time. What makes you think he's so different?"

"Ted, just read this from today's paper," I replied.

> **Employment on Merit. Patronage takes a Back Seat:** declared *The Bugle* in an editorial headline. The new leader of our city is dispensing with the old ways. No longer will the spoils of victory belong just to the winner. New Democrat boss, Michael Doyle, has a new policy for city jobs whereby those best suited will be appointed to fill the task. Doyle campaigned on this promise. It is heartening to know that this new breed of politician is keeping its word. There are no free lunches in City Hall now.

"In early February, 1923, Doyle played his trump card. I didn't realize what was behind the proposals for a new city charter. The St. Luke League, a group of city businessmen and concerned citizens put forward suggestions to modernize city government. The changes seemed reasonable and offered a progressive charter instead of the old, antiquated one. The changes comprised a reduction of the number of wards in St. Luke from twenty-two to ten, more than halving the number of direct ward representatives. Additionally, there would be five councilmen elected 'at-large', making the council fifteen strong. The council would appoint its leader from the fifteen.

"The reforms were hardly revolutionary and seemed to give no new advantage to the ruling party. Furthermore, the St. Luke League was viewed as a Republican leaning body, not one which would favor the New Democrats. What was not understood clearly was the effect of having five council men at-large. The entire city electorate would vote for these positions. The five candidates receiving the most votes would be elected.

"The New Democrats would benefit most from this change because they already had faces well known to the public as proclaimed war heroes. Voters would likely vote the New Democrat slate. Assuming the five New Democrats were elected as council men at- large, Doyle would only need three Ward seats for an overall majority on the council."

It was now early evening. Suddenly, I felt tired. "Ted, that brings us pretty well up to date."

Ted stayed silent for a minute or so. "Quite a story, David. What do you make of all this? Is Doyle on the up?"

"Probably, but please remember I knew Mike fourteen years ago. I'm only just getting to know the grown-up Mike Doyle. When we were boys, he was a lot of fun, but he had a hard side and he was street-wise. I now detect a harshness, a determination to come out on top at all costs. It's easily explained. It was a lesson his Uncle Joe instilled in him and you don't go through a war like he did without being scarred."

"To date his track record in public life is pretty good. Will he keep it going? Can he be trusted? That's what we need to know."

"I can't say for sure, but he has done nothing to make me think he's going to change."

"Listen, you're the one who brought the endorsement suggestion to the paper, you are going to have to stand by your judgment if Henry Brady goes ahead with it. I mean to say that if this goes wrong, and it could do, there will be no doubt who'll be on the firing line. Is that clear?"

"That's harsh. I'm new here."

"So what! This is your idea. If you want to be a newspaperman, you have to be responsible for your judgments. So, do we go ahead, do I take this back to Mr. Brady?"

"Ted, what does *The Bugle* lose by going to the next stage? If Mr. Brady finds he can't trust Doyle, that'll be the end of it."

"Okay, I'll go back to Mr. Brady and see what he says."

What Doyle and his men kept quiet, something that I didn't discover for quite a while, was the deal made with Charlie Brooks, the chief executive of one of the country's largest insurance companies, the Perpetual Insurance Company of America. Perpetual had its head office in St. Luke. Brooks was also the chairman of the St. Luke League. Twenty -five years older than Doyle, Brooks was shortish, slim, good looking in a matinee idol way, impeccably dressed, and looking every inch the millionaire he was. He gave the clear impression he was used to getting his own way. Brooks had watched Doyle's disposal of Hanrahan and swift rise to power with a mixture of respect and admiration.

Soon after Doyle's election victory, Brooks arranged a meeting. He arrived at Doyle's City Hall office, wearing a custom-made gray pinstripe, three-piece suit, and spats. He had slick black hair, parted in the middle, and sported a slim mustache. Doyle sat with Tom Berman. Brooks addressed Doyle imperiously, flattering him on his victory and covering Doyle in soft soap.

"Mr. Brooks," Doyle asked, "I'm sure you're not here just to praise me to the skies. What can I do for you?"

"I assume our conversation is private."

Doyle nodded his assent and glanced at Tom Berman. Berman nodded back.

Brooks continued. "My community knew where it stood with Hanrahan. Effectively, it paid him tribute and he left us alone. Do you understand?"

"No," replied Doyle. "Spell it out for me."

"Every year, my friends and I contributed $200,000 in cash to Hanrahan's machine. We received tax breaks, city contracts and other help, like tips on likely real estate development spots, to compensate us. We got the licenses and franchises we needed too, although we would often pay extra for them."

"Let me see if I understand," said Doyle. "You paid Hanrahan, not the City. In exchange, it was business as usual. Everyone benefited, except the tax-payer."

"Well, the tax-payer benefited as franchises kept the price of the services cheaper," replied Brooks.

"As it's just between us," chortled Doyle, "in a pig's eye. The tax-payer got screwed. So what is the deal you're looking for from the New Democrats?"

"Not the New Democrats, you." Brooks winked at Doyle. "I'm doing business with you, not your party. I'm sure my friends can spice up the fee."

"Mr. Brooks, I need time to absorb this information and discuss it with my colleagues."

"Mr. Doyle, you realize that nothing with Hanrahan was ever in writing and, as far as I am concerned, this meeting never took place."

"Of course, Mr. Brooks. I'll be in touch."

After Brooks left, Doyle looked at Tom. "Any thoughts?"

"Oh yes," replied Tom. "What a crook, that Hanrahan! No wonder he is angry about losing power. He probably got millions in pay-offs from Brooks and his friends."

"How would Hanrahan have disguised the payments?"

"The books most likely showed political donations," Tom answered. "No need to identify where the funds came from. And the payments were tax free if there were equal expenditures, such as salaries to employees, like Hanrahan's relatives. I don't know if Hanrahan or Brooks is the biggest crook?"

"So how do we deal with this? I need to think and we need to call in the others. This is too big to keep to ourselves."

The next day, Doyle met with his closest colleagues. Uncle Joe, Tom Berman, Alexei Gann, John Santino and Harold Levy, a county judge and old army friend of Doyle's, were there. Doyle laid out what happened in the meeting with Brooks. "I realize this is a lot to absorb, but we have to move quickly." Levy stroked his chin as he gave his advice.

"It seems to me we have options. First, we could report the conversation to a state judge with a view to his convening a grand jury to indict Hanrahan and Brooks for fraud and conspiracy. However, all we have is Mike's and Tom's evidence and Tom thinks Hanrahan's books will have been written well enough to disguise the payments.

Second, we could do what Hanrahan did and take the money. My guess is that the payment will be nearer half a million dollars a year. Personally, this is my least favored option because, in addition to breaking the law, it puts us in the pockets of Brooks and his friends.

Third, we tell Brooks 'no' and close the tax loopholes. I don't like this, because we create enemies out of potential allies for comparatively little gain. We'll win no extra votes and we'll probably get no extra tax revenue because Brooks will go to his friends at state level and they'll help him out."

Joe Doyle chimed in. "Why did ye dismiss taking the money so quickly? We can disguise the payment as easily as Hanrahan. No one will be the wiser and Brooks and his people won't tell because they're as implicated as we are. We're not in his pocket."

"How do the rest of you feel?" asked Doyle.

Alexei Gann broke the silence. "Doyle, if I know you, you have another option. What is it?"

"We horse trade. We tell Brooks that city executives do not accept bribes, but the New Democratic Party is always happy to accept contributions, provided amounts are, let's say, appropriate. We also tell him that we will be considerin' the closure of business tax loopholes, but not this year. We may have to do something before April, 1924, but any action will be a reduction of a tax benefit, not removal. He'll read between the lines. Finally, we tell Brooks about the revisions to the city charter that need support from Republicans and the St. Luke League. He'll cotton on that he'll get something in exchange for getting the League's support."

"Remind me, what's the big deal about the new charter?" asked Joe.

"Joe, we've been through this. It's a process that gets us control of St. Luke for years to come and we have a quiet life. We'll always get the vote for the five councilmen at-large because we'll always have enough registrations and votes to win. We'll always have control of at least four wards. That will give us a minimum nine to six majority in

Council. St. Luke will stay New Democrat, end of story. Provided we give the voters what they want, the opposition can go hang."

The next day Doyle telephoned Brooks. "Let's meet for lunch at the Pyramid, one o'clock today," said Doyle. Brooks confirmed he'd be there. The Pyramid was a diner close to Doyle's City Hall office. It was Doyle's number one choice of watering hole as it was not fancy, its prices were low enough for city office people to use and it was known that the leader of the New Democrats was happy to dine with ordinary folk.

Doyle had a corner table reserved every day. The Pyramid was glad to do this for him. Doyle attracted business. Brooks arrived at one o'clock sharp. "I'm happy to meet you here," Brooks opened, "but are you sure you want to be seen with me in a place like this?"

"Why not?" asked Doyle. "The people need to know I don't do things behind closed doors. I have nothin' to hide." This was said with a huge grin. "Let's order. The pot roast here is great."

Brooks got down to business straight away. "Have you thought about our deal?"

Doyle hardened his stare. "Let me be clear. Whatever deal you had with my predecessor as leader of the Council is over. This is a new administration. We start fresh and clean. There are no deals to be had from me. If you don't like it – tough."

Inwardly, Brooks was shocked, yet he hid it well. "Mr. Doyle, I think there has been a misunderstanding. I don't believe you accurately considered..."

Doyle cut him off. "Don't mistake me for someone who is green, Mr. Brooks. I've been under fire and risked my life in battle. You haven't. I didn't misunderstand anythin' when the Germans were shootin' at me and I didn't misunderstand you."

"I didn't mean to imply..."

"I say again, let me be clear, I'm not Hanrahan. No private deals. We have a lot on our plate, takin' back government of St. Luke from special interests and restorin' the city to the people."

Doyle paused and took a breath as the food arrived. "I don't know when we're goin' to look at tax breaks and franchises. My guess is that we will be too busy to make any decisions this year. Now, my Party can't stop anyone from offerin' a political donation, but if it makes us look like we are bein' bought, we won't accept it. You can depend upon it that we will publicize the refusal. And we won't leave any detail out. This is a clean administration." Doyle fixed his stare at Brooks as he gave the message.

"Mr. Doyle. I'm clear. My friends will be disappointed to hear we can't do business."

"Mr. Brooks, it seems I didn't make myself clear enough. Far be it from me to say this administration won't talk to its law-abiding citizens about the businesses they represent. The New Democratic Party is a supporter of business. It's just that business with the New Democrats has to be conducted our way. Political donations must be within bounds."

"Mr. Doyle, perhaps we could arrange another meeting, preferably in private, to discuss matters to our mutual advantage?"

"No. I've been plain enough. Oh, by the way, did I tell you about our plans to reform the city charter?" Brooks looked quizzically as Doyle continued. "So many American cities now have a modern charter and St. Luke's could use reforms. I expect details will be published soon. Do you think the St. Luke League would be interested in studyin' these reforms? If so, I can arrange a presentation for League members."

Brooks leant back in his chair and a smile appeared on his face. "Do you have time for dessert, Mr. Doyle?" Doyle called the waiter over. They both ordered apple pie and ice cream.

The details of the meetings with Brooks were unknown to me when I talked with Ted. All I could tell him was that the St. Luke League endorsed the new city charter enthusiastically. There were no important tax reforms in 1923 and a special city election in July saw the new charter passed with a huge majority.

There was something else I didn't know until years later. Doyle himself told me about a conversation he had had with his uncle the day after his 1922 victory.

"Listen, Michael," Joe said, "the results are wonderful but I'm a good few dollars out of pocket. In fact, I'm over a hundred thousand dollars down. Remind me how ye and yer people are going to get me replenished with these policies of yers?"

"Uncle," Doyle replied, "if you live to be a hundred, you couldn't spend all the money you have, even if you went on the biggest spendin' binge of all time. I've told you, it will take a while to refund you. For the next two years, the New Democrats will govern St. Luke in a way that our opponents will find impossible to challenge. Then we'll be re-elected and if we do things right, we'll rule St. Luke for many years to come. I've not done all this just to get into City Hall for two years.

"As for getting' your dollars back, look at our city buildings. They are old, inadequate and not fit for a growin' American city of the twentieth century. With New Democrat popularity, we'll get city bonds approved which will get us into a huge buildin' program. Red Circle Cement Company will benefit. The St. Luke Construction Company will benefit. I'll see to it. There will be millions of dollars for you. So, please be patient. Just trust me. I know what I'm doin'."

Joe Doyle nodded. He had started Red Circle Cement and St. Luke Construction in the 1910s, when his influence at City Hall made it certain that city contracts would come his way. "Okay, Michael," he replied, "I'll keep my powder dry, but I'll be watching ye."

"Good," said Doyle, "because the Party needs more funds. We're going to open an office on Main Street. The St. Luke New Democratic Party Committee will be open for business to all citizens. The Party will be there to help anyone who needs it. We'll get people jobs, homes, food and take care of medical bills. Think of the popularity and the votes. And I'll need $25,000 right away."

Joe groaned. "Why do ye need to do all this?"

"We are going to be different from Hanrahan's machine. We're lookin' after the poor so they can get homes and jobs. They want a decent life. We'll help provide it and we need seed capital. We'll get other funds when we help businessmen with their licenses and permits. We are goin' to be close with big business. It won't matter if they're Republicans or Democrats. We'll get them the franchises and tax breaks they want. People from all walks in this city will want us kept in power."

Joe shook his head. "You're nuts. This is pie in the sky. How are you going to pay for it all?"

"To begin with, you are," replied Doyle. "But after 1924, big money will come through. I'm goin' to change the way we do business in St. Luke. I'm goin' to be the Great Reformer. People will like it. Joe, this isn't like the old days with quick returns. I'm plannin' a long way into the future."

"And how are ye going to protect yourself from all these friends of yers, these new aldermen, who'll want your job?" asked Joe.

Doyle grinned. "I'll be so popular that no one will want to unseat me until I'm ready to go. It will be bad business for them if they try. And they are goin' to do well because in their wards, they'll be the bosses. I won't interfere as long as they are keepin' to the message. Also, I'm creatin' a team of my closest colleagues to watch over things. Anyway, in two years' time I'll be standin' down as leader."

"What? Where's my protection coming from?"

"Me. I'll be much less visible when I'm only Chairman of the New Democratic Party Committee. I won't be accountable to the electorate. Then I can run St. Luke my way behind the scenes."

"How did ye get so clever?"

"From you, of course. Also, it's interestin' what you learn in the army."

Chapter Five

There was a note on my telephone that a lady was waiting for me in Reception. I called down. "There's someone here to see you," was the receptionist's greeting. "She's been waiting for thirty minutes."

"I read the note," I said testily. Who is she?"

"Don't know. She refused to give a name."

"Didn't you ask her?"

"Yes, that's when I found out that she refused to give a name. 'Someone from the past', she asked me to say."

"Okay. Is there a room free downstairs? Send my apologies to the lady for keeping her waiting and tell her I'll be with her in a few minutes. Maybe you could offer her a coffee?"

I went down to the second floor. The receptionist told me my visitor was in Room 4. I opened the door. A woman sat perched, cross legged on a small conference table. I didn't recognize her. She appeared to be about my age, a gamin figure with bobbed hair. She wore a stylish brown coat with a fur collar and a matching pillbox hat. She sported two-tone brown and cream shoes with high heels. Her legs were fabulous. Altogether, she presented herself very well indeed. And I had no idea who she was. I approached her, holding out my right hand.

"David Driscoll, what can I do for you?"

She drawled, "David Driscoll, what *can* you do for me? Hmm, needs thought. Well, for one, you could say 'hello'."

"Hello." I started to smile.

"I need to think about the other thing."

"What other thing?"

"What other thing you can do for me."

"Okay."

"Well, you could say, 'How are you, how have you been?' or something like that." She grinned at me. She had to be someone from my past.

She laughed. "I'm not being entirely fair. It's been quite a while."

Then I realized who she was. I took two steps back, put a hand to my mouth and gasped, "No. It can't be."

"Yes, it can be."

"Adele? Adele Doyle?"

"In the flesh."

"How are you?"

"We've done that."

I looked at my watch. "Do you have time for a proper coffee?" I telephoned upstairs to my sub-editor. "Got a lead, I'll be back," not giving him a chance to reply. I grabbed Adele's elbow as I escorted Doyle's twin sister from the room and out of the building as fast as I could.

On the pavement outside, I stopped, twirled Adele round to face me, smiled at her and planted a kiss on her cheek.

"In public, sir," she sighed. "What will people think of me?"

"This is St. Luke. This is a modern city. 1924, these are modern times. And old friends can greet each other in public here without being excommunicated."

We both laughed and headed for a coffee shop. After ordering our beverages, we fell into conversation. Adele told me she had been out on the West coast for the past two years and lived in Los Angeles. She was home for a visit. Doyle had told her of my recent arrival at *The Bugle*. Her curiosity had got the better of her and she decided to renew an old acquaintance. I had not seen Adele for fourteen years. The skinny, large-eyed, awkward duckling had turned into a beautiful, brilliant, stylish swan.

I was captivated.

"How's life with the family?"

"Ma's not ageing well. Her memory is awful. William and Tom aren't good family men. 'Too much time in the speakeasies,' she says. Mike won't speak with them, but I don't know why. And ma doesn't care for Michael's brand of politics or his women. She spends a lot of time in church being a miserable old woman. We're not much of a family, these days. What about you? Are you married?"

I mumbled, "No."

"Is there someone special in your life?"

"Yes, *The Bugle*."

"Aha, well all work and no play makes David very boring. I must remedy this."

"Adele, it might be difficult. I'm really busy, my work isn't nine to five and it will soon be election time."

"David Driscoll, is this the cold shoulder? All I'm suggesting is dinner. Even great reporters have to eat, surely?" she mocked gently. "Meet me at The Metropolitan tonight, eight o'clock," she growled with a severe frown and stare. "Dress appropriately. And don't be late or I'll have you arrested."

She rose quickly, shook my hand and swept out of the coffee house without another look. I paid the bill and returned to my desk. I thought about how dangerous a casual flirtation with Adele could be both for my paper and me.

That night, I arrived at The Metropolitan, attired as requested. It was not my favorite form of dress. Tuxedo, starched shirt and black tie doesn't suit me at all, nor the Midwest on a cold winter's night.

The Metropolitan was a St. Luke landmark. Gerald Butler built it in the 1870s. His grandson, Gerald Butler III was now the proprietor and he ran the restaurant in much the same way as his grandfather. It was a place to eat well and hearty, American style. Thick soups and other starters, huge steaks, pork chops, veal chops and other dishes were on offer with great desserts to follow, like Boston cream pie and Key Lime pie. Some ingredients were imported by rail in refrigerated cars from all over the States. There were French wines advertised as "special European coffees" if desired, served in habitual coffee cups. Gerald Butler III was used to having the St. Luke Chief of Police as a guest and a blind eye was turned to unusual beverages.

The restaurant was built for cabaret, as well as food. At one end of the restaurant, there was a stage. In front of the stage, the eating area was horseshoe shaped. If you wanted to be seen, you sat in the lower floor space. At the rear and raised around the horseshoe were booths for privacy, each with its own gauze curtain, which allowed the diners to see out, but prevented the general throng from seeing in.

I gave my name to the maître d' and was shown to one of the booths. There was a couch alongside a table where food and drink had been laid out. I poured myself a shot of bourbon from a coffee pot and added a little branch water. Soft music was played by a quartet. Some fifteen minutes later, the curtain was drawn back. Adele glided to the couch and sat down next to me. She wore a white organdie full-length coat and scarf to match. Her hair was adorned with a white-feathered hat, which she removed. I detected expensive French perfume. The overall effect was intoxicating. She was just beautiful.

"Pour me a drink," she whispered.

"Bourbon and branch?" I asked.

She nodded. I went to the table, fixed her drink and turned back to hand it to her. In those few seconds, she had removed her coat to reveal, putting it simply, virtually everything. She wore a white choker around her neck and white silk stockings to match, held up by white garters. Her well-formed legs were crossed and a scarf rested on her breasts. "You approve?"

I tried to take everything in whilst keeping my cool. I quickly remembered advice given to me in college about seducing girls, "Always look deeply into a woman's eyes." But she was seducing me.

Adele noticed my stare and giggled. "Had I known it was my eyes you were after, I would have worn spectacles and slowly removed them."

I smiled back at her and laughed. "Guilty. You've got me. How about moving your scarf?"

Adele tossed her scarf aside, revealing small, pert breasts. My previous experiences with the opposite sex paled next to Adele's potent vitality. I took a sip of bourbon and, leaving some liquid on the tip of my tongue, bent to lick her left nipple while placing my hand on her right breast. She placed a hand at the nape of my neck and stroked my hair, bringing my head up. She placed the tip of her tongue in my ear. I let her do this for just a few seconds before I moved my face towards hers and kissed her. Momentarily, our tongues met. Then she drew away.

"We should talk, shouldn't we?" she said.

"I'd rather talk later."

"Men don't talk after. They just leave."

70

"Well, okay, but I can't talk with you when you're dressed like that."

"I agree. Take your clothes off."

"But I went to all this trouble to dress for you. I just love wearing black tie," I teased.

Adele eased off my jacket and slowly helped me remove my socks, trousers, shirt and underwear. Suddenly I panicked. "What if a waiter walks in?"

"He won't. I've locked the curtain," she joked. Adele assured me nothing and no one would disturb us. I lowered myself onto the couch and she snuggled on top of me. "So," she said, "let's talk about you. Tell me what has happened over fourteen years."

I struggled to concentrate as I told her of the mine accident, my father's death, life at Culpepper and at college. I glossed over my experiences in St. Louis, bringing her up to date with the move to St. Luke and my renewed friendship with her brother. I was cautious to keep the conversation away from city politics, but Adele was smart as a whip.

"Aren't you a New Democrat? Don't you support Michael?" she asked.

"I'm not partisan," I replied. "In my job, I need to stay neutral so I can be fair to all sides."

"Why would you give those Republicans and old Democrats the time of day? I might have to change my mind about where this evening's going."

I couldn't tell if Adele was serious, but I wasn't going to mess up my chances. "Listen, I don't like those guys in the White House or Congress on that side of the aisle, but in St. Luke, I have to keep my powder dry. You understand?"

Adele thought for a while, smiled at me. "Maybe."

"You haven't told me what you've been up to," I asked. "Fill me in on the past fourteen years."

"Afterwards," she said huskily. She rolled over and uncrossed her legs. She let out a laugh as she saw my look of surprise. "Haven't you seen a girl shaven before? What do you think?"

She looked below my waist. She knew what I was thinking. "Don't worry," she whispered in my ear, "the first time doesn't usually work well. Let's just do it."

I lay next to her, determined she would enjoy the next half hour, rather than go through a two-minute fumble. So, I stopped her stroking my penis.

"Why the rush?" I asked. "I have nowhere else to go tonight."

I held both her wrists in one hand and placed her arms above her head. As I kissed her, I started to stroke her legs, one at a time, first outside her thighs, then inside. I caressed her breasts and kissed them, returning to her legs.

After a while, I felt her getting impatient. She whispered, "I'm wet. Fuck me now." I got on top of her and put my penis inside her. No resistance at all, it just eased into her like liquid satin. Soon we were in a rhythm as I pumped inside her and then stopped to let her move up and down on me.

I moved to lie on my left side, lifted her left leg so her foot rested on my right shoulder and my hand sought her clitoris. She moaned as I found it and she let me massage it gently, placing a hand on top of mine. Not long afterwards, she bit into my neck as I felt her shudder underneath me.

We lay for a few seconds and she growled, "Go on, finish". Clearly, the sex was at an end for her. I didn't understand the change of mood, but I lost my erection.

She rose, put on her clothes, such as they were, and began to leave.

"Adele, stop. What have I done?"

"It wasn't meant to be like this. I just needed some fun, not this."

"May I see you again, soon? Please."

"I don't think so."

"Why not?"

"I'm married." And she left.

The next morning, I awoke with a start, feeling that I had a tiger by the tail. I wasn't anticipating death, but the events of the past day and night were overwhelming. I was suffering from self-doubt and inexperience. I just could not imagine how a boyhood friendship would develop into a potential sea change in political policy for the newspaper. And my feelings for Adele would swamp my career if I let them. It was little wonder that I felt confused and alone. There was no one in St. Luke I could confide in.

I walked over to Ted Page's office. "Ted, may I have a word?"

Ted nodded. "Can you spare me until Monday? I need to get home to Culpepper."

He looked at me. "Family problem?"

I decided to tell some of the truth. "Not exactly. I need to clear my head with everything going on and a weekend away will help. Is this okay?"

"Are you sure you need to do this? I'm happy to listen."

"Thanks," I said, "but I want to see an old friend of mine. No disrespect to you. I just don't know you well enough."

Late the next afternoon, I arrived in Culpepper. I was greeted like a long-lost hero. My mother fussed over me. Jane, my sister, usually shy and withdrawn in her relationship with me, wanted to tell me her news – how her piano playing had improved and how she might make classical music her life's work. Mother, now retired from teaching, still spent time at her school, helping the little ones learn to read and write and doing good works in the community.

In the early evening, I walked over to see Sam Perkins. We spoke for a short while, but I told him I needed to be home. We agreed to see each other the next morning. My mother made dinner, her scrumptious meat loaf, followed by blueberry pie. I fell asleep in no time.

I strolled to Sam Perkins' office the next morning. It was smaller than I remembered. Mr. Perkins too seemed to have shrunk. His eyes were sad. He had aged. He had a distinct stoop and his speech was slower. He still handled *The Post* virtually on his own, and published it weekly now. He seemed pleased to see me but he told me Lily was unwell and that he spent much of his time caring for her.

"Now, David," he said, "how about coffee and a talk? It's been a while."

"Yes. It's good to see you."

"Let's get one thing out of the way," said Sam. "I know what happened in St Louis. Your private life is your own affair. What you get up to is your business provided it doesn't tread on your integrity. But it did. And what you did for that advertiser was just plain wrong. And you knew it. I'm not going to ask you to explain yourself. I just want you to promise me you'll never do it again. If you do, we're through. Understand?"

"Mr. Perkins," I answered, "I'm ashamed of what I did. I can't put it right in St. Louis, but I can make good in St. Luke. You have my word that I'll never take money for my writing again." I then added, "Except for my job or unless a publisher wants a book from me."

Sam smiled. "Good enough. We're all entitled to one mistake. Now what's on your mind?"

"Mr. Perkins, do you remember my talking about a friend from my days in Rawlings, Mike Doyle?"

"Don't recall, but go on."

"I lost touch with him and haven't seen him for fourteen years. He's now the leader of the City Council in St. Luke. He won the election in 1922 under the banner of New Democrats."

Sam nodded to me to keep going.

"Last week, I went to see Doyle. It was as if the long gap in time had never existed. As we talked politics, I got this idea. *The Bugle* should endorse the New Democrats."

Sam sat up. "What!" he exclaimed. "Henry Brady will never do it."

I explained the logic I had put before to Doyle, Brady and Page. "I see," said Sam. "Who'd have thought that my printer's devil would be an angel in disguise? David, this is very clever, if."

"If?"

"If Doyle is on the level. But you've played it right. It's not your decision. It's for Henry Brady and he's smart."

"You're not exactly right. Ted Page has made it clear that if the endorsement goes ahead and it goes wrong, I'll be held responsible. Mind you, if it goes well, it helps me to make a mark in St. Luke," I explained. Mr. Perkins nodded thoughtfully. I continued, "I've only told you half the story. Doyle has a twin sister, Adele. She came to see me a day or so ago. I haven't told anyone at *The Bugle* about this because I'm embarrassed."

"What happened?" asked Sam.

"She seduced me." Sam's eyebrows rose a tad. "And I'm infatuated with her. My emotions are all over the place. This is why I came to you. I don't know what to do."

"Is she pretty?" asked Sam with a gentle smile on his face.

"She is beautiful and difficult and confused and what makes it worse, she told me afterwards she was married."

"Oh, that would complicate things somewhat. Give me a moment, David." Sam sipped his coffee and took out his pipe. In a practiced ritual, he filled it, patted down the tobacco, struck a match, lit the tobacco and started to puff. "It's all about integrity, really. Did Adele ask you to do anything for her brother?"

"No."

"Then you have done nothing wrong as a newspaperman, at least so far. If you continue the relationship whilst supporting Doyle and the New Democrats, a conflict of interest could arise. You know this. You didn't know she was married. I assume she wore no wedding ring?" I nodded. "Therefore, you need only bother your conscience about having future relations with a woman outside marriage but this has no bearing on matters with *The Bugle.*"

"But what if Mr. Brady or Doyle find out?"

"Well, one way for Henry Brady to find out is for you to tell him. Henry is a broad-minded man. If you tell him what you've told me, there should be no comeback. But, as a friend, you need to think carefully about the relationship."

"And if she is lying to me, if she is not married?"

"Do you want a relationship with a liar? Either way, David, you'll be playing with fire."

I sighed. "I know. I'm so torn. I want to do the right thing but she is just... Well, how did you feel when you met Mrs. Perkins?"

"Those were different times. I can't tell you what to do about the lady. That's for you. Let me put it to you this way. There are a million girls out there but only one *Bugle.* Now, tell me more about Mr. Doyle and his politics."

So we spent time talking about St. Luke politics and the way things were in Culpepper and what we thought of Mr. Coolidge and the 68th Congress. Every now and then, Mr. Perkins went to check on his wife. He told me she sent her love but wasn't up to seeing visitors.

I left Mr. Perkins late in the afternoon, promising to write and keep in touch. I spent the rest of the day with my mother. Jane was out with friends until the evening. When she came home, she played the piano for us. She was better than good.

The next morning, I took the early train, getting back to St. Luke late on Sunday night. I had thought things through and was resolved in my course of action.

Chapter Six

On Monday afternoon, I sat with Henry Brady and Ted Page. Brady looked me in the eye. "David, Ted has reported your research on Doyle to me and the board. With considerable misgivings, the board has decided to consider endorsing the New Democrats. Please would you arrange for me to meet Mr. Doyle? It's up to him to convince us he's on the level."

"Okay, Mr. Brady. There are some questions."

"Yes?"

"Who do you want present from *The Bugle*?"

"Me, Ted Page and you."

"And where do you want to hold the meeting? It might be awkward if Doyle came here and we can't go to City Hall."

"I don't agree. Let's see him here. We have nothing to hide. I doubt he'll be spotted by other newspapers and if he is, so what? See if he can meet us tonight."

"There is one other thing and it's awkward, but I need to tell you about Mike Doyle's twin sister, Adele." I then relayed exactly what happened, except for the more salacious details of the restaurant encounter, which I kept to myself.

Brady stared at me. "Why are you telling me this?"

"It's the right thing to do. I wouldn't have said anything to you if you hadn't decided to take things further with the New Democrats. And I won't be seeing Adele Doyle again." I decided not to mention Sam Perkins' role in my decision. Why make it more complicated than it already was?

Brady nodded. "Good enough. Let me know when we're meeting Doyle."

My next step was to speak with Doyle. "I have a green light here to go to the next stage. Brady wants to see you. Can you meet him and Ted Page at our offices tonight? I'll be there."

Mike agreed to come at 10:00pm. He made no pre-conditions other than that Tom Berman would accompany him. I asked him if he was sure he didn't mind meeting at *The Bugle*.

"Why should I? I'm a public servant. I'm happy to meet with the fourth estate people when and where they like."

"What if you're seen by a reporter from another newspaper?"

"What if I am? David, what's the problem?"

I let the issue drop. It was his funeral if anything adverse happened.

That night, Henry Brady, Ted Page and I sat on one side of a conference room table, facing Mike Doyle and Tom Berman. While we all introduced ourselves to each other, I served coffee and cake. Then Doyle started the conversation.

"Mr. Brady, we all know why we are here. So, please ask anythin' you want."

"Thank you. Mr. Doyle, exactly what are your plans for St. Luke?"

"Briefly, the plans are to continue to provide good services for all St. Luke citizens at reasonable prices, to balance the city budget and to employ city workers on merit. The New Democrats also want to help the unfortunates of our city and encourage charitable givin' to establish better medical services for those who can't afford it. Sounds too good to be true, doesn't it? Let me explain how we propose to do it."

Doyle then spelled out the process, revealing nothing new. Under the new charter, a City Manager would be appointed. City services would be broken down into directorates, each under a director who would have responsibility for his department and who would report to the City Manager, who in turn would be accountable to the council. This way the council would emulate accountability in large corporations.

"What will be the directorates?" asked Brady.

"We're still workin' on this, but probably public affairs, accounts and finances, public safety, streets and public improvements, parks and public property. We are still considerin' home rule and how to administer the police and whether the director should be a policeman or civil servant. We are also thinkin' about taking control of education administration, too. We'll need agreement from the State Congress for both."

"How are you going to save costs?"

"What we found when we took over was huge waste. Say your Metro section was staffed full of your friends who didn't know the job? If you get rid of the time wasters and replace them with fewer people who can do the job, you get a better product much cheaper. That's the same with government. Services will continue to be streamlined and eliminatin' waste and inefficiency will pay for the additional costs. Hanrahan left a lot for us to do. We couldn't get it all done in two years."

"How will the City Manager be appointed?" Brady asked.

"He won't be appointed. He will stand for election. Some time ago, the New Democrats made a shortlist of names of the most suitable candidates and we chose our man."

"Who is your candidate?"

"Tom Berman, here. He fought beside me in the Great War, so I can vouch for him. Since getting stateside, he has become an experienced accountant and manager, working for my uncle and, for the past two years, the Party." Berman smiled at the people around the table.

"Mr. Doyle, we have some issues with the new charter. For example, how will voters have a relationship with the councilmen-at -large?"

"I know you have queries about the charter. I'll be happy to be interviewed on the record to deal with the detail. However, let me say this in answer to your specific question. If you look at our federal and state elections, to what extent do voters really know the candidates? Do voters get to talk with a presidential candidate or a feller runnin' for governor? This has not been viewed as a disadvantage, has it? Otherwise the system would have been changed.

"As for the council, I'm hoping that the councilmen-at-large will exercise greater independence. We need people on the council who can see a bigger picture."

"What do you mean by 'bigger picture'?"

"That they will look out for the interests of St. Luke as a whole, not just a ward they happen to represent."

"Give me an example."

Without a pause, Doyle answered. "Assume a business wants to open a new factory. There might be a fight between wards, based purely on self-interest. Councilmen-at-large will take a wider view, positioning the factory where it suits the company and the city best."

Brady continued with his questioning about the policies of the New Democrats for almost an hour and Doyle answered everything frankly. Then Henry said he would like to know about Doyle's personal and family life.

"I don't mind answerin' about my public life, but private is private. I'll see, dependin' on the question. What do you want to know?"

"There's a rumor that your brothers are involved in organized crime and that there are links between them and the New Democrats."

Doyle replied angrily, "I have no relationship with my brothers. We have been estranged for more than two years. And there is no truth that there are links between them, and the people they associate with, and the New Democrats." Doyle looked Henry Brady in the eye. "Absolutely no truth."

"So your brothers are involved in criminal activity?"

"I have no evidence of that. Off the record, I think this may be so, but I just don't know."

Brady nodded. He then asked, "Mr. Doyle, you live in your mother's home with her and your sister?"

"Okay, you're really treadin' on private territory. Yes I do, except my sister doesn't live in St. Luke. She lives in Los Angeles, but she stays with us when she visits."

"There is no Mrs. Doyle."

"Yes, my ma. Am I married? No."

"Do you have anyone in mind for this post?" Brady asked with a kindly inflection.

Mike leaned back in his chair, looking wistful. "If only I had the time. Mr. Brady. In my job, you work eighteen hours a day. I'm city leader but it doesn't stop there. I have ward people to look after. There's no time for a home life, really."

After a pause, Brady asked if he could confer with us for a moment. He asked if any of us had any questions. Ted Page indicated he was happy. I didn't want to ask anything.

"Okay," said Brady to Doyle. "Is there anything you want to ask me?"

"Yes," Doyle said, "do we get the endorsement?"

"I must confer with my board but I think you may well be happy with the outcome. There can be nothing formal between us yet, but you might want to read *The Bugle* in a couple of days."

Two days later, Henry Brady himself wrote *The Bugle's* leading editorial.

The St. Luke Bugle
Established: 1875. 28' ^*h* *March, 1923. Circulation: 298,452.*

THE BUGLE ENDORSES
THE NEW DEMOCRATS

Since its incorporation, this newspaper has supported the Republican Party in federal, state, county and city elections. However, in the past six years, the Republicans who represent this city have not seen fit to adapt their policies or propose new initiatives to the voters of St. Luke. We have argued that changes need to be made in the way the St. Luke Republican Party conducts itself but our advice has fallen on deaf ears. We have now lost confidence in the St. Luke Republican Party.

We have investigated the policies and proposals of the New Democratic Party, headed by Michael Doyle. The conduct of their administration in governing St. Luke for the past two years has shown they are fit for the job. Unlike their Democratic predecessors under Ed Hanrahan, the New Democrats have employed city personnel on merit and sought to balance their budgets. The services provided for the city could still be improved and the New Democrats are aware of this. To this end, they will propose substantial revisions to the way the city is administered and we will report on their plans in the coming weeks.

Michael Doyle, the leader of the New Democrats, is a veteran of the Great War and a war hero. Most, if not all, of his co-councilmen and party colleagues also fought in the Great War with credit. These men may not be the most experienced in government, but their first administration has been a success. They deserve a further two years in City Hall.

Accordingly, this newspaper is pleased to endorse The New Democrat Party candidates in both the forthcoming primary elections and the city election proper.

Chapter Seven

From around 8:30 a.m. on Friday, my telephone rang off the hook. First, Henry Brady asked if I liked the morning's editorial. I said it was excellent. What else was I going to say? His actual words to me were, "So what do you think of my purple prose?" Then Ted Page called me in.

"I'm putting you onto the city election full time. Your role is to do the research and get the stories. I need more experienced reporters to write them, but I'll give you what opportunities I can. And go talk to Doyle and his people. See what you can get."

Then Doyle rang. "This is a cause for celebration. Lunch?"

"Yes, why not." I was getting out of breath.

"Meet me at the Pyramid, one o'clock."

At lunch, Doyle was ecstatic. "Who'd have thought of *The Bugle* endorsin' the New Democrats? How did you persuade all those cynical newsmen? I still can't believe it."

A waitress brought some menus and we ordered. People came to our table every few minutes to say hello to Doyle. He introduced me as, "an up-and-comer from *The Bugle.*" After lunch, I settled the bill despite Doyle's protests. "*The Bugle*'s paying for this one."

Doyle suggested I go with him to his Main Street office. "We'll be talkin' election business so I should keep it away from City Hall," he explained. On arrival at his office, we walked up a flight of stairs, past a long queue of people. Doyle said, "Give me thirty minutes to deal with these people and then I'm all yours?"

I was offered coffee and waited. After almost an hour, Doyle appeared. "Sorry, it took longer than I thought. Come on in."

"What was that all about?" I asked.

"People want help, jobs, money, food, medical stuff, that sort of thing," Doyle replied.

"Why do you do this?"

"David, it's my job. These people need help. We don't ask lots of questions or have them fill in forms. I'm as good a judge of character as any charity organization and I know if people are trying to pull the wool over my eyes. So, if I can help them, I do."

"And secure more votes," I asked.

"Absolutely, but what's wrong with that? The federal and state governments do pretty well nothin' for these people. Those politicians sit in comfortable chairs makin' policy for the middle classes and don't care about the poor. City government is at the sharp end, retail politics. And sometimes, when that kind, Hanrahan's kind, gives little or no help to the people who really need it, it's left to people like the New Democrats – people like me – to sort things out. The New Democrats are here to help all the people, not just the rich and middle classes."

Doyle had a grim expression on his face as he spoke. Was he thinking of his own childhood? I sat quietly. The outburst was unexpected, especially from someone like Doyle who was usually so measured. Doyle broke the mood. He smiled at me. "Like a real drink?" I took a beer.

Over drinks, we agreed a plan of action. I would give him a broad outline of the areas that would be covered in an interview. I explained that I would conduct the interview then give my notes to Ted Page and someone else would write the story.

"That's a tough break for you."

"No, Mike, it's fair enough. I'm very new at the paper and this is a big story."

Doyle shrugged his shoulders. *Bugle* reporters would talk with the five New Democrat candidates for councilmen-at-large, the ten New Democrat ward candidates, as well as Tom Berman and any other candidates put up for city office. There would be feature articles and pictures accompanying them.

I made it clear to Doyle that everything we discussed had to be disclosed to Ted Page. "What if I tell you something off the record, David?"

"I'll relay it to Ted, but he won't use it. He'll respect your decision."

"Okay, I guess I can live with that. Now, why don't we relax a little?"

Over the next hour or so and more beers, Doyle talked about politics and life. Colleagues came and went. He introduced me as, "our man at *The Bugle*." I was too naïve to realize that I was being seduced, not so much by Doyle, but the proximity to power. Not only did I now have access to the center of St. Luke government and its politics, I had caught the better eye of Henry Brady. My future was on the up.

Casually, I asked about Adele. Doyle told me she had returned to Los Angeles. I felt both relieved and disappointed. When I left, I walked back up East 23rd and pushed my hands deep into my pockets.

Chapter Eight

Just before the February primary, Ted Page showed me the article which *The Bugle* was going to publish the following day under my by-line, a first for me.

The St. Luke Bugle
Established: 1875. 5th[h] February, 1924. Circulation: 293,130.

MICHAEL DOYLE AND THE NEW CITY CHARTER

When this newspaper endorses a political candidate or party, it does not do so blindly. It tests constantly and should a candidate or party fall short on promises or pledges, this newspaper will not hesitate to publish that fact, as well as both clarify and reconsider its position. *The Bugle* will review regularly both the policies of The New Democratic Party and the actions and statements of its candidates.

Last year, *The Bugle* aired its concerns on the speedy adoption of the new St. Luke charter, although many of its proposed changes were welcomed. In an exclusive interview last week with the leader of the New Democrats, Michael Doyle stated why city government in St. Luke needed to change. "St. Luke," he said, "is an important city whose population will grow rapidly as it welcomes new people, new businesses and new technologies. The demand for additional housing and increased services cannot be satisfied under the old government structure."

Asked about the City Manager's role, Mr. Doyle commented, "St. Luke government will look more like a well-run corporation with modern lines of communication and accountability. This is a change for good."

On councilmen-at-large, he said "St. Luke needs them, regardless of political affiliation, because they will help decide the big issues of the day, how much government needs to spend and where. They'll settle the turf wars between wards so that new factories, offices and homes are built where they are needed in the interests of St. Luke as a whole."

When asked about the loss of contact between the public and their politicians, Mr. Doyle was clear. "There will be plenty of help for the working people of the city. They need have no fear. I promise there will still be as much service as always under a New Democrat administration. If I am found to be lying, then the people will not vote for us again." Mr. Doyle concluded, "Overall, we are sure that the majority of our citizens will welcome the changes brought by the new charter. If not, we will be told in the election two years hence."

Ted asked, "Any comments?"

"I'm not happy that the new charter has sufficient checks and balances. Any party with a big majority on Council will be able to do pretty well what it likes because the legislative and executive functions will effectively be in the same hands. Separation of powers won't apply because the City Manager as Chief Executive and nominated by the party in power will not be able to resist the demands of those who nominate him. The New Democrats have less than a two-year track record and we all know that old saying: power corrupts. Mind you, I am impressed with Doyle and his colleagues. I've met lots of them and they seem pretty genuine."

"There is always a risk of overwhelming power, whether you have the old charter or the new one," replied Ted. "Whoever is in power calls the shots. It's Andrew Jackson all over again. You know, to the victor the spoils. David, maybe you should press Doyle on these points. It will be an interesting line to pursue in the run-up to the election. You are onto a good thing here. Keep it up."

After the February primaries, the election campaign proper started. The rallies were boisterous and rowdy as the Democrats and New Democrats vied against each other for the voters' attention. The Republicans hardly made a ripple. There were parades and marching bands and plenty of ballyhoo. And, as usual with city politics, there was little of substance, no details of new policy initiatives, just loads of personalities and boilerplate. The old Democrats campaigned on back to business as usual, the New Democrats on continued change to benefit all and city jobs on merit, as well as asking voters to look at their record.

I spoke with Mike about the prospects for St. Luke if the New Democrats were re-elected, but what Ted Page really wanted was copy for a Doyle feature article. We met at his City Hall offices on a cold, wet March morning and I welcomed the offer of a coffee.

"Let's have a brief run through about what we're coverin' this morning," Doyle said to me.

"I want to examine your plans for St. Luke for the next two years and to examine your motivation for the political career you've undertaken."

"Is that all?" Mike replied, ironically. "I thought we were goin' to talk about serious stuff!"

"Let's get started. So, what exactly are your plans for the next two years?"

Mike replied immediately. "First, you're makin' the assumption that the New Democrats will win the election next month. I'm confident, but let's not pre-empt the vote. If we win, we'll want to see how the new City Manager and the six directorates work out, as well as the councilmen-at-large. I won't be keen to see changes to the St. Luke municipal structure until the heads of department have had a good opportunity to get their departments workin'. One year in, we'll have a review with Tom Berman and then look at what changes might be needed."

"Fair enough. What else?"

"We'll have to consider the nature of the services that an expandin' city needs. There are goin' to be poor people living in St. Luke and the federal and state governments don't provide for them. There will be sick people here who can't afford doctors and a modern city should have somethin' in place. We must improve the sewers. The poor areas are a serious health hazard. This has to be fixed. We can't risk outbreaks of typhoid and cholera and those kind of diseases.

"We need to be sure that business can work effectively here, so regulations mustn't bite off the hand that feeds. Jobs are important. Let's face it, without business, the city will go downhill."

"That's a big agenda. Mike, can you put some flesh on these bones? For example, how will you get doctors to treat people who can't afford them?"

"Now don't put words in my mouth, *Bugle* man, I didn't say we had a plan. What American city does? I said it needed to be looked at. I don't want to prejudge issues. Our many St. Luke charities, which do a great job, have the thing partially covered. Maybe not enough, if we get the expandin' numbers of people I expect. I mentioned health as just one of the issues to be looked at. I expect to make a personal appeal to the hospitals in St. Luke to get them to join in a strategy."

"So what are the other issues?"

"Who should control our police? Why should we allow the state, the people in Cameron, to tell us what to do? If St. Luke citizens want home rule, then we should petition the state government to change the status of our police department. But there are no concrete plans in place yet. No point until we know the voters want this change. Education is the same."

"What about roads and public buildings?" I asked. "Are you satisfied with the status quo?"

"Well, what do you think? We are sitting in City Hall, the home of St. Luke government. The building is too small, old fashioned, drafty, cold in winter, almost unbearably hot in summer and ill-suited for the numbers of employees who will be workin' for the city in years to come. Our law courts are an embarrassment. They are shabby and depressin'. The prison cells are fit only for a system envisaged in the Dark Ages. The expansion of new suburbs has come with a road system that is the envy of the state but further out our farmers still use bumpy dirt roads. This is not the modern way and bad for the agriculture business. We need better roads for trucks and motor cars.

"So, no, I'm not satisfied with the status quo. If re-elected, we'll be concentratin' on this area. Harold Levy is standing for Chief County Judge and he'll be the one leading on road buildin'. I've talked with him, too, about our public buildins' and he may well get this brief, but I doubt that we'll make much headway on this side of things before 1926. It would cost a great deal and I don't know if we would be successful in selling city bonds to cover the cost. Anyway, there are other things that'll have priority."

"Like I said, you have an ambitious agenda?"

"I think so. There's a limit to what can be done in two years but I've outlined a lot of things we're goin' to try and tackle or at least look at."

"Indeed. Mike, what happens if things go wrong? For example, what happens if the City Manager proves to be a failure? How will you deal with this?"

"If we win, I can assure you that Tom Berman is up to the job. But, acceptin' your premise for a moment, anyone who can't do the job will be fired. Simple as that. And that goes for everyone on the city payroll. All we asked in our first term was for city government people to do their jobs well and, by and large, they did. Why change?"

"Okay, but what happens if the charter doesn't operate as envisaged?"

"I guess if the people don't approve, they'll have to wait until the next election and throw out the politicians they don't like."

"So there are gaps in the new charter?"

"Maybe but there were huge gaps under the old charter. And the sanction has always been that people in public life have to stand for election. If we are re-elected, we have to run again in '26. Anyway, a charter is not like a huge bandage to fix all problems. The new charter has much more protection built into it than the old one. You need to see the new charter as an experiment, much the same as the people regarded the Constitution one hundred and fifty years ago."

We talked more about the details, but Mike would not concede that with a big majority, his power would be almost uncontrolled. His answer was that the voters would decide.

"Let's move on, Mike. Let's talk about Michael Doyle, the man, what motivates him and what are his ambitions?"

"Shoot."

"What made you decide to go into public life?"

"It didn't happen all at once. I didn't have – what is the word – an epiphany. I grew up with an uncle who served the people of one of St. Luke's wards. I watched him work and I liked what I saw, how he helped people. Then, when I went to France, I had to grow up fast. Life in the trenches was surreal. You could spend a day being bored out of your skull and then, within seconds, you could experience fear that you wouldn't believe. That fear still stays with me. The mud, the stench, even the dreary routine fades away very quickly when shells are fallin' around you and you hear the screams of men dyin' in agony."

"Can you put those experiences out of your mind?"

"You mean do I have nightmares? No, I don't, but I shall never forget those war years. 'Man's inhumanity to man,' isn't that the phrase? But there's more to it. I made friendships that will last a lifetime. Look at the New Democrats standin' in this election. Many of them were in my regiment. I shared the sergeants' mess with some of my closest colleagues. We fought together. That creates a bond that I hope will prove unbreakable."

"After the war, you took your time coming home."

"Yes, by then I decided that I wanted to be in public life, partly to try to make some sense out of the war, to make the world a better place. David, don't quote me on that, please. I sound like an ass. The thing is that most of us who came back from France wanted to live in a better world, one where poverty was not a sin and where privilege didn't entitle some people to live better than others."

"Are you a socialist?"

"No, my beliefs are not communist or socialist. My beliefs are based on fairness, I suppose. If you've been shot at fightin' for your country, then you should be entitled to a chance of a good job and a decent life in return. Anyway, I took my time coming home by spendin' it with politicians, public officials, businessmen and workin' men of other states and cities, learning more about how things get done in America."

"Are you saying this was your version of going away to college?"

"You'd know more about that than me, college boy. I guess so. There was an opportunity for me and Uncle Joe made sure I took advantage."

"Does this mean that in years to come you have ambitions to serve in the state legislature or governor's mansion or even in Washington?"

"No, it most certainly does not. I have absolutely no ambitions in that area. I like livin' in the city where I grew up, where I know people and where I think I can be a force for good. That is where my ambition lies and where I'll stay."

"So, you see yourself serving on the city Council for years ahead?"

"Who knows? That's for voters to decide. But I will be very happy if the New Democrats are re-elected."

"And to lead the council?"

"If asked, yes. But that's for another time and other people to decide."

"What about your own time? What do you do with it?"

Doyle gave me a look. "You're gettin' into the private life here. I don't think it's your business."

"Come on, Mike, our readers would like to know the real Mike Doyle, who he is, what makes him tick."

"They'll be disappointed then. My private life belongs to me, not your readers."

"Okay, off the record, why aren't you married or in a relationship?"

Doyle glared at me. "Why aren't you? We're the same age. When do I have time? You've seen me at work. I start early and finish late. I don't have a chance at a personal life."

We sat in silence for a while. Doyle calmed down. He leaned close to me, almost whispering. "Books, let's go off the record, just you and me, nothing for Ted Page or anyone else."

"Okay."

"No one knows about what I'm about to tell you. If you tell a livin' soul, we're through forever."

I looked Doyle in the eye. "You have my word."

Doyle leaned back in his chair and closed his eyes again as he began to talk.

Versailles was surprisingly undamaged by the war. A billet was found for Doyle's platoon in an imposing residence on the Avenue de Paris, close to the Palace of Versailles and the shops and cafes of the town. Duties were light and the men had time on their hands whilst peace talks continued.

In early January of 1919, Doyle stopped at Café de la Palais for his morning wakener. Instead of being served by Gilles, the patron, a girl of Doyle's age came to his table.

"*Monsieur, vous avez choisi?* What would you like?" "*Merci, mademoiselle*," replied Doyle, "*café, s'il vous plaît. Ah, café au lait.*"

The girl looked surprised to hear French spoken by an American. When she brought his coffee, she addressed him. "*Vous parlez francais? Bien. Pourquoi les autres soldats ne parlent pas en francais?*"

"You got me there. *Oh, je ne sais pas. Alors, je m'appelle Mike Doyle. Et vous?*"

"Claudine, monsieur."

Claudine was called away and as the café became busy, Doyle had no further opportunity to talk with her. The next day, he returned and the day after and the day after that. Each time, Doyle and Claudine exchanged pleasantries but nothing further.

Claudine was his height, of striking good looks, especially her green eyes that were shaped like almonds. Her fair hair was cut short. She was very well proportioned in body and legs. On the fourth morning, she came over to his table. Doyle was about to order when she spoke to him.

"You don't have to come here every day, you know. If you want to see me, ask me out. My day off is *Dimanche*, Sunday."

"I would very much like to spend time with you. May I take you out this Sunday?"

"Yes, of course."

"When shall I collect you?"

"*Midi*"

"Where do you live?"

"Oh, meet me here."

That Sunday, a watery sun shone on a cloudless, chilly day.

"Let's walk," said Claudine. The vast gardens of the Palace were open to allied soldiers.

"There's a restaurant about a mile into the gardens, I think," offered Doyle.

"If not, you'll have to carry me back," giggled Claudine, amused by Doyle's seriousness. As they walked, they exchanged their life stories. Doyle omitted all the seamier aspects of his life, but he was also modest enough to keep his gallantry medal to himself. He told her how he was itching to get back to the States. "That's where it's happening now, and that's where I need to be. Opportunities aplenty and I'm missing out, while President Wilson takes his time here." He described St. Luke as, "a city for the twentieth century, where people will not want for anything, if things are handled right." He told her of his ambitions as a politician and how he hoped to be a force for good.

Over lunch, Claudine explained how her life was very different to his. She had grown up in the village of Chatillon, near Verdun, with her parents, two brothers and a sister. Her father had been a prosperous businessman. Everything had been wonderful until 1914 and even then, times were not so bad until both her brothers were killed in 1915 at the Battle of Loos. The next year, a battle had been fought near her village. There was a skirmish with a lot of shelling from both sides. Who knew who fired the shells that demolished her parents' house? In the destruction and fire, her parents and sister were burned to death.

At the time, Claudine was at a boarding school outside Paris. Orphaned, she stayed at school until she was eighteen and had recently come to live in Versailles where she worked until she could renew her studies at college. She didn't know what she wanted to become, but maybe a couturier. She was being cared for by Gilles, her father's younger brother, who had taken her in.

Doyle soon realized how much he liked Claudine, but his uncle's advice to care for no one but himself rang in his ears. "Not this time, Joe," he told himself. "This is different." Doyle and Claudine returned to the café by mid evening. Claudine shook his hand to say goodnight. "That's not how we do it in the States," Doyle whispered.

"Really, and how is it done in America?"

Slowly, Doyle took her into his arms and kissed her gently at first and then strongly. "That's how. *Bonne nuit.*" He walked away, grinning to himself, knowing that Claudine was staring at his back. In that kiss, he knew she was no innocent. Maybe life at a French boarding school had had its surprises.

On their third Sunday together, they went by train into Paris. Claudine showed Doyle the sights. They dined at Brasserie de Balzar, near Notre Dame. When dessert was served, she asked him, "Why are you not an affectionate person? You are nice but a little distant, I think."

"Why do you say that?"

"We hold hands only when I take yours. You seem uncomfortable when I put my arm in yours. But you like kissing. I think you are one of those men who is a proficient lover, but who doesn't know love."

"What's brought all this on, Claudine?"

Claudine just stared at him and looked wistful. "Just a feeling. Don't mind me. Soon you'll be gone and we will forget each other."

"I hope not." Doyle felt hurt. Was this what he had become, unfeeling, uncaring, just out for what he could get?

"Why do you care what I'm like? Do I matter to you?"

"Of course you do," Claudine murmured as she moved close to him and he kissed her.

Every Sunday after that, Claudine and Doyle spent time in Paris. First, they would have lunch at one of the many restaurants near the Place de Vosges. Then they retired to a room in the elegant Hotel Turenne. Doyle was surprised on the first occasion. Claudine made all the running. She told him she wanted to be with him, "as a man and a woman should" and that she had made the arrangements. After they had registered and were alone in their room, Doyle told her he had not expected the day to turn out quite like this.

"Mind you, Claudine, I have no objection."

"Cheri, I like sex and if I had waited for you to make a move, it would have taken an age."

Doyle thought he knew the ways of sensuous pleasure, but Claudine was his match. She set the pace, brought him forward and pressed him back until he finally exploded and collapsed, exhausted. She left him dozing. He awoke, refreshed and ready. This time, she let him take control, as passion engulfed them both. Later, as they sprawled on the bed, legs linked, Doyle asked Claudine how she had lost her virginity.

"At school with the son of my English teacher. I was fourteen, he was sixteen."

"Was it good?"

"Not really. The boy's father was so much better!"

"Good grief! You had sex with your teacher?"

"Why not? He didn't seduce me. I liked him."

"Have there been many other lovers?"

"Some. I told you, I like sex and who knows how long we will live."

One Sunday after they had made love, Doyle told Claudine he wanted to talk with her seriously. "The peace talks are coming to an end and I'll have to go back to the States. Have you thought about this?"

"I know. I will miss you."

"You don't have to. I don't want us to part. Come to St. Luke and be with me. You know I'd look after you."

Claudine bit her lip as she spoke. "I like you very much but I can't go half way around the world just like that. What if things don't work out?"

"Claudine, what assurances do you need? Is it money, is it security, what?"

"Michael, it's not that. It's so basic. I'm old France, you're new America. Our cultures, our ways of life are so totally different. Tell me, do you have wine in St. Luke?"

"What an odd question. We can get wine but people don't usually drink it. So?"

"Do you have fresh brioche and croissant in the morning?"

"No, we have black bread and rye bread and brown bread and bagels. I don't understand."

"Are there dressmakers, hairdressers, jewelers, places just for women in St. Luke?"

"Sure. Not like here on the Rue de Rivoli, but we have them."

"The point is that my life is in France. Everything I am used to is French. What is there for me in America?"

"Me."

"Why can't you stay in France?"

"I have people in St. Luke waiting for me, depending on me. I can't let these people down."

"But I can't just leave here? Michael, it won't work."

"Claudine, will you at least think it over? There's not much time, but couldn't we try?"

"Okay, I will think."

When Claudine and Doyle met later that week, Doyle could see she was unwell. "It's just a cold," Claudine told him. She was wrong. Sadly, the influenza pandemic, which was to kill more than twice as many people after the Great War as died in it, soon claimed Claudine as a victim.

Doyle had known death since he was ten. In Rawlings, in The Trench, in the war, there had been funerals and death aplenty. Many people Doyle knew in his young life, some very well, had passed. Even with his father, he had not felt pain. He thought he was immune to loss.

With Claudine, it was different. The night he heard the news, he took himself to his room. Alone, he started to cry and then he sobbed. Tears had never come like this before. He was out of control. He didn't care. He wanted to cry for the rest of his life. The reason for living had gone. He didn't care about his future, St. Luke, none of it.

The light left Doyle's eyes. The remainder of his time in France was played against a black curtain. Periodically, he would repeat the sobbing of the night of Claudine's death. He delegated most of his duties and spent a solitary life in his room.

His men knew something of what had happened and rallied as best they could to help. Crossing the Atlantic Ocean to New York City, Doyle spent most of his time in his cabin. He found life without Claudine to be unbearable.

Thankfully for Doyle, he experienced a catharsis when he saw the Statue of Liberty and the lower Manhattan skyline. He felt a physical change and his spirits started to rise. "Just a girl," he told himself. "Tell yourself she was just a girl. You have years of your life ahead of you. Never again. No woman will get close to me ever again."

And that, Doyle explained to me, was how things had remained ever since.

Chapter Nine

Days merged into one another as election-day neared. There was enough political mud-slinging to start a landslide. Most of the mud emanated from the Hanrahan camp. One outrageous story in a rival newspaper, *The St Luke Star,* depicted Doyle as a coward who had won his Congressional Medal for Gallantry through the ruse of falsely taking on the identity of a dead soldier, killed in the incident in question. Five men, supposedly independent, came forward alleging that they took part in the battle and had seen the dead soldier carry out the acts of bravery. Another three swore that Doyle was in a hospital five miles to the rear of the battle, faking a broken arm.

The story had legs for just a day. Colonel James Rapier, the commander of the Eagle Regiment, called a press conference. He confirmed Doyle's medal had been won legitimately and that he was one of the eyewitnesses to the action. He produced seven officers and men who backed up the story. The matron of the field hospital, now a senior nurse in a St. Luke hospital, confirmed that Doyle had never been a patient although he had often visited his men.

Very quickly, Doyle's vindication carried the day, but the story didn't go away. Instead, the Hanrahan machine was vilified in the St. Luke press for spreading rumours, emphasizing the desperate efforts of Hanrahan to re-take power at any cost. Doyle himself kept silent, despite my efforts to get him on record. "People have done my talkin' for me. Hanrahan's gettin' his, you'll see."

Ten days before the election, the St. Luke press reported a raid on a speakeasy in the downtown area. A number of prominent citizens were arrested, including Ed Hanrahan. The next day, stories were published, naming Hanrahan as the owner of the building and landlord of the speakeasy. In all probability, the story would have done Hanrahan little damage, had it not been for his strong support of

Prohibition. New Democrats and Republicans alike openly criticized Hanrahan for his hypocrisy.

St. Luke's old Democrats were now in a bind. Would they distance themselves from their leader so close to an election? They did, and quickly. Abandoning Hanrahan, they selected George Bolen, the former mayor, as his successor.

The press reported the story not so much as a nail in the coffin of the old Democrats, but more of a coffin lid nailed and shut tight. With their leadership in such disarray, there was no hope for the old Democrats to recover lost ground. They had become a hopeless cause.

In the meantime, the New Democrats continued to advertise their slate of candidates daily, with pictures in all newspapers. The New Democrat candidates for councilmen-at-large spoke at well-attended meetings each day and night, until their names and faces became almost as familiar as Doyle's. As each man was a Great War veteran, he would usually appear in uniform and be accompanied by a military-style band. The candidates were well disciplined, keeping to the New Democrat message.

Two nights before Election Day, Doyle asked me to meet him. He wasn't worried about meeting in a speakeasy. "Everyone knows I'm a wet." After a drink or two in a private room, Doyle said, "I need to tell you something."

"What's wrong?"

"Nothing. It's almost certain that the New Democrats will win on Thursday. There are goin' to be changes in City Hall. I'm resignin' as leader. I'm stayin' on as Chairman of the Party, but the two jobs are too much for me."

I looked at Mike, dumbfounded. "How long ago did you decide this? You've blindsided me and, what's worse, you've got *The Bugle* to endorse you under false pretenses."

"You're wrong. I've only just made the decision. Uncle Joe isn't well and I have to take over runnin' his businesses. He can't do it anymore. I can look after his businesses and run the Party, but I can't lead the city government as well. Don't you see?"

"Is this off the record?"

"I'd prefer it, but you can tell Brady and Page. If they run the story, it might hurt me a bit but it won't change the outcome, especially when I tell my side to the press. *The Bugle* will look petty, bad."

"Mike, I can't pretend I'm not disappointed." I thought it best to go. We didn't shake hands. Walking through the lounge, I saw one or two people I knew and talked a while. As I left, I saw Doyle by the bar, his arm around a redhead. "Well," I thought, "maybe he's starting a private life now!"

The next morning, I waited for Ted. "Don't you ever learn? I don't need you and whatever you have first thing in the morning. Come back after I've had a coffee."

"Not this time, Ted. I think I've been played." I waited till we were both seated in his office and told him what had happened last night.

"David, we've all been played. We can't use this. Doyle was off the record. If we print the story, he'll deny it and delay his decision. For what it's worth, even if Doyle admitted the facts, he's right, it won't make a difference to the outcome of the election. I'll let Henry know. I doubt there will be any comeback. But it's a bad day."

The election was won in a landslide, a colossal victory for the New Democrat candidates. All five of their councilmen-at-large were elected. In eight of the ten wards, New Democrats were elected with the remaining two seats going to the Republicans. All offices up for election went to the New Democrats, including the key post of City Manager. The old Democrats were wiped out completely. Even the habitual charges of election fraud and vote rigging were muted this time round.

For St. Luke government, it was business as usual, as control of the City Council had not changed. However, there was consternation and panic within the Democratic Party. A delegation of state Democrats rushed from Cameron to St. Luke to carry out an investigation. They demanded the resignations of all senior party officials allied to Hanrahan, who was now finished politically.

In City Hall, the New Democrats convened early on the morning after the election. Most had spent the previous evening together and, undoubtedly, they had sore heads after celebrating. Doyle bounced in, ready to hit the ground running.

"Congratulations. A stunnin' victory. We have to prove to the voters they did the right thing. Today and tomorrow, I'd like to meet with all councilmen individually to agree portfolios for the next two years. Then we'll all meet together to agree how we run things internally. Now we have to elect a leader of the council. May I ask if there are any proposals?"

There was uneasy laughter. John Santino chimed in. "Boss, there's only one leader for us, that's you."

"Thank you, John," Doyle replied, "but I'm not willin' to be leader of the council as well as being chairman of the New Democrats. I think it best for us to have another face as leader. I was hoping that Alexei Gann might take this on."

Alexei grinned. He knew what was coming. He was an imposing five foot ten, balding, of swarthy good looks, with a reputation for numerous affairs, something that did not escape the notice of Mrs. Gann, who had given him three children thus far. Alexei owned St. Luke's largest cinema and was not short of a dollar or two. He was greedy for money and power and a natural for city government. Doyle had selected him as one who would not enjoy popularity but who would command fear, not respect, from his co-councilors.

The others in the room were stunned into silence by Doyle's announcement. None felt immediately able to challenge the proposal of Gann's advancement. "Okay with me," was all Alexei needed to say.

"So we're done for now. I'll meet with each of you later. I'm callin' a press conference for tomorrow, when I'll introduce Alexei as the new council leader. Alexei, then you'll take charge." Alexei Gann nodded, careful to look only at Doyle.

The next day, the St. Luke press and other journalists around the state gathered in the East Room on the top floor of City Hall. The place was packed. At 11:00 a.m., the newly elected New Democrat councilmen and senior city staff entered the room. Doyle strode to the rostrum and took the microphone.

"Ladies and gentlemen, good mornin'. I have an announcement. I have decided to resign as leader of the council. I will serve as councilor for the First Ward and I have accepted re-appointment as chairman of the St. Luke New Democratic Committee. So, without further ado, may I introduce the new leader of the St. Luke City Council, Councilor Alexei Gann."

There was an audible gasp around the room and press hands were raised. Several reporters shouted Doyle's name, but they were waved off. Alexei came to the rostrum, shook hands with Doyle and took the microphone.

"Good morning. I'll take questions later. I, too, have a number of announcements for you. First, I have pleasure in confirming the election of Mr. Tom Berman to the post of St. Luke City Manager. As you know, the City Manager will have responsibility for the day-to-day control and decisions affecting St. Luke services. Mr. Berman will assume his duties immediately.

"Second, the council will restructure the city's services within the following five departments: public health and safety; streets, roads and public improvements; parks and public property; public and business affairs; accounts and finance. During the coming week, Mr. Berman will seek to appoint directors for each department. Where possible, he will promote from within. If this is not possible, he will recruit from within state. As you know, this is an experiment in city government and the changes are not written in stone. We will report to the citizens of St. Luke one year hence as to the benefits of the changes to the city.

"Third, it will be for each department director to make his own appointments. Therefore, we will require the resignations of all city officials and employees with effect one week hence. Our reason for this action is to ensure appointments made by directors are entirely on merit. They must be free to choose their own people." There was another audible gasp in the room. Alexei Gann, ignoring the murmurs, continued. "Of course, we expect a large proportion of existing employees will be re-engaged.

"Fourth, the additional services which the citizens have voted us to provide have to be paid for. We have decided not to increase property taxes. Instead, we propose to experiment by imposing a new city tax of 1% on all retail sales, excluding food and rent, to take effect six months hence. This will give time for debate on the new tax laws, which we will need to pass. In the interim, any deficit spending will be covered by a loan facility which has been agreed with the First Bank of St. Luke." At this, there were shouts and hands raised for questions.

"I will take questions in a moment," said Gann, who was visibly growing in confidence. "As they say, we live in interesting times. The Great War ended over five years ago and we are now enjoying economic prosperity, with the resulting increase in our city's population and demands on services. We hope our citizens will

101

support the changes we are making in the best interests of all. Now, I'll be happy to take questions."

I moved to get the ball rolling. "David Driscoll, *The St. Luke Bugle.* Mr. Gann, why has Mr. Doyle resigned?"

"I'll let Mr. Doyle answer for himself."

Doyle returned to the microphone. "This isn't easy. I guess the best I can say is this. I returned from the Great War to improve the lives of our citizens, but I had no ambition to be leader of the St. Luke government. I never asked for this and I was always uneasy in the role. Also, in the past few years, I've had no life outside my work for the city and the Party. I believe I am entitled to some time for myself and those near and dear to me. I'm much better suited to the roles I am taking on. I will be a better servant of the people as a result." Doyle refused to take follow-up questions and left the rostrum.

A reporter from *The St. Luke Star* asked Gann, "What increase in government expenditure is envisaged for the next year and what level of loan will be incurred?"

Alexei Gann responded, "Our calculations are best estimates only and much depends on circumstances beyond our immediate control, for example the increase in city population. We anticipate an additional $750,000 in annual expenditure in year one. The bank loan is adequate to cover this sum." There was mumbling in the room. Three quarters of a million dollars was a massive sum.

Gann added, "Last year's city budget was $2,800,000. Expenditure was within budget. However, we had insufficient funds to deal with some public health problems. You will be aware of the risks to health caused by open sewers. Now we will be able to deal with this problem. A modern city cannot have such a glaring health hazard, as I am sure you will all agree."

Doyle worked to suppress a grin. Unknown to me, he had struck a deal with Gann and Berman. One of Doyle's companies had already been awarded the contract for the repair and construction work. There was plenty of room in the price to kickback cash to his colleagues.

Gann continued. "A budgeted increase this year of 30%, taking into consideration services which have not been provided in previous years, is not so fierce. We are in uncharted territory and I stress these figures are estimates. Over time, St. Luke will enjoy enormous benefits from the changes, especially in the efficient delivery of existing and new services, as we attract new businesses and new people to our wonderful city."

I raised my hand again and Gann acknowledged me. "Isn't the 1% sales tax a tax on the poor?"

"We are conscious of this and this is why we propose to exempt items where the poor are most vulnerable. The sales tax will be aired and debated over the coming months, so I would ask the press not to prejudge the outcome."

I raised my hand again. "The division of services you announced? Are you saying the city has not provided them?"

Gann was relaxed as he replied: "Yes and no. Under Hanrahan, the provision of services was haphazard. It depended on who was available to deal with an issue. There was no streamlining, no development of expertise. The New Democrats spent the last two years sorting this out. Now we will formalize things. We will resemble a big corporation. There will be hiccups but soon you will see the provision of services improve."

The remainder of the press chimed in with their questions. Gann handled them with ease. Clearly, he was enjoying his promotion. Mentally, I prepared a story, but I admit I didn't think deeply enough about Doyle's apparent demotion and the reasons why he wanted to remove himself from the executive leadership. I didn't spot its real significance. I could accept he didn't want to lead. I failed to see what he would be able to do when the spotlight was no longer focused on him.

A few minutes after I returned to *The Bugle*, my telephone rang. A familiar voice said, "I've got something for you. Can we meet?"

"Ah, if it isn't Mr. Doyle, the private citizen? I assume you want to use me again. What could it be this time? How can my newspaper assist you in increasing your personal wealth and influence?" I had the right to feel sore. I had persuaded my editor and his newspaper to back this man and he had fooled us.

"Come on, Irish, surely I'm entitled to go my own way. And may I remind you that this whole thing with *The Bugle* started when you used me."

"Of course you are entitled to a life, but I think you had this move planned all along. *The Bugle* didn't just back the New Democrats. It backed you too as leader. You blindsided us. And now you want to use me again."

"Okay, I'll give the story to someone else and you'll kick yourself. Please understand this is my way of saying sorry and I promise you the story is big."

"Fine, come by my office and we'll talk."

"No, we have to meet on neutral ground. Let's meet at our place for coffee. Four o'clock. Okay?"

I put the phone down and went to speak with Ted. "What do you think?"

"It can't hurt to listen, David. Just pray the place doesn't get raided!"

Shortly after four, I arrived at the speakeasy. Doyle was waiting for me.

"Let's dispense with the formalities," I said. "I'll have a coffee and I don't mean bourbon and branch. I want you to explain why you hoodwinked my editor and made me look like a complete ass. Are votes more important than truth? Why would you do this to me? I don't know if I'll have a job by the end of this week. You were a bastard when I first met you, you haven't changed.

"Okay, you're pissed at me. I get it. But let's be civil at least."

I calmed myself. "I guess. So what's so big you can't talk over the phone?"

"There has been an approach from the Democrats. They want to merge with the New Democrats. If this happens, Hanrahan will be more than out, he'll be finished for good in city politics for all time and St. Luke gets back to bein' a two-party city."

I took time to think. Uniting with the Democrats would be a good move for Doyle's New Democrats, if they could get the right terms. The Democratic vote would not be split in future elections, allowing the Democratic Party to unite against their traditional Republican foes. Although St. Luke was essentially blue collar, new industries were providing good jobs and people with money were more likely to vote Republican. If a united Democratic Party could persuade voters that their party's policies were the main cause for St. Luke's prosperity, they would solidify their political position. The Republicans would never get a look in.

"Okay, so what can you tell me?"

"The discussions are closed to nearly everyone. Only two of my colleagues know so far. We can't let it go wider yet in case anythin' that's said by any of our people messes up the talks. We can't keep everyone silent, so it's best they don't know. That's why you can't write the story yet. Until we have a deal, we need to keep the lid on."

"I have the story. I can guess where the problems lie. Why should I wait? You can always deny it because I can't quote you or any other New Democrat."

"Really? And if you publish, how exactly do I keep the deal on the table? It's like gettin' toothpaste back in the tube after you've squeezed it out. Once the story is out, negotiatin' positions will collapse. I'm askin' you as a friend, don't publish anythin' yet. In exchange, once the deal is solid, I'll give you the exclusive from the New Democrat side."

"I can't be a friend here. Look, I'll take it to my editor. I know you have to get the deal done quickly. How near are you?"

"All bein' well, the next meetin' will resolve outstandin' points. We then have to take it to the Party, as do the Democrats. This will be easier for us, although I don't suppose the Democrats will object to the merger. They're in such a weak position, any deal they do with us will make them look better."

"So Hanrahan's out for good?"

"Yeah." Doyle sat back in his seat, smiling. "After what he did to me a while back, my heart's bleedin'. What goes around, comes around."

"A sweet and kind business, politics."

"David, seriously, you can't go public with this yet. The thing is on a knife-edge. I know you think you have the whole story, but you don't. It's in *The Bugle's* interest to hold off. I have to tell you, if the story gets published early, that's an end to the relationship between the New Democrats and *The Bugle*, whether the merger goes through or not."

"It doesn't help to make threats, especially after what you did to us."

"What did I do to you? Did anyone die? Was anyone wounded? You backed a political party that gets things done right and is a winner. As for me, you don't know the half of what I have to do."

"For heavens' sake, Mike, you have people to help you everywhere you look."

"Oh, do I? Okay, get your coat. We're goin' on a visit."

He jumped up, got his coat on and left with me in his wake. We got into the Buick, he gunned the motor and we sped off. We reached The Trench. He pulled the car up in front of a six-storey tenement building. Outside, Doyle explained. "There are eight apartments on each floor of this building. Come inside with me and knock on any door of any floor. You choose. I'll go in with you."

"Why, what are we doing here?"

"You think people help me do this work. I'm goin' to show you what I do. Me, no one else."

I went inside and climbed to the third floor. I knocked on a door. A woman answered. She looked like she was in her late forties but in fact she was thirty-three years old. She was short, dumpy, tired and ashen looking.

"Oo are you?"

Doyle moved into sight. "It's okay, Mrs. Caparelli, I just came to see if everythin' is okay. This is my friend, David Driscoll."

"Come in, Mr. Doyle, come in," she said with a broken Italian accent. She brushed down her apron as she tried to tidy a table. At that moment, the front door opened and four children entered.

The eldest couldn't have been more than ten years old. "Bath time done, Mama."

There was one bathroom on each floor, serving all the occupants of that floor.

Mrs. Caparelli looked at us. "My bambini. Okay kids, go in the bedroom and I'll call you when dinner's ready."

Doyle talked with Mrs. Caparelli for a few minutes. Her husband had recently been given a job repairing roads. They were an immigrant family who had made their way to St. Luke. She made it clear to me that she and her family owed everything to Mr. Doyle.

When we left, Doyle explained, "This floor is mainly Italian. Other floors are Irish, eastern European, Scandinavian. We find it easier if the nationalities keep together. Pick another apartment, another floor."

"What are you trying to tell me?"

"My uncle owns the tenement and another five besides. They are always full. We don't charge tenants any rent, we find jobs and help

106

the families until they can stand on their own feet. I have three hundred families who depend on me. My uncle is too old to do the work. I have four guys who help with the tenements but it's me who makes the decisions.

"In addition, I help people who come to the Main Street office. There are two people in the office who help do the bits and pieces. All of this work, the decisions, everythin' is down to me, but I sometimes can delegate the problems to ward leaders. And I run Uncle Joe's businesses too."

"How do you afford it, looking after the poor?"

"Good question. Federal don't provide welfare, the state doesn't help and the city can't provide either. My uncle and I and the Party cover the cost. The point is, you need to appreciate that now I've stopped bein' the leader, I have plenty of other things to do. Maybe you can give me a break?"

I felt ashamed that I had doubted Doyle. He broke the silence, "Now do you want a real drink or what?"

When I talked with Ted, he agreed to hold off publishing the merger story. He suggested I meet George Bolen, the leader of the defeated Democrats. Bolen stressed that he didn't want to be quoted. "We're off the record. If you want to use a particular quote, tell me. Attribute it to 'a Democrat party official'."

I opened my notebook. "Let me make it clear why I am talking to you, Mr. Bolen. There are rumors that the Democrats are merging with the New Democrats. Is this true?"

"You're asking me to confirm a rumor? You need to do better than that Mr. Driscoll."

"All right, let's take a hypothetical position. What if?"

"Let me stop you there. I don't answer hypothetical questions."

"Mr. Bolen, is the Democratic Party in talks with the New Democrats?"

"Better. Mr. Driscoll, the two parties are in constant discussion about the affairs of St. Luke."

"For someone who is off the record, you are being as opaque as a bathroom window. Let me revise the question. Is the Democratic Party in discussions with the New Democrats about merging the two parties?"

"We're off the record?"

"Yes."

"Yes."

"Pardon?"

"Yes, we are in talks with the New Democrats."

"Why didn't you say so in the first place?"

"I'm just getting you to do your job."

"Okay, you've had your fun. Can we now get into the particulars? What are the sticking points of the merger?"

"I wouldn't call them sticking points. I'd rather describe them as areas of discussion. There are a few. For example, who will contest which wards in 1926? Who will stand as councilmen-at-large? What policies will the party adopt? Stuff like that."

"Are the talks at an advanced stage?"

"Hard to say. If we had one hundred points to agree and fell at the 100th, the stage we were at would be irrelevant."

"Are you optimistic that the talks will succeed and, if so, when would you expect an announcement?"

"Mr. Driscoll, I'm neither optimistic nor pessimistic. I've been in politics too long to get sucked into feelings about a political deal. If it happens, great. As for when, I think we need to announce by August before the primaries for the congressional and presidential elections."

"How does Ed Hanrahan feel about this possible merger?"

"Ed's out. He's responsible for Doyle's rise and success so he has to pay the price. Having Ed Hanrahan on the outside is a danger but the state party is involved and this is their decision."

"How do you feel about the merger?"

"Like I said, when you've been in politics as long as I have, you give up having feelings. You just react and protect!"

"Mr. Bolen, will you keep in touch, off the record of course?"

"Rely on it, my boy. I like to stay on the good side of the fourth estate."

Ted agreed to hold back the story for a week or so. Our risk was that another paper might get the story out first. But if we kept the lid on and got an exclusive, the nationals would want to syndicate. Ted decided to give Doyle ten days. If the deal wasn't done by then, it would never be done and we would publish a story on the failure. We would then expect to have all the skinny so we could tell the public why the deal broke down.

I spoke with Doyle to let him know *The Bugle's* position. A week later, Doyle called me. "Come by the Main Street office. I have news for you. Get over here as soon as you can." I was in Doyle's room fifteen minutes later.

"David, tomorrow, the Democrats and New Democrats are announcin' the merger of the two parties. We will cede one of our councilmen-at-large seats and one ward seat to a Democrat in the 1926 election. There will be a new St. Luke Democratic Party Committee. I'll be the chairman. Alexei Gann retains the leadership and New Democrats will hold 85 per cent of the offices while the Democrats will have 15 per cent. The Democrats are contributin' $300,000 to defray our election expenses for 1922 and 1924. $100,000 will be held by the Democratic Committee on account of future expenses and the balance will be repaid to those who funded us."

"You mean your Uncle Joe gets a pay-off."

"Not at all. You can't mention the money details, as this will be in a side agreement. I just want to show you I'm keepin' nothing from you. As for the rest, I hope *The Bugle* will support the merger as benefitin' the voters of St. Luke because Democrat will no longer be pitted against Democrat. You can publish tomorrow. Maybe you can use some words from Lincoln, you know, 'the heads of both parties realized that a house divided could not stand,' that sort of thing?"

"Mike, I don't write the story. I don't decide what or how it will be published. I have to mention the money side of things, but I'll ask Ted Page to keep it to the funding of the new committee. How's that?"

"Okay, I trust you."

I went back to my office, wrote up my notes. Ted told me to write the story. When I finished, he read my copy, gave me a stare, re-read the story, made a few changes and nodded. "Not bad, rookie. This one's the lead tomorrow. What's the headline?"

"How about, 'The Democratic House is no longer divided?'"

Chapter Ten

A week after my merger story was published, I was called into Henry Brady's office.

"I liked your work on the city election. As a thank you, I'm sending you to Cleveland as part of our team to cover the Republican National Convention. Coolidge will get the presidential nomination, but it will be good experience for you."

"That's marvelous, Mr. Brady, thanks," I blurted out.

Henry hadn't stopped. "And I want you to go to New York afterwards to cover the Democratic Convention. The candidates, Al Smith and Bill McAdoo, will make it an interesting fight."

I couldn't believe my luck. Good quality newspapers like *The Bugle* devoted pages to national and international news, using agencies like Associated Press and syndicated pieces. However, it was the custom to send reporters to important national events like National Conventions to choose a presidential candidate.

The Republican Convention was pretty unremarkable, much like the man it nominated. There was controversy and disagreement amongst Republicans over whether to condemn the Ku Klux Klan, with the typical political result of saying nothing either way. What would Honest Abe Lincoln have had to say about these modern Republicans? I shuddered to think. I cabled a story to Henry Brady.

REPUBLICANS CONVENE IN CLEVELAND

Tomorrow in Cleveland, delegates to the Republican National Convention will start balloting to choose the Republican nominee for president. Calvin Coolidge was elected Vice President in 1920 but following the death of

President Harding, Coolidge has the top job now. He wants to run in his own right. There's an old saying in politics, "You don't switch horses halfway through a race." It is unthinkable that Coolidge will not get the nomination, probably on the first ballot. However, he has presided over times of plenty where his "do nothing" style of government seems acceptable to voters.

The delegates I have spoken with seem unconcerned whether Mr. Coolidge would cope in an economic bust, which invariably seems to follow an economic boom. Time will tell.

My article was published the next day minus the final paragraph. All in all, Cleveland suited taciturn Cal Coolidge down to his socks. He won the nomination in a canter. In contrast, as I was about to find out, Madison Square Garden was an auditorium for an extraordinary Democratic experience. The Garden had a capacity of 20,000 people and rumor had it the place was going to be full. I booked myself into the New Yorker Hotel on 8th Avenue. The advantage was the hotel was very close to Madison Square Garden. The disadvantage was that my room resembled a broom cupboard. The window overlooked an alley where the garbage was left. I needed to keep the window closed to avoid the stench. At least the room had a fan.

I arrived in New York early, two days before the start of the Convention. None of my previous experiences, even in St. Louis, prepared me for The Big Apple. I spent that day and the next touring and marveling at the sights: buses, subway trains, noise, people in vast numbers, shops, offices and everything else assaulted my senses. How did this city work? I just couldn't believe my eyes and my ears.

In the summer, New York is hot and sticky. The press box at the Garden was high up in the roof eaves. Even the large electric fans in the rafters could not prevent us from sweating from the moment we got into our seats.

Two days into the Democratic Convention, the first ballot established the anticipated deadlock. As predicted by Henry Brady, the majority of votes were divided between William McAdoo of California and Governor Al Smith of New York. Neither commanded

111

an overall majority. The swing votes were divided, mainly among local, "favorite sons".

During interludes between ballots, when the press was allowed onto the floor, I met up with Doyle, who introduced me to delegates from around the country including a diffident New Yorker, Franklin Roosevelt.

"How are things going, Mr. Roosevelt?" I asked.

"Swimmingly, thanks. I think we are doing a real job for Al Smith. He's all for New York and for America."

"Are you going to win?"

"This is Democratic politics. A day is a long time."

We spoke for a few minutes more. I gained the clearest of impressions that Mr. Roosevelt was a consummate politician and a man on the make.

The Convention lasted for ten days and did not reach a conclusion until the 109th ballot, when the compromise candidate, John Davis of West Virginia, was approved with fake enthusiasm.

I regularly telegraphed copy to *The Bugle* throughout the ten days of the convention. I didn't see much of Doyle. There were rumors that he was camped in his hotel suite, spending time with a Ziegfeld Follies showgirl. Doyle was regarded as just an up-and-comer within his state and not likely to be a player in national politics, so his absence was not a problem.

On the second night of balloting, I returned late to my hotel to find a note waiting for me. "So pleased you are in town. Meet me tomorrow night for dinner. Lindy's, Times Square. 8:30pm. An Admirer."

The next evening it was clear that the Convention would remain deadlocked, so I decided to check the identity of the mysterious note writer. I arrived at Lindy's shortly after the allotted time. I found the maître d' and asked if I was expected. He led me to a table for two in a corner of the dining area. The table was unoccupied. I ordered a coffee, hoping it would be a whisky. To my dismay, I was given a cup of coffee. Prohibition ruled in Lindy's.

As I sipped the coffee, I recognized the aroma of a familiar perfume. I was cuffed on the back of my head, gently but firmly. I stood and turned to see Adele, looking radiant. She wore a black, off-the-shoulder cocktail dress, with a choker style black pearl necklace. If possible, she was even more beautiful than I remembered.

"Hello, stranger," was her greeting. "I'm famished. Let's eat."

"Hello, yourself," I replied. "This is a surprise. I thought you were married."

"Me, married? Heavens, no! What made you think that?"

"Nothing really, except that was the last thing you said to me."

"Well, that was then and this is now. Where's the waiter?"

The light banter continued over appetizers and a steak for me, grilled fish for Adele. We both declined dessert. As coffee – again the real thing – was served, Adele asked me if I wanted to go elsewhere for some fun. I hesitated, not knowing what she had in mind.

"Have you been to Harlem yet?" she asked. "If not, this is something you have to do. I'll get us into the Cotton Club."

So, we left Lindy's and took a cab north beyond Central Park into Harlem. At the club, Adele was greeted like she was royalty and we were shown to a table close to the stage. A coffee pot and cups were produced. I was happy to discover that the coffee was bourbon this time, although of a standard that was barely acceptable. At midnight, the show started. For the next hour or so, amazing black dancers and singers entertained. At the end, I felt breathless, although I hadn't moved. The audience, lively throughout, gave the performers a standing ovation.

When the show was over, we left the club. Adele asked if I wanted to go to her hotel for a nightcap. I hailed a cab and looked inquiringly at Adele. "Waldorf Astoria, cabbie," she said. She saw my eyebrows raised. "Stick with me, Mr. D., I do things in style."

Adele's suite at the Waldorf was sumptuous: chintz curtains, comfortable sofas and a cocktail cabinet sufficient enough to send the Prohibition police into a fit. I had a scotch and soda on the rocks. Adele took her scotch neat. I finished my drink, stood and reached for my jacket. I felt a hand on mine.

"You don't have to go yet, do you?" Adele turned me around and kissed my cheek. I held her at arms' length.

"Are you married or not? Be straight with me."

"No, I'm as free as a bird."

"And what are you suggesting?"

Adele glanced towards the bedroom door. "I assume my bedroom is a little more comfortable than yours. You should at least look at it."

She threw open the bedroom door to reveal a huge, circular bed, covered in peach silk sheets and pillows.

"May I have another drink, please Adele?" I needed time to think. If she was a free woman, where was the harm now? Adele handed me a drink.

"Adele, is this how it's going to be? You come in and out of my life as and when you want and we have sex?"

Her face hardened. "I'm just suggesting we have a brief, uncomplicated liaison where you have no obligations. I would have thought this was a man's dream."

I was angry too. "Brief – you said it. But uncomplicated? Do you ever think? I have a professional relationship with your brother. I report on what he does, almost daily. I have access to him. If I am with you, I am compromised and so is he."

Adele was taken aback. I guess she was surprised to find I had a temper. Didn't she realize the problems she was giving me and jeopardizing my career into the bargain? Of course I was angry.

She stood close to me. "Oh, the high and mighty David Driscoll, too good for the likes of me. I still remember living in that tenement in Rawlings, with you in your big house. You didn't care a jot for others then. You make me sick. Just get out."

Our noses almost touched. "Happy to oblige."

Hearing this, Adele took a step backwards and slapped me. She didn't hold back. My cheek was stinging. I wanted to hit her back. She slapped me again, tears in her eyes.

My head told me to walk out. Instead, slowly I raised my arms, placing my hands on the top of her shoulders. I ran my hands down her arms until I held both her hands. "Let's not fight anymore," I whispered.

Adele moved next to me so we were face to face. "I don't know what this is but you do something to me, David Driscoll. You make me want to do bad things." She kissed me. "Make love to me."

We tore off each other's clothes and I did as she asked. I do not know whether we lasted for two minutes or two hours. Never before had I been overtaken by such passion. We finished, spent, exhausted, too tired for words and I fell asleep. Adele woke me in the early morning.

"You have to go. Mike just called. He is coming to see me now and you won't want him to find you here."

"Right," I didn't want to leave. "Can we meet tonight?"

"I'll call you, I promise, but get dressed. Hurry, David."

I left in indecent haste. I didn't see Mike. Why would he need to see Adele so urgently? Was it just a ruse on her part to get rid of me? Had I made yet another mistake? The best thing I could do was to get back to the New Yorker Hotel, shower, dress and work.

When I arrived at Madison Square Garden I went onto the floor and mingled with the state delegation. Doyle wasn't there. Nor did he arrive in time for the first ballot that day. I looked for him at lunchtime without success. I put everything to the back of my mind and concentrated on the proceedings before me and my copy for *The Bugle*. At 8:00 p.m., I left the Convention Hall, certain that the convention would remain blocked for the evening. At the hotel, there was a note for me.

David, our ma died last night. Mike and I have gone back to St. Luke. I don't know when I'll next see you. You have a place in my heart. xx A.

By the time I returned to St. Luke a week later, Mary Doyle's funeral had taken place. I regretted not being able to pay my last respects and sent Mike a note of condolence. I secretly hoped that Adele was still in town, but she had left.

At the office, I talked with Ted about the race for the White House. The Republicans had chosen the sitting President as their candidate whereas the Democrats had agreed on a compromise nominee. I didn't see much hope for Davis. Nor did Ted.

Ted talked to me about how *The Bugle* might report the national election. "Do you want to be in the team to follow Coolidge or Davis?"

"Coolidge, I guess. Mind you, with the amount he speaks, we'll have to invent the copy."

Ted laughed. "Taciturn Cal, eh? Did you hear the one about the pretty girl sitting next to him at dinner in the White House? She says to him, 'Mr. President, I've had a bet with my girlfriends that I can get you to say at least three words to me at dinner.' Cal replies, 'You lose.'"

115

I laughed. "Yeah, yeah. Seriously, thanks so much for the opportunity."

For the next three months, I was away from St. Luke, covering the Coolidge campaign. It was even more boring than I'd imagined. The candidate had little to say, which was not surprising given his ideology about federal government. It could be summed up as, "Do as little as possible."

When the Coolidge campaign reached Los Angeles, I tried to find Adele. I had a friend who worked for *The Los Angeles Times.* He ran some enquiries for me, but came up with nothing. I thought of hiring a private eye, but to what purpose? Had Adele wanted to stay in touch, she knew how to find me. I assumed that my tryst with Adele could be summarized as a pleasant interlude, no more and no less. It was time for me to concentrate on other things.

As expected, Coolidge won the national election in a landslide. The Republicans controlled the 69th Congress. After ten weeks, I returned to St. Luke in mid-November. I tried to summon the energy to renew my interest in city politics, but I was exhausted, both physically and emotionally. I had been working fourteen or fifteen hours a day for months. I loved the work, but I needed a vacation. So I talked with Ted and he told me to take some time off. I had accrued a lot of holiday time, so I decided to spend Christmas, 1924 in one of America's holiday resorts, Miami Beach. Normally, I'd have gone home, but I needed some rest and relaxation. I chose Florida sunshine. I had heard good things about Miami and thought it would suit me well.

Book Two: 1934

The New York Standard
Est: 1894. 11th April, 1934. Circulation: 1,472,347.

Three days hence, voters in counties, cities and towns throughout the United States will go to the polls to select their local representatives for the next two years. Often, these elections are rowdy, replete with razzamatazz, and hard fought. This is the American way. As a nation, we like to exercise our franchise. American citizenship is nothing if not active.

However, when the election process gets out of hand, when First Amendment rights are threatened, great damage is done to our democracy. Last night in St. Luke, David Driscoll, a well-respected journalist and opponent of the Doyle machine that has ruled St. Luke for more than a decade, was attacked outside his home. The attackers used baseball bats and steel pipes. Mr. Driscoll is now in hospital, fighting for his life.

Both Alexei Gann, the leader of the St. Luke Democrats and Michael Doyle, the Chairman of the Democratic Party Committee, have expressed regret and shock and denied any responsibility for the assault, but their denials do not ring true. Both are enemies of Mr. Driscoll and the newspaper he represents.

Mr. Driscoll was not robbed, so the motive for the attack is almost certainly political. Witnesses to the attack have given descriptions of the

117

assailants to the police. The evidence suggests the attackers were ward heelers, members of the Doyle machine.

There are three victims of the attack. First and foremost are Mr. Driscoll and his family. No one should be attacked merely for publishing their beliefs, especially when those beliefs are invariably supported by evidence. Second is the electorate of St. Luke – they are entitled to read a newspaper that reports the news fairly and with balance. In this, *The St. Luke Bugle,* Driscoll's newspaper, is a highly regarded exponent. Third, our democracy is damaged. The First Amendment upholds the right to freedom of speech. Whoever ordered the attackers to do their awful business seeks to deny First Amendment rights.

This newspaper and all titles around the country deplore what has happened in St. Luke. The St. Luke Police Department must bring the criminals to justice. Sadly, there is scant evidence that the police are putting resources or energy into the investigation. It is all the more suspicious because Police Chief Eddie Rupert and Machine Boss Michael Doyle are known to have a close relationship.

We wish Mr. Driscoll a speedy recovery and that he is soon restored to his family.

Chapter Eleven

My first awareness was light, a kind of dull, yellowish-white glow all around. I had no idea where it came from. I felt I was floating. I heard a groaning sound. A voice said, "Wake up, David. Wake up." The voice was gentle, soft, but not one I recognized. I opened my eyes, no, just one eye. My right eye seemed to be blocked. My left eye saw a shape of a person who seemed to be wearing a white apron and a sort of starched white hat thing. Then everything went black.

Later, I repeated the process. Whether later was a few seconds, minutes, hours or even days, I do not know. I heard a different voice this time. "I think he's coming round. I'll fetch the doctor."

I remember thinking, 'Doctor? What doctor? Where am I? Who are these people?' The light had changed. There was a sharp yellow glare from above. I tried to focus. I seemed to be in a garden. Flowers were everywhere. Then a head leaned over me. Out of my good eye, I saw my wife.

"Abby?"

"Yes, David. Thank God you're awake."

I mumbled, "Why are you here? Am I in Culpepper?"

"No, darling, you're in St. Luke Veterans Hospital. You've been hurt." I heard a strange voice say, "I'll get the doctor."

A few minutes later, a man leaned over me. "Hello Mr. Driscoll, I'm Dr Bullock. I'll be looking after you." The moaning noise happened again, the one I heard when I woke up the first time. "What's that?" I mumbled.

"Don't worry," said Dr Bullock, "we'll have you right as rain in no time. You've been in a bit of an incident and you're in hospital. Soon we'll have you on the mend."

I wanted to ask what had happened, but fatigue got the better of me. I fell back asleep as I heard Dr Bullock say, "sleep is the best thing for him. He'll be more aware in the morning."

He was right. The next morning I was aware. I was aware of the worst headache I had ever suffered, and body aches, too. There was pain everywhere. I was alone, but my yelling brought a nurse into the room very quickly. "Why, Mr. Driscoll, you're awake. Excellent. Let's have a look at you."

"Okay nurse, but let's reciprocate. I want to look at you," I thought. I still couldn't speak properly. The nurse was in her fifties. She had a worn, but loving face and a matronly figure. I could see her looking me over with concern. The pain was overwhelming. My head and right eye were bandaged, my left leg was plastered and suspended in a hoist and my right arm and shoulder were in a sling. My face felt bruised and battered and I was aware that I was mumbling rather than speaking.

"What happened to me?"

"You were beaten up three days ago. You have a fractured skull, a damaged eye, a broken leg and serious bruising to your arm, shoulder and face. Your spleen is also damaged and you have lost a lot of blood. Apart from that, you're fine," she smiled. "You'll be staying here a while and you and me, we're going to become good friends. We will take real good care of you. Mr. Doyle insisted we treat you as a very important person."

"Doyle," I growled, "that… that…" A lady was present. "I want nothing from Doyle."

"But Mr. Driscoll, Mr. Doyle has arranged this private room and has confirmed he will pay all your bills."

"The Bugle will do that. Doyle is to have no part in this!"

"Okay," replied the flustered nurse, "please calm down. I'll have this dealt with for you. What we need to do is get you better and worry about who pays for what after."

I calmed down. "What's your name?"

"Nurse Maynard."

"What's your first name?"

"Marie."

"That's a lovely name, now Marie, please contact a friend of mine, his name is Nathan Scott, and ask him to come see me. I think my wife is here. Please have her come in."

"Well, I want the doctor to see you first, and then we'll see about visitors but I will tell Mrs. Driscoll you're awake and fighting back."

"Marie, I barked at you, didn't I? I'm sorry. It's all a bit much for me. Okay with the doctor, but I need to see Abby and Nathan Scott as soon as possible. Please?"

Marie smiled at me. "We'll see."

A few minutes later, Dr Bullock came in. "Young man, you've had us worried but I gather you're shouting at my nurses. Good. Won't do them any harm. Are you hungry?"

I realized I was famished. "We'll just give you something light to begin with. Now, we've removed your spleen, and the swelling in your skull needs to go down but, all being well, we won't have to operate. The other injuries will heal. It's just a matter of time. We'll keep you here for a week or two and then you can be moved to somewhere more suitable for your recuperation. How does that sound?"

It sounded all right, but I felt the tiredness return. "If it's all the same, Doc, I'd like a little shut eye before breakfast."

When I woke up, it was evening. Abby and my sister, Jane, were watching me. "Hi, darling," I breathed to Abby. "How are you?"

Abby started to cry, mostly from relief. Jane smiled at me. They both looked washed out.

"You had us worried there, Cisco," said a recovering Abby. "Welcome back. The children send their love. I don't want them to see you when you look like this. As soon as you're presentable, they'll come to visit. You have friends and people from the office lining up to see you. And my folks send their love."

"Thank you. Hi, Janey."

"Hi, yourself. It's good to have you awake."

Abby wanted to tell me more. "You have so many get well messages. Editors around the country, senators and congressmen, the Governor and even the President have left messages. And look at all the flowers. You're a popular guy."

"I was really popular with whoever gave me the bumps and bashes. Listen, it's difficult for me to talk and I just want to rest. How long have you two been here?"

"Abby's been here since you were brought in three days ago. I got here yesterday," Jane replied.

"Who's taking care of Louie and Charlotte?"

"Christine and Alex came from Richmond," said Abby. "They are loving it. Honey, please rest. Don't worry about anything."

I drifted off into a light sleep. For how long, I don't know, but I awoke to see Nathan Scott watching me.

"How is the fearless editor?"

"Bruised, supine and very angry. I am an example of Doyle's democracy. And the man has the infernal cheek to tell the hospital that he'll pay all the bills. Nathan, please make sure my people countermand that order. You're a federal judge. What can we do to stop this man and his machine?"

"David, take a look at Thursday's paper." Nathan unfurled the broadsheet. I could see my name in the banner headline on the front page.

Bugle Editor-in-Chief Driscoll
Badly Injured in Fierce Attack
Democrats and Republicans Accuse Each Other

"I'll leave the papers for you. They've carried the story every day. Titles all over the country are telling the story. There are editorials, too, denouncing what happened to you and calling for the machine to clean up its act. *The Bugle* has declared that it will no longer endorse either party and has called on Democrats and Republicans alike to disavow violence, not just at the voting booths, but also in all elements of politics."

"Okay," I replied.

"As for what I can do, you know this well. If I'm brought evidence against the machine, I'll convene a Grand Jury enquiry. It's evidence I need, witnesses to tell the truth and stand up to Doyle. You and *The Bugle* have been lambasting Doyle for two years. I never imagined he would go to these lengths against you. Peter Garibaldi and your team are holding the fort at *The Bugle*. You have nothing to worry about."

I disagreed. I was lying in hospital, having been beaten half to death, the police evidently had no leads, and I had nothing to concern me except pain and frustration, not to mention threats to my family and that I would not be able to run my newspaper for a while. I knew Doyle was behind the beating. I now had hatred in my heart. I wanted to destroy Doyle.

Nathan left. I was alone. The room was in twilight. I felt myself drifting and I wanted to go to a happy place, Miami Beach, December 1924. I slept.

Chapter Twelve

In mid-December, 1924, I left St. Luke in snow and freezing temperatures. The train ride from St. Luke to Miami Beach took the better part of two days. Miami Beach was a balmy 78 degrees. I hailed a cab from the station and was driven to, "America's Winter Playground." I had a reservation at The Flamingo, which overlooked the Atlantic Ocean. My room and balcony were expensive, but I had earned good money recently and I was determined to spoil myself.

When I was at university, I had made friends with Charlie Stewart, who worked at *The Miami Herald*. I contacted him before I left St. Luke and on my first night, he drove out to the Beach to join me for dinner.

Charlie told me about some of the local spots. "Make sure you eat at Joe's Stone Crab." A stone crab has a peculiarity. Fishermen cut off one claw, which is cooked and eaten by Joe's customers. The stone crab is tossed back into the ocean and its claw is regenerated. I asked Charlie how this was discovered. I took a secret pleasure as he shrugged his shoulders, as if to say, "You got me there."

Charlie filled me in on the political scene. The conservative Florida state government saw the need to improve the state's transportation and public services to accommodate the huge visitor boom. As a result, businessmen like Henry Flagler had borrowed large sums of money to build railroads, hotels and other facilities.

The Florida legislature had passed laws prohibiting state income tax and inheritance tax in a series of moves designed to convince wealthy visitors to make Florida their permanent residence. "Do you think these ideas would suit a Midwest state?" I asked Charlie with what I hoped was casual insouciance. He shrugged, I had got him there again.

Politics rules wherever one travels in the United States. Florida was no exception. Miami Beach had casinos and drinking parlors, notwithstanding the Prohibition laws. The arm of federal law enforcers was not long enough to reach the Beach, which was one of America's wide open cities. Anything went.

The next night, Charlie took me to a speakeasy on Collins. Unlike St. Luke, there was no attempt to hide the true identity of the place.

"This is Miami Beach, the vacation spot of the United States," Charlie told me. "It is unthinkable that Prohibition will be enforced here. The police chief would get voted out if he tried, that's if he survived with his life until the election!"

Charlie left in the small hours. I awoke around noon. I'd missed breakfast. I fumbled into some clothes and wandered down to the lounge, which overlooked a huge swimming pool. I asked a waiter whether they could fix me some coffee and toast.

"Breakfast is still being served, sir, if you want."

"So late?" I asked.

"This is Miami Beach, sir." This phrase was irritating me. Were we not all on the same planet? Was this place an alien state of mind?

"Right. Can you fix me a bloody Mary?"

"Officially, sir, we can't. We can offer a Virgin Mary. Oddly it tastes like the real thing."

"Excellent, then I'll have a Virgin Mary, black coffee, two eggs, sunny side up and some toast. Do you serve outside? It seems to be a nice day."

"Of course." The waiter disappeared.

I strolled onto the terrace and chose a table. The hotel was quiet. I had been told that it would be peaceful, but that the hotel would be full for the Christmas holidays. There were people about but few of my age. "No harm," I thought. I could always wander into the places on Collins if I wanted company.

I wolfed down breakfast and took a stroll around the hotel. I then went to a poolside cabana to change into my swimwear and started doing laps of the pool. I needed exercise after the campaign trail. After taking some sun, I went upstairs for a nap. I slept until the early evening. I dressed and decided to try a local spot for dinner. I found a small Italian restaurant in a side street between The Flamingo and Collins. After devouring a green salad and a grilled veal chop with zucchini, washed down with a glass or two of Prohibition-free Chianti, I was ready for what the night had to offer.

Charlie had told me to try a nightspot called The Blue Lagoon on Washington. The cab dropped me there at around 11:00 p.m., a time when most of St. Luke was shutting up for the night. In the clubs and bars of Miami Beach, things were just starting to hot up. Once inside, I was met by a blast of Latin American music. On the dance floor, couples were gyrating to a samba beat. I was shown to a table. A bottle of bourbon and an ice bucket appeared as if by magic.

"Want anything else?" the waitress asked.

I shook my head. My eyes became attuned better to the dim lighting. The place was three quarters full and more people were coming in, mostly couples. I sipped my drink and took in the sights. One thing was certain, I needed to alter my wardrobe. Floral shirts might not be fashionable in St. Luke, but if I wanted to fit in here, I needed to buy some. I also needed to buy some light colored slacks and loafers. I'd go on a shopping expedition in the morning.

At around 1:00 a.m., there was a slight commotion as a party of six entered the club. They were ushered to a table next to the dance floor. A thickset man, accompanied by two other flashily dressed men and three glamorous women, sat at the table. The thickset man faced me from about twenty feet. He wore a white suit, black shirt and white tie. He weighed maybe two hundred pounds. He was clean-shaven, but had a swarthy five o'clock shadow. He was clearly the leader of the group. He laughed as he cuddled the blonde next to him. I saw a scar on his left cheek. There was no mistaking his identity. Al Capone had arrived.

Charlie had told me Capone stayed at the Clay Hotel on Espanola Way. I felt a frisson of fear, but told myself that this was the last place where there would be trouble. I suddenly felt tired. I settled my exorbitant bill and left.

The Flamingo was just the place to recharge my batteries. One week before Christmas, the hotel was full. I came down for breakfast one morning and was seated beside a recently arrived family, father, mother and three children. I reckoned the parents were in their late forties and two of the children were young teenagers. The third was maybe twenty. She was beyond pretty: slim, long blonde hair, blue eyes, pert nose and poised. She noticed me, stared at me and looked right through me. I felt as if I had been hit by a thunderbolt. It was so physical, as though a powerful blow had been struck to my chest and stomach. I lost my breath. I knew I was staring back at her. What was happening to me?

A waiter approached my table. "The usual, sir?" he asked.

Relieved to have my concentration broken, I smiled at him, saying, "Yes, thanks." I couldn't stop my gaze returning to the girl. She was no longer looking in my direction. I saw her in profile. "She's perfect," I thought, "just perfect." I was smitten. I had not met or talked to this girl, but I fancied myself to be in love.

They say you don't find love, love finds you. What next? How could I get talking with her? What if she wouldn't talk to me? What if she didn't like me? What if…? So many questions. I told myself to get a grip. I barely touched breakfast and went to the hotel gym, but to no avail. After ten minutes, I stopped working weights. "Just think," I told myself. "Work out a plan, as if you're interviewing a big politico."

I went to Reception, found my new buddy, the concierge, and asked him about the family who had just arrived. "Ah yes, the Porters. He's a doctor from Richmond. So is his wife. They're here until New Year."

I thanked him Miami Beach fashion with dollar bills. Later that day, I was sunbathing and saw the father taking a swim. I dived into the pool and found a way to bump into him. I apologized and engaged in small talk. We talked about the weather, Miami Beach and trivia. He asked nothing about me. Just as I started to get desperate, his wife dived into the pool and swam to us. She joined the conversation. Unlike her husband, she wanted to find out about me. Ten minutes later, she excused herself.

"Too much sun on my first day isn't good, Mr. Driscoll. As you are here on your own, why don't you join us for dinner tonight? I'm Christine Porter. This is my husband, Alex." Mr Porter said nothing but his look spoke volumes. I'd have to work on him.

"That would be a pleasure. What time?"

"Shall we say eight o'clock for mocktails?" She winked at me.

"Admirable."

I dressed carefully. Something conservative, this was not an occasion for one of my floral shirts. At eight o'clock, I presented myself in the lounge. The Porters were there. Christine introduced me to her children.

"David, this is our son, Peter and our baby, Geraldine. We call her Gerry." Gerry winced. "And here is Abigail. She answers to Abby." Abby looked stunning. She wore a dress that matched the color of her eyes. A strap on one shoulder held it up; her other shoulder was bare. Her hair was parted to the side and a fringe covered her left eye. She looked pure Hollywood.

I shook hands with each of them in turn, saying, "David Driscoll. Good to meet you." Abby's hand was cool. As she touched me, I wanted to keep hold of it. The waiter came over to us and asked what we would like.

Christine said neither she nor her husband thought Prohibition made any sense. "I know there are families where the weekly wage is drunk away, but why penalize the whole population for this? Surely, there are other ways of dealing with the problem. We're doctors. We understand addiction."

"Christine," said Alex, "we're on vacation. Mr. Driscoll, Prohibition is one of my wife's pet hates. We like Miami Beach because Prohibition is observed more in the breach, as they say." He ordered for the family and asked me, "What's your poison?"

"I'll have a bourbon and branch, please, but let me get these."

"Plenty of time for that. Now, Mr. Driscoll, I gather you are a journalist. Who do you write for?"

"I'm a journalist with *The St. Luke Bugle.*"

"Isn't that Henry Brady's paper?" Christine asked.

"Indeed it is. Do you know Mr. Brady?"

"I knew him when I was growing up. We both come from Boston. I couldn't stand him."

I laughed. "May I quote you when I see him next?"

"Not sure about that. Henry was full of airs and graces when I knew him, one of those people who is always very pleased with himself."

"He must have changed quite a lot. He's a highly respected editor. Might I ask about you? Where did you study medicine?"

"Harvard. There were three other women in my year in answer to your next question."

"It must be interesting, having two doctors in the family."

"Alex and I have practiced together for many years. I don't believe in this separate sphere nonsense. Alex did once, but I beat him into submission eons ago."

127

Alex Porter looked at his wife with a mixture of disdain, admiration and love. It couldn't have been easy for them both to establish a working partnership in the South at the turn of the century.

Alex asked me what I knew of Virginia. Rather than try to show off, I replied that I knew little about the South, save for the Civil War and Reconstruction. I said I had made no detailed study of southern politics, although I was aware of so-called Southern Democrats, men who sat in Congress as Democrats but whose sympathies were Republican.

After another round of drinks, we went into dinner. Abby walked next to me. "I can see you're charming my mother. Did you know she is a Harrington?"

"Sorry, I'm none the wiser."

Nothing further was said as we reached our table. We read menus and ordered. Dinner was a happy affair. The conversation flowed. No topic was taboo. After dinner, we all strolled along the boardwalk. Back at the Flamingo, Christine said goodnight, taking Peter and Gerry upstairs. Soon after, Alex said it was time for him to turn in.

"Don't keep this young man up late," he admonished Abby, as he kissed her goodnight.

"No, sir," she smiled.

Alone with Abby, I couldn't relax. "Would you like a drink?" We went to the bar and I ordered a white wine for Abby and bourbon for me.

"Who are the Harringtons?" I asked.

"They're a major political dynasty in Massachusetts. Senators, congressmen, mayors, the family is absolutely crammed with men in public life. A lot rubbed off on mother."

"What about your father?"

"Ah, there's the difference. His family owned plantations. His grandfather was a slaveholder, which embarrasses father. My parents provide the local black community with free medical help. I often wonder if it's a sort of penance for father. I'm really proud of them."

"What about you? Are you at college?"

"I'm at Virginia State."

"What are you studying?"

"English literature. I want to teach."

"Like my mother."

"Where does she teach?"

I told Abby about my mother and, prompted by her questions, talked about Jane, too. I gave Abby a potted version of my history. Abby told me about her childhood and her life at home and college. Abby accepted she had lived a privileged life, but did not think she was spoiled. "I've been encouraged to be independent, to look at life in all aspects and to think for myself."

We finished our drinks and went outside. It was still warm. That night there was a fingernail moon and the stars were easy to identify. As we strolled, we continued to talk. I lost all sense of time.

When I checked my watch, I saw it was past two in the morning. I told Abby I was sorry to have kept her out so late, and would get her back to the hotel. Without thinking, I reached for her hand. The touch of her hand made me jump. She reacted as well.

"What is it?" I asked.

She reddened. I whispered, "Did you feel something too?"

Abby bit her lower lip and nodded.

I faced her and held my other hand out to her.

She took it.

"May I kiss you?"

She nodded.

I bent my head and touched her lips with mine, gently, carefully.

"I'm not porcelain," Abby said softly, "I won't break and you're not the first boy I've kissed." I grinned at her and kissed her properly, firm and long. We broke away and held onto each other. Somehow, I knew this girl, this Virginia belle, was the one, the person with whom I wanted to spend the rest of my life.

Chapter Thirteen

I awoke in my hotel room with my stomach churning. I was a bundle of nerves but euphoric too. "So this is what love is," I said to myself, "wonderful but hopeless. Abby lives over fifteen hundred miles away, I'm leaving here in a few days and I probably won't see her for months, if ever, and she is far too young to make any decisions about being with me." It was just my luck to fall madly for a girl who lived so far away. It'd take an 80 hour bus trip just to meet her for lunch.

I went into breakfast. The Porters were finishing, but there was no sign of Abby.

"How late were you up?" asked Christine.

"Much later than we should have been, I'm afraid"

"Well, we don't believe in curfews and we trust Abby," said Alex.

At that moment, Abby arrived. She was wearing a white blouse and navy blue shorts. I couldn't help notice her legs, long and shapely. She smiled broadly at her family. She looked amazing. She asked for coffee and toast. Her parents bade her good morning, as did I. Peter and Gerry came to the table. I excused myself, feeling that I was intruding on family time.

The rest of the day passed with me spending more time with the Porters. That night, Abby and I were again left to our own devices, although nothing more than kissing took place. I knew, beyond doubt, I was falling deeper and deeper in love with this wonderful, beautiful girl and that I wanted her with me for the rest of my life. I just had no idea of how to achieve what I wanted.

Our conversations were about our lives, our ambitions and ourselves. I suddenly realized how very narrow my life had been. I loved hot metal and printers' ink. I knew journalism and something of city politics and the national scene, or thought I did. But what else did I know? Abby knew all sorts of things. A liberal upbringing brought a wealth of choice.

Abby spoke to me about literature. "Shakespeare wrote about everything in life. That's why people study his work."

"I tried him. Could hardly understand a word."

"That's because he wrote in verse and old English and used a huge vocabulary for the times, words which are sometimes difficult for us. But if you get beyond the written word and into the meaning, the whole of life is there."

"Give me an example."

"Do you know the play *Macbeth*?"

"Yes, that's the one set in Scotland. Doesn't everyone die? Is that the message, we all die?"

"You goof. No, that's not the message. The play is about power, ambition, fear and love, of a sort. Macbeth is ambitious, but weak. It is his wife, Lady Macbeth, who is strong but villainous. She gets her man to do things he wouldn't normally do but he does them because he loves her. The play is about relationships."

"And your point?"

"Let me try something else first. Take *Much Ado About Nothing*, or as you would put it, What a Fuss. It's a comedy and hysterically funny."

"So?"

"Beyond the humor, it's about two people who know they love each other, but express their love in insults until they feel able to confess the truth of their feelings."

"As I asked, your point is?"

"If you're writing about politicians, politics, things people do or shouldn't do, that's the stuff of real life and you'll find it in good literature. It's in *Macbeth*. So, what you do and what I study is much closer than you think."

"So, maybe I should start reading some of the classics."

"Yes, you should, and I'll help you. At the same time, you can teach me the reality of politics."

The next day, Abby asked me if I wanted to play tennis. I agreed and we left the rest of the Porter family happily squabbling about their next activity. As we walked to the court, Abby asked me how I was feeling.

I smiled at her. "Wonderful, thank you. And you?"

"I'll tell you after we play."

We knocked up for a few minutes and started our match. I hardly won a point. Abby just demolished me. After a while, I took a white handkerchief from my pocket and waved it at her.

"You win. Remind me never to play tennis with you again."

Abby picked up a water jug, poured me a glass and motioned for me to sit.

"Are you okay?"

"Humbled, but I'll survive."

"I wanted to make a point to you."

"That you're a much better tennis player?"

"Not exactly, although I am. I wanted you to know that there will be times when I'll be better at things than you are and that I don't want to feel like I have to hide my abilities in case I damage your male pride."

"That's fair enough. To be honest, I suspect that you are better than me at lots of things." I then realized what she had said. "You see us lasting longer than just here?"

Abby smiled. "Let's walk over to the beach. I need to talk to you."

We strolled to the ocean and found a bench where we sat.

"So," I asked, "what is it?"

She clasped her hands tightly together and stared at the ocean. "Where are you and I going? Is this just a holiday fling for you?"

I sat quietly. I needed to choose my words carefully. "Abby, don't interpret my silence as anything except me thinking carefully. I know what I want to say. I just want to find the right words."

She nodded, not looking at me.

"This is not a holiday fling for me. Never has been. I fell in love with you the moment I saw you. I know it. Every time I see you, I feel happy. You take my breath away. I want to be with you all the time. Please don't doubt this. But what can I offer you? I live so far away from you. It's at least two days' journey. I'm a reporter on a local newspaper. My prospects are okay, but who knows if I'll ever get a job with an East Coast newspaper. How can I even hint that we should get involved? How can we even think you should move away from your family, your friends, your studies, and everything you know? I could try to find a job in Richmond or elsewhere in Virginia, or even DC, but this will take time to arrange and it would mean my starting again at the bottom. If so, what could I offer you? If we continue together, it seems to me that I get all the pluses and you get all the minuses."

Abby looked less than happy with what I said. "But we would have each other. I feel about you the same way you do about me. I know you are the one for me. Please don't think of me as some silly girl, I'm nearly twenty-one. I'll graduate next year. I've seen plenty of life. I've been brought up to go after what I want. And, David Driscoll, that's you."

"Alright, Miss Porter, let's assume we continue this relationship. Where do we go from here?"

"We get married here and I come back to St. Luke with you."

"What! Are you mad? Now I need a proper drink. Abby, you're crazy. We can't do this."

"Why not?"

"A thousand reasons."

"Name one."

"Well, for one thing, I doubt that state law would allow it given your age."

"Call your friend Charlie Stewart. I bet he knows a judge who will dispense with the formalities."

"Assuming we can get past this impediment, what about your parents, what about your studies? Where will we live, what if... everything?"

"If you're the man I think you are, you'll answer these questions and talk my parents round. As for school, there's a college in St. Luke, isn't there? I can enrol and complete my degree there. David, don't you want to fight for us?"

"Abby, I'll go to the ends of the Earth and back for you, but give me time to think. Your parents will have one heck of a shock, won't they? I'm in shock myself. I never anticipated this. I have to think this through, be ready to deal with their questions. You know, like how would I support you? Who are my friends? Who in St. Luke would help look after you? Abby, put yourself in their position. What would you do if your daughter came to you with such a hare-brained idea?"

"So, I'm crazy?"

"No, you're not. But if I'm taken aback by this, how will they feel? I like your parents very much. I don't want to hurt them."

133

"If you won't fight for me, you'll hurt me. And you won't be the person I think you are."

"Darling, we're all damaged in some way. We all have weaknesses. But never doubt that I love you and want you."

I needed to think. I asked Abby to give me time to go through things in my mind. I worked the dilemma through. If I said no, this would end things with Abby. Would I be able to go back to St. Luke and live with the fact that the girl for me had slipped through my fingers because I was scared? But if I said yes, what were we getting into? What if we didn't work together?

Abby sat with me. She said nothing, but I felt her saying, "Make up your mind, David".

I decided. "Oh, hell, Abby, you only live once. Let's do it. Let's get married. I don't know if I can live with you, but I know I can't possibly live without you. I'll call Charlie. You, my girl, are a brazen hussy."

"Yes, I am," said the future Mrs. Driscoll, "but am I not worth it?"

It took Charlie an hour to organize a judge who would marry us the next day. The judge had told Charlie he was willing to dispense with all documentation on our promise to provide the necessary birth certificates in due course. After all, it was a wide-open town. Charlie had vouched for both Abby and me.

Abby agreed to meet me in her parents' suite at two-thirty that afternoon. I rehearsed what I might say, trying to sugar coat the words, but soon realized that it would be counter-productive to soft-soap the Porters. "Tell it like it is," rang in my ears as I knocked at their door. The Porter's suite had a sitting room overlooking the ocean. The windows were ajar to catch any breeze and an awning kept out the fiercest part of the sunlight.

The smiles on the faces of Alex and Christine told me that Abby had not even hinted to them what this was about. Alex and Christine looked at me. I cleared my throat. "Dr and Dr Porter, Christine and Alex, I'm here to ask for Abby's hand in marriage."

Alex raised his eyebrows. I detected no reaction from Christine. Alex looked at Abby. "May I assume this man has proposed to you? This is not a surprise to you?"

Abby rose and came to my side. "Actually, Daddy, I proposed to him this morning."

Both Alex and Christine froze when they heard this. After a long silence, Alex cleared his throat. "May I ask when the engagement will be formalized?"

I didn't understand the meaning but Abby did.

"We're dispensing with the formalities, Daddy. We won't marry Southern style."

"Isn't this a little unorthodox?" he enquired. I could tell Alex's anger was boiling just beneath the surface. Christine put her hand on his.

"Darling, I have a feeling there's more to come. Let's hear them out." Abby smiled at her mother and mimed, "Thank you."

"May I speak?" I asked. The Porters nodded. "This has come as much a surprise to me as to you. Don't doubt, don't ever doubt, that I love Abby. I've known it since the moment I saw her. And this is neither a holiday romance nor an adolescent fling. I repeat as earnestly as I can, we are in love and you know that is the strongest feeling in the world. I assure you, nothing inappropriate or improper has occurred between us. However, Abby is not on a pedestal. It is very clear to me that we are a partnership and that is how our married life will be."

I took a deep breath. Now for the really difficult part. "We want to get married tomorrow and Abby will come back to St. Luke with me."

At this, Alex stood, fists clenched. His face turned crimson. "Over my dead body, this will never happen." He faced Abby. "I do not consent and you're not old enough to go ahead without my consent."

Abby looked Alex straight in the eye and replied, "In that event, I will go to St. Luke as an unmarried woman and live in sin with David."

I looked at Christine despairingly. I was afraid this might happen. The last thing I wanted was to cause a family rift and destroy these fine people. Going over to Abby, I faced Alex Porter.

"Please let me express the respect I hold for you and Christine. The past few days with your family have been some of the most enjoyable of my life. You have accepted me and now you think I have stolen one of your crown jewels. I assure you this need not be a tragedy. I will marry Abby, some day, somehow. We are in love and there is nothing that you can do to stop us. It may seem to you that we are doing things

135

in indecent haste, but this is our decision. This is what we want and short of having me shot or arrested and deported from Florida today, Abby and I will be together. I hate to be blunt, but if I don't fight for her now, how will she trust me and how will you take us seriously?"

Christine spoke. "David, Abby is in her final year of college. Would you not agree to let her finish her year at Virginia, graduate and then get married?"

"Yes, I would, but Abby will not. She has decided to complete her degree in St. Luke and I will do everything possible to make sure she graduates there. But it is her decision to do this and I support her."

"Well, aren't we all being nice and polite," uttered Alex. "Abby, I tell you I don't consent, I'll never consent to this… farce. Have you lost all sense, all reason?"

"Daddy, I understand you're disappointed with me, that you're angry, but may I remind you and Mama that you brought me up to think for myself and follow my own mind. Just because right now I am doing something you don't want me to doesn't give you the right to tell me how to lead my life. David is the man I love. I know beyond any doubt that I will always love him. So, whatever your objections, we're going ahead tomorrow, one way or another."

"What a smart aleck," exploded Alex.

"Actually," interceded Christine, "Abby's right. When she acts in a way that doesn't fit in with our way of thinking, we really can't complain. Alex, let's you and me go outside for a while. We need to talk."

"No need," I said, "Abby and I will go. We'll be outside."

I was desperate to go. In the corridor, I felt sweat all over my body. Abby wiped my forehead with a hanky and put her arms around me. "You're dripping. Was it that bad? You were a lion in there."

"Maybe, but when we go back in, I might become a lamb for slaughter."

Abby giggled. "You are funny. They're not going to eat you. My parents are caring, rational people. Keep standing up to them and they'll come round. Just promise them we'll come back to see them as often as we can and that you'll enjoy the parties held for us. And if they mention 'shivaree', just nod your head and say 'sure.'"

"What's a shivaree?"

"A Southern custom. You'll enjoy it!"

"Why do I get the feeling you are not telling me everything?"

"As if," said this wonderful girl who wanted me.

We stayed outside the Porters' suite for quite a while. When Christine called us in, Alex had calmed down, although he was not smiling. Later, Christine told me she had persuaded Alex to reconsider because, logically, they had no choice. They could have returned to Richmond straight away with Abby but they would have had to watch her every minute to stop her running away to St. Luke.

Alex looked at Abby. "I have some questions for you."

"Okay."

"Is David kind?"

"Yes, and not just with me. He's been lovely with Peter and Gerry and he treats others, like the hotel staff, in the way I would like to be treated. He doesn't discriminate."

"Is he steady?"

"I believe so. I don't think he has lied to me about his job and prospects. But that's easy to find out. Mama, why don't you telephone that Henry person at *The Bugle*? I'd be quite interested myself."

"Good idea," said Alex. "David, have you any objection?"

"None, sir," I said, wondering what Henry Brady would have to say about me. I hoped he would keep my early career indiscretions to himself. I resolved to tell Abby everything about my past that night. Christine left the room to make the phone call.

Alex was speaking again to Abby. "Does he make you laugh?"

"David is very funny. You should have heard him just now when we were outside. I think he believes you're going to call in the mob to fix him."

Alex looked at me. "David, how much money do you have in the bank?"

"Not much. This vacation has made quite a dent. Maybe I have $300."

"And what is your salary?"

"I'm paid $25 a week before taxes. My rent is seven dollars a week and the only other regular expenses are food and laundry. I'm due a salary review when I get back. I'm told I've done well at *The Bugle* this year, as I hope Mr. Brady will confirm, and I'm confident I'll have enough to keep us."

"If, and I'm just thinking aloud, if we agree to let this madcap scheme go ahead, when will you come to Richmond? If we want to throw a wedding party for you and our family and friends, is that alright?"

"I'm afraid you won't see us for quite a while, maybe six months, unless you come to St. Luke. Travel takes so long and it's not cheap. I hope we will get back to Richmond as soon as possible after Abby graduates, so I'll do my very best to bring Abby home to see you in June next year. I'll need to clear it with my editor. It would be an honor if you gave a party for us."

"Six months? That takes me by surprise, but I see why coming sooner will be a problem. When you come, we'd want you to have a shivaree. You got any problem with that?"

I looked at Abby. "Of course not. Anything you want."

Alex shook his head. He looked at Abby. "This is complete madness, you know."

"Yes, father," she grinned at him.

"Abby, it's not a laughing matter. Just think, what happens if it doesn't work out. You're more than a thousand miles away with no family around you. It's your life at stake."

"Daddy, that's exactly right. You brought me up to make my own life decisions. Isn't this what I'm doing now? I'm responsible. If it's a mistake, and I'm certain it isn't, but if it is, it's my problem, not yours."

"That's the trouble, Abby, it won't just be your problem. But I take your point. We can't teach you one thing and then tell you differently when we don't like it. But can't you two be more patient?"

I was about to agree with Alex when Christine joined us. "Well, talk about memory lane. Henry seems to have changed quite a bit. He's nowhere near as pleased with himself as he used to be. But he is pleased with you, David. 'Very promising... hard worker... gets amazing results,' and, 'a pretty straight guy,' were some of the things he said about you." She looked at Alex. "What do you think?"

"I think we have a headstrong daughter who takes after your side of the family. She seems to have chosen someone with no money at all, who will struggle to keep her and be a burden on us both. However, he seems to be stupid enough to want to ignore the fact that Abby will keep him poor and force him to work very hard to keep her mildly

138

happy. She will freeze in the winter and burn in the summer and become even more ornery than she is now. However, it does mean we get her bedroom back."

I appreciated Alex's effort to recover, to mark his concern with a joke. It must have cost him dear. Christine looked at Abby and me. "In other words, you appear to have our blessing. Now, what have you arranged?"

Abby told her parents that we were due at the judge's chambers in Miami at 1:00 p.m. tomorrow and that our train for Chicago left at 11:00 a.m. the following day. She explained that my sister, Jane, was giving a piano concert recital after Christmas and we would be visiting with her and my mother for a day or so. "Good to know there's a modicum of talent in the in-laws," chimed Alex.

I laughed to ease my own tension. "She plays well with her knuckles."

Alex had recovered his equilibrium. "Let Christine and me sip a little wine to get over the events of the afternoon. You two go off and do what you young things do and we'll see you at dinner tonight and talk some more."

Outside, Abby put her arms around me. "See, you are a real lion. You fought for me, for us. I love you so."

"Anything for a pretty lady."

"Let's go to your room," Abby said in a smoochy voice. When we got there, we began kissing as soon as the door was shut. Her body was firm yet supple. I forced myself to draw away from her. "Don't you want to wait until tomorrow night?" I asked.

"No. If you're no good in bed, I'll have to throw you over."

I held Abby at arms' length. "I want to start married life with a clean sheet. There are things in my life that I'm not proud of and I want you to know everything about me. I'd like you to think I'm being noble by telling all, but there are people in St. Luke who know what I did and I'd prefer you hear it from me, not them."

Abby's mood changed. I realized she was upset that I'd asked her to wait before we made love. "Abby, darling, I want to make love to you more than you know and we'll make love all the way to Chicago if you want, but how would you feel if I'd had my wicked way and then told you about my indiscretions?"

"Okay, but you can't blame a girl for wanting to check the merchandise."

"Let me tell you everything I need to, and you can tell me about your dark moments and then we'll see if we are still speaking to each other."

"Okay."

So, I told Abby of my life in Columbia and what happened to me in St. Louis. I told her about Mike Doyle and the trysts with Adele. I didn't sugar coat anything. I'm not sure what shocked her more, my accepting a bribe or having sex in a restaurant. Abby then talked about her life before me. I was surprised to find she was not a virgin. In fact she had had two lovers before me, both, she said, good-looking jocks that were more pleased with themselves than her.

"Are you sure you don't want to put me on a pedestal? I think I'd look good on one," she told me when she had finished.

"No pedestals for either of us, I guess. There's more."

"Okay, let's have it all."

"Abby, this is harder for me than owning up to the other stuff. My parents weren't like yours. There was no joy in our house, no banter, no fun, hardly any conversation or love. When my father died, I felt nothing. When I left Culpepper for Columbia, I felt nothing leaving Mother and Jane. I don't seem to have feelings like other people. Maybe there's something wrong with my character. I know I like to work. There are times when I just love my job. I seem to put all my emotions into work and there's nothing left over.

"Until I met you, I had known infatuation. With you it's different. Believe me, the way I feel about you is so different to Adele and the other women. But what if this feeling stops? What if I do have a character flaw? What if I don't have normal feelings? I'm scared for me and you."

Abby smiled at me. "David, it's like this. Some things we know, the rest we'll find out. I know you are passionate, that you have feelings. It's just that people who were close to you haven't brought them out. And if I'm wrong, it's just something else we'll work on. I'm not worried. Right now, I have feelings enough for both of us." I checked my watch. "How much time do you need to change for dinner?"

"Half an hour."

"So, by my calculations, we have an hour to kill. Do you want to go for a walk, shall we go swimming?" I asked with a big smile on my face.

"I don't think so," Abby smiled back.

"Well, I'm fresh out of suggestions. Any thoughts?"

Abby moved towards me and unbuttoned my shirt. "Not really. What about you? Any ideas?"

We were both standing now. I took her in my arms and kissed her. I unzipped the back of her dress and slipped it from her shoulders. It fell to the floor. She wore only a brassiere and panties. I removed most of my clothes, too. We moved back onto the bed and explored each other's bodies. In the back of my mind, I thought Abby was probably yet to experience an orgasm. I whispered to her to stop what she was doing and just lie back. I slowly removed her lingerie and looked admiringly at her naked body.

"Have you any idea how incredibly beautiful you are?" I whispered.

"Please remember this moment when I have borne your fourth child, am fifty pounds heavier and have stretch marks."

The mood changed as I laughed with Abby. "Well you might as well look at what you're getting," I said, removing the rest of my clothes. "And please remember how I look now when I have gone bald and am fifty pounds heavier too."

We kissed and laughed and touched each other.

"I like what I see. I'm very pleased with my purchase. I'm so happy. I just know we're doing the right thing."

We made love quietly and lovingly. I knew I couldn't be happier. This wonderful girl who had chosen me replaced thoughts of Adele and the other women.

We finished, happy, exhausted and totally in love. My heart was pounding fast. I breathed to Abby, "was that *Much Ado About Nothing?*"

She laughed as she replied, "more *All's Well That Ends Well.*"

Chapter Fourteen

The following days were a blur. The morning of the wedding flew by in a rush of phone calls and messages to St. Luke and Chicago. Cabs for town came to the hotel on time. The judge was pleasant, but made it clear he had a tee time that afternoon and nothing would keep him from the golf course. On a warm day, the civil ceremony was delightfully brief.

Back at The Flamingo, arrangements had been made for a wedding breakfast. I've never understood why a meal taken after two p.m. is still called "breakfast." Alex persuaded the chef to produce his best efforts. Somehow, a wedding cake was procured with the traditional bride and groom figures on top. The concierge engaged a photographer who kept himself very busy.

Charlie made a delightfully funny best man's speech, detailing my many inadequacies at Columbia, while excessively praising my successes there. He read cables from my mother and Jane, also from Henry Brady and Ted Page, both of whom questioned Abby's sanity. Henry's cable apologized to the Porters for telling less than the whole truth about me but, "after all," he wrote, "I am a newspaperman".

Both Christine and Alex made their own speeches. In turn, they spoke in bitter-sweet terms about Abby and were more than kind as each welcomed me to their family.

When it came to my turn, I was overwhelmed. I was not used to public speaking and said so. I spoke from my heart. I said that the biggest stroke of luck I could ever have had was meeting Abby and her family. I promised not to let anyone down and to make them all proud of me and of us. I burst into tears. I put this down to nervous tension from the past few days. Maybe so, maybe not. My new family gathered round and made a fuss of me.

The Flamingo had provided a phonograph and we spent the rest of the afternoon and early evening dancing to the music of bands like

Bennie Goodman and Duke Ellington. At around 8:30 p.m., Christine came over to Abby and me, saying, "You have a big day ahead of you tomorrow. You need to leave here by nine-thirty in the morning, and you have to pack. So bedtime, my children, sleep well."

My luck had stretched to my choice of mother-in-law. I found Charlie and thanked him. He shook my hand, saying "Good luck, it's been an education."

Alex took me to one side. "Christine and I think you need a little something from the starter's gun. This is our wedding present for you and Abby, but you are the man of the house and I am giving it to you. Take good care of Abby. She is precious."

He passed me an envelope and shook my hand. Instinct told me not to open the envelope in front of him. I said thank you and hugged him. I found Abby and blew a kiss goodnight to everyone as we went upstairs.

In our bedroom, I looked at my wife and welled up again. I just couldn't help myself. "I've broken up your family and they've been so wonderful." I pulled myself together and took out the envelope Alex had handed to me. "Abby, your father gave me this. It's for both of us. You should open it."

"No, he gave it to you. You open it."

Inside was a brief note. It read, "Spend it wisely. We'll be watching!"

Alex had enclosed a check for $5,000 for Abby and me. It was a fortune. Abby started laughing and crying in the same breath.

"Aren't they sweeties?"

"I can't believe this. We can pay for your college tuition, put a down payment on a house, buy a car and still have money left over. I'm completely overwhelmed."

I sat on the bed, head in hands.

Abby walked over to me. "Sleep and pack in the morning, or pack and sleep?"

"I think pack and sleep."

Abby had done most of her packing earlier that day. It took me only ten minutes to pack my clothes.

"Before we go to bed, I need to do something. I want to write a note to your parents." It took longer than expected but when I finished, I showed it to Abby. "What do you think?"

Abby read:

Dearest Christine and Alex,

One day, I hope to write to you, beginning Dearest Mama and Father. I know the past days have been a roller-coaster ride for us all. I'm not sure when my feet will touch the ground. If I ever have a child who presents me with the dilemma that you both faced, I hope I will be able to behave in the same understanding way.

I want to thank you both for everything. The check was so generous. You know that it will make a huge difference to our lives. The funds will be banked in a joint account. They will be used first to pay Abby's tuition fees. We will use the rest as a down payment on a house and to buy a car, enabling us to visit you more easily. If there is anything left over, it's for a rainy day.

I intend to make Abby as happy as she can be and to make you proud of your decision to let me become part of your family.

With fondest regards and much love.

"It's a great letter. May I add a postscript?"
"Of course."
Abby added:
I know David is the genuine article. I want you to read this letter back to me five years hence and tell me I was right.
With all my love, Abby.

The rest of the night lived up to the events of the day. It was an interlude of love and peace.

The next morning was a rush to say our goodbyes to all the Porters. Surprisingly, Peter and Gerry, who hitherto had been matter-of-fact, became clingy with their sister. They both cried their goodbyes. Alex and Christine decided to say their goodbyes at The Flamingo. Abby hugged them both. I gripped Alex's hand and embraced Christine. Saying goodbye felt much more emotional than I had expected. The taxi took us to the station. The Porters had booked a private train compartment for us. The anticipated pleasure of traveling on our own was muted when we saw the couch opened into bunk beds. "Where there's a will, there's a way," I told Abby but the beds were uncomfortable for one, let alone two.

The compartment was hot and stuffy, so we decided to go to the lounge. Our fellow passengers were a motley crew, a mixture of salesmen, minor gangsters – that was Abby's take – and elderly people who had vacationed in the warmth, but whose funds were probably limited. There was no one in our age group. We kept ourselves to ourselves, dining on our own and keeping to our compartment, despite its lack of comfort.

The journey took us through Jacksonville, Atlanta, Savannah, Charleston, Raleigh, Richmond and Philadelphia, where we changed trains. We headed west through Pittsburgh and Indianapolis onto Chicago, arriving almost two days after we left Miami. We headed for the Blackstone Hotel on South Michigan, where my mother and Jane were staying. It was a stone's throw from Chicago's Orchestra Hall. Mother and Jane eagerly awaited the newest Mrs. Driscoll. They both fell on Abby, virtually ignoring me. I didn't mind.

Mother asked if we were hungry. I told her what we needed was a good night's sleep. Jane had changed. She was now a mere two inches shorter than me, lissome, attractive and poised. I noticed how beautiful her fingers were, pianist's hands. She was quiet and restrained, her usual mood before a recital. Abby asked what she was playing. Jane replied in a monotone, "Chopin's Sonata No 3, Prokofiev's Sonata No 5 and Brahms's Four Piano Pieces."

"Are you very nervous?" Abby asked with tenderness.

"Like you wouldn't believe. This is the biggest thing I've ever done."

"I'm looking forward to hearing you play and so is David."

"How did he manage to get a catch like you?"

"If you want to know the truth, Jane, I caught him."

Mother joined in the conversation. I feigned a yawn, apologized and asked to be excused. "Shall we meet for breakfast? Is nine-thirty okay?"

"That's a bit late. Jane has to be at Orchestra Hall by ten. Can you manage eight-thirty?"

I looked at Abby. "Is that alright for you?"

"Sure."

We said goodnight and went to our room. Abby looked at our quarters which housed a king-size bed. "There's hope for us yet. I'm not going to bother unpacking tonight." She went in to the bathroom. After a few minutes, she reappeared, not wearing a stitch. My wife was the opposite of coy. I loved the fact that she felt so confident about her body. "Care to join me?" she asked.

"Give me a moment." I stripped, went into the bathroom to wash and brush my teeth and came out naked. The light was still on.

"Shall I turn the light off, Abby?"

"No, I want to have another good look at you."

I stood still.

"Come to bed, David. We have things to catch up on."

The next morning, we met Mother and Jane as arranged. Elizabeth was chatty, Jane taciturn, as the nervous tension increased. I worried for Jane but Abby thought much of her non-communication arose from concentration on the task ahead. As for mother, she just suffered from worry for her youngest. After an hour, they left.

"What do you want to do?" I asked Abby. "We could go back upstairs."

"What a good idea."

"At some stage, I have to go to the Herald Tribune offices. There's a guy, Barry Springer, who I want to meet. Is this alright with you?"

"Ever the working man, eh? I suppose I'll have to get used to it. I might take a stroll through the Columbia Campus when you go. So, who is Barry Springer?"

"He investigates government wrongdoing. He was the man who helped uncover Teapot Dome."

"Teapot Dome? What's that?"

"Basically, it was fiddling oil leases for oil corporations to the advantage of crooked government officials."

"What nice people you mix with."

"Let's change the subject. You might want to do some shopping here? St. Luke's retail district is poor by comparison and you'll need some warm outfits for the winter. We can certainly afford it."

"I did my important shopping in Miami Beach! However, you have a point. I do need some clothes for the winter."

"Well, I have a sort of shopping list of things we need to agree upon before we get to St. Luke. It's time for us to be grown-ups. Sorry, that was patronizing. I didn't mean it to be. We just have to look at practicalities."

"Such as?"

"Well, let's take college entry. You don't have your transcript from Richmond with you, we'll need it."

"I talked about this with Mama. When we know where I'm going to enrol, she'll get the university to cable my details and send the transcript."

"Are you happy to go to St. Luke College? It's not necessarily the best place for you. The state university is in Paxton."

"I'm not coming all the way to St. Luke to be separated from you. St. Luke College will be fine."

"Okay, I'll ask Henry to get in touch with the University president. Next, my apartment is not suitable for two people. Are you happy to go house-hunting straight away?"

"Yes, but I want to get a feel of the place first. I won't know if I want to live in or out of town. I'd like a week or two to look around. Will you make time to do this with me?"

"If Ted Page will let me. I'll do my best, but a journalist's life isn't nine to five. I hate the idea of leaving you on your own, but there is a work ethic at *The Bugle* and I don't know how much time they'll give me to keep you company. I'm worried you'll be lonely."

"David, that's so sweet, but I'm tougher than you think. I'll find plenty of things to keep me busy. Listen, we're an experiment. We're young and modern and want a different way of life, not like the lives of our parents."

"Are we completely mad?"

"Completely."

"Can you cook?"

"Got me there. We have servants at home. I never learned."

"What about your time in college?"

"Refectory. Don't make me feel useless."

"You're not. I can't cook either. So, we need lessons."

"We?"

"Yeah. You'll be studying and I'll take on my share. If I don't get cooking lessons, you'll be getting a lot of canned beans on toast."

"Pooh, that's my specialty!"

After lunch, I headed to meet Barry Springer. We had not met before face-to-face, but I had read his pieces and we had corresponded. Barry was normal height and about one hundred and sixty pounds. He had a full head of ginger hair, clear brown eyes and a fair skin. I reckoned he was about forty years of age.

"Springer, is that German?"

"No, it's Dutch. My great, great grandfather came to New York from Amsterdam in the 1830s to help in the family banking business. Then the family name was Spriensma. Soon, we became Springers!"

"I see. You're a Yankee. Congratulations on the Teapot Dome stories, by the way. It's easily the biggest financial scandal of the decade."

"Or at least so far, but yes, that was a scoop. Our investigation into the Harding Administration uncovered plenty of bribes."

"Without you, those guys would have got away with it".

Springer shrugged modestly, then he surprised me. "I've read your stuff in *The Bugle*. Your coverage of the Doyle administration earlier in the year was interesting, but you've gone quiet of late. How come?"

"I've been out of St. Luke pretty well since August. I covered the Conventions and was part of the team reporting on Coolidge in the election. Then I went on vacation and got married. So, what do you hear from St. Luke?"

"Not much, but there are rumors about your guy Doyle."

"What's up?"

"There's a rumor that says his brothers are part of a criminal gang and that he is linking up with them. Another is that he's bought local real estate that the city wanted and sold it to the St. Luke Council at an exorbitant profit."

"It's not illegal to do this."

"No, but it should be. It's cheating the tax-payer."

"Doyle's being linked again to his brothers, is he? That will fire him up. He doesn't speak to them. Hasn't for years."

"Well, that's not what I'm hearing. The brothers are involved in organized crime and are putting the squeeze on your guy."

"Obviously, you can't disclose your sources, but how do you know so much?"

"This is Chicago. We have gangsters on the South Side and the North Side and *The Tribune* is in the middle. Don't like it much, but I love living here. And there's another story. It seems Doyle is squiring Mrs. Geraldine Frost, to put it politely."

"Who is she?"

"An heiress. Her family owns Frost Grains which is based in St. Luke. Her husband isn't too pleased. He's a Hungarian count or something, and he challenged Doyle to a duel. Evidently, the police ran him out of town. It's quite a scandal."

"Why am I not surprised? Doyle has a thing about a combination of ladies and danger. Boys will be boys."

I thought how odd it was. Here I am, settled down and happily married while Doyle is off playing the gigolo with a married woman and doing it in public.

We talked newspaper talk for a while. At around four, I excused myself. "My sister is playing in a concert tonight. Better not be late."

"Good to meet you, David. Let's keep in touch. I'll let you know if I hear any more about your guy and the mob."

I returned to the Blackstone. Abby was in the lounge, taking tea with my mother. "Hail the conquering hero," said my new wife, offering her cheek for a kiss.

"I assume you two have plotted my downfall."

"Worse than that, my boy, we're converting your head into a trophy which will be hung up somewhere."

My mother giggled. "You two, what are you like? I'm going to go upstairs to wake Jane. This is the worst time for her. We have to get back to the concert hall early. Here are your tickets. I'll see you there."

Elizabeth rose, kissed her new daughter-in-law fondly and pretended to slap me on my head. She was happy.

"So, you two had a good time?" I asked Abby.

"She's wonderful. What a life your mother's had, but no self-pity. I'll miss her."

"What about asking her and Jane to move to St. Luke?"

"You're a kind man, but you need to think with your head, not your heart. It wouldn't work. She's mistress of her house and I need to be the same in mine, even if…"

"Even if what?"

"Even if I can't cook."

Three hours later, I sat in the concert hall with Abby and my mother. Oddly, I became a bundle of nerves. No wonder Jane was a basket case before she went on stage. Yet when she began to play, her nerves disappeared and there was only the music. I need not have worried for her. Jane was beyond magnificent. She received a standing ovation. My mother had tears in her eyes, Abby was weeping.

"Are you alright?" I asked Abby.

"I am delirious. Your sister is so talented. I don't think I've ever heard the piano played so well. Mama would have loved this. She used to play when she was young. I must write and tell her about Jane."

After the concert, we made our way back stage to Jane's dressing room. She was surrounded by well-wishers and flowers.

"Congratulations," I said to her. "My little sister is such a star."

Abby joined us, speechless. She hugged Jane, not wanting to let her go. Elizabeth stood back, beaming. I don't think I had ever seen her like this, so proud, so happy.

When we returned to the hotel, Jane mumbled something about being hungry. She seemed withdrawn. The concern must have shown on my face, because Abby took my arm. "Don't worry. It's the adrenalin. It's gone. She's feeling empty, but she'll be fine."

We ordered sandwiches and tea. Jane became more animated. "Did you notice the missed note in the Chopin? I'm sure everyone did." We all assured her that only Jane would have known this.

Then a presence arrived at the table. A woman in her fifties stood over us. She had a shock of unkempt red hair. She wore an ill-fitting, long black dress with far too much lace embroidered on it. She seemed to be a throwback to the Victorian age. She was holding some newspapers. She ignored all of us except Jane.

"The Chopin was lyrical and the Prokofiev was musical ambrosia. However, both were superseded by the Brahms, which convinces this critic that the audience had a maestra of the highest class in its midst." Jane looked at the woman, nonplussed.

"Jane, my dear, these are not my words. This is what the music critic of *The Tribune* has written. And this one," the woman continued, holding up *The Sun-Times*. "There is a new supernova on the concert hall circuit, Jane Driscoll. Don't miss her, etc., etc." The woman paused for a moment and then continued. "It's a triumph of fantastic proportions. What are you drinking? Tea? My god, it should be the finest French champagne, if we only could."

My mother stood and shook the woman's hand. "Harriet, how good to see you. May I introduce my son, David, and my new daughter-in-law, Abby?" We exchanged greetings.

Harriet continued as if there had been no interruption. "Jane, I will have no more arguments. You have to move to New York, you have to go on a tour of the best concert halls. You have to do this or I will not be responsible for my actions."

Jane blanched. "I'm not sure," she started.

"Let's talk tomorrow," said my mother. "It's late and we're all tired."

Harriet bade goodnight to us all and left for a night of entertainment.

"Who on earth was that?" I asked.

"Harriet Shapiro, Jane's agent. I know she looks like the wreck of the Hesperus, but she is very highly rated in the music world. From what I gather, she was something of a musical prodigy but she had no financial support and the concert circuit passed her by. Instead, she has developed careers of young pianists. She is a bit odd but we like her, don't we Janey?"

Jane and Elizabeth made their way to the elevator, my mother holding the newspapers. "Good night. What time is your train tomorrow?"

"Twelve-thirty. Shall we have a late breakfast?"

My mother nodded and left with Jane. I looked at Abby, raised my eyebrows and moved my head to one side. She understood. We went upstairs in the next elevator.

I awoke early. Abby was dozing on her back with one arm behind her head. I watched her. Time stood still for me. If I did nothing else in my life, this would be enough. With her eyes closed, Abby asked, "What are you looking at?"

"You."

"Why?"

"I hired you in Miami Beach. I need to check you haven't gone off in Chicago. The weather might have made you rusty."

"I think not. I seem to be alive, well and shiny bright."

We made love. I now knew what Abby liked. Sex was wonderful for us both. As we packed and dressed, Abby told me that she now understood why there was such a fuss about sex.

"I am employing you for orgasms. You are my chef d'orgasms now."

"Okay, but could we talk about something else when we see my mother and sister?"

"Why? Don't you think they'd be fascinated?"

"Yes and let's get hotel reception involved. The head porter will be all agog. Maybe we'll get a discount in exchange for interesting conversation." We fell on the bed laughing.

We said our goodbyes at the hotel. Jane clung to me. "Congratulations. Abby is special."

Our train journey to St. Luke took almost a day. We arrived at eight-thirty the next morning, tired but happy. To my amazement, we had a reception committee. Ted Page and his wife, Mary, were there to greet us. Typical of Ted, he addressed Abby.

"I'm here because I just had to see the woman who was fooled into taking on our very worst reporter."

They shook hands. True to form, Abby replied, "Very good to meet you. I so wanted to meet the most hopeless Metro Section editor in the country. David says without his brilliance, you'd be out of a job."

Ted burst into laughter. He turned to me. "Welcome home, Ace, I have lots for you to do. I've hardly seen you since last August. Welcome to St. Luke, Abby. Did you two eat on the train?"

We hadn't, so we all went to the Station Hotel and had breakfast. I said very little. Abby took control and captivated Ted and Mary. After breakfast, Ted brought his car around and we all piled in with luggage on our laps. When we arrived at my apartment, Ted helped us with our bags.

"Upstairs, Mrs. Driscoll, now," I barked. At our door, I opened it, picked Abby up in my arms and carried her over the threshold. "Welcome home, Abby."

Later that day, I received a note from Henry Brady. He had spoken with both the President and the Dean of Humanities at St. Luke College. Abby enrolled on our second day home. She was involved immediately in term papers and exams. The dining area in our

152

apartment became her study. Her determination to graduate in May was matched by her enthusiasm for work. I was relieved that she was focused and engrossed so quickly.

Mary Page agreed to give us cooking lessons. On our first night in town, Mary cooked a pot roast for us. It was just delicious. Abby asked coyly how she had prepared it and how hot the oven had to be. She then confessed to Mary about her shortcomings in the kitchen and told her she would fall on her knees if Mary would teach her to cook. Mary was delighted to be asked and became even happier when I asked if I could join in.

Ted Page gave me a few days at home to help Abby settle in, but told me I was needed at the office the following week. I bought a second hand, red 1924 Duesenberg A Roadster for $350. What a beauty!

Letters were exchanged with Richmond, so the Porters were kept abreast of most of what we were doing. We planned a vacation in June, when we would drive to Virginia.

On my first morning back, I found out why Ted needed me. Alexei Gann, John Santino and Tom Berman were re-shaping the look of St. Luke city government with almost indecent haste. In the last week of December, there had been a clear out at City Hall. Any city employee known to be a Republican supporter had lost his or her job on a week's notice. All were replaced by Democrats. So much for employment on merit only; political affiliation had become a condition of a city job.

The merged Democratic Party, on the pretext of being short of funds, had called upon all 3,500 city employees to contribute to party coffers. For the low paid, the contribution was 3% of their annual salary, rising to 10% for the highest paid. Raising money in this manner was not illegal. Party machines in many cities were known to adopt the practice in an election year. However, not only was this was a new departure for St. Luke, but the levy was not made in an election year.

The bad taste that these moves left had been reported in *The Bugle*. Democratic councilmen made themselves scarce rather than be interviewed and Doyle had been unwilling to talk with *The Bugle*. "I'm not the leader now," was his line. "These decisions were not mine."

A new newspaper, *The St. Luke Democrat,* was launched with considerable fanfare on January 1st, 1925. It was wholly sympathetic towards the Democrats and interviews with Democratic politicians abounded. Doyle had been featured. Ted Page tried to make contact with Doyle. He was rebuffed.

Ted filled me in on the latest moves. "I don't understand. Why would the Democrats want to antagonize us? There are all sorts of rumors going around. First, there is talk of real estate being bought up by so-called friends of the Democrats, in other words Doyle's stooges, and that this real estate will be sold at a huge profit to the city. I'm trying to run down sources and find out details.

"If the St. Luke government is increasing both in size and spending," Ted continued, "and if additional services are to be provided, new people will have to be hired and they will need office space to do their work. So, it makes sense that there will be new offices built. But it has a nasty smell. It sounds like your friend is about to fatten the size of his wallet at tax-payers' expense."

"Interesting. Ted, I heard this rumor too, when I was in Chicago."

"Talking of Chicago, I'm sure you've heard of the Chicago Outfit and Al Capone?"

"Heard of him? I'm pretty sure I saw him in Miami Beach. Why?"

"The story is that organized crime is spreading its wings. Since the war, Midwest cities like Detroit and Minneapolis have had the mob in town and there is now a real concern they are headed to St. Luke. Bill and Tom Doyle are reputed to be part of the Chicago Outfit and the talk is they have been pressurizing Doyle to ease their path here. Capone's mob controls bootlegging in the Midwest. If the mob comes, it will bring drinking, gambling and prostitution."

"What do you want me to do?"

"Meet Doyle. Find out what's going on. If St. Luke has a problem, the people in Cameron need to know and help us out."

I felt unsure about this. I was worried that Doyle was turning into an old-style boss, that he had disguised his true colors from me and had used me. But would Doyle want the mob in St. Luke? I doubted it. He would want to be top dog, not be in debt to organized crime.

"I'll do it, but I don't know how things stand between Doyle and me now. I think we're okay, but we're both a bit bruised by what has happened. Anyway, how well do we know Governor Hyde?" Michael Hyde was the Republican governor of the state.

"Pretty well. He and Henry are great friends."

"Well enough to get me an interview with him?"

"Of course, but walk before you can run. Oh, talking of Henry, he wants to see you this morning. You'd better get up there."

I went to Henry's office. His secretary smiled at me, said "Congratulations," and told me to go right in. Henry was at his desk, reading. His head came up when he heard me come in.

"So, Christine Harrington is your ma-in-law. God help you!"

"She was equally complimentary about you, sir."

Henry grinned. "Actually, we had a nice chat. I was a little different when I knew her, as she may have told you. Mind you, from the sound of it, she has changed quite a bit too."

"I can't be hung for what I don't say, can I?"

Henry laughed. "Welcome back, David. Mrs. Brady and I would like to meet this new wife of yours. Would you come for dinner on Saturday night?"

"Thank you, sir. It would be a pleasure."

"Okay. Seven o'clock for drinks. Mrs. B. likes fancy, so please dress accordingly. Have you got a tux?"

"Yes, sir."

"Great. Now, has Ted filled you in on what's been happening here over the past few weeks?" I nodded. Brady continued, "My nose tells me we are in for a squall or two right now, but there's a big storm on the way. I'm certain of it. I don't think I can trust Doyle and his people anymore. We can't do much yet, but when you see him, warn him we can remove our endorsement any time."

"My experience of Mike Doyle is he doesn't respond well to threats. Better for me to give him a friendly word along the lines of, 'This is not what *The Bugle* expects.' Anyway, from what Mr. Page tells me, Doyle seems to be closed to us at the moment. I'll do what I can."

"Thanks, David, and congratulations."

At my desk, I read the correspondence and memos that had mounted in my absence. Then I went to the Library to read the back issues I'd missed for the past months. By four o'clock, I was done. I went back upstairs, checked for messages and put a call through to

Doyle at the Democratic Committee headquarters. I was told he was out and would be given a message. I decided it was time to re-acquaint myself with married life. I bade all a good night and made my way home.

Abby was at the stove. She had a pile of flour on a wooden board positioned lengthwise on the kitchen table. Flour was also all over the floor as well as her face, hair and clothes. Steam was pouring from a pot on the stove. The kitchen was baking hot. As I entered, she was bending by the stove door. There was a smell of incineration. She screamed her frustration.

"Doctor Driscoll at your service," I called, "burnt goods a specialty."

"Oh, damn you," shouted my lady wife. "Enjoy your dinner. It's only fit for the sink." She sped past me into the bedroom, sobbing all the way. I turned the oven off, took off my overcoat and jacket, waited a moment or two and opened the bedroom door. Never say I lack courage. Abby was lying face down on the bed. When she looked up, her face was blotchy.

"I tried to make something really nice for dinner. I messed up."

"You did make something nice," I replied. "You may just have cooked it a little too long." I tried to keep a straight face. It was impossible. "Before you hit me, please remember I'm laughing with you, not at you. Really I am."

Abby sat up, raised the oven gloves as if she was a boxer but put her arms around me. "Sorry."

I kissed her and told her I loved her, even if her cooking was a little off. After we finished making love, breathless, clothes all over the floor, Abby looked questionably at me.

"How long before we stop making love every day?"

"Maybe when I'm ninety. Actually, I plan to do it forever. Not sure with whom. You'll be a bit wrinkly by then."

"What are we going to do about dinner?"

"I think we had better clean up the kitchen first. I know a place near here. It's a diner, but the food is good. Oh, talking about food, we have an invitation for dinner on Saturday night from your mother's biggest fan, Henry Brady no less. You might remember that he's also my big boss, not that that's of major importance. But I hope you have something amazing to wear to impress the Brady's and for me to remove as soon as we get back home."

An hour later, we sat at a booth in the Pyramid. It was quiet.

"What's good here?" asked Abby.

"I like the chicken pot pie, but everything is okay."

We ordered and started to talk about our days. I felt a presence at my shoulder, and, looking up, saw Mike Doyle.

"Hi, Mike, how are you?"

"Fine. Who's the lovely lady?"

"Mike Doyle, I have the pleasure of introducing you to Abby, Abby Driscoll."

Mike frowned. "I don't remember you having two sisters. Is she a cousin?"

I laughed. "No, Abby is Mrs. Driscoll."

Mike did a double-take. "No! You're not! Are you?" I nodded. "Really, you're married. Wow! When did this happen? Tell me all." I noticed a change of mood. He seemed happy for me.

A crowd was gathering at Mike's usual table. I whispered to him that he might want to talk with me another time as we were being stared at.

"You free for coffee in the morning?" he asked.

I agreed to meet at the Main Street office at 11:00 a.m.

"Congratulations and good luck," he said to Abby as he moved away. "With this shnook, you'll need it."

After he'd gone, Abby looked thoughtful. "So that's Mike Doyle."

"That's Mike Doyle. Now, tell me about your day, especially the cooking."

"Well, I have been looking around the area for a new home. I would prefer to live out of town. I am a country girl and I want to live where I can breathe fresh air."

"Whatever the lady wants…"

"I've found one. I want you to look at it."

"What's the rush? I thought you wanted to finish college first."

"Well, there's no harm in looking. It's beautiful. Four bedrooms and a yard. We'll be fine unless you decide you want more than three children."

"Let's look at it at the weekend. Dare I ask how much it is?"

"Seven thousand dollars, easily within budget," she said with a disarming smile.

The next morning, I traced my steps to Doyle's Democratic Committee building. There was a queue on the stairs to the second floor, all of them men. I eased past them into an outer office. A secretary looked up. Before she could tell me to get in line, I told her that I had an appointment with Doyle. After giving me the once over, she got up and went into Doyle's office. A few moments later a man in working clothes left and Mike called me in.

He motioned me to sit. He turned his back to me. I heard a champagne cork being popped. He handed me a glass. "Never too early to toast a newly-wed. Let's drink to love. So, tell me the story. What happened? Don't leave anything out."

"Michael Doyle, you are a romantic." I gave him the abridged version of my time in Miami Beach, the speedy wedding, the trip to Chicago and my arrival home. "By the way, I called you yesterday. Please note that this was on my first day back."

"Yeah, I got the message. I assume it was *Bugle* business."

"Partly. That's quite a queue you have outside."

"It's boom time in St. Luke but people still need me for jobs. As I'm running the cement and property businesses, we need labor. Never send anyone away. Everybody needs to work."

I noticed his diction had improved in the five months since I'd seen him. Also, he was wearing a custom-made suit and an expensive silk tie. No doubt Mrs. Frost had exercised her influence.

"What's this I hear about a new lady in your life, Mike?"

"Oh, Geraldine. Well, it was fun while it lasted but, truth to tell, she got very demanding and clingy and her husband was a pain, so I dumped her."

I remained silent for a moment or two. He sounded so callous, a typical Doyle move where a woman was concerned. How different my life was to his. I wondered if he would ever understand what it was like to be happily settled.

"What about politics, Mike?"

"I'm not the leader anymore. I'm happy to be Councilor for the First Ward and the Chairman of the Party Committee. That gives me a handle on the politics thing. But I'm a businessman now. I've told you, Uncle Joe is pretty old and he's not good these days. The business has gotten far too big for him. To be honest, Joe just can't crack it anymore."

"I'm sorry to hear it. Listen, I need to talk with you about some stuff. If you want to be off the record, I'll understand but I'd like you on the record."

"We're working now?"

"If that's okay with you?"

"So, not friends now?"

"Mike, since we were six years old, we've been friends. How does my profession change things?"

"Well, if you're not with me, you're against me. And sometimes Driscoll the reporter doesn't sound like the friend. What do you want to know?"

"Mike, what's up with you? I report the news. I don't take positions. You know that. I want to ask you some questions about the future intentions of the merged Democratic Party. As the chairman of the St. Luke Democratic Party Committee, you are bound to have views on what is happening at City Hall. The St. Luke public would be interested."

"David, we're off the record now. Okay?" I nodded reluctantly and Doyle continued. "I am not happy at the clear out at City Hall, nor the raising of funds from city employees. It's not my call anymore. What else have you got?"

"What do you know about the rumors of insider dealing on real estate deals and the involvement of organized crime in St. Luke?"

"Insider dealing: yes, I've heard stories. I know nothing about those deals. As for crime, organized or not, I can't seem to shake the shadow of my brothers but I have nothing to do with it."

"May I publish a denial on both on the record?"

"Yes."

"Okay. Would you help get me an interview with Gann, Santino and Berman? They're proving hard to nail down."

"Leave that with me. I'll get back to you. Listen, I have to say bye, I've a lot of people waiting for me. Good to see you and congratulations. Abby, she's quite a looker."

I went back to my office and called Barry Springer to ask if he had anything new about organized crime spreading its tentacles from

Chicago into St. Luke. He told me there was always gang gossip in Chicago, but he would not be at all surprised to find truth in it.

"Like any other business, organized crime has to find new outlets for its products, like booze. If the Outfit is really determined, they'll be hard to fight against. They're powerful enemies. But I don't have any more info since we met."

I spent the rest of the working week trying to run down the stories about insider dealing and organized crime. I got nowhere. Maybe Doyle had told me the truth. I was amused to see Doyle's picture in the Society page of Friday's *Bugle.* The caption read:

Man about town, Mike Doyle,
escorts Hollywood starlet, Meg Dickson
to the opening of St. Luke's newest restaurant

Meg fitted the template: blonde, pretty, buxom. How long would she last with him?

We saw Mary Page two nights a week for cooking lessons. It was working out well, especially as Abby and I could obtain half drinkable wine from an illegitimate source. We were trying to get into a routine, but I found it difficult to keep to a schedule because a journalist's life means working outside normal business hours. At least I made the effort and only missed about one lesson in four. Needless to say, Abby was not altogether impressed with me.

On Friday, I received a call from City Hall. Appointments were made for me to see Gann, Santino and Berman the following week. For the rest of the day, I worked out the questions I wanted to ask and the structure of the story I might write. When I got home that night around seven-thirty, Abby met me at the door.

"Please come in, master of the house. Let me take your coat and jacket. Are you hungry? Dinner will be ready in about fifteen minutes. There's time for you to wash and change. I'll have a drink waiting for you."

I looked at her with surprise. "I could get used to this."

I did as I was told. I washed, changed and came into the dining area to find a bourbon on the rocks waiting for me.

"Where did you get the booze?"

160

Abby tapped her nose with her forefinger. "So, the brilliant reporter doesn't know everything. Actually, it was a gift from Mr. Doyle."

"Really?"

"And I expect high praise for the dinner. I have had several lessons with Mrs. Page. Shame you couldn't make them all"

Abby served a chicken casserole. The gravy was a little thin and the chicken was overcooked but naturally, I said only complimentary things.

She beamed with pride. "My first banquet. Okay, I know it's not brilliant, but I will get better." And her cooking did improve, although I confess I spoiled too many of Abby's dinners by getting home late.

The next night at the appointed hour we presented ourselves at the Brady mansion on an exclusive street opposite the park and a kitty corner from City Hall. Henry Brady had an easy stroll to work.

The place was huge. We were shown into a reception room the size of two bowling alleys by a maid. On seeing us, Henry came over to us and shook me by the hand. He shook Abby's hand as I introduced her.

"So, you're Christine Harrington's daughter," Henry said to Abby. "It's a pleasure to meet you. Is this young man looking after you properly?"

"He's a treasure," replied Abby, "especially in the kitchen. Who knew?"

Henry laughed. "Let me introduce you both to our guests." There were two other couples in the room: Michael Hyde, the Republican state governor, and his wife Reggie; and Anthony Clarkson, the state's senior US Senator, a Democrat, and his wife Jill. Henry gave us both a glowing introduction. Both women smiled at Abby and took her to one side. I stood with the men, listening to their conversation, which seemed to be limited to the best vacation spots in California and Oregon.

The doors to the room opened and a woman, apparently in her early sixties, glided in. She wore a stunning white silk dress. At a distance, she looked regal.

Abby sidled over to me. "That's what I call an entrance," she whispered.

161

Close up, I noticed the woman's skin had a grayish, translucent pallor. She greeted her other guests and asked Henry to introduce her to Abby and me.

"Connie, this is David Driscoll and his new wife, Abby."

"So, you're the infamous Driscoll, the daughter-stealer."

"Guilty, Mrs. Brady."

"Call me Connie, please. And this is your beautiful wife. You're a lucky man, David."

"Yes, I am."

"Henry tells me you have achieved a lot in the year you've been with *The Bugle*. Are you having fun?"

"More than I ever expected. I am really pleased to be in St. Luke."

"And you, my dear?" Connie addressed Abby. "How are you finding things here?"

"Feet haven't touched the ground yet. It's all so new and different."

"And difficult, isn't it, talking with the boss's wife and having to be polite."

Abby and I burst out laughing. Before I could reply, the butler entered and whispered in Connie's ear.

"Everyone," she said, "dinner is served. David, please escort me in. You're sitting next to me tonight."

I was seated between Connie and Jill Clarkson, who knew each other well. They talked animatedly about St. Luke and Washington D.C., but made sure to include me in their conversation. On Connie's other side, Governor Hyde and Henry talked literature with Abby, putting her on home ground. I could see her charming both of them. Dinner consisted of a Waldorf salad, roast beef and apple pie à la mode. Connie remarked, "It's appropriate to have a good American dinner."

Wines were poured. The politicians toasted law-breaking, which I enjoyed almost as much as the wine. After dessert, Connie rose and indicated that the ladies would leave. The four men gathered at Henry's end of the table. Over cognacs and cigars, Senator Clarkson said he despaired about events in D.C.

"That idiot in the White House, I tell you an ostrich could do Coolidge's job just as well. We have made it crystal clear to him that the US trade surplus is not healthy. Sometime soon no one will have the money to buy American goods. And what does Coolidge do about

162

it? Nothing. He won't listen and says even less. At least you could talk to Harding."

The Governor agreed. "Looks to me like there are tell-tale signs of hard times ahead. I know we're used to boom and bust in these United States, but I've never known a spike in real estate like we have today and it's all over the country. Soon, the market will slide. We have bubbles appearing everywhere, not just in real estate. Just look at the stock market."

Henry Brady looked at them both. "I provide, at enormous risk of arrest for a heinous crime not to mention expense, some splendid liquor and you two become maudlin old women. David, have you any thoughts?"

"I'm thinking seriously about buying my first house, so now I'm really nervous. Economics is something I've never understood, but if what the Governor and the Senator say is right, what happens to the poor, the people who lose their jobs?"

"Nothing," said Senator Clarkson, "if the Republicans are in charge. No offence, Michael. Poverty is a sin, isn't it, if you're Republican?"

I understood his Democratic irony. "This country will never agree to welfare, so people will starve and die unless the charities do their work." Michael Hyde coughed. "I'll not get partisan tonight, Tony, but my seconds will attend you in the morning."

Everyone laughed.

"It's true," I said. "We ignore the poor." I looked at Henry.

He was brisk and non-committal. "Interesting. I know we could talk the night away, but the ladies would never forgive us. Shall we join them?" So the conversation was over.

Henry led the way to another reception room where coffee was served. Within moments of our entry, Connie stood. "Will you all excuse me? I think I am coming down with a cold. Please stay as long as you like." She made a special effort to say goodnight to Abby. "I think you're perfect for him. Keep him on the straight and narrow." She gave us all a weary smile and left. Henry faced us, saying, "I'll be back soon," and followed her.

Henry returned after a few minutes but it signaled the end of the evening. People began to say their goodnights. The men shook my hand. The Governor pulled me to one side. "Be careful with Doyle's people. I have grave suspicions about what's happening. My door is always open to you."

I thanked Henry for a splendid evening. He looked at me wistfully. "Yes, it was. I wonder if we'll have more nights like this."

On the way home, I asked Abby what she thought Henry had meant. "Was it that times are changing, like at the start of the Great War? Hyde and Clarkson think we have very bad economic times ahead."

"No," she answered. "I think it was personal. I have a terrible feeling that Connie is ill."

Abby was right. We didn't know that Connie had cancer.

Chapter Fifteen

On my arrival at Tom Berman's office at City Hall, I was offered coffee and cake. Instead of serviceable mugs and plates, bone china was used. Standards had improved, no doubt at the tax-payers' expense, but I thought it best to say nothing except, "good java."

Leader of the council, Gann, bailed out at the last moment. "Pressure of business," was the message given to me.

I assumed that the law had been laid down in no uncertain fashion to the others to let me interview them. The only person with power to do this was Doyle.

Santino spoke. "We're pleased to have an opportunity to talk with you and to put the record straight."

"So this is on the record?"

"Sure, unless Mr. Berman or I say to the contrary."

"Am I not seeing you separately?"

"No, we'll do this together. If we disagree with what the other says, we'll tell you."

"Okay, are you ready?" Both nodded. "My first question is to Mr. Berman. Recently, there was a cull of city office workers. Those fired were all registered Republicans. Is this right and, if so, why?"

"The publicity on this, Mr. Driscoll, was not accurate. We have replaced a number of city workers since November last year. The first round of dismissals was indeed limited to registered Republican voters, but these people had already made it clear to us they did not want to work under a merged Democratic council. They were happy to work for the city only if they worked for New Democrats or Republicans. And I'd like you to print that."

I thought this explanation was unlikely, to put it politely. "Exactly how many Republican workers were dismissed in the first round?"

"I don't recall. Not many."

"Will you get back to me with the numbers?"

"I'll do my best."

"After the first round of dismissals, how many other city workers were fired and how many of them were Democrats?"

"I'd need to check on that."

"How were their replacements chosen?"

"On merit, in accordance with normal practice."

"How was this achieved?"

"Interviews."

"No written applications, no references?"

"That is the new-fangled method used by corporations. We don't need it. We are experienced army veterans. We know men."

I thought that was odd. Usually the council employs women too. I continued, "In the interviews, did you ask for verification of political affiliation?"

"You mean, did we ask if they were Democrat or Republican? No."

"Why not?"

"We don't discriminate."

"How did people know that jobs were available? Did you advertise in the press?"

I knew the answer to this question already. The jobs had not been advertised. Word of mouth had been used in Democratic wards. Republican applicants didn't stand a chance.

"We didn't have to advertise. In many ways, St. Luke is still a village. People tell people."

"Would it surprise you if I told you that all new employees were registered Democrats?"

Berman had the grace to smile. He knew I had him. Berman and his people had put the fix in. "I guess it wouldn't, but I want to make it clear. The policy of the St. Luke Council is to employ people on merit, regardless of their politics. All we are concerned about is that they do their jobs."

"I asked Mike Doyle about the council's employment policies some time ago. He told me that all people had to do to keep their jobs is do them properly. Did you compare notes with him?"

"I don't have to. We agree on this policy."

"In that case, why were the second and subsequent rounds of dismissals all registered Republicans? They didn't resign. They were fired. Before they were fired, they had been doing a good job under the New Democrats. It doesn't add up."

"They were fired because they refused to work for the newly democratically elected Council, controlled by the merged parties."

"That's what you said about the first round of dismissals. Why weren't these people included? Will you give me the names and addresses of the people fired?"

"No. This information is confidential, as is any information about city employees."

"Mr. Berman, I had understood this interview was to clear the air between the Democrats and *The Bugle*. You're stonewalling me."

I wondered what was happening in the council offices to cause Berman to be so defensive. Why was Berman avoiding the truth? I didn't have to wait long.

John Santino asked to go off the record. "Okay, what if I said we fired people because they voted against us? Is that so surprising? We are embarking on radical changes for St. Luke, a new model of government, new taxation, altogether a sea change from the old ways. The people we fired would have thrown spanners in the works, or at least tried to. We could not afford to take risks."

"Fine, tell the truth to the public. Let readers and voters decide. Don't come up with some cockamamy story that doesn't hold water."

For a moment or two, Santino chewed on his lower lip. "You're right, Mr. Driscoll." He turned to his colleague. "Tom, let's go with this. The other line doesn't work and it will bite us in the rear end if we stick to it."

Berman nodded.

I asked Berman questions about the levy on city workers and got the same runaround. I was exasperated. I decided to move on. "Mr. Santino, you plan to increase the number of employees on the city payroll. How many extra people will be employed by the city and what is the likely cost? Supplementary to this, how will the cost increase be paid for and where will the new people work from?"

"These are all good questions. The directors are working out their numbers and costs and the council will review policy over the next few months, following which the figures will be published."

"With respect, your answer gets me nowhere."

167

"Mr. Driscoll, this is not as easy a matter as first appears. There are no figures on which we can rely to project numbers and costs. So we're investing in a new political science. It's called 'demographics.' We intend to publish our findings by the autumn, but the process is difficult."

"Would you explain the difficulties?" I wanted to add, "by all means continue to patronize me," but I refrained.

"Well, first we have to predict increases in population numbers and the ages of the increased population. Some corporations are planning ahead and are helping us with their anticipated numbers for new jobs. This only gets us so far. Not all corporations will give us the information and most look only one or two years into the future. We have to look five and ten years forward."

Santino took a breath and continued. "Then we have to factor in our own home-produced growth. You're newly married I understand?" I nodded. "My congratulations. How many children will you have?" I shrugged my shoulders. "You don't know. You see, we need to assess probable increases as well as estimating numbers of deaths too. When we have likely population growth worked out, we can plan the levels of services that will be needed. We need to distinguish these from services that are desirable. For example, we need to have good public health, but we cannot afford to provide medical help. We also need to consider other issues: will St. Luke run its police under home rule, who will provide education services? The costs are different if these services are provided by the state.

"Now," asked Santino, warming to his theme, "how will these increases be paid for? We have floated the idea of a tax on retail purchases. However, we have other options. We could consider a property tax hike and a city income tax. Nothing is included or excluded at the moment. Until we know our likely expenditure, I don't want to speculate further."

I repeated my question about where new employees would work. Santino replied, "We are undertaking a review of our available space here in City Hall. City Hall is old and in need of much more than a fresh coat of paint. It needs a proper refurbishment. We can't expect people to work long hours in excessively uncomfortable conditions. We may need to find additional office space. However, until our research is concluded and analyzed, I cannot comment further."

I searched Santino's face for signs of embarrassment, following his unquantified responses. I wanted to ask why, after two years plus in office, there were no numbers to be tested. My suspicions concerning City Hall were not assuaged. Santino must have seen my concern.

"Mr. Driscoll, I'm sorry to give you such long, complex and incomplete answers but your questions are not straightforward, even though you may have thought so."

I was not in the mood to let Santino off. "Isn't it disappointing that after more than two years in office, the administration seems to be stuck in the long grass? On a different topic, there is a rumor that sites have already been chosen for new city buildings and that land has already been purchased by third parties in anticipation of selling to the council at a huge profit. Would you care to comment?"

"No politician comments on a rumor. For all I know, you have made this up!"

"So you don't deny it?"

"Don't deny there's a rumor?"

"No, that land has been bought in the knowledge that it will be sold on to the City at an inflated price and huge profit for the sellers."

"That is easier to answer. I have no knowledge of any such purchase or purchases. That said, can you tell me what land has been bought in anticipation of this alleged deal, who bought it and the extent to which these people expect to profit? Come back to me when you have something concrete.

"As for your comment about being in the long grass, you seem to think that governing is easy. Try it some time. Then you will realize how difficult it is."

"I have one more set of questions. They concern the council's attitude to fighting crime. It is an open secret that Midwest cities like Chicago are ruled as much by organized crime as by their city councils. Will you confirm that you will prevent organized crime from getting any foothold in St. Luke?"

"The responsibility for fighting crime in this city rests with the St. Luke Police Department. The St. Luke P. D. is ruled by the state, not this council. Until we achieve home rule, I cannot give you the categorical assurances you seek. We will be using every effort to persuade the State Congress to direct the P. D. to fight organized crime."

"Will you be seeking home rule?"

"I believe so. In the meantime, the council will support every action to fight crime, organized or otherwise."

"How will it do this?"

"By trusting the St. Luke P. D. to do its job, as it has done since I have served on the council."

"Is that the policy, to keep out organized crime? No more than that?"

"What else would you have us do, Mr. Driscoll? Are we to react to every rumor? We'd get no governing done if we did."

I could recognize a block as well as anyone else. The Hanrahan machine was back under a different name. I thanked Mr. Santino and Mr. Berman for their time. I said we were now off the record.

"Have you heard stories about the Doyle brothers?"

Santino answered. "You need to be more specific. I can't deal in hearsay."

"I was in Chicago recently. The word is that Bill and Tom Doyle are leaning on Mike hard to allow the Chicago Outfit into St. Luke."

"Off the record?"

I nodded.

"We had an approach from Chicago people. We referred them to Mike. He rebuffed them. End of story."

"Okay, but surely you don't think the Outfit will leave it there. How will you fight them?"

"Interesting question. We have lots of options. Beyond that I can't answer you."

I felt very uneasy but accepted I would get no more.

"Expect to see something in *The Bugle* tomorrow or the next day. I assume *The Democrat's* rebuttal is ready?"

They both had the grace to laugh. At least lines of communication were open. Two days later my story was published.

170

The St. Luke Bugle

Established: 1875. 7th November, 1925. Circulation: 324,262.

IS ED HANRAHAN BACK IN CITY HALL?

Since April, 1922, aspects of St. Luke government have changed dramatically, in particular the employment of people working for the city. When the New Democrats were elected in 1922, hangers-on, people who were the beneficiaries of patronage without commensurate skills, and relatives and friends of those in power found themselves dismissed and replaced by people whose abilities matched the job description. With the "employment on merit" policy in place, the level of public service in our city improved beyond all expectation.

Therefore, *The Bugle* regrets the recent moves by the merged, ruling Democratic Party that cast doubt about whether the merit policy will be maintained. First, Republican voters employed by the city have been dismissed and replaced by registered Democrats. City Manager Tom Berman alleged the Republicans were fired because they refused to work for the new, democratically elected Council. However, Mr. Berman refused to identify any of the employees dismissed, nor did he explain why those jobs were not advertised and were, instead filled by Democrats whose abilities may not match the job description.

Second, the Democratic Party has raised a levy of between 3% and 10% of salaries on all Council employees. There are many examples of the governing party in other cities procuring funds in this fashion in an election year. But this is not an election year. Mr. Berman and John Santino, the party treasurer and councilman respectively, said

171

the party was left very short of funds after the election, but were unwilling to explain why funds were needed for the party this year. They refused to confirm that no further levy on city employees would be raised next year.

Voters whose memories go back more than three years will recall the tactics of the Hanrahan machine in the way they employed and treated people working at City Hall. Those voters may be concerned by the current antics of the Democratic Party, whose committee chairman, Michael Doyle, refused to comment on the changes. His attitude was that this was nothing to do with him, not his concern. As chairman, surely this is wholly his concern and his duty is to tell his political colleagues that they should consider their actions more carefully.

There was little overt reaction, except a phone call the next morning from Doyle, who screamed his head off at me. "How dare you quote me like this?"

I said I would talk to him when he had calmed down. He didn't accept my calls. It was his own fault. Doyle had turned his position as St. Luke leader on its head. I guess I always knew politicians couldn't be trusted. I would have to be ready to defend myself in our future dealings, but I couldn't help having a soft spot for him.

The Bugle was now on its guard with the St. Luke Democrats. I could see its endorsement being withdrawn for the 1926 election. Not that an endorsement was crucial for the Doyle machine. The Democrats were firmly in charge in St. Luke, despite the strength of the Republicans federally and elsewhere in the state.

Henry's appearances at the office became irregular and brief. He was uncommunicative, according to Ted Page who took over much of the day to day running of *The Bugle*. Too soon, all became clear. Connie Brady died in April, 1926.

Her death affected everyone at *The Bugle*. Henry Brady was the big cheese, the editor-in-chief, the man with day-to-day control of the newspaper, but Connie was the proprietor. She had been a member of the board of directors for many years. She owned 95% of the shares, the remainder being spread amongst the other directors. On her death, Connie's shares passed to Henry. It might have been thought that at *The Bugle* things would not change. Instead, Henry's heart went out of the business.

Connie's funeral spoke volumes about her. Virtually everyone from *The Bugle* came to the service. In addition, the many charities she supported were represented, not only by executives, but also by people she had helped. She was a true benefactor. Henry invited more than a hundred people to the mansion for Connie's wake. It was a somber affair until he came in.

"What a sorry bunch of people we have here. Connie would be appalled." He went over to a secretary from the office and started to reminisce with her about his late wife. There were hoots of laughter as stories were told. The shared memories made me wish I had known Connie in her younger days.

Governor Hyde came over to talk to Abby and me. "Good piece on the new rulers of St. Luke. Keep it going and press them on the organized crime links too. That's a real worry for us folks in Cameron." So he was watching.

As we were getting ready to leave, Henry spoke with us. "Connie was a very good judge of character. She liked you, David. She believed you were a real newspaper man and destined for great things, although not necessarily just as a reporter. We'll see. And she fell in love with you, Abby. Keep David's nose to the grindstone, please."

We both told him again how sorry we were for his loss. He shook my hand and hugged Abby. A month passed until Henry returned to his office. His visit was short. He announced to the board that he was taking a leave of absence for at least six months. The board had appointed Ted Page as temporary editor-in-chief immediately after Connie's death, so it was logical for him to stay in place. I was surprised when Ted asked me to take over as editor of the Metro section.

Ted put it like this, "It will do you good to see how the other half lives, looking after people like yourself who can't write and can barely spell. You'll have to double up. I can't find a full-time replacement reporter that quickly, so you'll keep some of the political beat as well as taking on editing. And you'll have to cope with those of your colleagues who think they should have the job."

I looked aghast. "Abby and I are about to move house, things will soon hot up for next year's elections and you want me to do both jobs? Have you got the blueprint for a 36-hour day?"

"You'll handle it. We'll get you some help. You can't write your stuff and edit it too. And there will be a salary bump. How does a twenty-five per cent raise sound?" I grinned. "Fifty per cent would sound better."

"Get out of my office. Now! Seriously, think about it over the weekend. Give me your answer on Monday."

When I got home, I was greeted with a hug from Abby. I threw my jacket onto our bed. "Want to talk?" I asked.

"Later. We have a visitor. Indeed, a visitor bearing gifts." Abby led me into the lounge come dining room come study. Mike Doyle was standing with his right hand outstretched towards me.

"Hi. My apologies for the intrusion. I've got you a sort of combined wedding and house-moving gift."

Abby pointed to the kitchen. There was a case of scotch, a case of French champagne, a case of bourbon, two crates of beer and food in abundance. "Good lord, Mike. Thank you." I was astonished by such largesse.

"My pleasure. Now, I know you're busy with the house move and everything. I'll say goodnight."

"You'll do no such thing," I said. "Let's get a drink. You've brought enough food to feed your old platoon. I insist you break bread with us. It's your bread, after all."

"Well, thank you. The food was meant to keep you supplied while you moved house. I can get some more."

"Will you relax? Abby, I'll do this." Mike wandered into the kitchen to pour the drinks. As I followed him in he said, "Sorry I didn't return your calls. I was mad at you. Since Joe's death last month, I've been struggling. His death is a huge loss personally. It is also a serious business loss. I'm going to announce my retirement from being a ward councilor. You have an exclusive," he laughed. "Are we okay now, you and I?"

"What do you think?" I gestured to the goodies.

We returned to Abby. I passed beers around and brought in the food. We sat around the table and ate pastrami and corn beef sandwiches. Mike told Abby how his days were filled helping newcomers to the city find places to live as well as jobs, while ensuring locals secured jobs if they didn't have the skills to be employed in new factories. He took his role as Chairman of the Party seriously.

"We've got to get training for new skills on the agenda. If not, a lot of good St. Luke people will be out of a job. It's not something that government will do or should do. We have to persuade the corporations to do this."

Mike Doyle with a social conscience! I took a good look at him. He was as smartly dressed as ever, but he was thinner than I remembered, twitchier that I had ever seen him, his hairline was receding further and he looked tired. The essential vitality of the man was missing. Maybe it was just the effect of a long working week.

I didn't want to press alarm bells yet.

Two hours and four beers later, Mike had relaxed. I teased him about Meg Dickson.

"Okay, I know she's young, but so am I, sort of. It will be fun for a while. Anyway, soon she'll be off to Hollywood and better things."

"So, no wedding bells, then?" For this I got an old-fashioned look.

"David, would it be possible for just us to talk?" Mike asked.

I replied that there was nothing he could say to me that he could not say in front of Abby.

He looked uncomfortable.

"Mike, Abby knows everything about me. You won't shock her."

"What I am going to tell you is very important, but not for publication." I nodded. "You know my brothers work for the Chicago Outfit, something I ain't proud of. I try to keep clear of them, but they've been leaning hard on me. They refuse to listen to me or anyone. I think they're going to act and we won't be able to stop them. It will start with gambling. They will force the speakeasies to take their slots."

"What are slots?" asked Abby.

"Slot machines," replied Doyle. "You put a nickel in a slot, pull a lever and win or lose, depending on where the pictures land. Usually they are pictures of fruit and you need to get three of the same fruit in

175

a row. The operator sets a win/lose ratio to the machines. Usually it's eighty-five per cent win, so the operator gets fifteen per cent of the amount wagered."

"I see," said Abby.

"Slots will just be the beginning. Then they'll force their booze on the speakeasies. Next will be prostitution and worse, maybe drugs. St. Luke will be a different town in no time because of the people this stuff attracts. News will get around that St. Luke is a wide open town and all sorts of low-lifes will come in."

"What can I do?" I asked.

"Go to Gann and get him to fire up the P. D. Chief, Eddie Rupert, so he throws my brothers and their people out. Go to the Governor and alert him. Write about it. Kick up a fuss, a real fuss. That might deter those brothers of mine or at least delay them."

"Mike, what proof have I got? I can't go back to Gann on a rumor. He's too wily a politician for this."

"I'll let Gann know you're coming and that he should believe what you're telling him."

Abby interjected. "Wouldn't it be simpler if you both met him?"

"Can't do that," replied Mike. "Alexei is a very proud man. If I am seen to dictate the moves, he'll get hot under the collar about his being just a puppet leader and that if St. Luke wants a puppet as council leader, he'll step down. Suddenly, it's all about him, not the mob."

"What do I say to the Governor?"

"Get him to delegate police powers to the St. Luke Council. If we have to wait for the state to give orders, we will lose. They'll take forever and a day. You have to realize how quick things happen. The mob don't like taking 'no' for an answer. There could be violence, guns on the streets, terror, who knows what else?"

"I see and if the change to home rule is publicized, it serves notice on these criminals, tells them we're ready for them. Should we also warn them about other things?"

"For example?"

"If they bring in slots, the police will remove them and take sledge hammers to them in front of City Hall?"

"Great! I like it. Listen, I have to go. Keep in touch on this one. I'll get a message to Gann today."

"Thanks for coming, Mike, and for all the gifts. I just hope our new neighbors don't see us bringing in all this booze when we move into the new place tomorrow. What will they think?"

"All you need is a Dry reporting you to the cops, right? What an entrance to your new home that would make!"

At the door, I asked Mike if he was alright. "Just tired. I need a vacation. Talk with you later."

I went back inside. Abby was sitting in an armchair, sipping a drink. "Let's talk," I said.

"It will keep."

"No it won't. What's up? You have something on that clever mind of yours."

"It's our plan. I graduate. I told you when we first met that I wanted to teach. This hasn't changed. I still want to become a teacher. You're a reporter. We live happily ever after."

"We have a plan?"

"Be serious, please. My professor spoke with me today. If I do just a reasonable job in my exams at the end of the month, I'll graduate summa cum laude."

"That's fantastic. I'm really proud of you, Abby."

"There's more. He wants me to stay on to do a master's degree and maybe even a Ph.D. Ultimately, I might teach at the college. What do you think?"

"Is this something you would want to do?"

"Yes, but can we afford me not earning a salary for years while I study?"

"Assume the money is not a factor, what then?"

"I'd jump at it, but I can't ask my parents to finance me. Maybe the college would help?"

"Decision made. I have news for you. I'm taking the job of Metro Section Editor. The offer came today. I have to do both the editing and my reporting job for a while but I'll get a huge pay raise. So, Professor Driscoll, what do you think now? How do you like them apples?"

Abby gave me her familiar smile. "I'm happy". She took my hand, caressing my fingers.

"David, do you want to be an editor?"

"You remember my talking about Sam Perkins?"

"Yes, the man who got you interested in newspapers."

"He was a lot more than that. He put me on this road years ago. Yes, I want to make the change."

"Won't it be a huge strain on you, editing and holding the political brief? And your working day, will it get even longer? I don't see enough of you anyway."

"Ted said he'd get me some help on the reporting side, the editorial team is experienced and who knows how temporary the appointment will be? I think it's an offer I shouldn't turn down. But I have to admit, I'll be spending more time at work. It's the life of a journalist. Things don't happen just in normal working hours."

Abby looked wistful, but soon she smiled again and murmured, "Let's go to bed. We have a big day tomorrow."

The next day was spent in a flurry of activity. For two people who hadn't accumulated much in the way of possessions, it still took us half a day to load the removal truck.

We reached our new home in the early afternoon. New neighbors came to take a quick peek at the newcomers. We waved to them. A couple of guys asked if we wanted help in shifting things. Sadly, I had to refuse – politely. I'd have liked the help, but I was worried about the booze treasure trove being discovered. We had quite an audience as I carried Abby over our new threshold.

By early evening, the truck was gone and cartons and cases were in their correct rooms. Abby and I sat on tea chests in what would become our dining room. We made sure we couldn't be overlooked and broke open the beers. We set out the leftover food from the previous night and ate and drank.

"What next?" I asked.

"I think we should unpack tomorrow. I found the sheets and blankets and made the bed. Tomorrow, we'll unpack the upstairs and get done as much as we can downstairs. I can take Monday away from my studies and finish the move then. Does this work okay for you?"

"I have to be in the office on Monday, but I'll try to get home early. The timing of Ted's offer couldn't have been worse, could it? Sorry."

We went upstairs, showered and went to bed. We were too tired to do anything but flop. On Sunday, we did nothing but unpack, and shift, and clean. By the evening, nearly everything was in the right place.

"We're in good shape," Abby observed. "Mind you, the yard needs work." Memories of my childhood flooded back. I had yard duty in those days. "Piece of cake," I replied with as much irony as I could muster.

On Monday morning, I met with Ted Page and told him, "I want to accept the job on two conditions."

"Talk."

"I promised Abby's parents that we would go to Richmond as soon as she graduated. That will be next month. I'll need three or four weeks away. When I get back, I'll be all yours."

"And the second condition?"

I told Ted of my meeting with Doyle. "I need to continue report on City Hall. I seem to have been put in the role of go-between and I suspect that if my name comes off the by-line, it will send the wrong message to Doyle's people."

"That's not so easy." Ted looked worried. "I've told you about wearing two hats, writing City Hall politics in the Metro section and editing your own work. It won't look right."

"Why don't we reorganize? Let's take City Hall politics at high level away from Metro and pass it to you? I'd write the copy and report to you. I will only get called in at election times, or when the politicians start behaving badly, or if outsiders start interfering with City business and life?"

"Good notion. It might just work. By the way, there could be all sorts of changes here."

"What are you getting at?"

"Henry is selling out; the newspaper, the mansion, everything. He's moving east to Boston. I think he's taking a teaching post at Harvard. So, we don't know who our new masters will be. Henry's assured me jobs will be safe, but you can never be certain."

"Ted, what do you mean about jobs? My personal situation has changed. I need job security now."

"Let's have dinner before you go on your holiday. Sort out the newspaper problems of the world. Don't worry about your job. With the new responsibilities you're taking on, any new owner would be completely mad to let you go."

I went back to Ted's old office. I couldn't think of it as mine. Pushing these thoughts to the back of my mind, I put in a call to the Governor. His office said he would call back. I said I would be with Leader Gann at St. Luke City Hall and asked if he could call me there in about an hour. Then I called Alexei Gann. "I've been expecting you," he said. "When can you come over?"

"Give me thirty minutes?"

Half an hour later, I sat with Gann, mugs of steaming coffee before us. "I see the good china has been put away."

He laughed. "Now, Doyle told me to treat you seriously and that it was urgent. What's up?"

"The organized crime thing is no longer a rumor. As you know, Doyle's brothers are part of the Chicago outfit. Doyle says they are leaning on the speakeasies here in town to take slots and he believes this is just the beginning. Now he's not the only one to warn me. I have it from the Governor himself. He's been hearing things from his people. There is real concern in Cameron about the mob getting into St. Luke. The Chicago Outfit probably sees St. Luke as a soft touch. The federal government won't help, so it's up to both you and the folks in Cameron to act."

"Christ almighty! Have you any ideas?"

"*The Bugle* will publicize what's going on, get it out in the open and encourage our Police Department to get tough. We can also get the radio stations to help with live interviews, maybe with you and Chief Rupert."

"Okay, this is very bad news. But how can I direct Chief Rupert to do so much as blow his nose? I don't have the power."

"I'm working on it."

At that very moment, the phone rang. Gann lifted the receiver. With eyebrows raised, he handed the phone to me. "Governor Hyde is on the phone for you."

"You should listen to this on an extension."

Gann nodded and moved to another desk phone. He called his secretary, who took the necessary action. We both heard the Governor's voice say, "Hello."

"Governor, this is David Driscoll. I'm sitting with Leader Gann. He is on an extension phone at this end and can hear you."

"Good morning, David, Mr. Gann."

180

I looked at Gann, asking if it was alright for me to do the talking. He nodded. "Governor, when we last met, you warned me about the invasion of organized crime into St. Luke. I have it on good authority that it's happening now. Please don't ask me to disclose my source, because I won't. Trust me when I tell you the source is very reliable. Leader Gann needs your help right away. He wants you to delegate control of the St. Luke Police Department to him so Chief Rupert is under no misunderstanding as to whose instructions he obeys and what he is to do. We need local control. Furthermore, Mr. Gann needs your express authority to fire Rupert if he fails to carry out his orders."

"What will those orders be?"

Gann interjected. "To enter the speakeasies and seize the Outfit's slots, when they come and believe me they are coming. No more, no less. We can't stop all gambling, but we don't have to have organized crime running it. If we halt the mob straight away, maybe they won't be tempted to bring their other foul practices into the city, at least for a while."

There was a silence as the Governor considered his position. "I need to make sure I have the power to do what you want without referring to the State Congress. If so, I will consider implementing what you ask. However, without better proof than just your word, David, it may not be so simple. Will you wait there with Mr. Gann? I'll call back as soon as I can."

Gann looked at me with seeming admiration. "Ever thought of running for office? You're a natural."

"Nah. No disrespect, but I like the company I keep! Here's the bottom line, I'm far too thin-skinned for politics. I'm better suited to newspapers. I'm easy with the 'tell the truth at all costs' kind of life."

"So, let's talk about the plan if the Governor gives us the go-ahead."

"I go back to *The Bugle* and write the story and an editorial to be published tomorrow. You call your council into emergency session, get a resolution approved to prevent the incursion of organized crime into St. Luke by whatever legal means and instruct Police Chief Rupert accordingly. Have him set out what he proposes to do. Then get yourself and Rupert on the radio, telling the Outfit to stay out." I gave Gann my suggestions as to the specifics and what Rupert ought to announce.

181

"Okay. I'll make doubly sure the manpower is available to back it all up. Once this is done, I can find an intermediary to pass the message back to Chicago that they will not be welcome here and will be met with force if they try. While you're here, that piece you wrote about our new employment processes. I see it didn't catch fire."

"I don't know what your administration is up to, but we're beginning to get a bad taste."

"There's an old saying. You campaign in poetry, you govern in prose. Governing's a tough, difficult business. Why don't you put your hat into the ring and seek election? Then maybe you won't be so quick to criticize."

Gann and I spent about an hour talking things through. Then the Governor called back to confirm his temporary Order. It would be sent by telegram immediately.

Gann shook my hand. "I prefer working with you than not. Let's stay in touch. I look forward to reading what you write."

I returned to the office and told Ted what had happened. I knew I ought to go home to give Abby some help, but I had to stay in my office and write.

Oddly, much later in my life, I would find it easier to write the important pieces at home.

We didn't have a telephone in the house so, riddled with guilt about leaving Abby alone, I dashed home to find her washing the insides of the kitchen cabinets. I told her of the morning's events and that I had to get back to the office. She took it well, considering the work that needed to be done at home. She asked if I wanted a coffee and a sandwich, but I was already half way out the door.

I rushed back to the office and started to write. It took quite a while. I went to Ted's office and interrupted a meeting. "Sorry, people, but this is urgent." Ted asked if he could have the room. When we were alone, he read what I had written. It comprised a factual report and a draft editorial. He made some alterations.

"This is better than good. Old Sam Perkins would be proud of you and so would Henry. I'm running the story with a 48 point headline. I'm also putting the editorial on the front page. Go home. You've earned your salary today."

The Bugle was delivered to me at six thirty the next morning. Abby was already awake and studying but she came over to me as I opened the paper.

The front page read:

The St. Luke Bugle
Established: 1875. 6th May, 1925. Circulation: 338,831.

NO TO THE MOB

In a startling turn of events yesterday, Governor Hyde temporarily ceded control of the St. Luke Police Department to the City Council. "This is not home rule," said the Governor. "However, a clear case has been made to my office that the St. Luke City Council should have day to day authority to direct the Police Department in a fight to avoid the threat of organized crime infiltrating St. Luke."

It is an open secret that speakeasies operate in St. Luke, both in the downtown areas and in some of the old wards. For years, people who do not want to adhere to Prohibition have taken their pleasure peaceably and without disturbance to their fellow citizens. Bad liquor would be just one of the mob's dirty businesses that would become part of St. Luke life.

The City Council appealed to the Governor for special powers. "If adults want to drink and gamble in a free society like ours, they will always find a way," said Mr. Gann, "but their freedom may be affected if organized crime gets its foot in the door. If it did, what would happen next? Will it be more dens of iniquity?"

There is evidence that representatives of the criminal gang known as the Chicago Outfit have been pressuring St. Luke speakeasies to take gambling machines known as slots into their premises. Leader Alexei Gann said, "This would have been just the beginning of organized crime taking control in St. Luke? Will we suddenly find prostitutes on our streets? Will protection money be demanded of our local businessmen? Will the other filthy practices of organized crime wreck our city and what it stands for?"

At an emergency session of the City Council, a unanimous resolution was passed, directing Police Chief Rupert to take all steps necessary to prevent organized criminal elements from St. Luke. Soon after receiving his orders, Rupert gave the following statement:

"Let me make things clear to anyone from the criminal gangs of Chicago or any other American city. You will not be permitted to bring your business here. If you install your slot machines in our speakeasies, they will be removed, brought to the plaza in front of City Hall and sledge hammered to pieces by our police. You and your kind are not welcome here. I have a clear message for you. Keep out and stay out."

Police Chief Rupert confirmed he received instructions direct from Governor Hyde to take orders from the city leadership and would comply with the directions of the City Council. "The St. Luke Police Department always stands ready to serve the people of St. Luke. I commend Governor Hyde and Leader Gann on their firm stance."

Leader Gann made the council's position abundantly clear. "We will contest and defeat any attempt by anybody, no matter how powerful they may be, to disturb and disrupt the life we have built in St. Luke. We are proud of what we have here. It is the inheritance we want to pass to our children and our children's children and we will protect the city at all costs."

Underneath the story, the editorial had been printed.

Defeat Organized Crime

For months, rumors have abounded that organized crime was seeking to spread its poison into St. Luke. Yesterday, the council struck. In a startling series of moves, temporary control of the St. Luke Police Department was ceded to the City Council. Leader Alexei Gann persuaded Governor Hyde that the danger to St. Luke was clear and present and the Governor responded. For this alone, our leaders deserve praise.

Some may wonder what all the fuss is about. Speakeasies in St. Luke have subverted the law for years and no action has been taken to close them down. What does it matter if some slot machines are available to grown adults? Why should anyone have the right to tell these same adults that they can drink but not gamble? Is it not hypocrisy, especially as people can find other ways to gamble in St. Luke?

The line taken by our leaders, and rightly so, is that it is not the supply that is questioned. It is the supplier. Independent businessmen who pay their taxes and owe no obligation to others run St. Luke speakeasies. The slot machines would have been supplied by the mob, organized crime, people who, once they have their tentacles gripping you, won't let go. Leader Gann rightly set out what might happen if the authorities turned a blind eye to the slots.

It is not known whether the messages sent by our state and city governments will fall on deaf ears in Chicago. If they are not heeded, this newspaper stands ready to report on the subsequent actions of our Police Department.

It is good that we have a state Governor willing to cede his own authority for the benefit of the people of St. Luke. It is good that we have an active council, willing to take action to protect us. It is good that we have a Police Department ready and able to fight organized crime. This newspaper will continue to support these efforts, but will be as vigilant as the council in ensuring the enforcement of our ordinances and laws so that organized crime never gets a foothold in our city. Indeed, we call upon all our politicians and city officials to pledge their efforts and support in keeping our city safe.

Abby finished reading. "I'm taking this edition with us to Richmond. My parents will be interested."

That was it. I had expected some reaction but not this. I followed her. "Didn't you like it?"

"No, I loved it. This is one of the reasons I married you. You're a crusader."

An envelope with my name on it had also been delivered to the house. Inside was a note, "Good job, Irish."

Chapter Sixteen

We left for Richmond at the end of May, five days after Abby graduated summa cum laude. The drive took three days. On reaching the Richmond house late in the afternoon, Abby was welcomed with all the love one would have expected. Peter and Gerry were ecstatic to have their big sister home. Abby was praised to the heights for her degree.

Alex beamed about his eldest beginning her postgraduate life in the autumn. He took me aside to ask if Abby's studies would put a strain on the finances, and was delighted to hear that I could afford it. "You gave us a wonderful start and I can't thank you enough, but we'll take it from here. No offense intended." I thought it best to keep the uncertainty about *The Bugle's* future to myself.

"None taken." He must have told Christine because she called me Mr. Moneybags at dinner, which we ate outdoors, or "al fresco," as Christine described it, remembering her salad days in Italy. After dinner, Abby excused herself and returned with the edition of *The Bugle* on the fight against organized crime. Christine and Alex showed no surprise. "We have a confession. We are *Bugle* subscribers. It gets delivered every day, although a few days behind, so we keep up with what you write. What's happened since?" They both wanted to know.

"Good question. Lots of local attention, but everything has gone quiet for the moment. I can't think the mob will quit, but St. Luke may have bought a few months peace." Soon after this exchange, I confessed to being exhausted. "One thing I'm looking forward to is time to relax. The past six months have been so frantic, what with the newspaper and moving house. Now I have a while to just think and rest." With that, Abby and I retired for the night.

Almost immediately, I fell into a deep sleep, but suddenly awoke to the sounds of shuffling feet and I could hear people breathing. Sitting up, I saw hooded figures at the foot of the bed. My shout of "help" was drowned by a cacophony of noisy hoots, drums and whistles, as well as some unrecognizable musical instrument being played outside. I was dragged out of bed.

Abby got up, laughing and hugging herself. "It's your shivaree!" she yelled. I hadn't a clue what she was talking about.

I was half-pushed, half-carried downstairs and into the front yard. Outside, there was a collection of people, virtually none of whom I recognized. They were singing and dancing and liquor was being passed around. Alex and Christine were laughing with Abby. I was pushed and pulled by the throng, who were clapping to the music that was now very loud. Without warning, a hood was put over my head. I was lifted off my feet and carried fireman-style over someone's shoulder. A minute later, I was thrown onto something hard, heard an engine start and realized I was in the back of a truck, being driven away. I couldn't believe it. What started as high jinks seemed to have developed into capture. Was a shivaree a kidnapping?

After fifteen or twenty minutes, the truck stopped. Hands roughly pulled me out and shoved me upright. I was hit over the head by something, maybe a shovel. I fell to the ground and felt sick. Crouching, I put my arms over my head and round my body to protect myself while kicks and punches landed on my head, arms, stomach and ribs. Maybe a shivaree was being beaten to death?

Why would Abby and her family have wanted me to endure this? How could this really be a Southern custom? I don't know how long the beating lasted. In the end, I became numb to the pain. "That's enough," I heard someone say. "Leave him."

"Not yet." I felt more kicks and punches. Then there was a shuffling of feet, the sound of an engine starting and I heard the truck tear away. I removed the hood and struggled to my feet, and fell over feeling really ill. I had no idea where I was but a head wound was bleeding while awful bruising pains were everywhere. The heat of the night had dissipated and I shook with cold. I was in shock. It was hard to walk, especially with the pain in my ribs. "Find a road," I told myself, but which way? I figured the truck had driven out of the Porters' drive turning right which meant it was headed north. I guessed the way south from the stars and limped my way along. After a while, I came across a road. I was exhausted and I stopped.

I must have passed out. Minutes or maybe hours later, I awoke, frozen to the bone, to see a watery sunrise. Hearing the sounds of a motor, I tried to get to my feet, but threw up instead. The engine sound came closer. I saw a car and fainted. The next I knew, I was having my head cradled in my wife's lap, her tears splashing my face, telling her father to drive faster. I was taken to a hospital and admitted for treatment. Ten stitches were needed for the cut on my head and ointments and bandages helped soothe my bruises. The hospital doctor thought the shock, exposure and exhaustion would pass after a couple of days in hospital. I managed what I thought was a grin but probably looked like a grimace to the members of my adopted family who surrounded my bed.

"Thanks for that wonderful Southern welcome," I mumbled.

Abby hastened to explain to her parents, "It's his sense of humor, he's not being sarcastic."

"Who says?" I countered.

Christine sat by me and held my hand gently. "We are so sorry. We were a little inebriated last night when you were brought downstairs and just didn't notice what those Cooper boys were up to. I had no idea they would be so rough with you. It really got out of hand."

Alex chimed in. "Please don't judge Southerners by what happened. I'll make sure those boys regret what they did to you."

I couldn't nod my head. It hurt too much. I slept instead. Hours later, when I awoke, Abby was there alone. She spent much of the night looking after me and the next day, too. Eventually, I was allowed back to the Porters' house, where I was made very comfortable. Alex and Christine sat with me, apologizing yet again.

"A shivaree is an old Southern custom, dating back a hundred years and more. It's meant to be lively, a party as well as kind of a rite of passage for the groom before the wedding night. Sure it's meant to get him coping with a bit of embarrassment, but not like this. It's not meant to be physical. What were those Cooper boys thinking? When we realized you were gone, we went looking for you but these roads are so dark, we had to give up. We started again just before dawn."

"Not to worry. I don't bear grudges." I asked the Porters what they wanted me to do about my attackers. They didn't understand. "I don't live here. You do. If it's just something that got out of hand, I can forget it. I'm going to be fine in a few days."

"I have to say," said Alex, "it would be unfortunate for those boys if you had them prosecuted, but we wouldn't blame you. Are you content if they come and apologize, the boys and their parents, too?"

"Wait a minute," said Abby, "I'm not content. Look at what they did to him!"

Alex answered her. "The eldest boy, Cal, he was sweet on you, Abby. He was jealous and he let it get the better of him. The other boy, he's a thug and I'll warn old man Cooper this must never happen again or they'll go to jail."

"That's okay with me. Abby, let it go."

The next day, three Cooper men and Mrs. Cooper presented themselves. The two boys lowered their heads as they mumbled apologies. I told them to look me in the eye. "If this is personal, when I'm recovered I'll meet you in a fair fight, one at a time. If you're really sorry, then let's shake on it and forget it." The boys didn't know what to do. Eventually, Cal offered his hand, followed by his brother.

Their father looked at me approvingly. "Thank you, young man. Maybe you and your lady wife would break bread with me and my family while you're here?"

"I don't think so, Mr. Cooper." I didn't want him to think for a minute that I was a pushover. "What has happened today is through the respect I have for Abby's people. Mrs. Cooper, I mean no disrespect to you, but Mr. Cooper, you and your boys should not come near me again ever, if you know what's good for you. If I see your boys, I won't be responsible for my actions." I looked Cal in the eye. "Understand?"

The rest of our visit passed quietly and far too quickly. I mended fast and soon got into the swing of things down South. I especially liked the late afternoons when my new in-laws returned from their surgery to, "Hoist one for purgatory," as Alex liked to call it.

It proved fortunate for me that Alex had taken a subscription for *The Bugle*. I was able to keep abreast with St. Luke news. There wasn't too much reported on the local scene but I wasn't happy with what I read. It seemed that Gann and his people were moving away from the high standards of the New Democrats' first term in office. For example, there was no movement on employment fairness at City Hall. Quite the reverse in fact. Soon, I was itching to get back to my political beat to find out what exactly was going on.

190

Shortly before we intended to head back to St. Luke, a telegram arrived from Jane. My mother was seriously ill in a New York hospital. I felt guilty. In the six months since the piano recital, I had been so busy that I'd hardly kept in touch. I knew it was wrong but at least I was consistently wrong. Abby had written to my mother regularly. It was an emergency, so we packed immediately, but promised to see the Porters just as soon as we could.

Alex floated the idea of meeting in Miami Beach at Christmas. I replied that I would try, but getting more time off this year would be a problem. Would they consider coming to St. Luke?

"Christmas in the Midwest has its advantages," I explained, trying to lighten our mood, "It's usually white— well light gray, and you're unlikely to be attacked!"

I cabled Jane that we would be in New York within a day or so and we left Richmond the next morning. I drove the direct route through D.C., Baltimore, Philadelphia and New Brunswick. It took 28 hours to get to Jane's building on 8th and 79th in Manhattan. There was a message with the hall porter that Jane was at the hospital. We took a cab east across town to Sloan-Kettering, a specialist cancer hospital. We found my mother's room. She was sleeping. Jane was holding her hand.

When Jane saw us, she burst into tears. We helped her outside into the corridor. She hugged Abby, then me. Making an effort to control herself, she looked at me. "Mom's going, David, it's just a matter of time."

"What happened?" asked Abby quietly.

"For a while, Mom was complaining of headaches. About three weeks ago, they got a lot worse. The doctor referred her here. They did some tests. On the day I sent the telegram, we found out she had a brain tumor, it was inoperable and all they could do was to make her comfortable. I've been told she may die in the next day or two. How am I going to live without her?"

Jane broke down as Abby comforted her. I tried to take in the news. My brave mother had battled through life, brought up two children almost on her own and when, at last, life should have been a real pleasure, this happened. "No time for feeling sorry for ourselves." I thought. I needed to give Jane the support she needed.

Later in the day, Harriet arrived. She greeted Abby and me as long lost friends and took us aside to a lounge area while Jane stayed at Mom's bedside. "How's the patient?" she asked me.

"She's resting comfortably. That's all that can be done."

"How's Jane?"

"Shattered, broken. What can I tell you? Jane's never been the strongest. Have you any suggestions?"

"Right now, none. I'm so glad you and Abby are here. David, may I talk plainly?"

"Yes, of course."

"Jane has the potential to be one of the world's great concert pianists. Your mother believed in her, and pushed her. Without Elizabeth's influence, I'm not sure Jane will stick at it. She needs someone with her to urge her along. She has concert dates booked around the country months ahead. All of us assumed Elizabeth would be with her. Jane can't do this by herself. Have you any suggestions? Could Abby take time out?"

"Harriet, no. Abby is starting her postgraduate studies in the fall. And selfish as it may sound, I won't live without her. Please don't put the idea into Jane's head."

"I didn't. It was Jane's thought."

"I apologize." I paused for a minute. "Doesn't Jane have any close friends who would fit the bill?" Harriet shook her head. "So, we're left with one person."

"Who?"

"You, Harriet. I assume Jane is very well paid for these concerts?"

"Yes, she's paid between $250 and $300 a night."

"Wow! That's real dough. So, it could be made worth your while?"

"That's not the point, David. This isn't what I do."

"I know but could we persuade you to consider taking on just one client? You'd be perfect. You understand the business, you and Jane obviously get on and you might enjoy the experience. Surely there's enough money to keep you both happy. Why not try it for just six months? If it doesn't work, Jane will know she has to make other arrangements."

"Let me think it over. I can see good things, especially if she undertakes a tour of Europe. I haven't seen London or Paris for quite a while and Rome, Vienna, and Amsterdam, all are possibilities."

192

"Harriet, can we talk another time. What I will do first is take Jane home to St. Luke with me. She'll need some time after Mom passes. She should be with us. Could you cancel her concerts for a few weeks?"

"Leave all this to me. I'll see you tomorrow."

Harriet left and so did Jane, reluctantly, after I promised not to leave mother's side. When she woke up, I was glad to have some time alone with her.

"Hello my darling boy. How are you?"

"Mom, I'm terrific. I'm so sorry."

"David, I don't have long, so let's not get maudlin. I need to talk with you. Will you promise me something?"

"Anything."

"You'll look after Jane. She has a special talent, like you. I'm so proud of you both. But Jane doesn't have your inner strength. She's going to need you."

"Of course, I'll take care of her. But what can I do for you?"

"Just sit with me for a while. Where's Abby?"

"She's just out in the hallway."

While my mother slept, I spoke with Abby about Jane's wishes that Abby act as her companion and my promise to my mother to look after Jane. "I refused on your services on your behalf, of course. It would be unfair for you to take a lot of time out from your studies and I'm selfish. I couldn't do without you." Abby had the good sense to let me struggle with my guilt.

Mother drifted in and out of sleep. The pain medication helped. She woke in the middle of the night, waking us in the process. She talked with us for a while, reminiscing about the old days, remembering the scrapes I'd got into. Before dawn, a few minutes after Jane returned, Mother smiled at us all for the last time, closed her eyes and passed away peacefully.

We decided to cremate Elizabeth and scatter her ashes in Culpepper. To my relief and Jane's delight, Harriet agreed to become Jane's companion and would meet us in St. Luke six weeks hence. We left New York, taking three days to drive to St. Luke.

At home, we settled Jane into one of our spare bedrooms while we sought to get our lives back to normal. Abby arranged for Jane to use a music room at college, so she could practice but Jane had no inclination to do this. She was just stunned at the loss of mother. She became taciturn and remote.

The weekend after we arrived home, the three of us drove to Culpepper. The roads had improved and the drive took only seven hours. Culpepper seemed smaller than I remembered. Isn't it odd how the familiar places of one's childhood look so much smaller a few years on? I left Jane in Abby's company and wandered over to the old *Culpepper Post* building. Two people were working, but I didn't see Sam Perkins.

"Oh, Mr. Perkins is in a home now," I was told and given directions.

When I got back to the hotel, Jane was sleeping but Abby was sitting on the porch.

"Come with me, please?" I asked.

"Where?"

"To see an old man."

I left a note for Jane, telling her where I was going, and drove for five or six minutes to the Culpepper Rest Home. At reception, I asked for Mr. Perkins. "I think he's in the common room. Please come this way."

We walked along a corridor whose windows overlooked a garden. We entered a room where some fifteen or twenty elderly people sat in wheelchairs. I saw Sam. He had no hair to speak of, he was shriveled, but he was still the Mr. Perkins of *The Culpepper Post*. I walked over to him.

"Hello, Mr. Perkins."

Sam looked up, squinted and tried to focus. His hands shook as he reached for his spectacles. He put them on and stared again. After a few seconds, he mumbled "Young David Driscoll. Well, well."

"How are you, sir?"

"Old and ready for my maker. Who is this pretty young thing?"

"Permit me to introduce you. This is my wife, Abby. Abby, this is Mr. Sam Perkins, one of America's great newspapermen."

Sam took a good look at her. "Why are you wasting your time with him?"

"I love him. He's quite nice really."

Sam cackled, "I know. I quite like him too. Push me outside, will you please?"

We went out into the warm summer afternoon. "David, it's good to see you. I know what you've been doing at *The Bugle*. I liked your stuff on the Chicago Outfit. Got to stand up to those bastards."

"They're asking me to move up, to be the Editor of the Metro Section. See, all that training you gave me has paid off," I told him.

"Editing is a different ball of wax. Give your reporters plenty of credit and rope. Make sure you tell both sides. And above all, never move away from the truth. Remember what I taught you, a hundred years ago? Now, what are you doing here?"

"My mother passed away. We're scattering her ashes here tomorrow."

"I'm sorry for your loss. Maybe you'll do the same for me? It won't be long." Mr. Perkins looked wistful.

At that moment, a nurse came over. She told us visiting hours were over, but that we could visit again tomorrow.

The next day after breakfast, we scattered mother's ashes in her favorite spot out of town by a river where we had often picnicked in the summer. Jane and I talked about the old days, exploring memories for comfort. Her thoughts of those times were kinder than mine, but then she did not remember much about our father. What she recalled vividly was mother as a teacher, one who had had all the time in the world for her students and for us.

"I learned patience from her and the will to succeed," Jane told Abby.

My own memories were not as pleasant. I would have been more than happy to forget most of my childhood, although mother was not to blame for this. When we scattered her ashes, I felt nothing except sadness for the hard life my mother experienced. I was all the more determined to lead my life differently.

Jane visited some old friends and Abby and I returned to see Mr. Perkins. I told him about my life at *The Bugle* and what I had been doing. I hoped for some more nuggets of advice, but it was not to be. He was tired. We said our goodbyes and collected Jane.

Early the next morning, we headed back to St. Luke. I felt unemotional about leaving and just could not figure out why. Maybe I had suppressed memories of my childhood because they were so conflicted. Or maybe I had a latent sentimentality that would not be set free. I knew this would be my last time in Culpepper.

Jane retreated into her shell as soon as we got home. Abby and I didn't know how to draw her out, but I had an idea. She had liked Doyle all those years ago. Why not invite him for Sunday lunch? Abby didn't object and Jane was ambivalent, so I fixed it up.

I had recently built a cook-out, a brick oven structure, in the yard. It had a mesh wire shelf for cooking. It worked by putting charcoal in the bottom of the cook-out and lighting the charcoal.

I explained to Doyle that lunch would be casual. Typically, he turned up wearing a three piece suit on a hot summer's day. He brought a brewery and a distillery with him, which we appreciated. We persuaded him take off his jacket, waistcoat and tie. He even removed his detached collar and undid his top shirt button. Abby put on the radio, playing soft music in the background.

We sat around talking and drinking until Abby ordered me to the cook-out. "We have hungry people here."

Jane had hardly said a word, but with Abby working in the kitchen and me getting a fire going, she was forced into conversation with Doyle. Soon, the two were animated. I eavesdropped and to my astonishment, Doyle was talking about Mozart, Beethoven, Chopin and Brahms. Jane was on home turf and opened up for the first time in weeks.

Lunch stretched into the late afternoon. The ladies went into the kitchen to organize dessert. Doyle and I were alone for the first time that day. "Where did this interest in classical music come from?" I enquired.

"The trenches in the war. Do you remember me mentioning Jeremy Pressman? He was my lieutenant. He had a phonograph and lots of classical music records. We took a liking to each other and I spent many an evening with him. He taught me some of the finer things of life. You have to appreciate that a lot of the time in those days was spent sitting around. It's the old army thing, 'hurry up and wait.' Anyway, amid the mud, stench and boredom, Jeremy played his scratchy records. I developed a love of classical music."

"Good grief!"

"You should meet Jeremy. He had just graduated from law school when war was declared. He had been in the ROTC, so he took a commission with the Eagle Regiment. After the war, he moved here from Paxton and we stayed in touch. Years back, I asked him to help look after my interests. He still does. I believe I am his only client these days."

"You're looking prosperous, as usual," I told him.

"Can't complain. Wall Street has been good for me. Plus lots of new house building and some city contracts are keeping us going, too." I stored this item in the back of my mind. I wanted to know more about the city contracts, but Doyle changed the subject.

"That was a good job you did with the Chicago Outfit. But they won't give up, you know. I think my brothers have been sent elsewhere. Still, I can't help but wonder what will happen next."

"Next should be the federal government. Organized crime is a nationwide problem. Coolidge should get onto it."

"I can't see Old Cal winding himself up and getting involved. Can you? He'll just say it's for the states themselves to resolve their problems."

"He's no ball of fire, that's for sure. Have you had any thoughts about next year's elections?"

"Not really, David. The new St. Luke plan to modernize the city should be out soon. I guess the election will be about supporting the plan or not."

"It will be good for you and your business if it goes through. Lots of construction work to go around."

"It will be good for everybody."

"Ever the politician, eh, Mr. Doyle?"

The ladies joined us. Later, Abby and I said our goodnights. I was a little hesitant leaving Jane alone with Doyle, considering his reputation with the ladies but I was too tired to stay up. I didn't hear Jane come up to bed.

Chapter Seventeen

Harriet telephoned regularly to see how Jane was faring. After a month, she wanted to know when Jane would be ready to get back to work. I was honest. Jane told me she wasn't ready to play, and to stop nagging her. She would work things out in her own time.

Jane spent her time in Doyle's company. From my viewpoint, she spent too much time with him. Abby told me to be patient. I was grateful to Abby for not reminding me I had put Jane and Doyle together in the first place. I asked Doyle to encourage Jane to get her career back on track. He said he understood, but he didn't feel he was in a position to tell her to practice, let alone tour.

Weeks passed. Harriet was getting impatient with her situation. She was not being unreasonable. She had agreed to put her professional life on hold for Jane. Jane could not expect Harriet to sit around indefinitely. I suggested to Harriet that she talk face-to-face with Jane when Harriet visited the next week.

That night, I resolved to talk to Jane when she came home. By ten o'clock, Jane had not returned.

"She doesn't have a curfew. These evenings with Doyle can run late," Abby said, when I grew impatient.

Abby came over to me and gave me a hug. "Not easy being a big brother, is it?"

I sat back in my comfy armchair. Had I behaved as a big brother should? When Jane and I were growing up, I didn't recall talking with her much or even spending time with her. We were just members of the same dysfunctional family. After I left for college, I hardly saw her. Of course, she'd be home when I visited Culpepper, but she would just be in the same room. We had few emotional ties to each other. I had seen and spoken with Jane more often in the past few weeks than in the equivalent number of years.

I asked myself, did I love Jane? I knew I was in love with Abby. She was my granite base; nothing would shake how I felt about her. If pushed, I would give my life for her. It was axiomatic; I didn't have to think about it. Jane was just someone I had known since she was born. I felt no strong emotional tie to her, though I felt responsibility. I was taking care of her, partly because it was the right thing to do and partly because of a promise I had made to mother. It was not done out of love.

So, if I didn't feel close to Jane, why was I fussed about her career and her association with Doyle? Surely, these were her problems, her decisions? Yet I knew that she had a special gift, an ability to play a musical instrument like few others in her generation and that she owed it to herself to share that gift. I had also made a promise to my mother that I intended to keep. And I worried at Jane's vulnerability. Surely Doyle would understand? He wouldn't treat her like his other women. By the time Jane got home, I was asleep. I let the issue drop.

Harriet's visit was imminent. I shared my thoughts with Abby about talking things through with Jane and Doyle together.

"Be careful and don't lose your temper. Those two seem to be involved with each other and you're heading into treacherous waters," Abby advised.

Early the next morning, I went to Doyle's downtown apartment. He opened the door himself. This was my first visit to Doyle in this place. The apartment was opulent, ornately decorated and far too ostentatious for my taste. It was no secret in St. Luke that business had been kind to Doyle. The newspapers often reported his social activities and rise to wealth.

"To what do I owe the pleasure so early?" he asked.

"I need to talk with you and Jane. Would you ask her to come out please?"

Mike reddened but nodded his head. After a few minutes, Jane, without make-up, barefoot and wearing clothes from the night before, came into the room. "Shall we have coffee?" she asked.

Doyle and I thanked her. We talked idly until she returned with a steaming coffee pot, a creamer, and matching sugar bowl and fine bone china crockery. After coffee was served, I opened the discussion.

"Jane, your life is your own and I don't want you to think I am interfering but it has been almost three months since mother died. Are you ready to go back to the concert circuit?"

"No, David, I'm not. In fact, I'm not sure I'll ever go back."

Keeping my temper, I asked why.

"I'm happy as I am. The circuit is a constant round of pressure, practice and travel, not to mention loneliness. Odd isn't it, feeling lonely when you don't get any time to yourself. You're always doing something and you're always with people who want something from you. When you're not performing, you spend six hours a day or more in practice, practice, and practice. The pressure on concert day, the waiting, knowing that when you perform, the critics want to catch you out. Why do I need this in my life?"

"Because, Janey, you have a gift, an extraordinary gift, an ability to play piano better than virtually anyone else in this country. You could have the United States and Europe at your feet if you want. What's wrong with that?"

"Nothing if that's what *you* want. I don't want it."

"You don't want it now, but might you not change your mind? If you leave things for too long, you'll miss the chance."

"Well, you've heard what I have to say."

"Okay, I freely admit I don't know this world of yours, but Harriet does. She is on her way to St. Luke to talk to you. She'll be here tomorrow."

"You had no right to invite her."

"Jane, I didn't invite her. Please think back a few weeks. Remember, Harriet agreed to put her own career on hold and take mother's place to be with you on tour. She wants to know where she stands. I think she has every right to talk with you about your future."

"I won't see her."

"You have to. Jane, she's a friend as much as anything else. Look at what she did for you during the last four years. She helped put your name up in lights."

"But she'll want me to change my mind and she'll pressurize me and I don't want to change my mind."

"That's your decision but you owe it to her to tell her yourself."

Jane looked at Doyle for help. "Will you tell Harriet for me? I don't think I can."

Doyle pondered. "I'll sit with you when Harriet sees you if you want, but David's being reasonable and he's right. You should speak to her yourself."

Jane sat trembling, started to cry, and suddenly ran out of the room.

"Best leave her," Doyle said. "She gets like this. She'll be okay in a few minutes."

"You two close?"

"She's been staying here a lot."

I sat forward and cradled my hands under my chin. "May I ask where this relationship is going?"

"I love her, David."

"And she loves you? After two months?"

"Yes, that's what she tells me."

"So, what's next?"

"It's early days."

"I don't want to sound like a Victorian father but you're sleeping with my sister. She seems hell bent on throwing away a fabulous career and for what? You seem to be getting your vigorish here for no risk."

Doyle stood up, anger in his reddening face. "How dare you? I told you, we're in love. Why would you think I'd take advantage of her?"

"Because you have a track record of doing just this, taking up with a girl and throwing her away when you're done."

"Jane and I haven't talked marriage yet. And I'm not going to propose just because you say so." I took a breath as I raised my hands in peace. "Let's ease up on each other. I'm sorry. Please understand all I'm doing is taking care of my sister's interests."

"I know, but I'm not her enemy, or yours for that matter."

"I don't know, Mike. I get the feeling that you have something in your character that stops you committing. I think you like the chase and the kill but there's nothing afterwards. I want you to make me a promise."

"What?"

"You'll be honest with Jane and tell the truth if you end it."

"Who's talking about ending things? We're good with each other. And as for the commitment thing, that's the pot calling the kettle black."

"What?"

"My sister. I know you had relations with her and then left her to her own devices. You broke her heart and you didn't care. So, if I do that to Jane, doesn't that make us even?"

I glared at him. "Adele seduced me, not once but twice." I could not help raise my voice. "Yes, we had sex, but each time it was at her instigation. Our relationship, brief as it was, had no emotion in it for me. It was all physical. Adele has given you a bill of goods. You tell me, is Jane anything like Adele? Is there any of the temptress about her? She is a lovely, sweet girl. Have you got close with Jane just to get your own back on me?"

Doyle clenched his fists. He didn't like the accusation. "No, of course not. I treat her with respect and kindness. Ask her if you want, but not now. Wait till we've both cooled off." There was a pause. "David, you need to come off your high horse. What happens between Jane and me from now on is our business, not yours. I think you should leave."

"Not until I've spoken with Jane."

The door to the room opened. "I heard every word you two said." She stood next to Doyle and looked him square in the eyes. "Do you love me?"

"Yes Jane, I do."

Jane turned to me. "That's good enough for me. I don't care about marriage, David. Let me live *my* life *my* way."

"Mother made me promise to look after you and that's what I'm doing. I accept it's your life, but you have such a wonderful talent. Please don't throw it away, Jane. And what about Harriet?"

"Mike and I will see her together. But my mind is made up, David. I'm staying here."

I shrugged my shoulders. "I think you're making a terrible mistake. What would mother say? Did you think of that? Look at all the sacrifices she made for you. Doesn't that count for anything?"

"Tugging at the emotional sleeves again, big brother? You should leave now." Jane had made herself painfully clear.

Back home, I went into the study, slamming the door.

Abby came in and said, "Bad?" I nodded my head. I told Abby what had happened.

"I can't see how it will get better. Jane is going to throw away a career for a man who will leave her as soon as he gets bored. What will happen to her then?"

"Your job will be to pick up the pieces. That, my darling, is what big brothers do."

Harriet arrived in St. Luke the next day. I met her at Union Station and took her to her hotel. Once she was settled in, we sat together in the lounge. Over tea, I told her everything. I explained that Jane was in a relationship with one of St. Luke's prominent business men, that she was in love and that he was not encouraging Jane to return to the concert circuit. All I could offer was a meeting for her the next day with Jane and Doyle. I apologized profusely and offered to talk compensation with her.

Harriet was surprisingly refreshing and encouraging. "David, this is not the first time I've seen an artist go off the rails. Jane's a young girl who has led a somewhat sheltered life. You have to let her spread her wings. In many ways, an unsuccessful love affair is good for one's art. When an artist channels that anger into work, amazing results occur.

"I've been in this business a long time. Six weeks ago, I put all Jane's dates on hold. Nothing will be lost there. I've spread the word that she has been deeply hurt by her mother's death and it might be many months before she returns to the concert stage. The circuit is like a family and the people involved are sympathetic. Were Jane to return a year hence, little will have been lost, provided she keeps practicing. If she doesn't, it will be hard for her to get the artistry back."

"Harriet, she is very lucky to have you in her corner. I suspect you will not be given a pleasant reception when you talk to her. She'll be defensive and maybe even hostile. Please don't hold it against her."

"Of course not. I'm telling you this is not a novel situation for me."

"What will you do about reclaiming your business?"

"I never lost it. I always thought it was a fifty-fifty chance whether Jane would come back. Don't ask me why. Sixth sense, shall we say?"

We talked for a while longer until Abby joined us. We dined together. Harriet showed an interest in Abby's postgraduate course. "Never handled a writer before but there's always a first time. Where's your novel, Abby?"

"Ah," my wife replied, "I need to suffer more before anything I write would be worthwhile, though living with him," pointing at me, "I have high hopes."

Harriet called me before she left for New York. "I've just seen Jane. She was pretty belligerent, as you predicted. She was adamant that she was not coming back, ever. We'll just have to see."

"Did Doyle contribute?"

"Only when I mentioned piano practice. He told me of his love of classical music and why. Fancy listening to Mozart sonatas in the trenches? He told me Jane played piano for him most nights. He owns a baby grand, though it seemed like a stage prop for appearances' sake as he doesn't play. Maybe he bought it for Jane? Anyway, he said he would encourage her to keep playing, albeit in private. I guess that's something. Odd sort, isn't he?"

"Don't be fooled. He's a big shot in St. Luke."

We said our goodbyes and agreed we would keep in touch. I thanked her again. "Young man," she said, "I hope this is just au revoir."

Instinctively, I felt I should try to mend fences with Jane. I telephoned Doyle's apartment. Jane answered. "May I come over?" She agreed and in fifteen minutes I was ringing the door bell.

"Is Doyle here?"

"No, just me."

"Jane, yesterday was rough for both of us. I'm sorry I upset you. I want you to be happy, so if this is your way, I accept it. I think you're making the wrong choice, but I respect your decision. I'll say nothing more."

"Which decision, the piano or Doyle?"

"Well, both I guess. As you said, it's your life. Harriet seemed resigned when I spoke to her. She advised strongly that you keep up your piano practice. I can understand you not wanting to do this for six hours a day but will you do some?"

"Yes, of course. I still love the piano." She came over and put her arms around me. "I don't like being bad friends with you. This was our first quarrel."

"And the last, I hope. Remember, Abby and I are just a phone call and a five cent bus ride away. Ask Mike to call me. We should mend our fences, too."

"I will," Jane confirmed. But Doyle didn't contact me. Nor did I try to reach him. In the light of what had happened, this was hardly a surprise.

A few weeks later towards the end of the year, the Democrats started to gear up for the 1926 city elections. Alexei Gann launched his campaign with a huge parade through town. The St. Luke college band played well-known rousing marches. Floats were decorated to delight the crowds gathered along the pavements of downtown St. Luke. Banners were displayed everywhere and people were handed rosettes, campaign buttons and flags. The party atmosphere was contagious. I managed to contact Abby at college and asked her to join me.

At twilight, the culmination of the rally began in Fellway Park. By then the crowd had swelled despite the cold and covered an area bigger than four football fields. Fortunately, the police presence wasn't needed. The people were good humored. The rally continued with songs by a school choir. They could be heard by everyone through the effective public address system. John Santino was introduced. He praised his Democrat councilmen colleagues to the heights, listing their achievements over the past four years. Other speakers followed.

More musical treats were given. Local singers offered renditions of Al Jolson's *Danny Boy*, Fanny Brice's *Second Hand Rose* and nonsense songs like *Yes, We Have No Bananas*. Then the college brass band played more familiar marches, from Souza to Karl King.

After more than hour of speeches and entertainment, the rally reached its crescendo. Alexei Gann made a rousing speech, praising his supporters and denigrating the Republican enemy. He vilified them locally and then spread his criticisms out to include the politicos in Cameron and Washington D.C.

"Recently, this city was threatened by members of an organized criminal syndicate. These people operate all over the country. They should be stopped. They must be stopped. This country has a Federal Bureau of Investigation. It is in business to help good American citizens defeat crime. What did Coolidge and his administration do to get the FBI to help this city? I'll tell you in one word. Nothing. What did our Republican State Congress do for us? I'll tell you in one word. Nothing. Fortunately, we had a Governor who took action. As a result your council was empowered to stop organized crime from becoming an established part of the life of this city. If for no other reason, this is why you should re-elect us."

The applause and cheers were deafening. "Now, let me introduce a man who may have taken a back seat from active politics but who strives for the benefit of this community. He will have helped many of you. He is working with you and for you to build a new St. Luke, a modern city for all our citizens. He is a war hero, an innovator and a unifier and the best friend the working man of St. Luke ever had. Ladies and gentleman, it is my pleasure and distinct honor to introduce the Chairman of the St. Luke Democratic Committee, Mr. Michael Doyle."

Doyle took the stage. Despite the cold, he wore no overcoat. I thought I detected some make up. He looked less pasty than usual. Maybe Jane had helped him.

He took the microphone.

"Folks, we've been out here for a while and it's pretty chilly, so I'll not keep you long. This coming election is crucial." His delivery was crisp and engaging. "The Republicans are gearing up to steal this election by false registrations and voting frauds. We know this because of what they've done in other elections. How do we beat them? That's easy. We make sure that those of you who want to vote Democrat are registered to vote. We do this before the primaries and if any person isn't already registered for the general, we make sure they go to register themselves. Then we bring out the vote.

"All of you here have come because you want to make our dreams for St. Luke come true. We can't do this if we don't get elected and we won't get elected if you don't register and vote. So you know what to do tomorrow when registrations start. Let's get the people out, reclaiming the rights that the Founding Fathers enshrined in our Constitution. Thank you. Have a great night. And don't forget, my door is always open to you."

Doyle left the stage to thunderous applause, surrounded by party members. As he left the park, he walked past me. "Mike," I called out. He pretended not to hear me. Abby laid her arm on mine. "Leave him, you don't want a scene here." It was good advice. I saw Jane link her arm with Mike's, I let them go.

One of *The Bugle* Metro team came over to me. Joe Burton was covering the city political scene. "Any thoughts, boss?" he asked.

"Yes, 500 words about the rally on my desk by nine tomorrow morning." Joe grinned at me and went on his way.

The next morning, I asked Harry Reed, one of the Metro's most experienced reporters, to come into my office.

"Harry, how good are your contacts in the County Judge's office?"

"Not as good as yours in City Hall, but not too bad. Depends what you want."

"I want to know about all street and road contracts signed off since 1924. I want details of the streets and roads in question, the length of time for the contracts, the agreed contract sums – I'm assuming they are all fixed price – the name of the contractor and the identity of the cement supplier. I also want to know if there are any unusual terms in any of the contracts."

"Such as?"

"Large down payments in advance, no penalty clauses, bonuses for finishing on time, commission payments to third parties, stuff like that."

"Oh, is that all? That's going to take a while."

"One other thing. I want you to cover your tracks. I don't want it to get back to Gann and his people that there is a *Bugle* investigation. Any ideas?"

Harry stared at me. "What's this all about?"

"A while back, Doyle let slip that he is doing very well out of city contracts. I want to know if there is anything suspicious or corrupt going on."

"David, I can't just walk into County Judge's office and get this information. No one here on the staff can do that without alerting city employees we are looking into stuff." Harry thought for a moment or two. "What if we found a college student who is doing research into this sort of thing?"

"That's quite a notion. Do you have contacts at the college?"

"Not really, but I know someone who has."

"Who?"

"Abby!"

"Abby can't handle this."

"Of course she can't, but maybe she can find a student who wants to earn some pocket money?"

"Good idea. Meantime, see if you can come up with other undercover approaches we can use. If there is a story, it would be good to break it for the primaries, but at the latest, we would need to run before the general in April."

I raised the subject with Abby of engaging the services of a sleuth. "There's no risk to this, is there?" she asked.

"I don't see it. We'll ensure the student gets a good cover story and back up from his professor. It ought to be a postgrad, I think."

A few days later, Abby called me during the day. "Can you come over to college for three o'clock? I have someone you might want to meet."

Later that day, I met Emily Venn. She was in her early twenties, kind of mousy, thin and petite with brown eyes and long curly hair to match. As some of my old college friends might have remarked, she was no oil painting. However, I detected a cute body underneath her plain clothing. Not that I was interested, of course. More to the point, she was studying for a master's degree in accountancy. Abby had told her about me and that I had a paying proposition for her, doing some research at the County Judge's office. She had already checked with her professor and he had approved her taking on an assignment.

"Emily, let me tell you what I want you to find out, but it has to be just between you and me." I explained the brief to her in detail. "I want you to take your time, read every contract you're shown carefully and take detailed notes. If you're asked why you're doing this, just say it's an exercise for your master's degree. Most importantly, under no circumstances can you mention you're doing this for *The Bugle.*"

"I understand. I'll ask my professor to write a letter of introduction to the County Judge? I'll contact whoever you tell me to at City Hall and take it from there."

"A great idea. Emily, we seem to have covered everything. When can you start?"

"When we agree what you're paying me!"

"Of course." I gave myself a silent telling-off for the omission. "What do you have in mind?"

"Mr. Driscoll, I'm putting myself through college. I have no money behind me. I have to work nights to keep going. I reckon this assignment is not without risk to me personally. If I am found out, I don't know what might happen to me, but my college career may be in jeopardy. You say there's no real risk but I disagree, otherwise you wouldn't be asking me to do it. So, that being said, I think this is worth quite a bit."

"Emily, there is no chance of your damaging your college degree. If anything happened, the college would find itself getting a heap of bad publicity from my newspaper. Can we agree ten dollars an hour? My guess is you'll need at least fifteen hours to complete the task."

Emily started to reply, but I continued. "If your research produces nothing, that's an end of it. However, if I publish a story, there will be a bonus of $250 for you. How would that be?"

Emily tried to look serious but she could not hold the expression. She gave me a big smile. "That would be fine, in fact, more than fine."

I liked Emily. She did not procrastinate and she spoke her mind. "How about an advance, say $50?" I gave her five ten dollar bills. I thought she would burst into whoops of joy. "Now, if you need to talk with me, just let Abby know. Don't call me direct or speak with anyone on my staff. Okay?"

"Yes, Mr. Driscoll."

"I'll get you the name of the person at County Judge's office. Please show me the letter your professor will write. Then we're off to the races."

Within two days, I had approved the letter written on college letterhead, introducing Miss Emily Venn as a postgraduate student, researching the processes of city road and street contracts and requesting details from 1922 to date be made available to her. I had also passed on the name of a record keeper at the County office. I heard nothing for two weeks. Then one night, Abby told me that Emily wanted to see me. We met at a coffee shop near the college.

"How are you getting on?"

"It's done. I'm typing the results for you. I should have them by the weekend."

"Well done! What did you find?"

"The contracts themselves were quite lengthy. Mind you they were almost identical, but I checked each one. Also, I thought it would look suspicious if I went for the same length of time every day so I mixed it up. Here's a note of time spent."

The note was meticulous. It scheduled dates and times attended and an aggregate of seventeen hours.

"Can you bring the results to my house on Saturday? Come for lunch. Is one o'clock okay? I'll have your cash for you." I owed her $170, of which she had received $50 but I had in mind that I would give her an extra $30, rounding up her earnings to $200. *The Bugle* owed her $150. That would keep her going for quite a while.

Emily arrived on Saturday at one o'clock on the dot. Clearly, she had a tidy mind. She gave me the results. I quickly scanned them. In the last two years, the St. Luke Council had placed contracts worth $1.8 million for approximately one thousand miles of streets and roads. They had been spread among seven contractors, none of whose names meant anything to me. All were in-state corporations.

I checked the nominated cement suppliers. In nearly all the contracts, St. Luke Cement Company, Doyle's company, was the contractor. Doyle was supplying St. Luke with the vast majority of cement used for road construction. No wonder he was prospering.

"Emily, this is great work. I need to look at these results more closely, but I have the feeling there's an interesting story here." I had a thought. "Do you want to work in the Christmas break?"

"Maybe. What do you want?"

"See all these different companies named as contractors? I want to know who is behind them. The records are kept in Cameron. I'll pay traveling expenses, your hotel room, meals and a fee of $20 a day."

"I have to be at home until the beginning of January, but I don't go back to college until the 14th. I could do it in the gap."

"Great. And here's the money I owe you." I handed Emily an envelope. She peeked inside.

"Excuse me," she blushed. "I've never seen this much money before." She counted it. "You've given me too much."

"No, you earned it. Let's go in the kitchen and eat. Abby's waiting."

Chapter Eighteen

The Christmas break was special as Abby's family shared it with us. Luckily, Abby had a few days between the end of semester and the Porters' arrival to get the house ready. I offered to help, but she told me the best way of helping was to keep out of her way. "Just provide loads of money for food and presents," I was told unceremoniously.

I asked Jane if she and Doyle would join us for Christmas Day and meet Abby's family. She hesitated. "I'm not sure. It's Mike, you understand. He's worried that you wouldn't want him in your home because of what has happened between the three of us."

"Jane, we want to see you. We want Abby's family to meet you. I'm offering an olive branch to Mike. Please tell him the invitation is there. He would be welcome."

"Can I let you know?"

Sadly, Jane didn't contact me. I had to accept if I wanted to see my sister, I would have to go to her.

Ted Page called me upstairs on the Friday before Christmas. "Sit down, David. I have news for you." Ted looked drawn and tired. "The board has been in discussions for the last week with prospective new owners. To cut a long story short, all board members resigned today. *The Bugle* is now owned, as I understand it, by a consortium of business men from the East Coast. One of them will be here early in the New Year, when we will be given our orders."

"What are you saying?" I was staggered. "Why did the board resign?"

"Because of concerns over the businessmen buying the newspaper, I guess. It seems these men own some east coast titles, which tend to be at the populist end of the spectrum. I anticipate some major changes here."

I sat and thought for a minute or two. "Shouldn't we talk about this now?" I asked Ted. "Shouldn't we formulate a plan or something? Who are these new owners? Who are our bosses?"

"I don't think this is the time to talk, David. Anyway, I'm just too tired. This sort of thing happens. In fact, it's been part and parcel of the newspaper business since the end of the War. We've been lucky in St. Luke that this hasn't hit us before. I think the best thing you can do is try and put things out of your head and enjoy the holiday. Who knows, maybe the new owners aren't as bad as the board thinks."

I knew Ted was soft-soaping it. There were bound to be changes, but he was right in one sense. There was no point in speculating. We would know our fate all too soon. "Well, thanks for letting me know, Ted. Happy Christmas." I tried not to make the words sound too hollow.

"You, too."

I took myself home and checked in with Abby who had wound herself up into a panic. The family was due at Union Station in two hours. "Calm down, darling. They're here to see you, not a sparkling house."

"Are you saying this house is dirty? What's wrong with it?" Abby was out of control. At times like this, I found that humor was the best cure.

"I think you should dress accordingly to greet your parents. Some ashes dumped on your forehead, a sackcloth scarf covering your hair, dirty jeans. I'll dress likewise."

I hugged Abby and stared her in the face, putting a goofy look on mine. Eventually, her mood broke and she laughed. I couldn't see the point in telling her the news at *The Bugle*. It would keep.

The Porters were marvelous guests through New Year. They appreciated everything we did, from Abby's cooking which was by now very good – good enough to produce a turkey with all the trimmings on Christmas Day - to home comforts and just being together. I took Gerry and Peter to the ice skating rink to try out their Christmas presents; a pair of ice skates each. After some spills and bumps, both of them mastered the art of gliding.

Christine and Alex were the easiest people to please. I could tell they were delighted to see Abby so happy. They took us out to restaurants. I made sure that Gerald Butler gave us one of his best tables at The Metropolitan. We also went to the theatre. The hit show, *The Melody Man*, was in town.

The visit ended all too soon on New Year's Eve. We promised to make a trip south some time during the summer. "It's an election year here, so I have to watch my timing," I told them. "However, Abby and I are talking about getting away as soon as her semester ends, maybe in May, because the city and county elections here will be over."

"You two are welcome in Richmond any time. Just let us know," both the Porters said to us separately. We were sorry to see them go.

After delivering my in-laws to Union Station, I took Abby to the Pyramid. Over lunch, I told her what was happening at *The Bugle*. She was shocked, but typically sympathetic and supportive. After the past few days, the house felt empty. Abby looked sad. "How can I cheer you up?" I asked.

Her response was to take me by the hand over to our comfortable couch in the den.

"Have we done it here before?" I asked innocently.

"Only many times."

"And what do I do exactly?"

Abby had no trouble showing me. Later, we started clearing up the house. We didn't finish tidying until quite late. Just as we were going to bed, the doorbell rang. Jane was at the front door, suitcase in hand. We brought her inside. She was shivering. Jane stood in the middle of our hallway. Silently, tears fell down her cheeks. Abby took her into her arms, escorted her to the den couch and sat her down, rocking her gently. She removed Jane's coat.

"Build up the fire, David and make sure the spare bedroom is ready." I left them. When I came downstairs, Jane was dried off, in clean clothes and sleeping in Abby's arms. I carried Jane upstairs. Abby and I put her to bed.

"Did she say anything?" I asked.

"Only that Doyle threw her out on Christmas Day and that she has been staying in an hotel on her own."

"Why didn't she come to us?"

"She didn't want to spoil Christmas with my Mama and Father."

"Oh, no," I shook my head. Maybe I didn't love my sister in any accepted sense but I felt compassion for her. I thought quite seriously about going to Doyle's apartment and beating the living daylights out of him.

"What good would that do?" asked Abby. "What will it achieve? Nothing except your own self-gratification. Instead, think of what Jane would want? Maybe the relationship can be saved? Please, sleep on it."

So we went to bed. I was seething inside. That bastard Doyle, I hated him. I used all my restraint not to go to his place and hurt him like he'd never been hurt before. I didn't know if I wanted to do this for Jane or for me and I didn't care. I told myself to cool off, which is when I realized my wife knew best. In the morning, Jane was awake by the time I was ready to leave. Her eyes were red. I doubted that she had slept much. But I had no time to talk.

"Abby, I'll get home as early as I can. Jane, let's talk tonight." I drew Abby aside. "You've got a few days before your next semester. Please can you take care of her today? I have to find out about my new bosses and if I still have a job." I left before Abby could reply.

Chapter Nineteen

At the newspaper, news of the sale had got around. A message was sent to all editorial staff to go to the sixth floor boardroom for an 11:00 a.m. meeting. There would be an announcement for other staff at 1:00 p.m.

At the appointed hour, some thirty people gathered in the boardroom. We were kept waiting for ten minutes. Ted Page entered, accompanied by a short, balding man, maybe fifty years old. Ted told us all to sit.

"People, allow me to introduce Walter Jenks. He is one of the businessmen who have bought Henry Brady's shares in *The Bugle*. He represents the new owners."

Jenks spoke. "I am a businessman. Henry Brady was a newspaperman. I am not like him, nor are the people I represent. My colleagues and I have bought *The Bugle* for its future profit potential, not its reputation. Since I arrived here two days ago, I have been looking at the business side of the newspaper. There is a lot of waste. We have to cut it out. There will be job losses across the board. I know you won't like it but this is the modern way. Those of you who keep your jobs will have more security as the newspaper will now be run on modern business lines. As President Coolidge says, the business of America is business.

"Now let me tell you some changes we are going to make. We will beef up the popular side of things. More funny pages, more articles on show business and pictures of pretty girls. We will also give more space to sports. Above all, the format needs to be changed. We regard broadsheets as cumbersome and wasteful. A tabloid format is more convenient and easier to read. This was our experience when we implemented the change very successfully at *The New York Sentinel*."

My stomach churned. *The Sentinel* was a cheap rag, as different to *The Bugle* as it could be. Jenks was still talking.

"As you are editors, you will appreciate the prime importance to the business of advertising and high circulation. Advertisers' business is essential. Therefore, we will expect feature articles in support of advertisers. We don't expect you to lie but we do expect you to encourage our readers to buy our advertisers' products. Advertisers will be happy to place their ads with us and our sister newspapers all the more."

I raised my hand. Jenks nodded in my direction. I stood.

"Mr. Jenks, my name is David Driscoll. Recently I have edited the Metro section. Are you familiar with the expression, truth to power?" Jenks nodded. "I feel obliged to be the truth to your acknowledged power. I don't question your right to make changes, although *The Bugle* has been a successful publication for over seventy-five years. If you want to 'beef up' some parts of the newspaper and abandon others and change the nature of the format and risk losing readership, that's your privilege. However, when you tell us we must praise the products of advertisers and help sell those products, I say you are asking too much. What you advocate is unethical. I want it to be as clear as day, I will not be willing to accept this instruction."

Jenks was taken aback. "Maybe you misunderstood. Maybe I misspoke. We'll sort this out, Mr. Driscoll. Thank you for your frankness. And thank all of you for your time. People, there will be changes. It's unavoidable. We'll let you know decisions on jobs as soon as we can."

Jenks left with Ted Page in his wake. My colleagues talked with one another. Some looked at me admiringly. Others showed they thought I had signed my own death warrant. Later, Jenks addressed the journalists and other staff. From what I was told, he was more upbeat but indicated there would have to be some job re-organization. My bet was Ted Page would be handed the axe and ordered to wield it. I was proved right. Over the next few days, ten people from the editorial team were fired, as well as one hundred and twenty journalists and ancillaries. Some fifteen per cent of employees had gone.

I felt sorry for Ted. He had not signed up for this. I also felt sorry for those who had lost their jobs. I couldn't help curse the name of Henry Brady. Surely he would have known how Jenks and his colleagues would act, yet he had not cared. He just wanted the money.

I had to admit, I was worried about my own job and the problems that might follow. Would I be able to afford to live in our present style and cover Abby's tuition fees? I felt queasy.

Late in the afternoon, it was my turn to be interviewed by Ted. I assumed I was for the firing squad. Ted smiled when I came in. "You scored big with Jenks. He's not quite as bad as he appears from first impressions. He likes people who get in his face."

I just stood there, mouth agape. "I truly expected you to fire me, Ted."

Ted continued. "Quite the reverse, you have a new job. We are merging city, county and state politics into one bureau and Jenks wants you to run it. You're *The Bugle's* new political editor and you have the right to run your own stories. You can even cover D.C. if you want, although you'll need to clear this with whoever the new editor-in-chief turns out to be. Jenks has read your stuff and he likes it."

"Slow down, Ted. Let me be clear. I'm the new politics supremo?"

"Yes. Jenks has given me a message to pass to you. No, it's not about the advertising thing. It's Doyle. He wants you to know that the consortium of new owners includes local business people. Mike Doyle has shares in the consortium. Jenks says you are not handcuffed. If you believe criticizing the St. Luke Democrats is justified, you must do so. However, be careful if you decide to take on Doyle personally. He has power within this newspaper."

"I've been mentally clearing my desk since this morning. I need to re-calibrate... By the slightest chance, do you have a drink in here?"

Ted went to a cabinet, removed a bottle of scotch and two glasses and poured us both stiff ones. "Water or ice?" he asked. I shook my head. I could never understand why anyone would adulterate good whisky with water.

"Leave the bottle out," I growled.

Ted eyeballed me. "Jenks says Doyle will take a close interest in *The Bugle.* I know he shouldn't use his position to influence stories but this is Doyle."

"Ted, you know the newspaper editors' code as well as I do. Proprietors are not to interfere with editorial comment or an editor's choice of story. Otherwise conflicts of interest arise. Just because Doyle has a share in *The Bugle* doesn't mean he's exempt from the rules."

"David, you're not being smart. What do you think Doyle will do with *The Bugle*?"

I sighed and took a long pull on my scotch. We talked over the events of the day. I had so many questions. How much power did Doyle exercise in the consortium? How would he show his teeth? If Doyle held a large share, how could he have afforded to buy in? What influence would Doyle have over my future? Who would be the new editor-in-chief? I was distinctly unhappy at the course of events. Three drinks later, I suddenly remembered Jane was waiting for me at home.

"Ted, I have a little local problem to resolve. I have to say goodnight."

He clapped me on the shoulder and sent me on my way.

"You bastard, you complete, bloody bastard." I opened our front door to be met by a tirade from a wife whose face was contorted and crimson with rage. I had seen Abby annoyed; I had seen her angry but I had never seen her like this. A tornado would have been less terrifying.

Abby continued her rant. "For months I have seen a different side to you. You rarely get home at a decent hour. You seem to care more about your precious *Bugle* than anything else in your life. You have been so selfish and you take me for granted. This morning you were uncaring, dismissive and even cruel, yes, cruel."

Abby continued in this vein for a minute or so, not missing any particulars of my shortcomings. She ended with my treatment of Jane. "This morning you gave her ten seconds, you just couldn't be bothered. When you knew she really needed you, you have come home late. If that isn't bad enough, you're three sheets to the wind, drunk! Lord knows I love you, David Driscoll but I don't know for how much longer and at this moment, I surely don't like you."

The storm seemed to be blowing out, at least a little. The dressing down had taken place in the hall. I hadn't even taken my coat off.

"I have things to say, Abby, but may I say them somewhere else? Could we go into the kitchen or something so I can sit?"

She nodded and marched away. I removed my coat and jacket, dangling both on a hook on the hat stand, and then I followed her into the kitchen. We sat in the breakfast nook where I could face her.

"Whatever I've done or failed to do, never let it be said that I don't love you and that I'm not in love with you."

"What's the difference?"

"When you love someone, they become your friend and you are my best friend. I get a warm, happy feeling when I'm in your company. I know you and trust you and I would do pretty well anything you ask. And a best friend doesn't shirk when a person needs to be told he's done something wrong. You're as close to me as a person could be."

"So?"

"But when you're in love, there's something added. It's a mixture of anticipated happiness and fear. You want to be with them, they give you that feeling inside your stomach that there's nothing more important on the face of the earth. But you live with two fears. One, that you will stop feeling like this; the other, and so much worse, that they will stop feeling like this about you.

"So, Abby, never, never let it be said that I don't love you and that I'm not in love with you. As for the other stuff, yes, you're right, but I didn't intend to take you for granted. And I didn't mean to hurt Jane. I have a career which, as we speak, is hanging by a thread and when you hear about today, I hope you'll understand better what I'm talking about. But that's no excuse for my shortcomings. I don't know what I can say except I'm really, really sorry."

"Spell out why you're sorry."

"I am very sorry for all my shortcomings and making you unhappy and for you building all this up inside."

Abby fought back a smile. "Comprehensive list. Anything else?"

"Yes, of course, for not finding time for Jane, especially tonight."

"Anything else?"

"What? Yes. Can we be friends now, please? This is killing me." I moved towards her. Slowly, my hands linked with hers over the table. I hoped my beautiful wife was almost in charity with me again.

"We've had our first really big row," I told her, "and there's a time honored tradition about making up. Shall we?"

Abby tried to stop me finishing my sentence but I ploughed on. "Shall we? Oh Jesus, I should talk with Jane. Do you think she might wait just a little while?"

Abby giggled. "Probably, why don't you ask her? She's right behind you."

I turned to see my sister standing, legs crossed at the ankles, resting her shoulder on the jamb of the doorway. "You were saying, brother?" She had clearly been there for long enough to hear me grovel and she had obviously regained some composure after yesterday, not to mention a sense of fun. She looked at Abby.

"I think you should put him out of his misery."

"Pity," said Abby, "I had prepared the woodshed and a two-by-four especially for him."

I turned to Jane and embraced her. "How are you?"

"I have my dry spells, but most of the time I'm like Niagara Falls. Poor Abby has drenched shoulders from me."

"Am I okay with both of you now? I have had quite a day, topped off by this most interesting homecoming. I'd like to get a shower and change. Dare I ask if there is anything for dinner? I'm really hungry. I'll tell you about my day when I come down."

Abby smiled at me. "Go get your shower. Dinner is just pasta and won't take long."

After I left, Abby must have excused herself from Jane, because when I came out of the shower, Abby had come upstairs and perched herself on the bed. As I dried off, I started to give her a shortened version of my day. Abby suggested I wait until dinner so Jane could share in the conversation.

"Not so easy," I told her. "Mike Doyle is now one of the owners of *The Bugle*. In a manner of speaking, he's my boss. How's that going to play?"

"Jane isn't going to be able to face this business any better if we don't mention Doyle. Tell her everything, the whole truth. Don't sugar coat it. Oh, but you do still have a job?"

"It seems so, although I was very close to losing it and I'm not sure I'll be able to tolerate the changes that are coming at *The Bugle*."

We went downstairs. Jane looked at us indulgently but sorrow was written all over her face. Abby busied herself preparing a pasta bake.

"So," I looked at Jane, "I assume 'how was your day dear?' won't play too well. Would you like to talk?"

"Maybe after dinner. Abby has been amazing. I found out today that I have a big sister."

220

"You two are pretty well the same age!"

"I know, but she's been Abby. You know?"

"Yes, I understand."

Abby served dinner and we ate. "So, shall I tell you two about my day?" I went through it in detail. I tried not to beef up my "truth to power" conversation with Jenks, but I couldn't help making myself out as a bit of a hero. I told them about the people who had been fired and that there were more sackings to come, the changes that would be made to the paper and finally, who now owned *The Bugle*. Jane flinched at hearing Doyle's name, but she didn't cry. Abby asked questions about the newspaper's future. I told her it was hard to predict, but people in our state weren't good with change. I doubted that changing the layout and appealing to the lowest common denominator of reader would play well with *Bugle* readers.

"If the circulation drops, advertising revenue will almost certainly fall, there will be more cuts and who knows how long the paper will last. It will be a slow death, but it may happen. *The Bugle* could be starting a slow slide south. Sorry to be a gloom and doom merchant. I think the new owners are making a big mistake."

"Will you be telling this to the new owners – more truth to power?" Abby asked.

"I'd be outside my comfort zone," I replied. "I have only so much courage."

After dinner, Jane told us she was tired and suggested that she and I could talk the next day. I didn't mind. I was worn out. In bed that night, I held Abby. The nape of her neck was in the crook of my shoulder. I whispered my apologies again. "At least I cleared up the dinner things. That's a start."

Out of the blue, she asked, "Have you thought at all about our starting a family?"

I was instantly on my guard. Was this part of the reason that Abby was so annoyed? I replied cautiously, "Yes, maybe, not just yet, but one day. It wouldn't be a good time right now. My job is at best uncertain and you've just started your postgrad studies."

"I've been thinking about the past few days. I don't want us to have children unless you commit to being a full time dad."

"What does that mean?"

"When I was growing up, my father was always there, or at least he seemed to be. He sat with us at breakfast, he came home for lunch, and we always had dinner together. In between, he often took us to school or collected us. He was around just as much as Mama. He was never distant, he was always approachable. He and Mama were a real partnership. I never appreciated all of this until quite recently. I just took it for granted."

"And you want me to be a dad just like yours?"

"No, that would be unreasonable. I just want to be sure you're committed to being a father before we start a family and you won't leave me to raise the kids alone. I want you and me to be a partnership, like my parents."

"If I tell you I need to think this through, am I in deep trouble again?"

Abby sighed. "No, you idiot. I said this was serious. You should think it over. Just don't take too long."

"You're not… are you?" I asked in a mild panic.

"No. I'm not pregnant."

"Just checking. Okay, answer me this. How do I arrange work so I get home at lunchtime?"

"Maybe we get a second car? It would take you just a few minutes to drive home."

"Isn't that a bit extravagant? I'm not sure we could afford another car as well as children."

"Get a bicycle. Good exercise for you. You'd be home in quarter of an hour."

"To be here for just thirty minutes before I had to go back? Also, my day is not structured. It doesn't run like clockwork. There are emergencies, decisions on the spot, that sort of stuff. I seem to have a new editing brief at *The Bugle* and I suspect there will be a lot of travel involved, if I keep the job. Abby, my career is really important to me. It's something I have to do, I'm not sure that I'll ever be able to meet your partnership ideal."

"David, you wouldn't have to come home every day at lunchtime. And I know you'll be late home more than just now and again. I respect your ambition. It's part of who you are. But I need to be sure I can count on you to be with me in raising our family. I won't raise our children on my own. You would have to change some things."

222

"You can always count on me to be with you. I'm not going to make promises that I know I won't keep, but I will do my best. Can we leave it there for the night? I'm really tired."

The next morning, I sat with Jane over breakfast. "Jane, I don't have to get into the office straight away. Shall we talk?"

"Not much point. I poured it all out to Abby yesterday and I'd rather not hash it all up again. Mike came home on Christmas Eve. He ordered me to pack my bags and leave there and then. I was frantic. I begged him to explain. He told me he was going to be more high profile in the community and it would look bad for him to be living with someone. I said we should get married. After all, we had talked about it. He laughed in my face."

Jane started to cry. "That son of a bitch laughed at me. 'Why would I marry you? Where do I benefit? I've taken what I want. Anyway, you'd never convert to Catholicism, so what's the point in discussing it? Just go.' That's what he said. I couldn't believe it. So here I am, telling you what happened and waiting for you to tell me, 'I told you so. I warned you.' I'm such a fool. I gave up everything for that bastard."

"I'm not going to say anything of the sort. You're not to blame here. Do you want me to go over there and punch his lights out?"

Jane laughed at the thought. "I'm inclined to think that if you don't get the first punch spot on, he'll hit you back and you'll find yourself in hospital. So don't do that. I just want to stay here for a few days while I work out what to do."

"You can stay with us till you're a hundred. You're family. Abby and I love you."

"Do you? Honestly? We've never been what you'd call close, you and me."

"I know, but at times like these, blood matters. We only have each other now mother's gone. What would she say if I didn't look out for you?"

"Hey, you have Abby."

"And so do you, Jane. The three of us, we're tight. Have you had any thoughts or plans?"

"I know what I don't want to do. I won't go back on tour. I'd come to hate it well before Doyle. But I still love playing piano. I'd like to teach, maybe in school, maybe privately. I earned lots of money so I don't need your help to keep me. Like I said, just a few days here will fix me up."

"You're very resilient. Are you sure you're okay?"

"No, I'm not okay, but I will be. Mike Doyle will not beat me. You really don't know me that well, David. I may give the impression of being a bundle of nerves and very frail and theatrical, but I'm grounded. The way I see it, Mike was there, I loved him and now he's gone and he won't ever come back, whatever is said or done. I'll be sad, I'll cry from time to time, but I'll dry my eyes. Life goes on and I have to accept this. What other choices are there? I wasted a week on my own, feeling sorry for myself. I think that's enough."

"I don't get it. He was nuts about you."

"There's stuff in his past. Once or twice he started to talk about it. The lessons he learned from his uncle about life. Evidently, his uncle drilled into him to look out only for himself, that life was war. And something happened to him in France at the end of the Great War. Occasionally, he'd mumble in his sleep, Claudia or Claudine, something like that, but he refused to talk to me about her."

"Yes, he's a complex one. Jane, his behavior is inexcusable and the day will come when I'll tell him what a shit he is. I don't care what happened to him with his Uncle Joe or in the war."

I noticed an alarmed look on Jane's face.

"Don't worry, I'm not going to do anything silly." I checked my watch. "Janey, I have to go but we'll talk more tonight."

Abby came into the room. "Sorry but I couldn't help overhearing. Is there any question about staying here, Jane? I sincerely hope not. This is your home until you tell us differently. Right, David?"

"Absolutely. No argument. Look, at the risk of getting myself back into hot water with both of you, I really have to go. I have a newspaper to help write and edit, at least for this morning. After yesterday, who knows what is going to happen and how long I'll have a job? But I need to be in my office thirty minutes ago."

Abby mimed, "We'll be fine, go."

I blew her a kiss as I closed the front door.

At *The Bugle*, the atmosphere was awful. Not a surprise really when so many had been fired and when things were so uncertain. I called the remaining Metro people into my office.

"I don't know exactly what's going to happen but until we're told differently, life will go on. Let's have no gossip and let's just do our jobs to the best of our ability."

Apart from losing five journalists and ancillaries from Metro, that's the way things stayed for a while. I was not moved up to a new politics brief just yet. Jenks had other priorities that month. No doubt, his attention would fall on me eventually, but until it did, what choice did I have?

Jane left us for a while to visit friends in New York. Towards the end of January, Abby told me she had seen Emily Venn, who had said she had the information I wanted. I asked Abby to invite Emily for dinner the following night.

Abby was surprised to see me at home early the next evening. I wouldn't be late for Emily. "This is not to convince you to start a family," I told Abby. Abby did her best to make a crestfallen face, but she couldn't hold the look.

The doorbell rang. I let Emily in, took her coat and headed for the kitchen table. Abby looked surprised when we entered. "Don't you want to use the den?"

I told her the kitchen was fine, especially as I wanted her to hear what Emily had to tell me. "Abby and I share our thinking processes," I explained to Emily.

What Emily told me, as she unfurled her research, shocked me. It was fraud, pure and simple, on the taxpayers of St. Luke. She told me she needed to check one aspect but it was clear, as I questioned Emily closely, that she and I had uncovered serious wrongdoings by some of the political rulers of the city. The facts, all independently verified by Emily, spoke for themselves. As we ate, I asked Abby for her views.

"I'd check the facts again, no disrespect, Emily. If you can find other independent sources, it would be so much the better. This story has huge consequences."

After dinner, I asked Emily if she had her invoice for me. She produced the familiar neatly written and itemized account. I told her I would have cash for her the next evening if she wanted to come by.

"Let me get those road construction costs verified first," she told me. I drove her home.

When I returned, Abby looked worried. "You're going to take Doyle on, aren't you?"

"Maybe."

"He's going to be a tough nut. Make sure you're not doing it as revenge for Jane."

"Why?"

"Because that's personal. This should be about business. The story is St. Luke taxpayers being screwed, not your sister."

"I admire your delicacy of language."

"You know I'm talking sense."

"Yeah, I know. But I can get him where it hurts. Abby, I've told myself to be an editor on this one, not just the reporter. Check the facts, and then check them again. I will be professional. But you are right. I want to hit Mike Doyle where it really hurts him, reputation, wallet and maybe the criminal courts."

I contacted Barry Springer in Chicago to ask him to find someone who knew about road building contracts. Barry gave me a name the next day. Fred Harris was a construction engineer who had worked for the State of Illinois for eighteen years. In a long telephone conversation, he confirmed the figures that Emily had provided. He also told me that it was standard practice for both the Illinois cities as well as the state to put road contracts out to tender and to have at least three corporations bid. What was important for me was Fred was happy to be on the record. I had Emily check again with her contact in the County Judge's office whether any of the St. Luke road contracts had gone out to tender. None had.

I kept the story close to my chest for a week until I was ready to put it to Ted Page. I knew he would demand that I put any allegations to the parties involved before he approved publication. Hence, on the day I was ready to place the story before Ted, I contacted Jeremy Pressman, Alexei Gann, John Santino, Eddie Rupert and Tom Berman. Doyle did not take my call.

Gann, Santino, Chief Rupert and Berman gave me identical answers. It was as if they had been schooled in what to say, should the facts ever come to light. Each denied any knowledge of the corporations which owned the road contracts, despite the fact they were named as shareholders. Each of them demanded written evidence to prove they had agreed to accept their shares. Pressman had a harder time with me. At first, he refused to tell me anything about the road building corporations. When I presented the written evidence that he had participated in their formation, he responded with a weak, "I may have had an involvement."

"So, please would you explain why Gann, Santino, Rupert and Berman were named as shareholders in certain corporations?"

"I acted on instructions."

"From whom?"

"That would be confidential."

"Don't you think the public, the taxpayers of St. Luke who paid for these roads, are entitled to know who is behind the contractors?"

"That's not for me to say, I am merely the conduit."

"What about the corporations where you are the sole shareholder?"

"I acted as nominee."

"So you had no personal financial interest in the road contracts?"

"I didn't say that."

I knew that his tax return for the next tax year would declare the earnings from the road building now. "So who has the financial interest?"

"The person for whom I acted as nominee."

"And that was?"

"Confidential. Professional ethics prevent me from telling you."

"What if a crime was committed?"

"What are you alleging?"

"For example, the city did not go to tender on these contracts."

"Are they legally obliged to do so?"

"It is acknowledged best practice to do so."

"But not a legal requirement." Pressman had me there.

"So, why were these corporations chosen to carry out the work?"

"I suppose because they have a good track record with the city."

"But these were newly formed corporations. How could this be?"

"I guess you'd have to ask the City Manager."

"I did. Tom Berman told me to ask you."

"So you have asked the City Manager and you have asked me. This comes under the heading of 'asked and answered'. Is there anything else?"

I sighed at such obfuscation. "Yes, I have evidence that you have formed three corporations to buy land and property in St. Luke."

"So what?"

"Mr. Pressman, I have also seen the option contracts. Why have the corporations you formed taken the option?"

Do you understand options Mr. Driscoll? To explain, an option is a right to enter into a contract at a future date on previously agreed terms. It's normal commercial practice."

"Not when the council will soon announce plans to develop the land and refurbish the buildings in question. The city will have to buy from your client. Isn't this just graft? *The Bugle* will point the finger at you, as sole shareholder of record."

"As I recall, some decades ago a New York politician coined the expression 'honest graft', not that I am admitting anything of the sort. The kind of deal you're outlining is within the law."

"Maybe, but it's not within the clean government promise made by the Gann administration. It's dirty practice by the Doyle machine. Let's stop pussyfooting around, shall we? I'm asking you straight out, is the person behind all this, the one for whom you act as nominee, Mike Doyle?"

"I can't answer that."

"Can't or won't? You were on record a year ago that Mike Doyle was your only client."

"Things change."

"Have they?"

"I've answered your questions. I want to end the interview now."

"I should tell you that tomorrow's *Bugle* will headline a story that the city rulers have conspired with Mike Doyle to favor themselves with road contracts at an exorbitant price. In other words, the current administration has become as corrupt and as fraudulent as Ed Hanrahan's. And I will be naming you as one of the architects of this business. The article will also mention your war record and lament that you and others have failed to honor the promises given by council survivors of the Great War that St. Luke will be a home fit for heroes? Care to comment now on anything I have asked? It will be on the record."

"No comment."

"Oh, by the way, the article will also name you as a practicing homosexual."

"Print that and I'll sue you and your rag for every penny it has."

The allegation was just bluff on my part, although rumors about Pressman's private life were rife. I wanted to see him react and the goad was better than expected. Interestingly, I'd struck a chord. Of all that we had talked about, that was the only time he had threatened to sue.

I returned to my office, completed the story and called Ted. "I need to see you straight away. Are you free?"

He told me to give him an hour.

I went to his office an hour later and presented him with my story.

"Why are you the reporter in this story?"

"The story is dynamite. I had to keep it to myself."

"Okay, give me time to read it."

City Hall Caught in Fraud
Massive Road Building and Insider
Dealing Scams Uncovered

This morning, *The Bugle* can disclose serious wrongdoing and fraud at the heart of City Hall. In the past two years, Tom Berman, the City Manager, placed ten contracts with six corporations to carry out road and street construction work in St. Luke. The contracts are public documents filed with the County Judges' office and are available for inspection, should any of our readers wish to verify the facts.

Additionally, documents filed at the Companies Registry in Cameron confirm that attorney Jeremy Pressman is named as shareholder and director of all six corporations. In two of the corporations, he is named as the sole shareholder. Those two corporations were granted five road contracts over an eighteen month period. Council Leader Alexei Gann is a shareholder and director of another corporation that was granted two road contracts. Three other corporations were granted one road contract each. Councilman John Santino was named as shareholder and director of one of the corporations, Chief of Police, Eddie Rupert, was also named as shareholder and director of another corporation and the City Manager too is named as shareholder and director of yet another corporation.

Separately, two companies were nominated as sub-contractors for the supply of cement for each of the ten road contracts. This newspaper believes that Jeremy Pressman acted as a nominee for City boss, Michael Doyle who is the real owner of these corporations.

The Bugle is not claiming that the men named in this story have acted illegally in the contract process. However, the standard, acknowledged best practice in most American states and cities for placing of street and road building contracts is by open tender, where at least three contractors are invited to bid. In this way, the city or state gets the best deal. The tender process was not followed for any of the ten road contracts. When asked to comment about the failure to follow best practice, City Manager Tom Berman failed to give any plausible explanation for the omissions.

Messrs. Pressman, Gann, Santino, Rupert and Berman have been asked to comment on the alleged ownership of the road contracts. Mr. Pressman said he was acting as a nominee for a principal he would not identify. A year ago, Mr. Pressman said he had only one client, Michael Doyle. Mr. Pressman refused to confirm or deny whether the situation had changed. This newspaper has reached the conclusion that Mr. Pressman has acted in these matters for Michael Doyle. If there is nothing untoward or wrong with the transactions in question, why does Mr. Doyle feel the need to hide behind his lawyer?

When asked to comment on their participation in the road and street contracts, Messrs. Gann,

Santino, Rupert and Berman denied any knowledge of the shareholdings. There is no obvious explanation as to why the records of the corporations in question, all of which are documents of public record maintained in Cameron, are incorrect.

Evidence from independent sources, including a State of Illinois road engineer, confirms that the street and road contracts have been placed at an inflated price. The contracts confirm the city paid approximately $1,800 a mile. The proper charge ought to have been in the region of $1,300 a mile (the price paid in neighboring states), including the cost of cement. It would appear that the contractors have benefited from an additional profit of some $500 a mile, a grand total of approximately half a million dollars overpayment.

The Bugle has also discovered that Mr. Pressman was involved in three other recent company formations. These corporations have entered into options to buy land and buildings in and around St. Luke city center which are now marked out for the development of new city offices. Mr. Pressman refused to identify for whom he acted in these transactions. However, he insisted that insider trading was not illegal in this state. Even so, this newspaper alleges that Mr. Doyle has benefited from insider knowledge and is selling land to the city at an inflated price.

The taxpayers of St. Luke need to know what is happening at City Hall and should demand answers from the City Manager and the council. If the denials of Messrs. Gann, Santino, Rupert and Berman are to be believed, who benefits from the contracts? Should not the person or persons be identified and asked to explain why they have charged an inflated price for the works?

This newspaper demands answers from the council and Mr. Doyle to the following questions:

1. Who are the principals for whom Mr. Pressman is acting?
2. If Messrs. Doyle, Gann, Santino, Rupert and Berman are indeed the beneficiaries of contracts, why did they not disclose their interests?
3. What was the price charged by Mr. Doyle's companies for the cement used in the contracts?
4. Why was no tender process used for the placing of the contracts?
5. On what basis were the contract prices agreed? Was independent advice taken by the council on pricing beforehand?

On many occasions since 1922, the New Democrats and, latterly, the Democrats have proclaimed they stand for open and honest city government. Let them prove it now by answering our questions and dispelling the notion there has been graft at City Hall.

As far as I was concerned, the story was solid. It contained who, what, where, when, why and how, as prescribed by Mr. Sam Perkins to me all those years ago. It did not give opinions, just facts. It might need a little editing here and there, but it was pretty well done. As an editor, as an objective reader, I would have checked the facts with the writer. If I was satisfied the facts were correct, the story would be published.

As Ted read the article, his complexion paled. By the time he reached the end, he was white. "David, I can't publish this story. I won't publish it!"

"Why not?"

"Don't be naïve, David. I can't do it. Orders from on high. I had a call a few minutes before you came in. Jenks knew what you were writing and has ordered me explicitly not to publish the story."

"Since when do you take orders from a proprietor? That's way outside their rights and the editors' code of practice. Ted, ignore him."

"I can't. Apart from anything else, if I print the story, I'll be fired. The presses will be stopped and the story removed. Jenks told me in no uncertain fashion that I would be sued, too. So defiance on my part would be futile. I might add that I won't jeopardize my family in these circumstances? Why are you being so pig-headed? You'll just have to accept that you've lost on this one. Mind you, it is a very good piece of journalism."

"That will never be read. You know Doyle has even more power over the other newspapers in town and in the neighboring towns the editors are just as scared of taking Doyle on as they are right here in this office."

Ted remained silent for a moment.

"Ted, there's a principle here. We have to fight!"

"Jenks is here, he's in the building. You go fight him."

I stood, anger burning through my body. As I opened the door, Ted told me to hold on. "Don't confront Jenks when you're angry like this, it won't help you."

"Jesus, as if I care. I have a bomb in my hands, primed to explode. I have the facts that put Doyle and his people in the same league as Hanrahan. They're thieves and hypocrites."

I stormed upstairs to Jenks's office. I didn't bother to knock. In his outer office, his secretary saw me. She got as far as, "Mr. Driscoll, I'll let Mr. Jenks know you're here." By then I was in Jenks room.

"Come in, David, I was expecting you."

"I bet you were. What you are doing is interfering with editorial rights. It's monstrous, the worst thing I've ever seen in my time in newspapers. You've even threatened Ted Page with the sack and litigation. What the hell!"

"Okay, I want you to sit down and calm down. I know you're angry and upset, but that won't help you. I'm going to explain something that very few people know."

"Thanks. I'll stay standing. I don't want to calm down. I'm ready to walk out right now."

"Up to you. The long and short of it is that Mike Doyle now controls *The Bugle*. My colleagues and I between us have only a 25% share. He has bought the rest. When you interviewed Pressman and

233

the others, they must have warned Doyle what was coming. He personally called me this morning and told me he wanted your story spiked. He made it an order. He's vicious about you and dangerous too."

I collapsed into a chair. Breath left me for a while. This was the worst news. I knew I was beaten by a man who had no scruples about how he made his money or who he cheated and hurt in the process. Furthermore, any doubt that I now worked directly for Mike Doyle was dispelled. He would have no ethics about what went in *The Bugle*. My story was spiked for sure and my career at *The Bugle* too. I guess that if I had been honest with myself, I would have seen that my story would not reach the light of day. I was challenging Doyle the person, not Doyle the politician. I had blinded myself to the truth.

"Sorry David," said Jenks, "this time power talks to truth."

"Mr. Jenks, I may not like your methods, but at least you've been straight with me. Ted Page will have my resignation within the hour."

"Understood. By the way, don't try to publish the story elsewhere. We'll have an injunction on you in no time. Face it, you've lost this battle."

I looked at him, shaking my head. Doyle had wrecked the hopes of a Driscoll family member for a second time in a matter of days. There was nothing I could do. I felt hatred in my heart.

"David, you should take a little time. Don't submit your resignation yet."

"I have no choice."

"What about your future?"

"I have to leave St. Luke."

"To go where?"

"Mr. Jenks, this is two minutes old. How the hell should I know?" I apologized for my language.

"I've heard worse. When you are considering your options, think about New York. I might be able to help you."

"Why would you do that? You're the enemy."

"Nonsense. I'm now just doing a job here, looking out for the 25% shareholding interest. I'm leaving here soon anyway. You're a good newspaper man. I know some people who could use you in New York."

"Due respect, Mr. Jenks, but that seems like out of the frying pan into the inferno. This story apart, I can't accept your modern methods, not to mention your lack of professional ethics. I don't want to work for you again if the title will be managed like *The Bugle*."

"That's why I want you. You're not scared of anything or me. But I understand what you're telling me, Mr. Truth. How about my putting in a word with *The New York Standard?* It's a newspaper more to your liking. Even in New York, the newspaper world's a village. And despite what you think, I don't like what's going on here. It's wrong. Lucas Vine is the editor and proprietor of *The Standard.* I'll let him know you might be in touch. And call me Walter."

I took a moment and looked at Walter Jenks as if I was seeing him properly for the first time. "Thank you. I appreciate what you're doing for me, Walter. If I've misjudged you, I apologize." I offered my hand, which he shook.

Back at my desk, I wrote my resignation letter and took it to Ted. He read it, aghast. He asked me to think it over. I refused and thanked him for everything, except today. Harder than that was when I called my staff together and told them I had resigned on a matter of principle. I refused to be drawn on the reasons.

So I left *The Bugle* building and the newspaper that had been my home away from home for nearly two years, where I had learned so much and where I had had my triumphs and disappointments. I reminded myself that in professional life, everything usually ends in tears.

The next day, insult was added to injury. *The St. Luke Democrat* ran a piece praising the City Manager for his road building program, complimenting him on its efficiency and how it was brought in at a low cost. The story detailed neither facts nor figures. It was shoddy journalism and the author ought to have been ashamed of himself. If nothing else, it confirmed my view that it was time for me to leave St. Luke.

Chapter Twenty

Abby was astonished to find me at home when she returned from college. I was in the kitchen preparing dinner. I was making chicken paprika, a dish that involved getting one's hands dirty. It was just what I needed. It seemed appropriate. When Abby came into the kitchen, I raised my hands so she would not get smothered by cooking ingredients.

"I don't have a gun here, Cisco," kidded Abby.

"Good, Pancho, but you might want one when you taste the food."

"You're in a good mood, my darling."

"Gallows humor. Let me do this fast and dirty. My story on Doyle got spiked, I got mad and I am now unemployed."

"You were fired?"

"No, I resigned."

"What happens to us?" Unsurprisingly, Abby was worried.

"Remember that richer or poorer thing you vowed? You did make a promise. I know. I was there when you did it."

"So?"

"This is one of those poorer times. Walter Jenks is recommending me to a New York title, *The New York Standard*. Odd, isn't it? He effectively forced me to resign, but he wants to help me. I don't know anything about *The Standard*, but how does a move to New York sound? Your parents will be much nearer. There are some great schools in New York and all of them would be lucky to have you."

Abby's face moved from shock and concern to fury. "So, you've got it all worked out. Why, when I'm finally settled, when I've got friends, a career path ahead of me, a life sorted out, why would you think you have the right to move me on a whim? And then you just drop this news on me with no explanation, no warning. You can be such a bastard, David."

Slowly, I washed my hands at the sink, avoiding her eyes. Then I turned back to her. "Abby, you'll see I had no choice and New York is only a suggestion. We can stay here and I'll do something else."

She expelled a deep breath. "Sorry. It's just such a shock. You left here this morning and everything seemed fine and you had a great story ready to be published and now our world has collapsed. And you have decided the future and not given me a chance to say what I want."

I removed the apron and hugged her. "I had no intention at all of excluding you from decision-making. I was just trying to soften the blow, to show you that I may have an alternative for us. We'll get through this together, I promise."

Abby and I sat at the kitchen table as I re-lived the events of the day in detail. I showed her a copy of the story that got spiked. Abby looked contrite after she read it.

"Doyle's covered his trail, just like a mob capo," Abby said.

In bed that night, Abby kissed me. "I'm sorry for before. You just shocked me, I guess. I don't care where I study, where I live, just so long as you're home with me at night. Something tells me New York will be good for you. I think you're ready for the big time."

Two days later, I headed for New York to meet Lucas Vine. Abby couldn't spare the time. She had a big assignment to deliver by the end of March. My research about *The Standard* told me it was middle of the road politically, with perhaps a slight Democratic bent. It was a broadsheet publication with a circulation of some one and a half million readers. Crucially, its political editor was in his late sixties. There would be a future for me with *The Standard*, if I fitted in.

I liked Lucas Vine. He was, a tall, blonde-haired patrician in his forties. He was an alumnus of Princeton. "Not a real university you know, just a college. No medical school."

I replied, "That's like saying an orange is not really a fruit, just something to squeeze and drink."

We talked politics. I explained my background and that my experience was mainly city politics, limited to St. Luke, though I knew something of the workings of Cameron.

"My experience of Washington is virtually nil."

"Walter told me you didn't bullshit. You scored big with him. Let's have a trial period. Work with us for two weeks. If we like each other, I'll give you a year's contract."

"I need to ask you one thing. Has Walter Jenks got any financial interest at all or any power over this newspaper?"

"He also told me you'd ask that. The answer is no. I am the sole proprietor as well as the editor-in-chief. I'm one of the last independents."

I said a silent thank you to Walter Jenks. He really understood me. "May I give you my answer in the morning? I want to think it over tonight and speak with my wife. I need to be sure she's willing to move here."

"If she is, I can put in a word for her at Princeton for her postgraduate degree."

"Thanks, that's very kind. I'll tell her."

Abby told me to take the try-out period. In those two weeks, I liked what I saw of *The Standard* and its methods. Lucas Vine liked my writing and me. It was mutual. New York politics was lively. Like St. Luke, the city had a boss and a political machine but on a phenomenally larger scale. At the turn of the century the five New York borough machines had united into a single entity. Tammany Hall ruled the whole city, not just Manhattan. There was internecine political warfare and corruption aplenty. I felt completely at home.

Abby agreed to move to New York and join me. I found a rental on West 75th and 7th. So after my two-week trial, I returned to St. Luke in April to pack up the house and drive Abby and Jane to New York. Abby and I decided not to sell our St. Luke home just in case New York didn't work out. Ted agreed to keep an eye on the place and to rent it out for us. Our belongings were shipped to New York, so we only needed small suitcases for the two-day drive. We left on the day the Democrats were returned to power in St. Luke, amid charges of election fraud and ballot rigging by the Republicans.

Some six hours into the expedition, Jane was dozing gently on the back seat. I asked Abby, "Still happy you married me?"

"That's an interesting question."

"Come to think of it, Abby, why did you marry me?"

"I felt sorry for you."

"Why?"

"You were no good in bed. Someone had to save you from yourself."

"Did I improve?"

"Not so much."

I heard Jane snickering in the back seat.

"I can drop you off in the middle of nowhere," I reminded her, checking in the rear view mirror.

"Two against one here, buster, you have no chance," Jane replied. Abby joined in, "Too right."

.

Book Three
1928-1934

Chapter Twenty-One

Jane stayed with us in New York for a few weeks. She renewed her relationship with Harriet Shapiro, who nagged Jane unmercifully to return to the concert stage. Eventually, Harriet gave up. As an alternative, she asked Jane to move into her apartment and become what Harriet termed, "a super-teacher" for gifted pupils. Jane agreed to this, provided the super-teaching took only two days of her time each week. She wanted to keep herself free to teach in grade school. So, my sister became settled and happy again in her life.

Our three-bedroom apartment would have been big enough for Jane to stay, but she wanted her independence. The apartment was not decorated to our taste but it was a rental and we lived with it. One bedroom became Abby's study. I had to contain her habit of filing papers on every seat, shelf and flat surface. New York suited us both. It was so different to St. Luke. It was a city where anything was possible.

Lucas, wanted me to get involved with the bigger picture of federal politics and the US economy. As political editor, I had access to and interviewed senior politicians and civil servants in Washington, D.C. with some frequency, as well as the leaders of business and financial institutions in New York City.

I attended both National Conventions in the summer of 1928. By comparison with the conventions of 1924, these were lack-luster affairs. President Coolidge couldn't be bothered to go to the Republican convention. He called the press to a remote Vermont location, gave a two-minute statement in which he stated that he would not run for re-election and refused to answer questions. Typical of the man.

Commerce Secretary, Herbert Hoover, was Coolidge's natural successor. In his acceptance speech at the Republican Convention, he included the words: "We in America today are nearer to the final triumph over poverty than ever before in the history of any land." That one came back to bite him on his butt.

The Democratic National Convention nominated experienced New York Governor Alfred Smith, a Roman Catholic, as their presidential candidate. Smith's stance as a Wet in the Prohibition debate, his opposition to the Ku Klux Klan and his Catholicism nailed him. Poor Al! He was a good candidate and possibly would have been a great president. It was only timing that was against him. But in politics, timing is almost everything. Hoover was the Republicans' blue-eyed boy. He entered the White House in March, 1929, on a wave of popularity.

Although I tried to put St. Luke behind me, I couldn't help keep an interest. I had plenty of friends back there who told me what was going on. My departure had marked the prelude to Doyle's taking the city over, political lock, business stock and corruption barrel, although my leaving and Doyle's virtual dictatorship were hardly connected. I couldn't have held him in check anyway. Rather, his true nature emerged. After Joe Doyle's death, but not because of it, Doyle no longer felt it necessary to present an image of anything but the Mr. Fix It of the city. Had Joe survived, no doubt he would have been very proud of his nephew, who resigned from public life, yet controlled the political and commercial life of St. Luke virtually unchallenged.

Doyle was unusual as a city boss. He was willing to operate behind the scenes without a public presence. Anyone who knew the city realized that Doyle was the seat of true power and that Alexei Gann could be replaced any time Doyle chose. Gann had been unable to create any power base of his own separate from Doyle and was resigned to his role, comforted by high remuneration.

Gann became a busted flush when the demographics study for the city he had so proudly vaunted in 1925 never materialized. True, the council put out some projections, but they didn't stand much examination. Doyle's power ensured that the St. Luke press collectively turned a blind eye to the omissions.

241

Doyle's corruption operated on many levels. At election time, he left nothing to chance. The Democratic slate received huge newspaper publicity before the primaries. Billboards sported photographs of candidates under the caption, "Vote the Democratic Slate." Doyle's Democratic candidates stood unchallenged, so hopeless was it to contest a seat in a primary election in many of St. Luke's wards.

Although the Democrats won the 1928 St. Luke city election with ease, crime was on the increase. It was obvious to me that the mob now had a foothold. Doyle remained chairman of the party and his personal fortunes rose. He was reputed to be a Wall Street player and as the market rose, so did Doyle's fortune. In 1928, he bought the Brady mansion.

Lucas added one weekly edition of *The Bugle* to the *Standard's* library. I was disappointed to see *The Bugle* laid low. As I predicted, its circulation dropped and there were fewer and fewer advertisers as the readers of St. Luke voted with their feet and read rival newspapers from other nearby towns, rather than continue to read a tabloid. Doyle continued to be featured in the papers with a succession of glamorous women on his arm. I felt no jealousy. Instead, I pitied him for his apparent inability to make a lasting relationship.

The Bugle featured regular stories on Doyle's charitable works, which read more and more like propaganda. His office at the Democratic Committee was open to all comers. No one who voted the Democratic ticket was turned away empty handed. It didn't matter what you wanted, whether it was a job, a place to live, clothes for the children, food to eat, legal help, medical aid – the Doyle machine was geared up for welfare. His office always had a long line of supplicants. He did not delegate the tasks. People who needed to see him got his time, or that was certainly the message *The Bugle* put out.

The Standard was one of very few titles to predict the stock market crash of October 1929, but we did not foresee the aftermath. In December, Barry Springer called me. After Teapot Dome, he made another reputation for himself, reporting on the events surrounding Chicago crime. In 1929, he became a nationally recognized journalist for his reports about the St. Valentine's Day massacre, when five members of Bugs Moran's North Side Gang and two others were lined up against a wall and shot, supposedly by Al Capone's men. He also exposed the bootlegging activities of Detroit's Purple Gang. I often

242

wondered whether Barry's days might be numbered, but he appeared unconcerned.

"David, news has reached Chicago that Wall Street hiccuped."

"Hiccuped? More like whooping cough. It started on October 24 with a massive stock market fall. Five days later, there was another huge drop, followed by a bloodbath. Did you know Coolidge was warned years ago that this would happen?"

"So far, there has been little reaction up here. I don't think there are that many in Chicago who invested."

"The smart people in New York say it's not just the stock market that's sick. We could be headed for a huge economic recession. Companies will fold and people will lose their jobs. They are saying that the Midwest could catch a real cold too. Crop prices could drop sharply, farmers won't be able to pay their notes and banks will be in trouble, the usual stuff."

"Yes, a rosy picture. Okay, I know you're out of the St. Luke loop these days, but my gut tells me you'd want to know my information. One of our New York stringers is chasing stories about big Wall Street losers and Doyle's name has come up. Evidently, he's lost a fortune. I mean really big money. His stockbrokers have closed his positions and it seems he owes millions. He was dealing on margin and his brokers have been making call after call."

I understood. Buying on margin permitted investors to pay a small percentage of the deal price, provided the balance was paid within an agreed period, usually seven or fourteen days. Doyle had probably been caught with his pants down, having to pay full price for worthless shares.

"Barry, if Doyle's caught a cold, the people of St. Luke will get pneumonia! If you hear anything else, would you let me know?"

In contrast to all the economic gloom, my career prospered. The irony wasn't lost on me as I wrote editorials frequently on the economic crisis and unemployment, not only for *The Standard*, but also as a guest contributor to other magazines and journals. I was signed up by *North American Review, Scribner's* and *Harper's Weekly.* I was paid well for my words.

The New York Standard
15th December, 1929

An event occurred two months ago in October which is now referred to as "The Wall Street Crash." If you speak with the man in the street, he will tell you the Crash was the fault of speculators and that almost all the adult population of this country have been wiped out financially as they have watched their investments in American companies fall through the floor. These investors borrowed money to pay for their shares, so they are probably bankrupt and the health of the banks is in critical condition.

Some of this is correct. The New York Stock Exchange witnessed the biggest crash in its history because a number of speculators invested in what is called "short-selling." A short-seller is an investor who sells shares he does not own in the hope that by the time he pays for the shares, the share price will have fallen. If this happens, the investor makes a profit as he then "buys" the shares for a lower price. However, if the share price rises, the short-seller is caught short! In October, there was massive short-selling, hence the Stock Market collapsed.

As for the rest, it is probable that not more than one in ten Americans invested in the stock market, although many of these people did borrow to buy their shares. However, the Crash was a mere symptom of the disease at the heart of the American economy. American manufacturers have been building inventories, their stock of goods, for the past two years as they experienced problems in finding markets where they could sell. Our domestic market is saturated with what we make and America's trading partners in Europe and Asia ran out of credit as long ago as 1927 and

244

cannot afford to buy what we make. It is a basic rule of economics that if you make goods but can't sell them, you will eventually run out of cash and go bust.

This is the real truth of what is happening in America today. Our businesses are running out of money. Our banking system cannot cope with the demand for loans to tide businesses over. If we are not careful, our banks will start to collapse. We do not have a robust banking system. Most of our banks have just one branch. They cannot cope with demand for loans as well as write off losses.

We are experiencing a recession as jobs are lost. However, this will be as nothing if our economic times turn into a full-blown depression. I take no pleasure being a Jonah, but the body of men who could help the economic situation improve are sitting on their hands. I speak of the Hoover administration and Congress who remind me of rabbits in car headlights.

Mr. President, please look at what is happening and use your ample powers to persuade Congress to open the nation's coffers, help American business and make sure people keep their jobs while there are still American businesses to save.

I dropped Ted a line to find out how things were with Doyle, a man who deserved his comeuppance, but if Doyle really had lost a fortune, it was the people of St. Luke who would suffer.

It seemed that my predictions of disaster for *The Bugle* were coming true. I felt no triumph in this. *The Bugle* was a St. Luke institution, brought low through greed and poor management decisions. *The Bugle* had changed dramatically. It never criticized the Doyle machine. No one accused Doyle of editorial interference. They wouldn't dare. However, *The Bugle* readers did not take kindly to a tabloid format, they found the funny papers and show business news too frivolous for their tastes and most trivial reporting was frowned upon.

Ted even admitted that Doyle pressured St. Luke businesses to make up losses by proposing the amount of advertising space corporations should take and raising prices at the same time, which didn't go down well. I knew Doyle had lost his touch, and couldn't help but feel a sense of satisfaction. It's called schaudenfreude: happiness at the downfall of others. Within months of the 1929 Wall Street crash, *Bugle* advertising revenues decreased rapidly. Soon Doyle found himself supporting *The Bugle* financially when he could scarce afford it.

The newspaper business is tricky. You need the staff to write the copy that encourages readers to buy the papers. In turn, advertisers are willing to take space because they reach so many readers. Good writers are expensive and they need back-up staff. So newspapers are heavy, both on working capital and investment. If business is good, profits are high but small losses can become big losses very quickly. Doyle was learning the lesson the hard way.

Chapter Twenty-Two

In 1930, shortly after Doyle's Democrats had won their fifth election in a row in St. Luke, I received a letter from an old friend, federal judge Nathan Scott. I had not seen him since I left St. Luke. He wanted information about the Doyle/Gann machine and asked if I would provide what I had, on or off the record. I replied that I had some evidence of corruption but it was a few years old. I no plans to visit St. Luke but if he was headed my way, I would be happy to spend time with him. If I was honest with myself, my resentment towards Doyle still burned and I would love to help someone cause damage to my old nemesis.

Nathan came to New York in June. I remembered why I liked him. He was an unimpressive physical specimen, spoke with a gravelly, low-pitched voice and dressed uncomfortably for the New York early summer but the quality of his conversation was more than compensation. He expressed himself with nifty phrases. He was clear in his intentions. The corruption within the St. Luke administration was running out of control and he wanted Michael Doyle, Alexei Gann and their colleagues removed from power.

His legal training had taught him to get the evidence first. I told him as much as I could. I had kept my story about the road contracts and the underlying evidence, which I passed to him. I also suggested he look for alternatives to the legal route, such as public relations.

"I don't do business like that. It's the rule of law for me, not public opinion. But home rule has got a lot to answer for," he stated.

"What do you mean? It was supposed to make the police more effective."

Nathan laughed. "The reverse happened. Drinking, gambling and prostitution multiplied in the seedier parts of town. The mob is in town."

"Well, that's no surprise."

"I have no proof but Doyle must have made a deal with the mob. Possibly, he thought it would cost less to allow the mob in and contain it by an agreement."

"So how much of St Luke has the mob got its hands on?"

"Interestingly the middle-class areas are untouched, although St. Luke now has the reputation of being the worst kind of wide-open city in the Midwest."

We laughed at the irony and agreed that things were only going to get worse. We promised to keep in touch. In fact, our meeting was the prelude to a long correspondence and a friendship that would last my lifetime.

In my time in New York, I became totally absorbed by my work. Likewise, Abby was fully engaged with her studies, researching for her doctorate and teaching too. We remained close and in love but the relationship had changed. I guess the relationship between two focused, career-minded individuals, whose work was so absorbing, would have to change. Balancing our lives to make time for each other became a luxury.

In July, 1930, I received a call from the New York State Governor's office. The Governor wanted to see me. An appointment was made for me to meet The Man at Hyde Park, the governor's country residence. Albany was in recess for the summer. I took the train from Grand Central Station up the Hudson River to Poughkeepsie. The journey was amazing for its contrasts. Manhattan was soon behind me. The train tracks paralleled the Hudson River. I was staggered by the number of factories along the route, and hoped they were still providing some employment for small communities.

After three hours, I reached my destination. A car was waiting for me at the station and took me on the short drive to Hyde Park. The house was large. It was clearly a home, not a showplace, as the paraphernalia of children growing up was evident. The house was set back on a hillock some three hundred yards from the Hudson River. The views were impressive, whatever the season.

I was shown into a comfortable reception room and offered a beverage. I asked for an iced tea. A few minutes later, I was shown into the Governor's study. He motioned me to sit opposite him.

Despite his paralysis, Franklin Delano Roosevelt remained an impressive man. He was handsome, behind spectacles his eyes were blue and clear and there were flecks of steel gray in his hair. His voice was unlike the oratory version I had heard from time to time. In private, it was a little squeaky, perhaps high pitched. Nevertheless, I had no doubt I was seated before a powerful man.

"Did they give you something to drink, Mr. Driscoll? It's a warm day."

"Thank you, Governor. I'm fine."

"Before we start, are we off the record?"

"If that's what you want."

"Now, I've been reading your editorials for a while. What do you think will happen in the country in the next two years?"

"I assume you mean the economy. I guess it's possible that Mr. Hoover will alter his stance and accept that the federal government has to do more to help the people but he has a whole host of problems facing him. First, he would not have the backing of his party. I wouldn't put money on it. Second, he seems hidebound to Republican ideology. The so-called 'rugged individualism' is important to him, facing one's problems alone and no government help. Third, I don't believe the government really understands what it faces. This is a global problem, not just an American problem. Fourth, and probably most important, our banking system is creaking under the weight of debt and repayment failure. Would any Republican politician dare to tamper with it?"

"So, if you're right, where does that get us?"

I felt a newfound confidence running through me. David "Truth to Power" Driscoll was talking with the state's leader. I told myself to keep cool. "Governor, why ask me when you're getting there yourself?"

"Meaning?"

"If the federal government won't help, the problem devolves to the states, the cities and the charities. The charities and the cities that help will eventually run out of money, so the states will have to act. Some will, some won't. In New York, I think you will."

"Interesting. Would you like a real libation? I'm not a Dry and I am on record that Prohibition was not the cleverest law ever passed. Want a beer?"

The Governor must have pressed a button on his desk because an aide appeared. "Two beers, please, Charlie, and how about opening those French doors? Let's get some air in. Thank you."

After a half hour or so, Roosevelt gave me a winning smile. "How would you like to join my team, become an adviser to me, maybe become a state administrator down the road and help me get New York State back to work?"

"Governor, I'm flattered, truly I am." I gathered my thoughts and continued. "I'm just a newspaperman. I don't have ideas. I just report on them and give them a critical viewpoint."

"Don't sell yourself short, Mr. Driscoll. I've read your criticisms of the Hoover administration. You're on record that to get the country going, the government has to restore credit and that the Federal Reserve should get off its backside. *'Mr. President,' y*ou wrote, *'nothing good will happen until the banks are sound and back in business. This is your priority now.'* Well you're right. I agree with you. I can do something in New York State, but it will hardly touch the sides. We have a federal banking problem because we have a nationwide banking crisis."

"Lucky guess, Governor," I grinned. I was enjoying the flattery.

"So will you come on board?"

"I don't see how I can, I'm a working editor. If I start advising you and you do something I don't like, I'll have a conflict of interest. There's also the small matter of keeping a roof over my head. I seem to have gotten used to a pay check every week."

"I can understand that. We're off the record, right? My ambitions don't rest at Albany. I'm thinking of running for the White House in 1932. I need people like you around me. I can put you on the state's payroll. I could use a great press officer."

"Governor, I'm amazed that you would consider me. I'm flattered, too. But there's a problem. It's like a pitcher for the Yankees moving to the Dodgers, it just wouldn't feel right. So, with regret, I'm going to decline your generous offer, while wishing you well."

I had been told that Roosevelt was the supreme pragmatist. Do what's necessary and move on. That's what he did with me. He thanked me for coming and dismissed me. In no time I was in the car headed back to Poughkeepsie station.

That day was a big day, a very big day. After Abby had received her master's degree, she had been encouraged by Columbia to continue studying for a doctorate and the defense of her thesis was taking place that afternoon. Before I left for Hyde Park, I gave her a gold necklace for good luck. "I'll be thinking of you every minute today. You're going to knock 'em dead."

I had hoped to be at home to greet Abby on her return, but my train was delayed. I entered our apartment to find Abby, head in hands, sitting on a settee in the lounge. Jane was there comforting her. I assumed the worst, and almost ran the few steps to Abby. "Abby, what happened?" Slowly, she raised her head from her hands, gave me the biggest smile and stated imperiously, "Doctor Abby to you. Pass, with minor corrections."

I fell back, then jumped, punching the air in triumph and began dancing around the room. I sang a spontaneous jingle, 'Doctor Abby, that's not shabby.' Do you think I can sell my services on Madison Avenue?" I asked her.

I went to the kitchen fridge, removed a bottle of French champagne I had secreted there before I left that morning. It wasn't hard to evade Prohibition any more. I returned with three glasses. "I am so, so pleased, thrilled. You worked so hard; you really deserve this." I hugged Jane. "A doctor in the family, what do you think?"

I popped the cork, bubbles flew out, but I didn't care. I don't think I have ever felt so elated. I poured the bubbles and passed the glasses. "I want to propose the first of hundreds of toasts. To my fantastic, clever wife, Doctor Driscoll. And I have reservations at The Palm for later. This is so great. Here's to my brilliant wife, one in a million."

"David, hold it right there," said Abby.

"What?"

"The toast is not quite accurate."

"I don't understand."

"You said I'm one in a million. Actually, I'm one and a bit in a million."

Jane gasped. I didn't get it. "Sorry, darling, I'm missing something."

"You won't be in a while. Her tummy will be staring you in the face," quipped my sister.

Then I got it. "No! When? How?"

Abby responded immediately. "Let me see. Yes, last week, the milkman or the postman or perhaps, a visit from the stork, and the usual magic dust. Do you have anything intelligent to add?"

"Yes, today I turned down a job offer from someone who may well be the next President of the United States. So, no, I know nothing except I'm completely speechless and pleased and proud and happy and, and you're much too good for me. Now, when did you find out?"

"Two days ago. I should have told you, but I wanted to get past the defense first. The timing couldn't be worse, could it? How can I go for a teaching job when I'm pregnant? All that work, for what? Forgive me?"

"Nothing to forgive. Anyway, I'm partly to blame. I don't know what to say about the job. Maybe universities will be a little more enlightened these days about hiring working mothers? Oh, let's not ruin the moment. I can't believe it! Have you told your folks?"

"I'm going to call them now. What a day!"

Later, The Palm was its extraordinary self and we left, stuffed to the gills. Janey said her goodnight at the restaurant and Abby and I walked a while. We got home late. "Want a nightcap?" I asked.

Abby shook her head. "No but I want to talk."

"Sure, re-live your day for me and don't leave anything out."

"No, I want to talk about us and how we move on from here."

"I don't understand. Things are fine."

"Not so much, David. You work ridiculous hours and I want a career, so Little Beppy is going to get in the way."

"Little Beppy?"

"Have to call him or her something."

"Any preferences, Abby? Boy or girl?"

"It doesn't matter. Healthy is what I want. But I'm worried about us. Can you change? Will you change? Can I change?"

"I understand what you're saying and you are right, our timing is awful. Look, I could tell you right now I'll change but I would be lying as I don't know how to do it. Let me have a little time to work things out in my mind and with Lucas. Please try not to worry. You're not speaking to deaf ears. I understand what you want. That's a start, isn't it?"

However, it turned out that Abby was speaking to my version of a brick wall. She didn't press the subject and I made no substantial

252

changes to my modus vivendi. I took some time out when the Porters insisted we see them straight away to celebrate Abby's news. It was only about six hours from New York to Richmond, so we made the trip as often as we could.

During Abby's pregnancy, I got busier and busier in the long run-up to the next presidential election. I found myself traveling all over the country, meeting state governors and politicians from both sides of the aisle. I thought that Abby was tired just because of carrying Little Beppy. I failed to notice that she was becoming withdrawn. Rather than confront the problem, it was easier to ignore it. I had a job to do at *The Standard*. In my defense, Abby said nothing to me. I thought she was just concerned about her own career and the pregnancy.

In February, 1931, Little Beppy, better known as our son, Louis, was born in Richmond, weighing a healthy seven pounds. Louis' arrival presented challenges. Fortunately, my salary was now substantial, so we could afford to live on one wage. In fact, we could have afforded home help, but Abby wouldn't hear of it. Abby's graduation was delayed until after Louis was born.

As often as I could, I would come home for lunch to play with Louis, but I have to confess this was rare. I would see him in the mornings and some evenings and try to spend time with him and Abby over the weekends. Louis was a happy and easy baby, which probably helped to conceal the growing gulf between Abby and me. I was totally engaged in my work and the traveling entailed. Abby was wrapped up in research projects. We were driven people and couldn't help pursuing our own interests.

We spent Christmas and New Year in Richmond. Abby felt a trip to Miami would be too much for Louis. Life flowed on. When Louis was a year old, Abby took a position with the City University of New York. CUNY was the right place for her. She agreed to take on part-time home help for those days when she was teaching, but teaching and raising a family brought tensions for Abby. Both made her happy but she found it increasingly hard to balance the two.

I didn't help. It was not a subject I wanted to discuss. Selfishly, I told myself that the less said, the more likely it was that the status quo would be preserved. Looking back, how could I have assumed I had the right to conduct my working life as if my wife and son didn't really exist? How could I have been so selfish? Eventually Abby decided that looking after Louis was more important than teaching. She didn't ask me to talk things over with her. Hindsight tells me this was a very bad sign but, at the time, I merely thought that she had come to her senses, realizing that my career paid the bills. I assumed that the reduction in our previously active sex life resulted from tiredness, not from other less obvious causes.

Jane was a frequent visitor. She doted on her nephew and in due course on her niece. Often, Abby would tell me, "Jane popped in for coffee or lunch today." We saw her very often and I was glad. I grew to like my sister very much, as well as love her.

CUNY offered Abby a leave of absence with an agreement to "talk at a later date" but we both knew her career would be put on hold for quite a while, especially when she told me in April, 1932, that Louis would not be an only child. Number Two, "Peanut", was due in November. And out Peanut popped, to be re-named Charlotte, blonde-haired, blue eyed and as beautiful as anything I had seen in my life.

When Louis was born, I was overwhelmed by the emotion of it all. For Charlotte, my feelings were stronger, if possible. Ten minutes after the baby arrived, a nurse was holding her. I recall thinking to myself, "Nurse, if you drop her, I'll kill you." Now I don't really have a violent bone in my body. Why on earth would I think like this?

I held Charlotte for ages. She opened her eyes and smiled at me. I know newborns can't see and the 'smile' was gas, but when it is your own child, you believe what you want to believe.

Our New York apartment, the one that had been very suitable for two adults, became cluttered with baby and toddler clothes and equipment, not to mention toys everywhere. Looking back, for most of those years Abby and I were worn out, tired to a state of exhaustion. Abby was the most wonderful mother. She loved our children and was firm about bringing them up in the way she had been raised herself. I was delighted, I told her, as I wouldn't have wanted them to have my kind of childhood. I saw some happiness return to her eyes and ignored the resentment that boiled under the surface. Maybe we weren't the happy, loving newlyweds anymore, but wasn't this the normal process of married life?

In contrast, I enjoyed my time at *The Standard* more and more. I had license to write about pretty well any political issue I chose. I read the results of the April, 1932, election in St. Luke. It was a mirror of 1930, the same allegations of fraud and same results. Doyle and his friends maintained a complete lock on the city.

Abby said nothing about my absences at the National Conventions. I assumed she had accepted that my work ethic prevailed above child-raising. I did not think in terms of winning and losing, more that Abby understood the way I was and was content or resigned to us continuing in this way. Her career didn't really feature in my thinking.

Chapter Twenty-Three

Gann sat with Mike Doyle at their regular monthly meeting. "Alexei, the demand for jobs in town is rising so fast, I'm having trouble keeping up."

"You can only do what you can do, Mike."

"You've gotta help more. The city has to make more jobs available."

"How? We've already taken on too many people. The voters won't like us putting taxes up to pay for it all."

"What's the alternative? Having people sleeping on our streets, robbing and thieving to make ends meet? I'll tell you how you can do it. Forget efficiency for a while. I'll give you a for instance. That new road you're gonna build along the Parkway. Forget machines for the digging and cement-mixing, use men instead. For every machine you'll use fifteen men."

"Easy for you to say, you're supplying the cement. The costs of building the roads will increase too much."

"I'll take some of the hit. We can reduce my contract price by, say, five per cent. The road contractor will do the same, as he's one of ours. Look at the advantages. Men in work, families fed, crime reduced. Use those famous brains of yours, you'll see I'm right. And so will most of the voters."

"Okay, okay, I hear you. I'll get the city people into this." Gann thought to himself, "You're a crafty so-and-so, Mike Doyle. I bet you added five per cent to your contract price because you knew you would be offering this deal."

"Mike, there's something else we need to talk about. I'm getting it from all angles that the mob wants more and won't take a no."

"I know. This one's for you, not me. The mob has targeted St. Luke and we can expect big trouble if we don't give in."

"I agree. So do we talk with them? What do you think?"

"I think we accept the inevitable and do a deal. The mob prefers a peaceful entry. My advice, let them in on terms. Keep them away from the good residential areas and limit the type of business they do. No drugs."

"Will you be with me in the talks, Mike?"

"Absolutely not. This one has you stamped on it. Take Santino with you. Want a re-fill?" Gann nodded and Doyle poured a shot of whisky.

"It's a bad business, but I just don't see the alternatives." Gann took a breath.

"How are things, Mike? I mean socially. You're rattling around in Henry Brady's mansion, you never throw a shindig and people don't see you much in town, except at your office."

"After years of our doing business, you have to ask? I like my own company and the business keeps me fully occupied. There's no time for other things."

"We all need other people, Mike."

"Yeah, yeah. Are we done? If so, get outta here. I have things to do." But, in truth, Mike didn't.

Chapter Twenty-Four

Doyle's people always ensured a high Democratic voter registration, by fair means and foul. The deceased of St. Luke rose again like Lazarus to vote. Falsely registered voters were always in the Democratic column. At the election proper, ballot-box stuffing provided an additional safety feature. Through corrupt organization, the 1932 elections ensured the Doyle machine triumphed in shows of raw power. Put bluntly, Doyle stole elections.

Nathan Scott contacted me shortly after the election to tell me that Doyle had set about creating a power base in the state capitol, Cameron. He had managed to get four state senators and ten representatives voted into the state Congress. Each one was handpicked by and obligated to Doyle.

Michael Hyde had been replaced as Governor in 1926 by an independent, but in the 1930 gubernatorial election, Doyle ensured that the Honorable Richard Monk was elected. Monk was a country lawyer with few, if any, credentials sufficient to make anyone believe he was governor material, except for one important quality: he was Doyle's man. He was known as 'Monk's habit' for good reason. His habit was to do Doyle's bidding whenever asked, increasing Doyle's patronage power. On one famous occasion, Doyle told Monk to veto a piece of legislation, passing through the state Congress. A note came back to Doyle. "I'd have been happy to oblige, had your note arrived in time. I signed the Bill yesterday."

Nathan feared that Doyle would soon turn his eyes to the federal stage. "What if he has men in Washington? Where will he stop?" Nathan wrote to me. I had no answer.

I wrote to Ted Page for local information and, as predicted, matters had worsened for both *The Bugle* and Doyle through 1933. Employees were laid off and syndicated columns were bought in to compensate for the lack of copy. The readership was quick to notice, bringing with it a deluge of complaints as reporting of local news deteriorated in quality. Jenks was long gone and in March 1933, Ted resigned in disgust. Doyle was left with little choice. He had either to invest heavily, borrowing if he could, or sell. If not, the paper would go bust.

Despite his Wall Street losses, Doyle's other private business interests were just about sufficient to keep him afloat, though his profits from business with the city were reduced as tax revenues dropped in the Depression. Even the city was limited in its options to place contracts for new buildings. Franchises and licenses also produced less revenue, as business demand fell. Doyle's personal income dropped as he continued to cover increasing demands from the poor and needy. Doyle was fast running out of options. As a result, he was forced to revise his deal with organized crime before they realized how weak he had become.

In early October 1933, Doyle called Charlie Brooks, who had remained the boss of the Perpetual Insurance Company of America.

"Charlie, we need to do some business."

"Well, well, Mr. Doyle, how nice to hear from you. It's a fine day."

"Charlie, cut the crap. You know the deal we have with your friends. I need to increase the fee. And I need it paid right away."

"Mike, my old chum, of course. We're here to help. But what do I get? I can't take this to my people with only one side of the balance sheet."

"How about if I get the St. Luke PD on your backs for all kinds of fraud? Don't fuck with me Brooks. I've been your friend for years. And now you crap on me when I ask for a favor?"

"Cool down, Mike. Insurers need a tax break this year. Will you fix it?"

"Can do, but in exchange I need $150,000 next week."

Brooks was silent for a minute. "That's a lot of money. I'll need the tax break in place for three years."

"No, two years."

"Three, Michael or I can't deal."

Doyle hesitated, then mumbled, "Okay."

I didn't hear from Barry Springer until the autumn of 1933. When he called, his news was chilling.

"It's your old friend Doyle. He's lost another fortune, this time on the gee-gees. It seems Mr. Doyle gets his fun losing large sums of money betting on horses. The rumor I have heard is that Doyle hasn't paid his bookies and Capone has bought his notes. If so, Capone won't settle for repayment plus interest. His vig will be an in into St. Luke, if he isn't already there."

"Barry, you've spoiled my lunch. I have a nasty, sinking feeling. My contacts in St. Luke are a bit cold. Please get back to me if you hear any more, especially if you can confirm any of these stories?"

"David, there's more. Max Torino is headed to St. Luke."

"I don't move in your elevated circles, my friend. Who is Max Torino?"

"How can you profess to be a journalist, and yet be so ignorant? Max Torino is the brains of Capone's outfit. If you met him socially, you would think he was an accountant. He wears Brooks Brothers suits, shirts and ties and appears to be the epitome of moral rectitude. But I would be just as scared of him as I would be of Capone. He is evil personified."

"Okay, I'm convinced. So what's happening?"

"The skinny is that Capone is moving Torino to St. Luke. The Outfit has its claws into Doyle and they will tear him to pieces and suck him dry, forgive the mixed metaphor. You should warn your people in St. Luke that Doyle can no longer restrain organized crime in your city."

"What do you think Torino will want?"

"Not for me to say, but at a guess, the Outfit will expect a good-size share of the St. Luke tax dollars to find their way to the Machine bank accounts.

"Thanks, Barry. We'll talk again. This is a lot of information to process."

That night, I talked to Abby about my plans. "With Doyle going down the tubes, maybe it's time for me to pay a visit to St. Luke, research what's happening and expose Doyle. This time, he can't stop me writing in *The Standard.* Doyle is notorious enough for Lucas to syndicate the story."

"David, I don't think you're being smart. What stories has *The Standard* published about Chicago or San Francisco, where the machines are equally as notorious? You haven't even exposed all the failures in Tammany Hall. Darling, I know you don't want to hear this, but I think you're taking things personally."

I was. I sulked for a while, but I knew Abby was right. I changed my mind. St. Luke was the past. There was more than enough in New York and D.C. politics to keep me interested.

Doyle was ushered into an office in a nondescript building on Chicago's south side. Sitting before him was a man who introduced himself as Max Torino. Seated to the side of Torino was a thickset man with a scar on his left cheek. He wasn't introduced. There was no need. Everyone knew Alphonse Capone.

Torino was the physical opposite of Capone. He was tall, angular and skinny. His complexion was clear. He was balding, and he wore spectacles; he looked more like a Wall Street banker than a gangster.

He motioned Doyle to sit. "Thank you for coming, Mr. Doyle."

Doyle nodded.

"We have several notes signed by you for gambling debts. You're not a lucky gambler, are you?"

"I guess not, but I will have all the money I owe very soon. You know I pay my debts."

"The game has changed, Mr. Doyle. You may treat the debts as an investment by us. To show good faith, here are your notes back." Doyle was handed five notes, totaling over two hundred thousand dollars.

"We know that your organization is involved in managing New Deal programs in St. Luke. I'm sure you do this for the benefit of all citizens to help them get back to work but what matters is that millions of federal tax dollars passing through your hands to be distributed. It's only fair that we have a share of the vig. It is time you made us your partners.

"Now, we are reasonable people. We will want only, let's say, half the profits you make. I've wanted to leave Chicago for quite a while, move my family to a smaller place, and I'll be relocating to St. Luke. My organization will help you and your boys oversee things. I'll be in touch when I get into town."

That was it. No discussion, no negotiation. Doyle knew a more powerful presence when he saw one. He nodded his head in agreement. He wanted to leave Chicago as soon as he could.

Chapter Twenty-Five

In May, 1933, our lives were changed by one phone call. Out of the blue, Ted Page rang me. "I'm in New York, David. Can we meet?"

Thirty minutes later, Ted sat in my office. "On the quiet, Doyle has put *The Bugle* up for sale. It's not much of a proposition unless you are on the inside. And I know the newspaper business inside out. If you buy it, you and I could run this thing so easily and bring it back to profit."

"Doyle hates me and everything I stand for," I told Ted. "Never in a million years would he sell to me. And why isn't it you and me buying? Don't you want a part of this?"

"Doyle doesn't like me much either. And at my age, I dare not risk what little savings I have on this venture. This is a young man's game. You're right. You'd have to buy in a different way. Remember how that crook Pressman operated as a nominee, hiding Doyle's identity? Do the same."

"Okay, I have a few questions off the top of my head. Leaving identities to one side, what's this going to cost to buy? What working capital will be needed? What will *The Bugle* stand for if I take it over? Are we staying with tabloid or going back to broadsheet? Do we need new presses? What staff is left? Where do we recruit? Will advertisers stay with *The Bugle* and come back to it? How do we increase circulation and advertising revenue, especially in these economic times? Is there any real chance of restoring the newspaper to what it was? And I have a few minor questions like how do I tell my wife I am uprooting her yet again, this time with two children? What do I tell my editor and boss here, a man I like and admire? How do I even think of coping with this during the worst recession we've seen this century? And these are just for starters."

"Who said it was going to be easy? Come on. This is America. This is your chance to be your own boss. Just think, you could be proprietor and editor-in-chief of *The Bugle*. You can be the next Henry Brady. If you like the sound of that, the rest is mere detail."

"What's the advantage of buying from Doyle? Wouldn't it be cheaper for me to let the paper go bust?"

"Cheaper, yes, but then you run the risk of the assets being broken up and sold separately. The building could go, the printing presses too and who knows what will happen to the staff? It's a risky option."

"If I buy as a going concern, I will have to take on debts and other liabilities."

"We'll get clever lawyers who'll reach an accommodation with creditors. Come on David, for now forget the detail. Concentrate on the big picture."

"If you don't want to be a part owner, Ted, what do you want from this?"

"I'd like my old job back. Not as editor-in-chief. Metro section head works well for me. I hate Doyle's guts. I really want to stick it to him. I want revenge."

That night, I returned home to a very tired Abby. I fed Louis and Charlotte, bathed them, let them play for a while and put them to bed.

"Abby, darling, you're exhausted. I want to get you help."

"I'm okay, really. It's just that Louis and Charlotte are so lively."

"Are you sure you don't need the doc to check you over, Doctor Driscoll?"

"Cisco, I'm alright. Please don't fuss."

"I'll fix dinner."

"There's a salad in the fridge and some cold chicken. Is that okay for you?"

"Sure. I had a good lunch today. Guess who with?"

"Excuse me, it's 'with whom.' No wonder you can't write. Okay, the Pope?"

"Yes, the Pope, and who else?"

"The King of England?"

"Yes, George the Something and the Queen too. Lovely lady. She sends her regards. Who else?"

"I'm fresh out of influential people. Tell me."

"Well, the Pope, the King and Queen of England and Ted Page."

"Ted! What did that old reprobate want?"

"Not much, just for me to go back to St. Luke as the owner and editor-in-chief of *The Bugle*."

Silence. It was rare for Abby to be lost for words. She soon bounced back. "And you're considering it!" That wasn't a question. It came out more as a shriek.

I told myself to tread carefully. "Well, right now I am neither considering it nor dismissing it. I'm reporting it to you."

"Well, you've done the reporting. What next?"

"Shall I get you the baseball bat?"

Abby relaxed a bit. "Do I scare you that much?"

"You scare me lots more! Ted dropped it on me completely out of the blue. I raised a hundred questions with him, but he told me there was just one question and the rest was detail."

"And the question?"

"Do I want to be the proprietor of *The Bugle* and its editor-in-chief? Do I want to be the next Henry Brady?"

"And do you?"

"I don't know, Abby. It sounds so tempting, but it's full of drawbacks, dangers, risks I haven't begun to consider. All in exchange for what? Massaging my ego? Getting one over on Mike Doyle, who, by the way, has to sell. Evidently he has big financial problems. Anyway, I would never make a decision like this without you. If you don't want it, then neither do I. Let's drop it for now and have dinner."

"Do you really mean that? If I said I didn't want to go back to St. Luke, it would be the end?"

I stopped to think. "That's a very big question and deserves an answer that isn't glib. But, yes, I would turn the deal down if you were against it."

Abby smiled at me. "I'm not saying 'no' but it's a huge step. How could we afford it?"

I refused to talk about *Bugle* business over dinner, but Abby didn't want to let it go. After dinner, we sat on our balcony, sipping iced tea.

"It would be good for you, David."

"What?"

"Running your own show. You have marvelous ideas. You've often mentioned a regular fashion feature for the ladies, better insights into sport and fitness, taking on social issues facing America. You care about employees, workers. You'd be a good boss."

"I'll tell you where my thinking is. First, we would have to get our readers back and sort out advertising revenues. The economic times make that a very hard sell. More importantly, where's the money to come from to buy the newspaper? I'll need capital to buy out Doyle, as well as working capital to run the business, take on staff, all that. I'm not a businessman. I'll need professionals around me, lawyers and accountants. I'll be working all the hours God sends. No more lunches with Louis and Charlotte for quite a while."

Abby smiled. "I have an idea."

"Abby, I'm really tired."

"No, not that! I could use a visit to Richmond and you can talk to Dad. He's very clever when it comes to money. He'll help you."

"Good thought. I'd like a break, even though Lucas will try to stop me. Let me check my schedule. Maybe we could go in a week or two?"

That night, I went to bed happier than I'd been for ages. Was the old Abby back, at least for that night, or was it the chase? *The Bugle* was the most seductive of targets.

I told Lucas that I was worn out and I needed a break. I didn't like lying to him, but I knew I had to be ruthless. I used the time before leaving for Richmond to contact key people. Ted agreed to get some figure work and proposals about staffing and other costs done for me. I contacted Nathan Scott. I needed a lawyer. He recommended his old partner, Fred McNulty. "He's strong, sensible and a lion. You won't regret it."

Abby had a brainwave. Get Emily Venn on board. I hadn't spoken with Emily for years. Within a day or so, I tracked her down to the St. Luke City Finance Department. I asked her to call me collect from St. Luke that night. When she called, she told me she liked her job. "I'm always happy with figures". However, she was unhappy with the department. "There is always pressure, especially to spend less, do more deals. Often I have problems tracing expenditures properly, that sort of thing. There's financial corruption going on here, right under our noses."

"Would you do something for me in strict confidence?"

She asked what I had in mind.

"I'm looking into buying *The Bugle*. If you're willing to help, would you work with Ted Page to let me have detailed figures? I'll need them in about ten days. Now here's the kicker, Emily. I will cover expenses. If it all comes to nothing, that's it. If by some miracle the deal goes through, you'll have a job with me at the newspaper, if you want it."

"What job?"

"Head of Finance and Treasury. I don't know about salaries yet. You'd have to trust me."

Emily went quiet for a minute or so. I was delighted when she said, "Okay, Mr. Driscoll. You treated me more than fair those other times. I'll do this for you. As for the job, let's wait and see."

When we arrived in Richmond, I spoke at length with Alex. Abby had let him know that I wanted to talk business. He thought it might be interesting for me to buy a newspaper. "I'll talk with some boys in town. Let's see what we can do. You got anything I could show them?" I handed over the paperwork Ted and Emily had sent.

Two days later, Alex and I sat with the board of directors of the First Bank of Richmond. After introductions and some small talk, the chairman, Sam Withers, gave me a long, hard stare.

"My boy, if it wasn't for Alex here, we wouldn't give you the time of day."

Alex had warned me to expect a hard time, and to be relaxed and calm. "Fully understand that, sir. In your position, I'd feel the same," I replied.

"This newspaper you want to buy is down the tubes. What's the point in buying it?"

"Mr. Withers, I'd like to answer as a newspaper man, not a businessman. I don't want you to have any misunderstanding about my credentials. I know the newspaper business. I have professional people to advise me on the business side of things and the financials. Now, I could try and start a newspaper from scratch. I'd need premises, a printing press and a reporting and editorial team with back up. Then I'd have to create a new title, as well as an advertising department.

"In the old days, some proprietors would do it all themselves. Those days are gone. *The St. Luke Bugle* used to have a daily circulation of more than 300,000 when I worked there. If I get that circulation back, advertising revenues will flood in. You have the figures prepared by my accountant."

"What makes you think you'll get the circulation back?"

"St. Luke people like their newspapers, they like both the local and state news of the day. And they're loyal. I'll wager Richmond is no different. How many years have you read the same daily paper?"

Sam Withers tried to keep a straight face, but I could see some board members smiling at his discomfort.

"If this is such a good deal, young man, why aren't others interested?"

"I don't know if they are, sir, but this proposal has been put together under the auspices of two former editors and employees who know the business and this newspaper backwards."

The questioning continued for a while from a number of bank people, indeed for much longer than I expected. "If *The Bugle* is dying, wouldn't it be cheaper to buy it out of bankruptcy?"

I gave Ted's answer to me, word for word.

"I've got one last question for you," Withers said. "If my bank decides to back you – and at the moment this is very unlikely – what collateral do you have to support a loan?"

Alex hadn't covered this question with me. To be honest, neither of us thought I would get this far.

"Apart from the assets of the newspaper, none in a form you would expect or could bank on. However, I would say this. I am married to a Richmond girl. My father-in-law is more a father to me than my own ever was. So, you won't be lending to me, you'd be backing my family. If I let you down, I let them down far more. You can't value this. You'd have to take a risk on me, that I'm talking newspaper truth to banking power."

"If we wanted to get a reference for you, who could we ask?"

"Not sure if he would give one because the last time I saw him, I turned him down for a job."

"Who's that?"

"President Franklin Roosevelt."

Withers appeared unimpressed. "Anyone else?"

"My editor, Lucas Vine, but please give me time to talk with him first. He doesn't know about this business. I saw no point in saying anything to him yet."

"That's fair," I heard a board member say.

"Mr. Driscoll, the boys and I will kick this thing around. We'll be in touch."

Mr. Withers talked with Alex for a few minutes while I went to the board members and shook their hands. Outside, Alex looked at me with astonishment. "I guess you Yankees can teach us a thing or two after all."

The day after my meeting with the bank, I received the offer of a loan. On hearing the news, I went to find Abby. She was less than enthusiastic. "David, does this mean I won't see you for a while?"

"I'm afraid so. I'll have to head back to St. Luke but I won't be able to show my face in town until the deal is done. I'll stay in an out of town hotel. This wouldn't be suitable for you and the children."

"Ever the practical husband. What if I said now, I don't want you to do this? Don't buy *The Bugle*. You'll be too busy for us if you succeed, you'll be miserable if you fail and either way you'll make a bigger enemy of Doyle."

"Abby, why are you thinking this way now?"

"I'm scared we're losing each other. We have a family but you won't be around. I still want a career but I don't seem to signify in your calculations."

Normally, I would have tried to placate Abby, but not this time. I felt it wasn't only my career on the line, it was everything. Surely Abby would see this? I recall her shrugging her shoulders as she turned away from me. Her body seemed to shrink as she walked back into the house.

I telephoned Lucas Vine and explained what was happening with *The Bugle*. I asked him to keep it to himself. "Lucas, I apologize unreservedly for leaving you, but this is an opportunity I can't turn down and I have to move on it fast."

Lucas was astonished. "David, I don't want to rain on your parade, but you don't strike me as much of a businessman. Take a bit of time, come back to New York, and talk things over with me. Owning and running a paper is a hazardous venture at the best of times."

"Thanks, Lucas, I appreciate it, but I really don't have the time. If things don't work out, I'll come back with my tail between my legs, begging you to take me back."

"David, I don't want to play the gratitude card, but you came to me for a job when you were in need. It's worked out really well for both of us. If it's more money you want, we can always look at salary levels. I don't want to lose you. I'll bet you haven't thought things through properly."

I could hear a little anger in Lucas's voice. "Lucas, I'm really sorry. You've treated me well and I know I'm letting you down. This is not a move for a salary hike. You know me better than that. An opportunity has come my way, and it's a once in a lifetime thing. If I don't go for it now, I know I'll always regret it."

I heard Lucas sigh. "Okay, David, if that's what you have to do, you'd better do it. Can't you give me a month? You know I can make you work your notice."

"No, I have to go for it now. There's no time to lose. Lucas, you have a good team there. They'll get things done for you. We'll keep in touch, one proprietor to another. Let's part friends. After all, I may well fail and I might be back very sooner than you think."

I heard a sigh. "Okay my boy, I know when I'm beaten. I can't say I like the way you've done this, but I wish you luck. Stay in touch, especially if things don't work out. I don't bear grudges and maybe I can give you some help if you need it."

"That's very gracious. I also have a favor to ask. The First Bank of Richmond might ask you to give a reference for me. It would be a kindness if you would tell them I am a not an axe murderer."

"You kill me, Driscoll! I'll think about it."

Later that night in our bedroom, I spoke with Abby. I apologized for the quarrel that afternoon. I also told her that I didn't have to leave. "I'll call Lucas and tell him I've changed my mind. I can live without *The Bugle*, but I can't live without you and the kids."

Abby got up and walked round to my side of the bed. She sat with me, so we eyeballed each other. In that so familiar movement of hers, she placed her hands on each side of my head by my temples.

"I didn't marry you so that you would change for me. I saw things in you that maybe you didn't know about yourself. Now you're finding them out. You're a newspaper man. It's in your blood. You are destined to run your own show and that's what you are going to do. I know this is the right thing for you and you will regret it 'til your dying day if you don't take the risk. I just don't know if this is right for us, right for me. It's not the deal, it's you. You get so involved, so focused that you forget everything else.

"I love you very much, David. Thank you for offering to stop the deal but that's not what I wanted to hear. I want to know how you will balance your needs with the children's and mine. I guess you just don't have the answers. But you can't stay here and I won't let you. You're going to do this thing come what may, so can I give you some advice?"

"Sure."

"You are not a businessman. You need someone at your shoulder that is on your side, making sure you hold onto your cash and that you make profits. My instincts tell me Emily Venn is so right for you. What she doesn't know about figures and numbers isn't worth knowing. Find a way to have her hold your hand before and after you buy the newspaper."

"I've offered Emily a job if I get the deal. I'll sweeten the pot for her so she says 'yes'. What else do you suggest?"

"Not much really. You'll make it up as you go along. Just remember that even though this is your chance of hurting Doyle, this is business, it's not personal. I only hope you get what you're looking for."

"But I'm not. I need to go with your blessing. I want you behind me on this one."

"I know, but if you won't tell me how you are going to have a newspaper and a family and give what is needed to each, how can I? I don't want our children to have an absentee father. And, yes, maybe I'm being selfish, but there's a lot more to me than just being a mom."

"Abby, you've made the position clear. I don't have answers for you yet but I have two days traveling to get to St. Luke. I promise I'll think hard on what you said."

"David, do you know when I was happiest?"

"When?"

"When Mary Page gave us cooking lessons and we ate those awful meals we cooked. We did things together then and we laughed so much. I'd give anything to get those times back."

"I know, but we've moved on, we're different people now."

Abby kissed me on the cheek, said goodnight and took herself to bed. I told myself she'd come to her senses, especially when we were all back in St. Luke.

I traveled to St. Luke with John Rayburn, a director of the bank, who would front the negotiations with Doyle's people. The plan was for me to stay in hiding outside town. If Doyle got wind of my involvement, the deal might collapse. I contacted Emily, who jumped at the chance of being involved. She would take some holiday time. Fred McNulty would sit with John Rayburn in the negotiations.

Pressman conducted the negotiations for Doyle, who was nowhere to be seen. I told Fred to bargain hard. After two days, the deal on the table was a price of $1,350,000 for the newspaper including the building, presses and other fixtures, as well as supplies such as newsprint and assets including *The Bugle's* name. There were other assets of $600,000 in the form of debts owed to *The Bugle*. The building was the most valuable asset. The newspaper owed almost $750,000 in bank loans. We agreed to pay off the bank loans on closing the deal, leaving a balance of $600,000 for the seller. The only other liabilities we would take over were trade creditors and *Bugle* employees for unpaid salaries, which amounted to some $25,000.

Emily had found an anomaly. The $600,000 owed to the newspaper comprised two loans made in 1931 to corporations where Pressman was the sole shareholder. The first loan was for $300,000 and the second was for $350,000, of which $50,000 had been applied in part repayment of the first loan. Therefore, the net figure of $600,000 payable to Doyle was eliminated by the $600,000 debt due to *The Bugle*. Undoubtedly, Doyle owed the debt. It meant that if my offer was accepted and the debt paid back, Doyle would come out of the deal with nothing. But I told Rayburn to demand repayment on closing the deal.

At a meeting, Rayburn told Pressman outright, "our terms are we will retain the whole of the net sale price until these debts are repaid. When are these debtors going to pay?"

"Mr. Rayburn, I am merely a nominee," came the reply.

"For whom?"

"That's confidential."

"Well, you can tell whoever you're acting for, they're not getting my clients' money until those loans are repaid in full, with interest."

For a day, we heard nothing. I knew I had Doyle in a cleft stick. The reality was that he could not repay the loans, so he would have to sell the newspaper for nothing. As *The Bugle* was making big losses and it was clear there were no other buyers hovering, Doyle was squeezed. I wondered what he had done with the $600,000 he had taken out of *The Bugle*.

Fred and John asked me if I wanted to chase the deal. I called Abby and Alex to talk things over. Abby was non-committal. Alex suggested I rely on Fred and Emily. "I haven't the feel of the room. I just don't know, David, but they will." The advice my team gave me was to sit tight. The next day, Pressman made contact.

"We'll meet you halfway. We agree to your retaining $300,000. If the loans are not repaid in full within a year, you keep the retention. If the loan is partially repaid, you keep one dollar for every two outstanding."

Fred spoke with John and me. "Probably the best we're going to get. What do you two think?"

John turned to me. "It's your crapshoot, but it's tantamount to paying another $300,000 for the newspaper. I don't advise it."

I agreed and told Fred to turn it down. I told him to say that if we didn't get our terms today, we were walking away.

We waited. Close of business came and we heard nothing. We had dinner. Still nothing. Then, at 10:15 that night, Pressman called Fred and told him we had a deal, provided we paid a token sum for the newspaper. We settled on $25,000.

It took the lawyers a day or so to tie up loose ends. John Rayburn signed the papers, together with a declaration that he acted as nominee for me. This document was kept confidential. I would not show my hand in public until all was settled.

John could not believe the deal we had done, nor, he told me, could the bank. I reminded John that the bank would still have an exposure. I needed to employ staff and invest in a new press before I could hope to improve circulation and attract new advertisers. On top of the loan to buy *The Bugle,* the bank had given me an additional facility of $250,000 and a stand-by credit of $100,000 if needed, subject to John's approval. John would visit St. Luke every other month to attend board meetings and protect the bank's investment, at *The Bugle's* expense, of course. I made Emily and Ted Page executive vice presidents of *The Bugle*.

I called Abby and the Porters to let them know I was now a newspaper proprietor. Alex and Christine sounded delighted with my success and congratulated me. Abby, too, said she was pleased for me. I told her I had been thinking over our way forward.

"I've not forgotten you want answers. Please give me time to get things sorted here and I'll be back to Richmond as soon as I can, okay?"

Abby told me she understood.

Emily resigned from her city job immediately and plunged into her new role at *The Bugle* with gusto. She negotiated terms with suppliers and persuaded the company supplying the new printing press to accept a 20% deposit followed by another 20% upon delivery and the balance, without interest, after two years.

On the evening the deal was concluded, I wrote to Doyle and had the letter hand-delivered. I tempered my elation with the knowledge that I shouldn't crow. After all, the venture could go wrong.

Dear Mike,

I wanted you to hear from me that I have bought The Bugle. I didn't want you to hear from someone else. It is business, not personal.

Much has happened between us over the years and I doubt that we will ever be friends again. Furthermore, The Bugle will focus its attention on council and city matters, so you and your colleagues may have to face much criticism. However, we will report fairly and put both sides of the argument.

Should you wish to contact me, my door is always open.

Sincerely, David Driscoll

Unsurprisingly, I received no reply.

Ted spent his days engaging staff. In all, Ted employed fifty-four people, of whom thirty had previously worked for *The Bugle*. It was now time for me to show my face. On the first Monday lunchtime after I bought the newspaper, Ted called all the staff together, editorial, reporting, printing, sales, administration and distribution.

"Ladies and Gentlemen, you know there are going to be changes here. I want to introduce you to the man who will make those changes. He is the new editor-in-chief and the proprietor of this newspaper. It gives me enormous pleasure to call upon David Driscoll."

I entered the room to murmuring and sounds of surprise. Ted continued. "The first time I met David was in 1924. He came to us from St. Louis, so we had to put a lot of work into him to make him a newspaperman. He's been working a while in New York City, so we'll probably have to put him straight again." There was laughter. "He wants to say a few words to you."

I cleared my throat. "Good day. And good to see so many faces I know. Over the next day or so, I hope to meet with all of you individually, but for now I want to tell you how good – and how daunting – it is to be here. These are tough times. You don't need me to tell you that. Starting a new venture in this economy at this time has enormous risks. And make no mistake. This is a new venture because we're getting rid of the changes made since Henry Brady left. Ted Page will resume his duties as head of Metro. The rest will be made clear over the next day or so.

"We've ordered a new printing press. A responsible newspaper is not printed in tabloid format, it is a broadsheet." There was a ripple of applause. "We're going to report news, not tittle-tattle. Local news, county news, state news and we'll even write about what the federal government is up to. With the way the new administration is doing things, there will a lot to write about.

"Our first job is to put the newspaper back in business. We are going to do this by exposing those who have damaged this city for the past decade and we will do this without fear or favor." More applause. "There will be fun stuff too but not pictures of semi-naked women – it's disrespectful. This is one editorial decision that is not up for debate.

"I enjoyed some very good times here in the 1920s, working for Henry Brady. It was a serious business then. We took pride in our work, but we worked with smiles on our faces. I hope to bring those smiles back. I look forward to meeting you and working with you. Let's get started now. I'd like to see all editors and senior reporting staff in my conference room, please. Thank you all."

I waved goodbye and returned to my office. Those requested gathered within ten minutes.

"Normally, I like to work from a script, have an agenda, but today I want to throw it open. We'll have free association. Suggestions, please, for tomorrow's paper?"

There was silence. Ted broke the ice. "They got used to orders from on high. People aren't sure what you mean."

"You mean that people in this room don't trust me, at least not yet. Okay, I can understand that. Listen, people, I'm happy to lead but not write. I mustn't do your jobs. What do you think of a 48 point headline, 'Under New Management'? The story will not focus on me, but on the changes we're making. I want you people to write it, so please decide among yourselves who will be the team to do this. May I have something by five o'clock, please?"

Four people broke away. "Next, I have a suggestion. Let's plan a run of 250,000 copies for tomorrow and the rest of the week and give them away free to the public. Emily, what will this cost?"

She shook her head, as if to say, "What do you care?" She said she would work it out, but probably not more than two cents each copy, depending on numbers of pages and how overheads were calculated. "What does everyone think?" Silence again. "Shall I leave the room? Listen, I am no Walter Jenks or Michael Doyle in disguise. You are my team. I have your backs. Your jobs are safe. In fact, those of you who are owed back pay will find envelopes on your desks by the end of the week."

Emily nodded her head.

"So, speak up, please."

The meeting drifted a little, but it was agreed that free issues were worth trying. The content of the issue was discussed. "Don't try anything ambitious yet," I counseled. "Let's keep to basics. What's happened in the courthouse and with the police? What's the social news? How bad are the unemployment figures? What's happening today in Cameron? This sort of stuff. We'll find our way. We need to plan features. What do we want to concentrate on? Who is in the spotlight? We're heading into election season. Who does *The Bugle's* new management endorse? What are the criteria? Think things over, please. We'll do this meeting again tomorrow, nine o'clock sharp, same place. The agenda is those items I've just mentioned. Okay?"

Heads nodded in agreement. We were off to the races. The next two weeks passed in a flash. The free issues caught the public's eye and there was a bump in circulation as a result. Torpid stories were replaced with those of interest to St. Luke readers. I made some agreements for syndication both to and from *The Bugle.* It felt good getting an agreement with Lucas Vine to syndicate some of *The Standard's* pieces.

I spent time going from department to department, listening to the people who now worked for me and encouraging them to bring forward ideas. Some mentioned pay rises almost as soon as they met me. I gave a standard response. "What if our roles were reversed? Would you agree to such a proposal?" Usually, that was enough to end the conversation.

I concentrated on the advertising department. I was not convinced we had the best person heading it up. He was in his late fifties and unwilling to consider new methods. I consulted with John Rayburn and Ted Page. We agreed the man would be retired on a third of his salary for two years. He was replaced by someone new, a woman Emily had known when she worked at City Hall. Henrietta Carson was thirty-two, unmarried, not unattractive and with a background in advertising sales in Chicago. She had moved to St. Luke four years previously in the expectation of marriage. The relationship floundered but she liked the city and stayed. I was sufficiently impressed to take her on.

"Henrietta, your target is to treble advertising revenue in eighteen months. I'd like you to present me with a plan of action within two weeks. By all means use Emily's team to help with the figures. Is this viable for you? Oh, the question is rhetorical," the last being said with a smile.

The printing shop was unionized. Here, I expected trouble. The new press I had ordered would halve the staffing requirement. The problem needed to be handled with care. Three men in the shop were nearing retirement age. I needed six others to volunteer to go. I had to avoid a strike at all costs. I called on Fred Kovach, the shop leader, and sat with him.

"Fred, I am leveling with you. The new press will be delivered in July or August. I want a smooth transition. But we have a problem. The print shop staff has to be cut. Nine people have to go."

"Over my dead body, Mr. Driscoll."

"If that's what it takes, Fred, I'll get my gun." I laughed.

Fred didn't.

"Fred, I understand you have to protect your people. Three of the men are retiring next year. I'll sweeten the deal for them. I am asking for six volunteers. Do you have anyone who wants to re-train and try another department here?"

Fred stayed silent. "I am asking you to work with me, Fred. If I can turn this newspaper around, it benefits all of us. You and your people will have secure employment."

"And you'll make huge profits which we'll never see."

"You think? I'm doing all this on a shoestring and a huge bank loan. If this thing doesn't work, I'm finished too."

Fred stopped short. "Okay, what sort of sweeteners?"

In two hours, I had worked out a deal with him. He agreed to try and sell it to his people. I told him I'd be happy to join with him in any discussions with his men.

After I left Fred, a secretary told me, "President Roosevelt's office called for you. They left a White House number." I rang it and was amazed to find the President answering his own phone. We exchanged greetings. The now familiar voice asked me what I wanted him to tell the First Bank of Richmond.

I answered, "I'm so sorry, I should have warned you. I've bought *The St. Luke Bugle.* Just tell them the unvarnished truth, Mr. President, I turned down the opportunity of a lifetime."

He laughed. "Sounds like you've fallen butter side up. Don't worry. The call came in a while ago and I dealt with it. How's it going over there?"

"It's much harder than running a state or the federal government. Once you've had a bit more experience, you should try it."

"I have a feeling I have enough on my plate but thanks for the offer. Now, I've given the reference as asked, would you care to return the favor?"

"How can I be of help?"

"I'd appreciate some supportive articles on the New Deal. Can you do that?"

"Consider it done. Would you be willing to give my senior political reporter time for an exclusive interview?"

"Sure, just let Hopkins know when. Here's Harry's telephone number."

"Thank you, Mr. President. You have a lot of people counting on you, including, I suspect, many of our readers."

"Thank you, David."

That night, I called Abby with a, "guess who called today?" She guessed the Pope again, but was impressed nevertheless when I told her. However, I could tell there was something wrong, although I couldn't put my finger on it. Abby didn't press me to encourage her to come back to St. Luke.

"I'm working eighteen to twenty hour days. It won't be like this forever, but I need to do this now. I have to concentrate on repairing a badly damaged newspaper." I asked her, "How about my coming to you next weekend for a quick visit?"

But it didn't happen, even when Louis fell from a tree and broke his arm. I simply hadn't the time. There was so much to do. I called Abby on the Friday afternoon to tell her. She seemed unfazed. I said I would get down the following weekend. Another week passed and I regret to say I cancelled again. On Monday of the next week, Christine called me.

"David, I know you're very busy, but I have to bring you to your senses."

"What? Is Abby alright? Is she ill? Is it Louis or Charlotte?"

"They are all fine, well physically. Louis's arm is healing nicely. But Abby is not right. She's very low. She thinks your marriage is over."

There was a silence. I was so tempted to yell, to tell Christine not to poke her nose in, that I was under so much pressure that I couldn't cope with another front being opened on me. Thank heavens I kept my mouth shut. I broke the silence by asking softly, "What would you suggest I do?"

"I don't want to be an interfering mother-in-law. I can't tell you what to do. You're both grown-ups, although the behavior on both your parts leaves me to question this. You and Abby have to work things out. You two need to talk and not by telephone. David, I'm scared for you both that if you don't take a lead in this, you will lose her. And that would be terrible for you and your family because I know for sure she loves you."

278

"Christine, I love all of you and Abby is everything to me. I know I have been negligent and I feel guilty. I just thought that if I could get the paper off the ground, everything would work out. Give me twenty-four hours to get things sorted out in St. Luke. I'll be with you as soon as I can."

That's what happened. I told my team I was exhausted and needed time out. I gave them the Porters' telephone number on condition they rang me only once a day, when I would resolve anything they couldn't handle. I gave them a lot of rope and told them I expected them to cope.

Two days later, I arrived in Richmond. The Porters were a bit shocked to see the way I looked. I had lost fifteen pounds. My complexion was grayish-yellow and the bags under my eyes stretched to the South Pole. I didn't care. Despite the exhaustion, I was happy to be back in Richmond with my family but I was also anxious. I knew I had found my vocation with *The Bugle*. More important, I knew that Abby, Louis and Charlotte had to come first. I needed to reorganize the newspaper's management structure while at the same time becoming properly involved in family life. Otherwise I would lose my wife. Maintaining the balance wasn't easy.

I spent three days in Richmond. I used a little of the precious time visiting Sam Withers and reporting in person. The office obeyed my instructions almost to the letter, calling just two or three times a day. In between calls, Abby, Louis, Charlotte and I got re-acquainted.

On my first night, I was too tired to talk. The next morning, Christine agreed to take the children. Abby and I took a drive. We stopped at a lake where she used to play as a child. "I have happy memories of being here," she told me.

"Do you still have happy memories of being with me?"

"Don't fish, David. You don't need to."

"I want you and the children back with me in St. Luke as soon as possible. I have been working twenty hours a day and if you had moved back to St. Luke, I wouldn't have seen you. But this will change, I promise. I hate living without you and I can't stand the rift between us. Your mother told me you were down. I should have noticed and I should have listened. I am so sorry."

"It's not just your fault, David."

"I don't agree. Can we work it out, Abby? Is it too late? I desperately don't want it to be." The big newspaperman was pleading and not before time. In that moment, I knew I would prefer to lose *The Bugle* and go broke if it meant keeping Abby. Abby didn't answer, so I spoke again.

"Let me tell you what I'm doing. First, I need another three or four weeks at the newspaper to get everything bedded in as I want it. It would be best if you stay here with your parents. Let's look at my coming to Richmond in August and taking you back home with me."

Abby looked at me as if to say, "What else?"

"Second, I will look for someone to act as my number two at the newspaper. If I can find the right man or woman, he or she will take a lot of time-consuming stuff off my desk. To be truthful with you, I had in mind freeing up time so I could get to D.C. and New York and travel round the country but, instead, I promise to use this time to spend it with you and the children. And I mean proper time, not just popping in and out for a few minutes."

I noticed Abby concentrating hard on what I was saying, but she still kept silent.

"Third, you must get your career back on track as soon as you can. There is no point wasting a hard-earned doctorate. I can create a Book Review section and I wouldn't give a flying fart about accusations of nepotism. What's the point in owning a newspaper if you can't employ anyone you want?"

At this, Abby smiled.

I continued, "I know you want to teach. We would need to hire home help. I can't cover the time for you. Worse, I can't afford the stay-in home help you'll need, at least not yet. I haven't the funds for a number two at the paper and home help. I'm drawing a salary, just sufficient to cover our bills. Things are looking optimistic at *The Bugle*, but it will be at least six months to a year before I know whether we have a financial success."

Abby looked me in the eye. "This is what I want you to do. Stay here for a day or two more and spend time with the children. Louis misses you terribly. Then go back to St. Luke and get that newspaper back to what it was before Doyle got his hands on it. Write to me and tell me all about these ideas of yours. Then we'll see."

"Are we friends again? I've hated being... estranged from you. Is that the word?"

"We were always friends, although I didn't like what you were becoming. If you're being honest with me and if you mean what you say, really mean it, I think we'll be okay. I just won't be shoved in a corner, be the only person raising the children, be a mere appendage for a man who has other ideas. So, let's wait and see."

"Okay."

"When you get back to St. Luke, I shall expect a phone call every day in addition to that letter."

I smiled at Abby. "Yes, Pancho. Anything else?"

"I missed you, too."

When I got back to St. Luke, I wasted no time in putting a team of reporters together to investigate Doyle and the St. Luke Democrats. I gave them what I had found in 1926 about road contracts and told them to be very discreet. After all, the actions back then were not necessarily illegal, and there was no absolute proof that Pressman acted as a nominee for Doyle. There was no rush. I would keep my powder dry.

Doyle still hadn't contacted me. I assumed it was too bitter a pill for him to swallow. But I wanted stories on the machine. I told the reporters that I would be happy to accept quotes from, "an official at City Hall" and, "a source close to the chairman." I didn't expect machine people to put their heads above a parapet.

Every night at six o'clock sharp, Eastern Time, I called home so that I could speak with Louis and Charlotte, as well as Abby. At least they could hear my voice. One night, a week after I returned to St. Luke, Christine answered the phone. She told me Abby was a lot better, not completely right, but getting there. However, as she put it, "My daughter is a royal pain because she's got two kids to manage. And whose fault is that, I ask her?"

Before Christine put Abby on the line, I thanked her for bringing me to my senses. "Well, I always had my baseball bat ready."

I told my senior staff that my working habits would change when Abby returned to St. Luke. "At least twice a week, I plan to go home for lunch. Most mornings, I will not be here before nine and on Wednesdays and Fridays, I will leave here at five, pretty well regardless of what is happening. In the light of these changes, I am hiring a number two who will cover for me at all times. If any of you have a problem with this, tell me now."

No one took me up on the problem thing. There were advantages to being a boss. I called Emily Venn into my office. "Would you help me with something? I don't understand the intricacies of finance and loans, but you do."

"Sure. What is it?

"What will it cost the newspaper to hire a number two for me for two years?"

"I guess no less than $4,500 and no more than $6,000." Why?

"I need you to talk with John Rayburn. Please arrange a loan to *The Bugle* for $6,000. I'll secure it with my personal guarantee."

"You're the boss. I'll get it done."

I recruited Peter Garibaldi at a salary of $2,750 a year. He had a journalism degree from North Western University and a business management Master's degree from University of Minnesota. A thirty year-old single man with no flashing looks to speak of and no money behind him but with a rapier brain, Mr. Garibaldi proved to be exactly what the doctor ordered.

My two ladies and Louis stayed in Richmond until the end of July. I dashed backwards and forwards to see them. Christine and Alex insisted on traveling back to St. Luke with us to help everyone settle in. Aunty Jane made frequent visits too. It was clear she wanted to be a hands-on aunt. I was very glad she made extended stays with us.

Abby was pleased with the way I was trying to re-invent myself, as I kept to a regime, balancing home and work as best I could. In fact, by Thanksgiving, Abby had relaxed sufficiently to make me believe she was enjoying life again. Abby herself decided that her teaching career would best be put on hold until both the children were in full-time school. She took me up on the offer of a running a Book Review section. Our lounge became a library as the delivery of books for review snowballed. Abby had weekly meetings there with chosen reviewers and woe betides anyone who interrupted those meetings.

At one of our daily editorial meetings, Ted Page brought up a story. "This one might appeal to you, David. You remember the opening of the new Dementia Ward at St. Luke General a month or two ago? Would you like to know the identity of the major donor?"

"Wasn't it American Beverages Corporation?"

"No, my friend, it wasn't."

"Who was it?"

"Mike Doyle. I have the story."

Evidently, Doyle had made an initial donation of $250,000 back in 1928 and had underwritten any shortfall between what the ward cost and what was raised. Phyllis Young, the wife of the chairman of American Beverages, had chaired the fund-raising effort. Doyle's sole condition for his donation was that it would remain anonymous. Dr Bishop, the man in charge of the project, had confided the truth behind Doyle's gift to our reporter.

I thought for a minute or two. "Ted, we're not printing the story."

"Why not? It's solid."

"Maybe, but Doyle's donation was private. He wants to keep it private and the story isn't news, it's just gossip. This one gets spiked."

"What about the source of Doyle's funds for the donation?"

"What about it? Do you have any evidence that it was provided from a corrupt source? If you find anything, bring it up again, but, at the moment, assuming you have nothing, we're not publishing this one."

Ted nodded his submission. Doyle, the man was like the curate's egg, good in parts.

Chapter Twenty-Six

September 1933 saw that start of an offensive by *The Bugle* to expose the corruption of the St. Luke Police Department, as well as the lax and wrongful handling of many of the city affairs by the Doyle machine, not to mention its corrupt deals behind the scenes with prominent St. Luke businessmen. We provided our readers with a barrage of articles exposing the working of organized crime in St. Luke, the illegal electoral practices of the Doyle machine ensuring only the men chosen by Doyle were getting elected, and the pervasive bribery, greasing all areas of city management.

I sent a message to Doyle himself, suggesting that he might like to put his side of the argument and that one of our senior reporters would interview him, on the record. Doyle didn't respond. I warned the staff that we were now in a full-scale war with the machine and it was not a popularity contest.

Typical of the reporting was an editorial that appeared in November, 1933.

The St. Luke Bugle
Established: 1875. 3rd November, 1933. Circulation: 294,369.

THE MOB IS IN CONTROL
Time to Rid Our City of This Menace

Almost a decade ago, this newspaper reported on the efforts of the Chicago Outfit to bring their lousy trade into St. Luke. A partnership between the Leader of the council, Alexei Gann, Police Chief Eddie Rupert and Governor Hyde thwarted organized crime and there was peace on our streets.

However, this is no longer the case. A while ago, the mob arrived. First they brought slots into

284

premises whose owners were bullied and threatened to take them. Next was the protection racket where many honest shopkeepers and business owners were forced to pay a "tribute" just to let them continue their trade.

Philip Collins, who ran three dry-cleaning shops in the Third, Seventh and Tenth wards, has left the city. We are printing an extract of the letter he sent to this newspaper before he left:

"I am leaving St. Luke, the town which welcomed me when I was ten and where my children were born. My life has been made intolerable and miserable by the outrageous demands of a criminal gang who imposed enormous financial demands on me in exchange for allowing me to trade here. I pay taxes, but that is not sufficient. I have complained to the authorities, but the St. Luke Police Department has ignored me.

"Ten days ago, my teenage daughter was attacked because I refused to pay protection money. The scars on her face will heal eventually, but my family is terrified. Nobody in authority is there to help us. I have no choice. I am closing my businesses and leaving."

We asked the Police Department to comment. All they would say is that the incident is being investigated. The council refused the comment, saying this was police business.

This newspaper fears for the citizens of St. Luke if the council just ignores the malicious influence of organized crime and the Police Department turns a blind eye.

The Bugle's anti-corruption campaign continued into 1934. Some of the local newspapers supported us. *The Democrat* consistently refuted all claims, unsupported by any evidence.

Occasionally, my editors would receive feelers from machine personnel to see if we could, "work our way through this misunderstanding." I assumed that Doyle, Rupert, Gann, Santino and the others were feeling the heat, probably from mob leaders and business mucky-mucks who wanted no adverse publicity. I drilled my people with the standard response, namely a demand for transparency, not opacity, in government. Oddly, despite my fears, no threats came directly from the mob.

In March 1934, the violence started. It began with vandalism, damage to my employees' cars and personal property. The violence escalated. My staff was hassled on the street by young thugs. I ordered them to report everything to the police and delegated to Peter Garibaldi the difficult task of seeking support from Chief Rupert's finest. Unsurprisingly, the senior police officers were unhelpful towards staff of a newspaper that was constantly critical of them, although a few in the lower ranks privately tried to help us. Not all police officers were corrupt, but it was clear there was little or no protection available. Peter reported the Police Department's failures both to me and our readers. He signed many articles himself to show he was not intimidated.

In April, 1934, shortly before the city elections, I was personally threatened. It started with a printed, unsigned letter, warning me that my health was at risk. Next, a brick was thrown through a window of our house and gunshots were fired. I decided that Abby and the children had to leave. Abby fought me tooth and nail, but I persuaded her to visit Richmond until things died down. When she left, I published a front-page editorial, detailing the threats and bullying we had faced.

THE St. Luke Bugle
Established: 1875. 12th February, 1934. Circulation: 301,421.

WE WILL NOT BE COWED

For the past few years, organized crime has become a part of St. Luke life. Our businessmen are required to pay for protection while the Police

Department stands idly by. Upright citizens have complained vociferously, both personally at Police Headquarters and council meetings, as well as through the medium of the press, including *The Bugle,* that their lives have become intolerable as a result of the actions of the mob, which has the tacit approval of the Doyle machine.

I, too, have been threatened. I have forwarded an unsigned letter threatening me with violence to the Police Department. My home was attacked this week when a brick was thrown through my window and gunshots were fired. I will not be cowed by threats but I have a wife and two young children to protect. They are no part of this fight.

The Bugle has published many articles about the poor government of our city by the corrupt Doyle machine. It has criticized our rulers, the Police Department and its head, Eddie Rupert, for numerous failures, in particular its apparent disdain when it comes to ridding St. Luke of the influences of organized crime.

This newspaper will neither rest nor cease its campaign until the unpleasant odor of mob rule is removed from our midst. If this means a change in city government and new people to head the Police Department, then we support these changes, provided the replacements are honest. This editor and his staff will never be cowed into acceptance of the status quo.

A week or so later, things seemed to have calmed down and Abby and the children returned. Three days before election-day, I drove home as usual. I parked in my drive and opened the driver's door of my car. Thugs jumped out at me. I don't recall how many there were or the weapons they used. The attack was swift, brutal and almost deadly. My injuries were severe. I was lucky to escape with my life. Whoever did it left me with a fractured skull, a damaged eye, a broken leg and serious bruising to my arms, shoulders and face. It was six weeks before I returned home and it took another two months to recover well enough to return to work. I still get headaches as a reminder. My father-in-law told me I would have occasional pains in my head for the rest of my life. Fortunately, their frequency and severity is fading now. I went through painful surgery and more painful rehabilitation.

The physiotherapy was slow and laborious. With Abby's and the medics' help and encouragement, I did get better. In my absence, Peter, Ted and my senior management team kept the newspaper going, conferring with me when it was possible. In all this time, there was not a word from Doyle. I had no doubt that he was behind the attack but I had no evidence. Unsurprisingly, the Police Department couldn't find anyone who knew anything.

When I returned home from rehab, Emily Venn, Henrietta Carson and John Rayburn came to the house. John told me he would be returning to Richmond immediately.

"My job here is done."

"John, I don't understand."

"Take a look at these figures, Mr. Driscoll," said Emily. She still couldn't bring herself to call me David. "We negotiated a good discount for paying the printing press manufacturer off early. Mr. Garibaldi approved. We have also paid off the loan from First Bank of Richmond."

"What! I don't believe it. How did we do this?"

Henrietta chimed in. "I've met my targets easily. The people here were desperate for a good newspaper and have supported us in droves. Daily circulation is now about 315,000 copies. Advertising revenues have probably plateaued for a while, but I doubled the target you gave me."

"The point is that your business is solvent," John continued. "You have a positive cash flow, you have no loans or debts and you don't need finance. If this position changes and you need new finance, The First Bank of Richmond will be there to help. This time, we won't need a guarantee."

"What guarantee, John?"

"Your father-in-law guaranteed the loan. Don't you remember this term of the deal? We wouldn't have done business otherwise. No bank would."

I muttered something about my poor memory but the guarantee was news to me. No wonder Emily had given me a strange look when I spoke to her about the loan to buy *The Bugle* being unsecured. She knew the truth.

The four of us talked for a while until Abby shooed everyone out. "He has to sleep and in this house, I'm the boss," she told my visitors brightly.

I shook John's hand and told him he was welcome in St. Luke anytime.

Later that night, I asked Abby about her father. "Did you know Alex had stood as guarantor for me?"

"Of course. Father and I have no secrets."

"Did you ask him to do it?"

"No! At that time, I was not exactly positive about things, was I?"

"But what if I had failed?"

"You don't fail. The thought never crossed his mind or Mama's or mine for that matter."

"Come on. If I failed, the bank would have called on the guarantee. What would that have done to the Porter fortunes?"

"Not wiped us out but there would have been a fair bit of damage."

I fell silent. I had never felt so humble in all my life. What Alex and Christine had done was beyond any kindness I had ever known. Apart from the financial aspect, they had showed faith in me and love, too, at a time when all was not well with my marriage to Abby. Silently, tears sprang from my eyes. It was too much. Abby put her arms around me. "You're their big son. They see how happy you make me, well most of the time! What they did is what family does, at least where I come from."

I asked for paper and a pen. I wrote a letter of thanks to the Porters that night, words from the heart. The prose wasn't polished, but it was real. My birth parents were dead, but the parents I inherited through Abby qualified in every way possible.

BOOK FOUR
1934 - 1944

THE St. Luke Bugle
Established: 1875. 12^{th,} November, 1944. Circulation: 347,888.

OBITUARY
Michael Doyle, 1900 - 1944

Mike Doyle was the unchallenged political boss of St. Luke from 1922 until his disgrace and fall in 1938. He grew up in Rawlings, where his father was a miner. Mike was ten years old when his father died. He and his family moved to St. Luke. Here he came under the protection of his uncle, Alderman Joseph Doyle, who taught him the political trade at which he became so adept.

Mike fought with distinction in the Great War, for which he was awarded the highest military honor this country can bestow, the Congressional Medal of Gallantry, presented to him in The Palace of Versailles by President Woodrow Wilson.

On his return to St. Luke, Mike formed the New Democratic Party, which won the St. Luke city election in 1922. The party merged with the Democrats in 1924 and the Doyle machine won every St. Luke election thereafter until 1938. Doyle ceased to be the official leader of the party in 1924, but as chairman of the St. Luke Democratic Committee, no one was in doubt as to the true identity of the political leader of St. Luke.

In 1938, Mike Doyle pleaded guilty to charges of conspiracy to defraud and federal income tax evasion. He was sentenced to twenty years in prison without remission. He was released a few days ago on compassionate grounds. He died the day before yesterday. He left no widow and no children. No surviving relatives attended his funeral.

These are the bare facts, but there is so much more to tell.

Mike Doyle was my friend from childhood, as well as my political leader in municipal government. I voted for him. He also became my boss, when he bought this newspaper. But he became my enemy, not only when he decided to corrupt the government of St. Luke, but also when he hurt people very close to me.

Yet, after I had bought this newspaper from him on terms that cost him dear, this same man helped me and my wife in the biggest crisis a family can face. Without a thought about our damaged personal relationship, he played a crucial role in resolving the situation of our daughter's kidnap, no questions asked.

At Doyle's trial, a federal judge vilified Mike Doyle as the worst kind of crook. Undeniably, Doyle committed serious breaches of our country's criminal code. He played the city government game to his enormous personal financial advantage. He corrupted the election process in our city to secure victory after victory when he had no need to do so; he would have won these elections anyway. He would just not leave election outcomes to chance because machine business had to be preserved at all costs.

However, no one truly in need of help was ever refused by Doyle and his machine. He spent long hours every week speaking to the needy and desperate and finding help for them.

Doyle ruined budding political careers because he would brook no opposition. He made sure fellow veteran Billy Walters was pushed out of the New Democrats before the 1922 election, but years later, when Billy was in financial difficulties, Mike was the first to put money in Billy's pocket and find him a job. During the Depression, unemployment figures in St. Luke hovered around 2% at a time when elsewhere in America, one in three adults could not find work.

Doyle looked after the poor, immigrant families. In The Trench, he owned tenement blocks where he housed hundreds of families, rent free. He provided food, clothing and medical aid. They didn't pay. He also found jobs for the man of the house. And all of this was done without fanfare.

Had Doyle used his considerable powers and skills for the betterment of our society rather than his own selfish ends, he would be remembered as one of the great men of this state and not be relegated to infamy.

But, to me, he will always be "Irish", the boy I met at school nearly forty years ago.

David Driscoll. Editor-in-Chief.

Chapter Twenty-Seven

Riverton is a miserable place. The town is in the northwest corner of our state. Little happens there. The weather is fierce. It's like an oven in summer and a deep freeze in winter. Riverton's main industry is providing supplies and personnel to the state prison, some five miles away to the northeast. Neither Riverton nor the state prison has a single redeeming feature. The prison grounds have neither trees nor natural cover. Existence there for guards is harsh and even more so for the inmates, especially those convicted of the most serious of crimes.

I was at the prison in November, 1944. I expected to find a crowd of reporters to witness the release of one of the state's notorious criminals. I was wrong. There was no one, just me. At nine o'clock on the dot, Michael Doyle exited the steel gates of the jail. He looked around, presumably hoping to see one friendly face. All he saw was me. He winced visibly. He walked towards me.

"Come to gloat?"

"No, Doyle, I came because this is news. I didn't think it right to send one of my reporters."

"Always the saint, eh Driscoll?"

"How are you?"

"Well, looking at this huge crowd here to greet me, I'd say I was not exactly the most popular man in the state these days. I'm told a bus will be along in a few minutes. So, much as I'd like to stop and socialize, I'd better go. It's cold and I don't want to miss it." He turned and started to walk towards the bus stop.

"Wait. Doyle, my car has a heater. I can get you back to St. Luke much quicker than the bus and in a lot more comfort. Take a ride with me."

"Aren't you going to be embarrassed to be seen in the company of a convicted felon? What about what happened between me and Jane?" Doyle was serious.

"You've paid your debt to society. As for Jane, she has a happy and fulfilling life and I can't bear a grudge. It would only eat away at me. Why should I be bothered by what people say or think? You don't have to say a word to me. Mind you, it's a six-hour drive, more or less, and I don't think there are many radio stations on the way. So it would be peaceful."

In truth, a long time had passed. We were getting on in age and there was no hatchet left to be buried. Doyle had got what was coming to him and suffered the just punishment. As far as I was concerned all scores had been settled.

Doyle thought for a moment or two. "Okay, where's your car?"

He took me at my word and said nothing for almost an hour. Then he started a conversation.

"How do you know I won't try to kill you?"

"You mean now?"

"Yeah. Grab the wheel. Cause an accident. Kill us both."

"I don't know, but it would be pointless, wouldn't it?"

"Not for me. I have nothing. For you, yes. You have everything. Wife, kids, a great business, friends, respect. In fact you have everything I don't. So, there's quite a lot in it for me if I bump us both off."

"That's fair. Are you a vengeful man now?"

"Not really, I was just exploring my options."

We came into a small town. "Want to stop for some coffee, Doyle? Maybe there's a Pyramid out here?"

I heard Doyle laugh. "Right!"

We found a diner. Steaming mugs of coffee were produced quickly. I ordered scrambled eggs. Doyle ate nothing. I noticed how thin and gray he was from temples to cheeks. Prison tan.

"What happened to you, Doyle? Back in '24, you had it all. You won elections, earned respect from all quarters, ran a clean administration."

"How do I know? Maybe I have a character flaw?"

"We all have weaknesses, and you're no different."

"This is too difficult for me, Driscoll. We were once friends, but not now... You nailed me good. You made me the number one enemy in St. Luke and the state. You got me a jail sentence. You ruined me. I'd like to go."

We went back to the car. I filled up with gas and we were on our way, each with our own thoughts. Mine took me back ten years.

After I was attacked in 1934, Doyle's machine had its usual electoral success but in the state election for governor, his chosen man to replace Richard Monk was defeated, as were most of his picks for the state Congress. The stories in *The Bugle* had caught the eyes of country readers, as well as those in Paxton and Cameron. People voted against the Doyle machine candidates in droves. The loss was bad news for Doyle. Patronage for state jobs, which had been in his gift, was either minimized or lost altogether. The new governor, Samuel Richardson, was an apple farmer by trade, and had no time for the likes of Doyle. Suddenly, in political circles Doyle was seen as fallible.

My friend Nathan Scott, the federal judge, had not been idle. He used his authority to investigate the primaries and the election. A grand jury was impaneled to take evidence. Efforts by the Doyle machine to stop witnesses from giving their accounts failed. Many witnesses took immunity from prosecution in exchange for giving evidence for the state. They told the grand jury of the threats and extortion they had imposed over the years at Doyle's command. It took Scott almost two years to get all the evidence together, but in January, 1936, the grand jury handed down 340 indictments against many prominent machine leaders and numerous operatives. Of course, Doyle himself, Gann, Santino, Berman and the most senior machine people had insulated themselves. They were not indicted because there was insufficient evidence to implicate them.

I cannot in all conscience give just one side of the St. Luke machine story. In the interests of fair and honest reporting, I have to give Doyle credit too. After the Wall Street Crash and the onset of the Great Depression, unemployment in St. Luke should have risen exponentially, as it did all over America but St. Luke seemed immune. The Doyle machine has to take the lion's share of the credit for this.

As makeshift shantytowns, "Hoovervilles," sprang up throughout the United States, even in Washington D.C., none appeared in St. Luke. The city had its vagrants, but no more than before October, 1929. Poor people did not starve, nor did their children run around wearing rags. In 1932, St. Luke charities ran out of funds and the state would not help. The Doyle machine stepped up to do what was needed.

Doyle and his people provided welfare when all other St. Luke institutions failed.

This was no idle or simple task. Welfare was needed not only by the poor but also by middle class people who had lost their jobs. Doyle found work and help for nearly all of them, regardless of political persuasion. Maybe it was not the kind of work they were used to, maybe clerical people had to learn how to drain ditches or repair roads but at least they had a job and a wage. Doyle and his machine weren't just villains. Thousands of people owed so much to Doyle for his skills as the real city boss.

Not that Doyle was out of pocket for services rendered. Work came through various sources, not just the city or the federal government. Corporations strong-armed by Doyle found work for people. Doyle rewarded the corporations with favors, usually tax breaks or city contracts. Many federal programs were managed by the machine, which took its cut. What Doyle achieved for St. Luke was business as usual throughout the years of the Great Depression, protecting its people from the worst hardships suffered by other communities.

That said, do ends justify means? Was it right that election after election was stolen by Doyle's machine? Of course not, but the probability was that the Doyle machine would have won anyway. Was it right that Doyle dealt with the devil, allowing organized crime into St. Luke? Absolutely not, but the probability was that the mob would have found a way in somehow. Exploiting human frailty is like water. It finds the weakest spots. Men who wanted to drink, gamble and consort with prostitutes will always find a way. Doyle felt that his deal with the devil was acceptable. Organized crime operated within defined non-residential areas of the city. The suburbs and better downtown areas of St. Luke were organized crime-free.

As for Doyle's trades with the business community, his methods were hardly new. Business got what it wanted, a milieu in which it could trade peacefully and without interference from the wielders of red tape. The big businessmen benefited hugely from Doyle's rule. A wide-open town, free from regulation, helped their concerns prosper mightily. The consumer might pay a few dollars more for what was produced but, in turn, the corporations could pay good wages because of tax breaks.

The crunch for Doyle came in the 1936 elections. By then, Doyle's people had been in power for fourteen years. Ruling a city had become too easy for them, too comfortable and too lax. Mike Doyle was nothing if not smart. He would have known this. So was he powerless to stop the decline or did he just not care? Was he so wrapped up in his own personal shortcomings that he couldn't see what was happening around him? Was it a kind of amorality? Was it the same demon that prevented him making a lasting relationship with the opposite sex?

The grand jury indictments did not catch the machine off guard. Doyle must have been pre-warned. The machine's defense team went into gear straight away. "All charges are groundless. Every prosecution will be fought, using all resources available to the machine," announced *The Democrat*. Teams of lawyers arrived from Cameron to assist those in St. Luke. Pressman was not involved, he knew too much.

The hearings started before the February 1936 primaries. It became clear that the federal government had very strong cases against those who were tried first; twenty in number. The state's witnesses weren't shaken in cross-examination. All twenty machine personnel were convicted before the city election proper in April. Sentences were deferred until the rest of those charged had been tried but Judge Scott warned those convicted, two of whom were women, that they would definitely face jail time.

The trials continued throughout the summer and autumn of 1936. Eventually, all 340 machine members had their day in court and all but five were convicted of a host of election crimes. The sentences varied from small fines for petty breaches to large fines for more serious offences. Those who aided and abetted in ballot box stuffing and crimes of violence received sentences varying from one to five years. No one was prosecuted for the attack on me.

Those who thought the Doyle machine was holed beneath the waterline and would be defeated in the April 1936 election were proved wrong. The machine won the election convincingly. Despite machine wrongs, voter loyalty and almost no unemployment ruled the day.

Doyle, in the guise of the machine, paid all legal costs and fines of those convicted and kept the imprisoned on full pay for the whole of their sentences. The strain on machine finances must have been enormous. Amazingly, the machine's business appeared to have continued seamlessly and unaffected. Doyle looked as if his people were set in power for as long as he wanted. Despite the efforts of *The Bugle* in reporting the prosecutions, disclosing wrongdoing at City Hall by senior executives and the close relationship between the St. Luke Council and the mob, by January, 1937, Doyle appeared as unsinkable as Titanic survivor Molly Brown.

Chapter Twenty-Eight

Months after I had recovered from the machine's attack, both Abby and I found ourselves busy, fulfilled people again in routines that we enjoyed. I found great comfort in seeing the newspaper recover from its dark times and return as one of St. Luke's institutions. I wondered if Sam Perkins was watching me from above and grinning.

Family life was good for me. I admit that physical relations with Abby were not enjoyed quite as often, or indeed as intensely, as they had been. I guess having children does that to a marriage, but we loved each other just as much, if not more so. I still got a big kick whenever I saw her.

Life was comparatively peaceful for us until one summer's day in 1936. Abby called me during the working day. When I picked up my phone, before I could say anything, even, 'hello,' Abby's panicked voice came through. "Charlotte's been kidnapped."

"Oh, my God! What happened?"

"Come home please, now!"

I tried to stay calm. "Did you call the police?"

"No, they left a note warning me not to do this. I've done nothing. Please come now. I need you."

"I'm on my way."

I flew out of the office, telling my secretary to have Peter Garibaldi deal with things in my absence and that I would call him as soon as I could. She started to phrase a question but I was already out the door.

The fifteen minute drive home gave me time to think about who was behind this. I saw Abby waiting for me at the front door of our house. She ran to the car as I got out, spoke no words, just put her head next to mine and cried.

I held her. "Darling, I'm taking you inside. We're going to stay calm, please. I need to ask some questions. Then we will decide what to do, you and me. Okay?

"I felt her head nodding. I half-carried her inside. I fixed a pot of tea and put some sugar in her cup. She gagged a bit as she sipped. She told me she had left Charlotte playing outside in the front yard while she was upstairs tidying the bedrooms. She heard a car screech to a halt outside, and the doors slam shut. Charlotte had cried out, but by the time Abby got outside, the car was out of sight.

"What will we do?" Abby wept again.

She handed me the note that had been thrown onto the grass. It said we would be contacted and not to call the police. That was all.

In order to cope, I became coldly matter-of-fact. "Abby, I think we should do three things. We have to call Jane and the police. And I'm going to call Mike Doyle. I bet he's behind this. If I'm right, I'm sure Charlotte won't be harmed."

"We can't call the police. You read what they said."

"We can't handle this ourselves. I'll speak direct to Rupert. I don't see a choice. Now, I'm calling Jane. Lucky for us, she's in town. We really need her. It's just in case. Trust me, please."

I went to my study. I called Jane, told her we had a problem that I didn't have time to explain and asked if she could come to us right away.

Next, I called the St. Luke PD and asked for Chief Rupert. I identified myself and said it was personal. It took a minute or two. Then I heard, "Rupert here, what can I do for you, Mr. Driscoll?"

"Chief, I need your help. My four-year-old daughter has been kidnapped. We have nothing but a two-sentence note to go on. One of the sentences warns us not to involve the police." I told him as much as I knew.

Rupert responded quickly. "I think the best way to handle this is low profile. One of my officers, Meg Letowski, will be over. She'll be in plain clothes and driving an unmarked car. Do everything through her. She is a specialist at this sort of thing."

"Chief, I don't know what to say. Given our history, this is awkward. Thank you."

"Mr. Driscoll, you and I don't fight our battles using children."

My last call was to Mike Doyle. It took a while to be put through. By then I'd lost my cool.

"Mr. Driscoll, it has been a long time. What can I do for you?" said the familiar voice.

"Listen to me, Doyle. You're all kinds of things I hate but what you did today, what you did to a defenseless child is the worst yet. I don't know why you did it but I want my daughter back and I want her now."

"Whoa! What are you talking about?"

"Charlotte!" I screamed then composed myself. "Less than an hour ago, she was kidnapped, taken away from our street. Bring her back now, back home where she belongs, not kept as a pawn in some disgusting game you have decided to play with me."

There was a silence. Then Doyle spoke calmly and quietly. "David, I swear to you on anything you call holy, on Abby's life, I know nothing about this. I had nothing to do with this, nor did any of my people. You must know this is not my style. I'd would never involve a child in my business. So, could we start this conversation again, please?"

I told myself to calm down. Maybe Doyle was telling the truth. As far as I knew, kidnapping had not been part of machine repertoire. Tom Berman's son had been kidnapped a year earlier. He had escaped unharmed and the local press agreed to kill the story for the sake of his family but no links were ever made to Doyle or the mob.

My thoughts were racing so I took a deep breath. "Charlotte is only four. Less than an hour ago, she was grabbed from our front yard. Abby didn't see the car. We have a note – it says we'll be called later and don't involve the police."

"What have you done since?"

"Apart from rushing home, I've called Rupert. He's sending someone."

"That's good. And that's all you should do. Let the professionals handle this. I'll make some inquiries. If I come up with something, I'll call you."

"Mike, I don't normally lose it, but Charlotte's so young."

"I understand. Stay calm. I'll get back to you, I promise."

I went to the lounge to join Abby. In short order, Meg Letowski and Jane arrived. Meg was short, blonde, fortyish and totally professional, yet not without feeling. Jane went to pieces when she was told what had happened. Abby comforted her until Jane realized it was meant to be the other way around and pulled herself together.

Meg spoke with all of us. "Kidnaps are usually one-offs. They don't follow a pattern, so I can't predict what will happen. We are

301

getting a court order to put a trace on your phone. This is a formality. Expect a call from the judge soon, Mr. Driscoll. After that, I'd ask you and your wife and Miss Driscoll to do nothing. Please trust me and let me handle things. There's not much else to do until the kidnappers call."

The phone rang. Despite Meg's warning, I jumped. When I answered, a judge spoke with me briefly and I gave my consent to the phone trace. I asked Abby and Jane to fix some food as none of us had eaten. They did so, reluctantly. Neither of them wanted to eat. Nor did I for that matter, but while they were in the kitchen, I spoke with Meg for a moment.

"Meg, you should know that I've spoken with Mike Doyle."

Meg looked surprised. "I thought you two were enemies."

"We are but we go back a long way and this is personal, not business."

"What did he tell you?"

"He says it's nothing to do with him. He's checking sources."

Abby and Jane brought the food in. Nobody ate much.

"What time should I collect Louis?" Jane asked.

Suddenly, I panicked. What if the kidnappers went after my six year old son, too?

Meg calmed me down. "Call the school now, make sure he's alright, tell them his Aunt Jane will collect him. Describe Jane so they make sure the right person picks him up. I have to wait here but I can send someone with Jane if you want."

I spoke to the school, which was in easy walking distance and asked Jane to go. Ten minutes after Jane left, the phone rang. A voice I didn't recognize said, "Driscoll?"

"Yes."

"$50,000 in small bills or she dies."

"Is she there? Can I speak with her?" I begged.

"I'll call again to let you know the drop."

Whoever it was rang off. When I told Abby and Meg the details, Abby blanched.

"I have to call my office. Get the money," I said thinking practically.

"That would not be what the PD would advise," said Meg.

"My daughter's life is at stake."

"I understand your concern, but she's worthless to the kidnappers if she's dead. You need to string these people along, make them panic. We find that's the best way."

"At least let me get the money. Then we'll have options."

I called Emily. "Please don't ask questions. I need you to draw $50,000 from the bank. It's a loan to me. I want it in cash, in small bills – tens, fives and singles – and I want it here today. Speak to the bank chairman. Have him call me at home. Please get here with the money as soon as you can."

To my infinite relief, Emily said, "Will do." I loved Emily. No questions, no frills. She was worth twice her weight in gold. When the bank called, I confirmed my instructions.

Jane arrived home with Louis. He loved having his aunt around to play games. He was unsure about Meg, but nodded in a grown-up way when I told him she was helping Mom and me. Surprisingly, he didn't ask about Charlotte.

Emily arrived shortly before five, carrying a satchel. I took Emily into the study and told her what was happening. She had figured it out already. She asked if I wanted her to stay. I declined, asking her to keep a lid on everything.

"Hopefully, this nightmare will soon be over," she said. She kissed me on my cheek and left.

We waited. Dusk turned into night and nothing happened. Jane put Louis to bed. She fixed some soup and sandwiches. We ate mechanically but no one had any appetite.

Hours passed. Finally the phone rang. I picked up the receiver, and Meg picked up an extension phone.

A voice said, "Just answer 'yes' or 'no'. Do you have the money?"

"Yes."

"Is it in small bills?"

"Yes."

"Do you know Butcher Station?"

"Yes." It was a disused railroad station by the old St. Luke stockyards.

"There is a garbage can on Platform One. Put the money there at exactly two o'clock this morning and leave. We'll tell you where the child is once we have the money. And no police."

"No."

"Whadda you mean, no?"

"How do I know she's alive?"

"Hold on." I heard the phone crackle and then a voice cry, "Daddy, help me."

"Now will you do as we say?"

"Yes."

The caller hung up. "Good," said Meg. "We have an hour and a half to get this done."

"No, I have to go on my own."

"You will, don't worry."

At exactly two in the morning, on my own, I placed the satchel bag with $50,000 into the garbage can at Butcher Station. I drove home. Meg related the rest of the story to me.

Ten minutes after I left, a truck with no lights on crawled into Butcher Station. A few minutes later, the passenger's door opened and a woman got out. She walked over to the garbage can, withdrew the satchel and walked back to the truck. Just as she was about to open the passenger door, bright lights were switched on, guns were fired above the truck and about twenty cops charged, dragging both the woman and the driver, a man, to the floor. Quickly, the truck was searched. Charlotte wasn't there.

The man and the woman were dragged away to an old waiting room. They were handcuffed to a bench and ringed by police who remained silent. Fifteen minutes later, the police left as Mike Doyle and a tall, well-dressed, slim man came in. They approached the woman and the driver. The tall man accompanying Doyle asked the couple if they knew who he was. They shook their heads.

"My name is Max Torino. I am a kind of super-policeman in this city. My boss is Alphonse Capone. You heard of him?" The couple nodded their heads vigorously. Clearly, they were terrified.

"Where's the girl?" asked Torino.

Both shook their heads.

Torino crouched down to their level, eyeballing the couple. He talked in a whisper. "I'm going to ask the question again. If I get the same answer, the police won't help you. I have men waiting with me. I'll call them in and we'll keep asking you the same question. Each time you give me an answer I don't like, you will be hurt. You," he said pointing at the man, "will lose a finger for each wrong answer.

304

For you, lady, we'll cut your pretty face. So, what do you say?" The couple shook, but said nothing.

Torino waited a few moments. Calmly, he addressed the pair. "Where is the girl?"

The question was met with silence.

He motioned one of his men over. The man brought out a knife with a six-inch blade. Torino gave the man a piece of wood. The knife cut through the wood as if it was butter.

"Cut her," Torino ordered the man. "Take four inches from under her left eye."

The terrified woman shrieked and sobbed an answer. She talked for a short while, as her accomplice growled at her. Doyle left with a driver and another man. Thirty minutes later, the other man returned to Butcher Station to confirm Charlotte had been found and was on her way home. Torino nodded and left with his men. The St. Luke PD took the couple away. The pair would not experience freedom for many years.

When I got back from Butcher Station, Abby, Jane and I waited. Meg told us that this was the worst time and to stay strong. Eventually, Jane took herself to bed, saying, "I'll be useless for Louis in the morning if I don't get some sleep."

Time seemed to stand still. Abby and I tried to sleep in our armchairs, but couldn't. We went to the kitchen and made cocoa. Shortly before dawn, there was a quiet tap at the door.

Mike Doyle stood there, holding a sleeping Charlotte in his arms. He handed her to Abby. "She seems okay," he said. "I'm sure she'll be fine. I know you'll have the doc check her out. Please let me know how she is."

Doyle left before we could say thank you. I ran out of the front door as he was getting into his car. I waved to him and placed my right hand to my heart.

He smiled at me.

Indoors, Abby was weeping and cuddling Charlotte. Jane woke up at the commotion. She lost her composure completely when she saw Charlotte. Meg grinned and said her goodnights, promising to return in the morning to finish things up

In the morning, I called Emily and asked her to collect the money the police were holding. I then called Chief Rupert. "Chief, it will be business as usual all too soon. Before renewing our battles, I wanted to thank you. Please read *The Bugle* tomorrow."

"Will do," replied the Chief. "Meg will be over later. She'll fill you in. This time, Mr. Driscoll, it's been a pleasure doing business with you."

Abby called our doctor. By the time he arrived, Charlotte had woken and was having breakfast. The doctor checked her out and, to our relief, told us she was fine, just one or two little bruises.

Meg arrived. She told us that the kidnappers were from Arkansas. They were not connected to any gang. Life for them had become intolerable: no jobs, lost home and living out of a truck. They knew that there had been kidnaps in states all over the Midwest. At first, they said there had been no reason for picking on Charlotte as a victim. They had just driven around a middle class section of town, looking for an unprotected child. However, under questioning, they admitted picking Charlotte because of me. I was listed in the newspaper as proprietor of *The Bugle*. They got my address and phone number just by looking in the phone book, simple as that.

"Meg, how did Mike Doyle know where to find Charlotte?"

"After the woman fessed up that they had stashed her in a disused shed, Doyle went to get her. They had made sure it was safe for a child and left blankets to keep her warm, but there was no food or drink. They didn't have any money left to buy anything."

"Just like that?"

"Ehm, no. Like I told you, Max Torino got the info."

"Torino? What was he doing there?"

"He was with Doyle. He talked to the kidnappers and the rest, as they say, is history."

"You know Torino?"

"Let's not get into things we don't need to."

"Are you suggesting the PD has relationships with the mob?"

"I've said as much as I can, Mr. Driscoll. Please don't ask me anything else. Look, it all turned out okay, didn't it?"

My mind was in turmoil. Who had helped Abby and me? To whom did we owe favors? To what extent was I compromised? I made myself stop. It would keep. *"Just remember Charlotte is home, safe and well,"* I kept saying to myself.

At that moment, Charlotte bounded into the room, apparently no worse for wear. She jumped into my lap and gave me a hug. "Where were you?"

"I'm here now, Lottie."

"Who is she?" pointing at Meg.

"That's Meg. She helped us look for you."

"She's nice. I like her."

With that, Charlotte jumped off my lap and headed to the next room and her toys. "Not too much wrong with her," observed Meg.

"Meg, how can we thank you? You have been such invaluable help. You have the admiration and gratitude of all our family."

Meg said her goodbyes. It was time for another call. I called Doyle's office. I was put through immediately.

"Mike, it's David. Why did you run off last night?"

"It was very late and your family didn't need to entertain me."

"I don't know what to say. You got Charlotte back. I now have a debt I can't repay. Abby and I are so grateful to you."

"Had the roles been reversed, you would have set everything aside and helped me. It's what people do."

"I have to ask you something and please don't get mad at me. I've been told that Max Torino got involved in the rescue."

"Yup."

"What do I owe him?"

"Nada. Nothing. This was not business."

"So, what can I do for you?"

"You might get that newspaper of yours to stop slugging me and Gann at every opportunity. We're not bad people. Just look at how St. Luke is surviving these days when the rest of the country is going to the dogs."

"Is St. Luke surviving or are we just putting off the evil day?"

"And I thought I was the cynic. We used to be friends. I know a lot has happened, but why don't we talk to each other?"

I thought for a moment. I was tempted to respond, "Because two years ago you almost had me beaten to death." Instead, I replied, "Okay. I have a deal for you. First, read the front page of tomorrow's *Bugle*. And second, as a token of gratitude to you personally, I'll hold off any stories about the machine until next week. In the meantime, I'll meet with you, and you can put your case to me."

"Just say where and when. I'll turn up" This was the old Doyle, always ready for a political deal.

"I guess you'd prefer neutral ground, but I don't think it's a good idea for us to be seen in public together."

"You mean it's not good for you. That's fair enough. Does Abby still cook meatloaf? I love an old-fashioned meatloaf. Will Saturday night do?"

So we agreed to meet. Abby looked astonished at the turn of events, but when I explained why, she understood. Jane was less understanding. "I'll never forgive that man. Never!"

That night, after the children were put to bed, I retired to my study to write. Abby came in to read the piece. She approved. I had an intern come to the house to deliver the copy to my night editor. I called him to make sure it would be printed in the morning issue. Peter Garibaldi had already told the typesetters to hold the front page.

The next day, this article appeared on the front page:

A Message of Gratitude

It is no secret that this newspaper is opposed to many of the actions of our city politicians and our Chief of Police. Indeed, for the past two years, it has campaigned hard for clean elections and the removal of organized criminal elements from our society. We have endorsed people who have stood against Alexei Gann, Tom Berman and Eddie Rupert and we have criticized the actions of Mike Doyle, depicting him as the prince of darkness of St. Luke, alongside his corrupt machine.

However, as the father of two young children, my attitude changed dramatically in the past 48 hours. On Monday afternoon, my daughter, Charlotte, was kidnapped. Details and evidence will be given at the kidnappers' trial.

I cannot describe the fear and panic instilled into Abby, my wife, and me. It was undoubtedly the worst experience of our lives. The kidnappers warned us not to contact the police but we could not deal with the kidnapping on our own. I contacted Police Chief Rupert. Rupert, while no admirer of this newspaper, acted totally professionally. He helped bring the desperate situation to a safe conclusion, appointing Officer Meg Letowski as liaison for my family. Officer Letowski was a calming influence, exactly what was needed. She was nothing less than brilliant.

It is well known that Mike Doyle and I were friends many years ago and in desperation, I turned to him for advice and help. Notwithstanding the opposition and criticism he and his colleagues have received from this newspaper, he accepted immediately that this was a personal matter. He set aside his feelings for me as a newspaperman and acted as an old friend. He used his many contacts to ensure Charlotte was rescued, virtually unharmed. Some sixteen hours after the kidnap, Mike Doyle himself returned Charlotte to Abby and me. The relief we and our family felt is beyond description.

Abby and I are glad to have the opportunity to thank the St. Luke Police Department for its professionalism and to single out and praise the actions of Chief Rupert and Officer Letowski. We are also pleased to acknowledge the invaluable part played by Mike Doyle and his associates in bringing our daughter back to us.

This newspaper will not retreat from its mission to explore and expose the wrongdoings we find in the public life of our city but today it acknowledges that nothing is black and white and that it is a mark of a good newspaper to keep an open mind about people and the institutions they serve.

David Driscoll, Editor-in-Chief.

Typical of Doyle, he arrived a little early on Saturday night, dressed to the nines, carrying gifts as if it was Christmas. His double-breasted suit was cut impeccably. When I remarked on it, he replied, "Brooks Brothers, only the best."

Jane was staying with friends for the night. "I have no wish to see or be polite to that low life," was her parting shot.

I introduced my children to him.

"Who's that?" Doyle asked them, pointing at me.

"Daddy," they both shrieked.

"No, it isn't."

"It is, it is, it is!" was Lottie's reply.

"I'll tell you who this is. This is Books."

"Who's Books?" asked Louis.

"Him," said Doyle pointing at me again.

"That's Daddy," insisted Lottie, speaking a little too loudly for her mother's liking. Abby appeared and smiled at Doyle.

"Hello, Mike," she said, miming "thank you."

"Abby, good to see you. I have these for you." He handed her a bouquet of flowers and a huge box of chocolates. "And Louis and Charlotte, these are for you." Louis unwrapped his present. It was a model train. Charlotte had been given a doll. Both looked at Doyle in astonishment.

"What do you two say to Mr. Doyle?" asked Abby. Both gave him a very loud "Thank you." Charlotte went to him and gave him a kiss on the cheek.

"Why did you call Daddy 'Books'?" asked Louis.

"When I first met your daddy, a long, long time ago, he always had his nose in a book."

"Why did you nose your book, Daddy?" asked Lottie. Why didn't you read it?"

"Nose in a book means reading," I answered.

"That's funny," said Lottie, "my daddy's a nose book."

"Thanks, Irish," I admonished Doyle. "Now look what you've started."

Abby told the children it was bedtime. They asked to stay up for a while to be with Doyle. Abby relented and they played for ten minutes more. Then I took them both upstairs and read to them, leaving Doyle to talk with Abby. When I came down, a bottle of red wine had been opened, another gift from Doyle. Typically he had brought a whole case with him.

"It's Californian." I'd forgotten he knew quite a bit about wine. "Did you know that in the 1890s, all the vines in the Bordeaux and Burgundy regions of France became diseased and had to be destroyed? Californian vines were used to get the French wines started again and now the French are so snobbish about their wine that they turn their noses up at ours. I often wonder why I bothered to go to France to fight for them! Can you believe that was nearly twenty years ago?"

Through dinner, we talked about nothing in particular. Small talk now came naturally to us. It was easy and comfortable. Abby asked if we wanted coffee. I said I would make it. It freed Abby to leave us and go up to bed. She was still tired after the kidnapping. She gave Doyle a hug, me a kiss and said goodnight.

After she left, Doyle suggested we talk and do the dishes at the same time. I liked that he still had no airs and graces, despite the style in which he supposedly lived.

"So," he said, "looks like the family is back to normal already."

"I hope so. I can't predict if there will be a backlash. Lottie seems unaffected."

"That was quite an article you published on Thursday. My people were pretty surprised. Did it hurt to write it?" he grinned.

"Like you wouldn't believe! I'm wondering if my staff will speak to me ever again."

He laughed. "It was big of you."

"And you, too. Abby and I are very grateful."

We talked a little of the old days as we finished the dishes. I fixed coffee. "I have a good malt whisky, Mike. Fancy a glass?" He nodded his assent. I put the coffee and cups, as well as the bottle and two glasses, onto a tray and took the tray into my study. We sat and toasted each other.

"Shall we get to it?" I asked.

"Why not?"

"How do you see us bridging our divide?"

"Maybe by your accepting some reality in city life these days."

"Hundreds of your people were convicted of election crimes, some quite serious."

"You're right. What makes you think that Gann or I or any of the leadership sanctioned what happened? That is simply not how it works. All our party and ward workers were called into meetings at the beginning of the year. They were told loud and clear that we wanted to win and jobs depended on it but we wanted a fair election. These people interpreted what we said as, "Win at all costs." The party workers in the wards are as ambitious as anyone. They think the more people they register, the more votes they get out, the bigger the victory, the better it is for them as individuals. They equate good results leading to a win as the road to promotion, more money and better life chances. For them, the end justifies the means. Machine life is very competitive."

"Mike, this might explain what happened, but it doesn't excuse it. You have twenty of your people in prison for crimes of intimidation and violence. Not only that, if I might remind you, two years ago I became a victim of your election practices."

"You can't think I had anything to do with that! Rupert couldn't find out who did it but Torino did. We settled it our way. I knew you wouldn't approve. You would have wanted a trial, but that is not how it happens in our world. Trust me, the people who hurt you have been punished severely."

I dreaded to think what happened to my attackers. I felt sick to my stomach. I doubted my attackers were still alive. I didn't want to be responsible for this, but it was too late. How could Doyle be so matter-of-fact?

"With all your election tactics, you leave no room for doubt as to who will be elected. The Founding Fathers would say that you have stolen the voters' birthright."

"If the Founding Fathers were so worried about city elections, why didn't they cover the rules in the Constitution? Why wasn't something added to the Bill of Rights? I'll tell you why. It didn't bother them. They were content to let the people sort out their own local affairs. As for birthright, let's look at this a little more carefully. Where does it say in the Bill of Rights that one man has one vote? What an omission that was! And how long did women have to wait to get the vote? Our Constitution is hardly a model of perfection. You know it got cobbled together in horse trades."

"Mike, in real terms I don't have a vote in my city election. Your people counter it with ghost voters. How is that right?"

"Tell me, are our streets clean? Is there a policeman on the beat regularly in your neighborhood? Do the sewers work okay? Have you or your family caught a disease through poor health management? Are the franchises priced so unreasonably that you can't use public transport? In other words, do you get the bang for your buck? The services you pay for, are they value for money? If you're honest, you'll say yes.

"This week and two years ago apart, have you personally been exposed to crime? Have you ever been a victim of organized crime? No. In other words, city government here in St. Luke works and it works well."

Doyle made good points. "I accept services seem to be provided well. However, I have received indications that city finances are in a mess. Every year, Tom Berman says the books balance, but the council has never permitted proper scrutiny."

"Personally, I'm not hiding anything. But this is one question you'd have to ask Gann and Berman direct. Get a court order if you want."

"You got pretty upset a few years ago when I was ready to expose the road contracts scandal."

"That was business. I had the inside track on city contracts. What's wrong with that?"

"The contracts should have been put out to tender. That's the proper process. Also, the contracts were overpriced. It was graft at the tax-payer's expense."

"Okay, let's say a tender came in at a lower price. What guarantee would you have got that the cement would have been the right quality or that the works would have been done right? None. With me it's different. How are those roads I built holding up, by the way? What I built passes muster. There was trouble with two of them last winter. I fixed the problems, free of charge I might add."

"I'm not surprised you didn't charge. Look at the vig you got from all those contracts. What do you do with all the money you get, courtesy of the tax-payer?"

"For starters, 340 sets of legal fees, 310 fines, 20 salaries for no work. We look after our own."

"Hopefully that will be a one-off. But you and the machine have taken millions of dollars from the system. Where did the money go?"

"Every two years, we have elections to pay for. There's no government funding."

"And every two years, you tithe all city employees to help defray the election costs, let alone the amounts you force out of business towards campaign funds."

Doyle paused for a moment and grinned at me. "Remember the politician's prayer. 'Lord, give me health and strength to get me through the day. I'll steal the rest.' Look at the money spent getting jobs for people, feeding and housing them, getting clothes for them to wear, covering medical and legal bills. It doesn't come cheap. Since 1930, the pressure on my organization has been enormous. The city helped a bit but where has the state helped? I've kept unemployment low, so low that you can't point to another machine-run city where the figures are better."

"Granted, you provide the jobs, but you don't pay for them. The tax-payer pays men who go on the city payroll. The jobs you find in corporations are paid for by the corporations."

"I pay for some."

"How many?"

"I don't know, I'd need to check."

"Where does the money go, Mike?"

"I told you, I provide welfare."

"Food is not that expensive, even on the scale that you provide it. I know you organize a Christmas dinner for thousands, but I also know that your lieutenants and captains and the restaurants cover most of the cost. As for clothing, you get some from The Salvation Army and church charities, pretty well free of charge.

"Face it, Mike, you run an expensive personal life. You have a big house to maintain, servants to pay for and a lifestyle that would be the envy of all but it still doesn't explain where you spend all your loot."

"That subject's closed, David. I don't see how this helps us."

"Okay, let's accept you're a modern philanthropist, a new breed of Robin Hood. The truth is you give to the rich."

"How so?"

"Franchises for wealthy corporations. There's a bus monopoly in St. Luke. The city receives a comparatively small annual sum in

314

exchange. The bus company charges twenty per cent more for fares than other bus companies in other Midwest cities. Can you tell me, honestly, you don't get a kickback?"

"I am paid a brokerage fee by the bus company, I admit that."

"But you act for the city. How can you take from both sides?"

"Is it against the law?"

"No, it isn't, but it's wrong, it's unethical."

"I can tell you, I break no laws. So what have I actually done wrong? If the voters don't like this sort of thing, air it, debate it and let's see if the law is changed. If this sort of thing is made illegal, I won't do it."

"Mike, the argument is circular. You control the City Council and the executive, not to mention the judges. How could the law be changed? You'd prevent it if it was against your personal interests."

"Then take it to state level. You'll find out how many others do business like me. David, you're a good guy but you are an idealist in a world run by pragmatists. Look at the way business is done in New York City, Boston, Philly, Minneapolis, Chicago, Cincinnati, Omaha, Los Angeles, San Francisco, Jersey City, Atlantic City, and any major metropolis in the USA. You will find it is done in exactly the same way that we do things here in St. Luke. And the people benefit from it. Maybe it is unethical, but will ethics put food on the table?"

"Is there organized crime in all those cities?"

"Yes, to some extent."

"And that's okay with you?"

"I kept my brothers' people out of St. Luke for as long as I could. You think fighting off the mob is easy? It was an unequal negotiation. They can do pretty well what they please, especially when the federal and state governments sit on their hands. What has the FBI ever done to help? Nothing! How do you expect a weak city government to fight the mob?"

"Strengthen our police."

Doyle laughed. "Get serious. Assume we trebled the St. Luke PD and that all new police people were completely honest. How long would it take to train them properly? At least two years. Look at the increased cost. I doubt the tax-payer would be happy to foot the bill, especially as the Police Department would need new buildings, more police cars and a much bigger bureaucracy. And when all of this is achieved, what makes you think the mob would not increase their numbers? As I think it through, I'm not sure this is even a state problem. It is a situation for the federal government to handle. Trouble is that the President has too much on his plate already and the FBI is just not interested. That guy Hoover says there's no such thing as organized crime. Can you believe it?

"So, Mr. Genius, what do we do about this? I'll tell you. We do a deal. You educated types would call it a Faustian bargain."

I had to laugh at that one. Doyle was as well-educated these days as anyone. He continued. "The mob sets up in agreed areas of town and controls criminal activities there. It makes sure that its protection is at a rate that business can afford. That protection is real. Other gangs are stopped from honing in. And you rely on your negotiating skills to hold the mob in check if and when things go wrong. You think I like this? Of course I don't. It's bad for business but when your back is stuck to the wall, what else can you do?"

We both fell silent. He was the supreme pragmatist. He worked all the angles. He had made a convincing case for those willing to sell their idealism for peace. I was not a seller.

"Mike, call me an idealist or whatever you like, but I know what's right and what's wrong. From your point of view, you believe in doing what you have to. I say that's wrong. I say you have to do the right thing. I don't see where we have a meeting point."

He sighed heavily. "It was worth a try. Are we back fighting on Monday?"

"I'm afraid so, but it's not personal. It never was."

"Really? Even after Jane? I felt very bad about that."

There was an awkward moment.

"As it's just you and me here, why did you do what you did to Jane? Why aren't you married with a family? I saw you with my kids."

Mike paused, gathering his thoughts. He held his glass out for another shot. "Are you willing to take it raw?"

I nodded.

"It goes back to my early days in St. Luke. Uncle Joe was no respecter of women and he taught me to kiss and run. Take what you want, and move on. There was a girl in France at the end of the war. Maybe if she had lived, I'd have been different. I know I have never felt so strongly about another woman since then. I think I would have given my life for her but this may be my memory playing tricks. Whatever, it's too late now."

We fell silent. I thought Doyle might have forgotten he had confided in me about Claudine. As usual, I underestimated him.

"One of the reasons I have time for you, Books, is that you keep your mouth shut, even when you might use confidential information to your advantage."

He paused again to gather his thoughts. "I was mad for Jane, but, suddenly, I felt nothing. There have been quite a few other women since. The relationships always end in tears. I can't stay the course. Maybe Claudine spoiled me. Now, I don't want to knock you off your throne, but I am not the only one in this room who has destroyed the women in his life. What about you?"

"What about me?"

"Adele was crazy for you. She was so in love with you and you spurned her."

"That is what she told you, but she was very mistaken and I've told you so. It was just physical between us. It couldn't have been anything else. We never spent any time together." I didn't want to dredge up old news, but I gathered my memories and related them to Mike, omitting the steamy details. "I liked Adele, I liked her very much, but I must tell you, our relationship was never anything deep and meaningful. It was about sex. I promised her nothing. I did not lead her on for one minute."

Doyle reached for the inside pocket of his jacket and produced an old-looking envelope which he passed to me. I opened it. The letter had no date. I didn't want to read it. I told Mike I'd read it later.

"David, I was given this in 1930, after her funeral."

"Adele is dead? I had no idea."

"She took her own life."

I just stared at Mike. I was lost for words. That beautiful girl was more troubled than I had ever realized.

"Do you blame me, Mike?"

"I did when I read the letter. Impossible relationships, eh? So now, what do we do, you and me?"

"We go on until one of us falls. It's just business, Mike."

"Shall we keep lines of communication open?"

"I'd like to on a personal level, but it will be too difficult. However, if there is anything I can do for you, I will try my best to do it. Before you go, there's something else I want to ask you. It's private."

"Fire away."

"The Dementia Foundation. After the new ward opened at St. Luke General, I spiked a story about you."

"Hmm."

"The story said you were the mystery donor who had put money into the project and towards a research department at Chicago University."

"Why did you spike it?"

"Our reporter was told you wanted to be anonymous. I respected your wishes."

"So?"

"I'm curious. You did a good thing, a very good thing. Why keep it secret?"

"That's easy. That money was, shall we say, a little tarnished. It came from the cement business. Had anyone investigated, the story you would have found wouldn't have been about dementia. Getting something done for sick people was far more important to me."

"Michael Doyle, you are a strange man. You have so much potential for good. Why don't you pursue it?"

Doyle laughed until he cried. "Why don't you stop trying to change me?"

"Oh, I'm not going to change you. Did you know we keep an 'I Like Mike' file at *The Bugle?* It's for those letters you had sent."

Mike smiled at me. "I'm sure I don't know what you mean."

"Let me read one to you." I grabbed a sheet of paper from my desk.

Dear Mr. Editor,

Your paper should stop saying bad things about Mr. Doyle. The bank took my Otto's farm away last year and everything with it. We were left with nothing except the clothes we stood up in. When we got to St. Luke, Otto went to Mr. Doyle. He got him a job in a factory, found us a place to live and gave food for our kids and us. Without his help, I don't know how we live.

Yours, Mrs. Otto Raben.

318

Mike kept smiling. "I didn't see any letters published in your rag. Too scared, eh?"

"You really didn't think you'd catch us out with those fake letters, did you? I guess we know each other too well. But I meant what I said. If there's anything I can do for you, you let me know."

"That's fair." We shook hands and he left.

Alone, I opened Adele's letter.

Dear David,
I saw you last week with your beautiful wife. I wish you happiness. I now realize there is no hope for me. I loved you so. I don't think I can go on.
Your Adele.

I sat for a while, shocked to my core. I understood Doyle better now. Abby was still awake when I went upstairs. "I couldn't sleep until he left," she told me.

"Were you listening?" I asked.

"No, of course not. I just wanted to be here when you came to bed in case you wanted to talk."

I smiled at my beautiful wife. Suddenly, I felt exhausted. "Not really. My friendship with Mike can never be revived. One of us would have to give up our way of life first."

I said nothing about Adele. Some things are best kept secret.

Chapter Twenty-Nine

In July, 1937, I received a handwritten note from President Roosevelt. "Are you coming through Washington this summer? I have something I want to discuss with you."

Abby and I were due to head for Richmond with the children. It would be good for them to see the nation's capital and to show them the sights. I replied saying it would be a privilege to see him whenever he wished. He cabled a reply inviting me for the 17th July and to "bring the family." So, we got into our 1936 blue Chevrolet Sedan and spent the next two days journeying from St. Luke. The children had been on train trips before, but not a long road trip. Abby kept them amused, playing word games like I Spy and reading to them, while I kept the car on the road.

Late on the 16th July, we reached our Washington destination. I had booked us into a suite at the Hay-Adams Hotel in Lafayette Square, across from the White House.

I was expected at the White House at ten in the morning. I was sure to have us arrive on time. We were kept waiting for only a few minutes before Mrs. Roosevelt came out to greet us. She was wonderful with the children. She offered them a cold drink and took us to the private quarters. Mrs. Roosevelt told Abby and me not to worry, there were plenty of things for them to play with, that FDR knew we were here and would see us soon.

A minute or two later, an aide came to escort Abby and me down to the Oval Office. There, the French doors were open and I looked out onto the Rose Garden. In the distance, we could see a game of what appeared to be hide and seek, where Mrs. Roosevelt was now entertaining six or seven children including our two. "It's what she loves best," boomed the familiar voice. FDR sat behind a large desk.

"How are you David?" he asked offering his hand. "And this must be the famous Abby. I have heard much about you." The twinkle in his eye would not have been missed at one hundred paces.

"Mr. President, good to see you. Yes, this is my infinitely better half. Abby is a very big fan, so if she gets tongue-tied, it's your fault."

He laughed. Abby nudged me in the ribs with her elbow.

I went on, "I hope you and the Vice President are recovering from baiting Supreme Court Justices." The Supremes had been a thorn in FDR's side, striking down much of his first New Deal program. FDR fought back, attempting to pack the Supreme Court by adding shadow justices, who he knew would approve his revised New Deal legislation. To FDR's shock, a large Democratic majority in Congress rebelled at the idea of increasing the numbers on the Court and voted the plan down. FDR didn't take the beating lightly, but just the threat had its desired effect. The Court had recently changed direction and was now upholding New Deal legislation.

"Looks like it. It was quite a blow, but we have to move on. Do you like the phrase, 'Rendezvous with destiny'? I'm working on a speech about political and economic freedom and how we need to fight the forces that seek to prevent many Americans from enjoying the rights envisaged by the Founding Fathers. What do you think?"

"I'm sure that whatever you and the speech writers come up with will be perfect."

"Ever the diplomat. What's happened to 'truth to power' Driscoll?"

"Still there, Mr. President. My ideals may have been shaken a bit by erosion of time, but I still adhere to them."

FDR addressed Abby. "Do you know he turned down a job with me?"

"I do, Mr. President."

"Did he do the right thing?"

"I couldn't say, but he has nearly always done the right thing by me."

"Now, I need to spend a little time with our man. Is that alright with you, Mrs. Driscoll?"

"Mr. President," I interjected, "if it's okay with you, I'm happy for Abby to stay and listen. She's a huge help to me. Oh, did you know she is Dr Driscoll? She has a Ph.D."

"No, I didn't know that. I'll have to execute a member of staff for poor intelligence work."

"Seems a tad harsh," said Abby.

"*Pour encouragez les autres*," was the President's quick riposte. Then his mood changed perceptibly. "I want to talk to you about a man called Michael Doyle. I assume you know him?"

"Yes, sir."

"Your state Governor, Sam Richardson, and I go back a long way. Sam tells me this Doyle fellow and his machine are really bad news. I know we have to put up with political bosses in the cities, but some of these fellows like Pendergast, Hague and Doyle give us Democrats a very bad name. Sam says Doyle has been too clever for his own good. Confidentially, my people tell me he's up to his ears in a state insurance scam, has stolen millions that rightfully belong to the tax-payer and hasn't bothered to declare his ill-gotten gains to the IRS. My Treasury Department is preparing a case against him. It's not ready yet. Treasury needs a month or two more.

"My people also say it's in the interests of the Party to start something in the local press to put Doyle in a very bad light, to hint at what a huge cheat this Doyle fellow is. As we're old friends, I thought I'd ask if you would do this for us?"

"I can't see why not, Mr. President. I have been exposing the excesses of the Doyle machine in *The Bugle* for years. But I can't do it in the interests of Party. It's in the interests of St. Luke and its tax-payers."

"Yes. You're right. One of my aides will brief you on the details. From what I've been told, Doyle has cheated people in your state on a huge scale. He has to be stopped."

"Mr. President. I will look at this very seriously. However, you should know that Doyle and I have a long history and that Abby and I are in his debt personally."

I explained the circumstances of the kidnap. FDR feigned horror but I'm sure he knew already.

"Is that her?" he asked, pointing down the garden. The effervescent Lottie was unmistakable.

Abby replied, "Yes, that's Charlotte. I'd better relieve Mrs. Roosevelt. Mr. President, it has been a huge pleasure and honor to meet you." Abby shook his hand and left.

FDR stared at me. "Do you know how lucky you are? If I didn't already have the best job in the world, I'd want yours, along with your family." He rang a buzzer. An aide came in. "Please take Mr. Driscoll to Atkins." We shook hands.

"Thank you and good luck with everything, Mr. President."

Henry Atkins was in his late fifties. He had long, brown hair with salt and pepper flecks. His patrician air came from being a member of FDR's New York State Brains Trust. He was a Yale graduate, independently wealthy and a complete whiz with figures. Emily Venn would have felt at home with him. He was charm personified.

"Mr. Driscoll, how good to meet you. I know you are here with your family. Is this a good time? I can meet you later, whenever you wish. I don't want to inconvenience you."

"Mr. Atkins, I am at your service and that of the President. My wife will not be shy about coming forward if she thinks we have outstayed our welcome. There is just one thing. Please, call me David."

"Certainly, so long as you call me Henry."

Atkins told me about the latest Doyle scam.

"There is an insurance syndicate who insure most of the city buildings in St. Luke, amongst other cities and towns of the state. The syndicate also covers other public risks. The premiums are in the tens of millions of dollars and the syndicate has a reputation for overcharging. In 1924, a legal case was brought against them because they had overcharged the state and therefore the taxpayers. Millions of dollars were involved. The wrong-doing was found out and the taxpayers got a lot of their money back. However, when the same thing happened a few years later, the legal action against the syndicate was stopped, to everyone's surprise. Instead of the taxpayers getting their money back, there was a quiet, unofficial settlement out of court, seemingly to the heavy disadvantage of the taxpayers of your state.

"My people in your state strongly suspect Doyle's involvement. They can't prove anything. We want you to check out Doyle and Charlie Brooks as well – he's the boss of Perpetual. He chairs the syndicate and seems pivotal to all this. I'm sure you know who he is." I nodded. "I don't have to tell you how badly we want to nail those guys, this could be our one and only chance. They give the party such a bad name."

There was a knock at the door. Henry called, "Come in," and Abby's face appeared.

"I am sorry, David. I need to take the children back to the hotel. They ought to have a nap. Will you be long?"

"Henry," I said, "may I introduce my wife, Abby. Abby meet Henry Atkins."

Abby asked Henry to forgive her intrusion. Ever the gentleman, he apologized for keeping me. "Mrs. Driscoll, I need just a few minutes more with your husband, if this is alright with you?"

Abby smiled at Henry, saying, "Of course."

Away from Henry's line of sight, Abby gave me a look that made me believe my conjugal rights were over for a very long time if I didn't get out of the room very quickly. After she left, Henry continued.

"I have a detailed brief for you, if you accept the assignment. Governor Richardson smelled a huge rat and tried to block the settlement deal. He ran up against your state Constitution and separation of powers. One branch of government can't impede another. He tried to get De Witt Souter, the State Insurance Commissioner, investigated by the State Congress but the Doyle Democrats blocked the move."

"I got wind of this a while back. Our chief political reporter couldn't find out what it was about."

"Well, now you know. The Governor is hopping mad and spoke with the President. The President cannot have this sort of thing on his agenda. As we say in D.C., it's too far below his pay grade. So this is why I am here with you. Your newspaper has crusaded against the Doyle machine. *The Bugle* has a heck of a reputation for good reporting and clean business and the President knows you."

"What do you want me to do, Henry?"

"I guess effectively work for the federal government, the IRS and nail whoever is behind this lousy deal. You're on the spot. We are almost certain that pressure to make the deal came out of the St. Luke machine."

"Henry, I'm sorry. I can't do what you ask, work directly for the government. I run an independent newspaper. Independence means my people and I are free from intrusion by government. However, this is an intriguing story, one that I will resource and investigate. If I find any possible breach of federal law, I'll pass the information to the authorities."

"Fair enough. Any help you can give will be much appreciated. Now, I think you should go and make friends with your wife. Blame me for everything. Have a good holiday and please keep in touch when you get back. Here's the brief." He handed me a fat folder of papers. "Good to meet you."

"Likewise. I'll be in touch."

I went to find Abby, expecting the worst. Instead, I found her with Mrs. Roosevelt, watching the children. They were both laughing.

"Ah, here he is," said Mrs. Roosevelt. "It was lovely to meet you, Abby. Come see us again in the White House or at Hyde Park. I love talking literature. You take care of your family, young man."

"Yes, Mrs. Roosevelt."

We all got in the car. The children had been given toys and they started playing on the back seat, bubbling away to each other.

"Abby," I asked, "exactly how much trouble am I in?"

"I'm pondering but as we've eaten and you haven't, we'd better stop somewhere. There's a hot dog stand over there," she said pointing across the street. "You have five minutes. Then I want the children to have a nap and afterwards, you are to take us to see the Capitol and the Supreme Court. And you will explain their significance to the children in words they can understand. Then, we'll see."

"If this is the City of Eagles," I mumbled under my breath, "it's full of eagle-pecked men."

"I heard that."

Chapter Thirty

Henry's brief was detailed so far as insurance documents and court hearings were concerned but totally short on evidence linking Doyle or Brooks to any scam or fraud. My first impression was there was little *The Bugle* could do.

The Porter's Richmond garden was a great place to think and reflect. Huge magnolia and aspen trees provided protection from the summer heat. In the afternoons, when the children napped, I used it as a place to ponder, not just about the insurance case but the future. What did I want for *The Bugle,* my family, me? For once, the peace of Richmond failed to provide me with any clear answers.

In the years since taking over the newspaper, I had become wealthy. I had not anticipated what could be made from publishing, even in a depression. Abby and I still lived in the St. Luke house we had bought all those years ago. I had changed my car once or twice, but that was it. I was not materialistic, nor was Abby. I had created trust funds for the children, sufficient to support them through college and early adulthood. Abby and I had what was, by any normal standards, a pretty big bank balance.

We returned to St. Luke in August. One of the few luxuries Abby and I enjoyed was a subscription to the St. Luke Country Club, a swanky, stuck-up place for rich people who wanted to avoid mixing with the inferior classes and, heaven forefend, black people. This didn't stop the Club from employing black cooks, cleaners and waiters or from using the skills of blacks and poor whites as gardeners, caddies and green keepers on the Club's two 18-hole golf courses. Why did I join? Great facilities for the kids and a good entrée for me to meet the St. Luke elite.

It took until October 1937 and a member of the Club Committee, to give me the initial breakthrough on the insurance case. We had returned from Richmond in early September to get the children ready for school. One evening, I went to the Club for a routine committee meeting, where we were presented with the usual list of applications for membership. One of the hopefuls was former State Insurance Commissioner, De Witt Souter. On the surface, there was nothing unusual about his application. He was a well-respected state administrator, who had decided to move from Cameron to St. Luke to take up a new position with the city, as head of its water administration.

My fellow committee men and I knew a few things about Souter. He was 52 years old, with a wife three years younger and two sons, both in state college. He had done no charity work to speak of in Cameron and had made few donations to charity, giving only $500 or so in each of the past three years. His recorded yearly salary of $46,500 as a state administrator meant a take home pay of probably $37,500. With such a huge sum for those years, his charitable contributions seemed modest. To become a member of the Club, a man had to show he was "charitable" and had a net worth of $200,000, excluding his main house. Evidently Souter had satisfied the membership sub-committee on this latter point. In addition, I knew his name had come up in the investigation of the insurance scam.

It was not unusual for the main committee to defer a decision on a membership application until the following meeting, so comprehensive checks could be made. Two committee colleagues took this view on Souter's application without my having to say anything. They just wanted to make him feel as though he hadn't got in easily. As a body, we liked to act unanimously, so the members as a whole agreed to keep Souter under review until the November meeting.

That weekend, the weather was fine, although there was an autumnal chill. Abby suggested we use the Club's facilities to take the children swimming in the indoor swimming pool. Abby and I sat by the pool, watching the next generation of Driscolls splash as much water as they could on each other. I resisted joining them for all of sixty seconds. Soon we were playing 'do the laundry,' which consisted of my holding one of the children and twisting him or her around in the water, washing machine style, splashing myself and anyone else in the near vicinity.

Louis loved playing 'throw the football,' which meant he scrunched up with his bottom in the biceps of my arms, urging me to throw him as far as possible. Knowing that these games could end in tears, I tried to be gentle. Both children punished me for this.

After twenty minutes, drenched and exhausted, I got out of the pool. When I suggested to Abby that it was her turn to play with the children, she reminded me that "Ladies don't indulge in such things." So, to the delight of my children and onlookers, I picked her up and jumped in the pool with her. We dried off and changed clothes, prior to lunch at a dinette which the Club provided for children. By then, I was thinking longingly of the Club restaurant, which was one of the best in St. Luke. I could have murdered a steak. Instead we dined on hot dogs and hamburgers.

After lunch, Abby and I took the children back to the pool area, promising them that if they rested on loungers for half an hour, they could go back in the water. As the children settled, Charlie Brooks came over to me. I made a "Be quiet," gesture to him by putting my index finger vertically on my lips, got up and strolled over to a table near the bar.

"Sorry to bother you, David. Want a drink?"

"No thanks, Charlie. What can I do for you?"

"I'll just get myself a small whiskey." Charlie was now in his seventies, but he didn't look it. He was trim and fit but had lost most of his hair. I towered over him but so did most people. He more than made up for his lack of height with the importance of his job. The Perpetual Insurance Company was a force to be reckoned with throughout the Midwest states, and as chairman, Charlie wielded real power.

He sat down, sipped from his glass and came to the point. "Just a small thing. What happened with Souter's membership?"

I was on my guard. Charlie would know Souter well as the state's former Insurance Commissioner but why would he know Souter socially?

"Some of the committee wanted to defer till the next meeting. You know how it is."

"Sure. Can I rely on you to get it done soon? Favor to the guy, new in town and all that."

"I'll do my best."

Not one for small talk, Charlie saluted me with his glass and left. I went back to the family. The rest of the weekend passed quietly. On Monday, I called the Club Secretary, Hamilton Frost. I asked him to send me all the paperwork on the Souter application, not just the précis that I had seen already and to keep this between us. I had worked with Hamilton for a while and trusted him. When I read the Souter documents, I was surprised to find nothing on his net capital wealth, except a statement by Charlie Brooks to the effect that Souter was worth the required sum and that if this were proved to be an error, Brooks himself would stand guarantor for any shortfall. This was extraordinary, not to say unorthodox. Prospective members could not rely on third parties to establish net worth.

Hitherto, I had talked about the insurance case with people on my staff who knew about state matters. They told me nothing that I didn't already know. I decided it was time to involve the newspaper fully in the insurance scam. There had to be something to uncover. I knew in my bones that if Doyle was involved, villainy was axiomatic. But where should I start?

I asked Emily Venn to join me. In confidence, I related my meeting that summer with the federal government, omitting any reference to any names. I passed the briefing documents to her. "They're just background." I told Emily how I had previously engaged newspaper staff to pursue an investigation but they'd gotten nowhere. "I might have let the scam lie, had it not been for yesterday." I relayed the exchange that I'd had with Charlie Brooks. "I have no doubt that there is something fishy going on here. I don't know what it is, but I want to know. So, I am asking you to become a financial detective and see what you can dig up. Are you interested?"

Emily looked at me, raising her eyebrows. "This story's outside my usual brief but I'd relish the chance to be a sleuth again. This has got Doyle written all over it."

"Maybe, but we don't work on guesses here. We need proof. Any ideas?"

"You've had this for months, me thirty seconds! I don't have any ideas. May I have some time, please?" Before I could reply, Emily added, "There's an old saying, 'Follow the money.' This could be the way through."

"There is no money trail," I replied. "That's the problem. If there had been a money trail, I'd have followed it. No one knows how much the out-of-court settlement was or where it went. All I have is that Henry told me to check out Charlie Brooks."

"And that's what is so interesting. You think like a newspaperman, I don't. Now, let me see if I have got it. Effectively, Charlie Brooks agreed to stand surety with the Club for Souter and the sum at stake would be $200,000?"

"That's right."

"Has Charlie, or any other member, agreed to do this before?"

"Not to my knowledge."

"So right there, the trail starts." Emily grinned at me. "Either Souter is due some money that Charlie knows about, or Souter has the money but can't show it."

"Which means what exactly?"

"I don't know. Just sit tight while I have a look around."

I didn't hear from Emily for two weeks. She telephoned me at home early one evening. She told me she had something worthwhile, that it was earth-shattering and that she needed to talk but not over the telephone. I asked her to meet me at the house after dinner. She arrived at eight-thirty. Abby greeted her warmly, fixed coffee and left us in the den.

"So what have you got?"

"The first thing I looked at was the filed accounts of the individual corporation members of the insurance syndicate covering St. Luke's public buildings and stuff. There were twenty-four member corporations in all. The only strange activity I could see was that each paid $75,000 in cash to The CB Corporation of Delaware."

"Why would each member of the syndicate make such a payment? And what was The CB Corporation of Delaware?"

"I have a friend who is an executive vice-president of one of the members of the syndicate. I spoke with him privately. I can't disclose his name. He told me that Charlie Brooks, as the syndicate leader, was given authority by syndicate members to negotiate an out of court settlement to compensate the state for being over-charged. A few weeks later, Brooks told syndicate members that he had found a broker who would guarantee an incredibly favorable settlement with the state commissioner, Souter, but that the broker's fee was a whopping $3.6 million. Furthermore, the payment was wanted in cash."

"I smell a rat."

"You certainly do. The syndicate baulked at these terms, of course, but the broker would not budge."

"Why didn't they just find another broker? Couldn't the syndicate revoke the authority they had given Brooks?" I asked.

"I don't know but I doubt it. Brooks is powerful. Furthermore, the only man who had sufficient influence and clout on this level with the state commissioner is Mike Doyle."

Emily continued. "Last year, it was agreed that half the broker's fee – $1.8 million would be paid to Charlie via his company, The CB Corporation of Delaware, who would release it to the broker after the settlement was concluded. The balance of $1.8 million would be paid a year later, provided there were no court proceedings challenging the settlement."

"Then what happened to the cash after it went into Brooks' account? Where does the trail lead?"

"Well, Charlie took his cut and passed the rest onto this broker but I can't prove it. If it was indeed paid in cash, there will be no trail."

"Okay, what else have you got on the CB Corporation?" I asked.

"I traced the corporation records to Delaware. I found out that our old friend, Mr. Pressman, formed it and the shareholders are Pressman and CB Enterprises. I also discovered that the bankers for the CB Corporation are here in St. Luke. I pulled a few strings."

"I'm sure you did," I smiled.

"Well, I am on good terms with one of their vice presidents. So, off the record, I'm reasonably sure I know what happened with the $1.8 million cash."

"Tell me."

"CB Enterprises belongs to Charlie Brooks. Pressman has nothing to do with it. CBE was formed over twenty years ago and holds investments for Charlie Brooks and his family."

"I almost feel sorry for Pressman, doing everyone else's bidding. What else has he been up to?"

"I checked which other corporations had been formed by Pressman in the past twelve months. One was the DWS Corporation. Pressman is the sole shareholder but for sure he'll hold those shares as a nominee. DWS is almost certainly De Witt Souter – the State Insurance Commissioner."

"An inside job."

"Brooks and our revered State Commissioner Souter have worked together in this deal. Souter had the power to sign off on the deal on behalf of the state and those insured. Somehow Brook's broker managed to get Souter to agree to a very small settlement."

"So how much did the taxpayers actually get back?"

"I don't have the exact figures yet. I'll get them soon enough, I expect. At a guess, they will have recovered some six million, when they should have got over twenty million.

"Emily, this is stunning work, really great. As ever, you exceed all my expectations. What I really can't understand is how the broker could have charged so much?"

"He got paid an enormous sum. Whoever the broker is, he wields real power and influence."

"Sounds like Doyle."

"In view of Pressman's involvement, need we look further than Doyle, especially as Souter has moved here and got a good city job, for which he doesn't seem particularly well qualified?"

"Maybe, but we have no proof at all of Doyle's involvement. The evidence is just circumstantial so far, all at arm's length and via shady businesses. How do we move forward on this?"

"I think Pressman might be involved in an illegal conspiracy. If he just formed the corporations and did nothing else, which I strongly suspect, then he can walk away clean, but if he was involved in the deal, he is a party to fraud. It won't do his practice any good to have a huge federal investigation. His reputation and his law practice would be badly damaged, if not destroyed."

"Not sure I like that. Those are the sort of tactics the machine uses. Anything else, Emily?"

"We can try the other side. If Doyle is the broker and has taken the money, he will be kicking back at least $200,000 to Souter. He should have paid Souter the first half already. We could try to find it. My guess is that Brooks has been paid off too. That payment will be harder to find."

"But Emily, the payoff, if there was one, was just enormous – preposterous." I was astonished at the discoveries.

"Doyle is reputed to be a very big gambler. Maybe he owed a lot of money. That would mean he owed the mob. You pay off those guys if you value your health.

It would explain the need for cash."

"Please keep digging. I also need you to think through what and when we tell the federal government. We should get our lawyer in. We seem to be headed into a criminal investigation and we must behave with caution, checking everything twice. Let's keep things confidential. I'd like to meet again no later than one week from tonight. Please bring that lawyer guy with you."

"That would be my husband?" asked Emily. She had married last year.

"It would indeed. It will be good to see him."

I showed Emily into the lounge to say goodnight to Abby. She was listening to a Brahms piano concerto on the radio and reading. She raised her head when she heard us. "Finished?" she asked.

"Yes, Emily is leaving." After they said their goodnights and left, I went back to the lounge.

"Listen, Abby, this business is highly confidential. Don't get upset but just this once, I can't tell you about it, at least not yet. I don't want to find myself giving evidence in court and being challenged about spreading rumors or talking out of turn."

"Don't worry. I understand, I think."

I kissed her cheek and returned to the den to tidy up. I needed to keep moving while thinking things through. Was Doyle so bored with life, so shallow, so worthless that he would rob the taxpayers of St. Luke only to spend the money betting on horses? Was it indeed taxpayers' money, wrongfully obtained? Questions led to more questions. I couldn't be certain about what answers would we find.

A week later, Emily came back to the house, accompanied by husband, James Rosenberg. After a brief exchange of pleasantries, I got the meeting started. "So, where are we?" I asked.

Emily started. "Bad news, good news, and very good news, I guess."

I looked inquiringly. "The bad news first, please?"

James answered. "The Pressman investigation is a negative. The court would throw it out. You'd just expose your hand."

333

"Okay, then there's good news?"

"Oh yes," said Emily. "The bankers who act for Charlie Brooks also act for Souter. I scared them into confirming, off the record, that $100,000 was transferred from the Commercial Bank of St. Luke into the DWS Corporation account, the one we think is Souter's company, shortly after funds were paid to the CB Corporation. My guess is Souter took out $5,000 in cash. The same bankers confirmed that Brooks himself transferred $300,000 into his personal account, on the same day. I conclude that Mr. Big, our broker, got his first payment of $1,400,000 the same day.

"So that accounts for the syndicate's first payment of $1.8 million," I said.

"There is a final piece of the jigsaw, the identity of Mr. Big," Emily continued. "I asked my banker friend if he knew who looked after Mr. Doyle's affairs these days. He gave me the name of the bank. Believe it or not, it's the same as ours. I suspect the $1,400,000 will have been paid in cash to Doyle. If we're right, Doyle did not make a deposit at his bank, but paid the cash out to his creditors. So, the real question is what is the state of Doyle's finances? So, I need you to talk to Edward North at the bank to get this information."

"I'll contact Edward tomorrow. Strictly, he shouldn't tell me anything, but I think I can get to him. Let's assume he confirms your hunch. What then?"

James Rosenberg came into the conversation. This was his turf. "Souter is the weakest link; he's out of his depth here. We should confront him and tell him we have evidence of a criminal conspiracy, which will be passed to the federal government. I suspect he'll want to tell his side early to seek immunity. Emily can take this one. I suggest I see Brooks and do the same thing. Once we know what each has said, we'll have to confront Doyle."

James continued, "Legally, there's no problem seeing Souter and Brooks. We know of no crime yet. If both confess, we have a problem as there will be evidence of a criminal conspiracy and we should inform the federal government and let them tackle Doyle. Of course, one or both of Souter and Brooks may stonewall. If they do, then you, Mr. Driscoll, have a decision to make on a, 'print and be damned,' basis. I think that's it in a nutshell."

I thanked them both. I felt an excitement that I used to get in my early days at *The Bugle.* I smelled blood. The next day, I went to see Edward North. He was an old fashioned banker. He had learned his trade from his father, as had his father from his grandfather. Edward's own son and grandson both worked for the bank, quite the family business. Edward asked what he could do for me.

"We've known each other a good few years now. I've never asked you to do anything unprofessional before, but I'm in a bind. May I speak to you in absolute confidence?"

I could see Edward was intrigued. I continued. "I believe one of your customers is involved in a criminal conspiracy to defraud the state, and some of our cities. My staff has put together a convincing portfolio of evidence, but we cannot find anything to pin the conspiracy on your customer because it is unlikely that any of the funds involved passed through his accounts."

"You mean he banks elsewhere as well?"

"No, Edward, he was paid in cash from a highly questionable, if not to say illicit, transaction."

"How much are we talking about?"

"$1,400,000." It was fun to watch Edward North go white.

"I see. I have a feeling I know the identity of the person you think was involved. Sadly, I can't help you. Client confidentiality and all that."

"Just so, Edward. However, may I put a hypothetical case to you?" North stroked his chin as he thought, "If you must."

"Say what I have described might actually have happened and that I suspected that the person concerned was running short of money. Would you be able to confirm or deny it, from a bank's perspective?"

Edward took his time. "Hypothetically, you would want to know if, for example, a buyer was being sought for a mansion in the city center. A property of that description might have been put up for sale quietly two months ago. I believe a sale might be concluded next week."

"What if that person had taken out loans, large loans, secured on the property?"

"Well, had that happened, the bank would be seeking repayment from the sale of that property. The bank would be secured by a mortgage or note."

"Edward, this is very helpful. Thank you."

"David, wait." North took a beat. "This is totally off the record. Mike Doyle's lost a fortune on the horses. He borrowed hugely and made larger and larger bets to chase his losses. His money's gone. And he's in a bind with the mob."

Back at *The Bugle,* I called my team together. I asked Ted Page to join us. I would need an experienced journalist to write the story, one who I trusted implicitly. I brought Ted up to speed and told the team it was time to put our plans into action. However, I was duty bound to let Henry Atkins know. Henry returned my call that night at home.

"Henry, can you get up to St. Luke quickly? I have something on the insurance case and Doyle. In fact, I'm almost ready to blow it open."

I could have taken us all to D.C., but I wanted Doyle to myself. I needed Henry on my turf to ensure I held all the cards. He came two days later, accompanied by Sheldon White III.

I assumed I would not like Sheldon White. I expected he came from an old family background, enjoyed a life of privilege and was serving his time in the Treasury Department until a seat in Congress opened up. How wrong I was. Henry filled me in. Sheldon was five years older than me, a graduate of the University of Wisconsin. He had served with honor in the Great War and had worked for the Midwest section of US Treasury since 1918. He was a solid citizen.

After introductions with my team were concluded, I chaired the meeting. Carefully, I took Henry and Sheldon through the steps we had taken, making sure to give credit to the team. Sheldon was sharp. His first question was whether Mr. Big was Doyle. If so, where was the proof? I took Sheldon through the main points of my meeting with Edward North.

"North doesn't bluff, nor would he give me a bum steer. My newspaper banks with him. To put me on the wrong track would cost him dear and he knows it."

Sheldon raised numerous questions of the team and eventually seemed happy with the responses. All that was left was to decide how to bring matters to a head.

"This is a matter for the federal government," said Sheldon who wanted to take charge. "We have conspiracy to defraud on a massive scale, federal income tax evasion and who knows what other charges."

I turned to Henry. "This is *The Bugle's* show. Without the people in this room, you would have nothing. We had a deal, the President, you and me."

Sheldon looked at Henry as if to say "What?"

I continued, "Let my people bring in the story. We'll hand it all to you on a plate. Anyway, I'm in a better position than you to get Doyle to talk." I know FDR had said no such thing but I needed to trump Mr. White. Henry realized what I was doing and I believe he saw fairness in my argument. We hammered out the details of how to proceed to avoid coming unstuck.

"The moon or bust, eh David?"

"Right, Henry. The moon or bust."

The next day, Ted made an appointment to meet De Witt Souter at his office. "You're the new Water Director. Our readers would like to know about you," was the line he used with Souter to get the interview. He agreed to see Ted at 2:00 p.m.

James Rosenberg also made an appointment for the same day and time with Charlie Brooks. "David Driscoll has asked me to run some ideas past you about insurance. I'd be happy to come to you after lunch. Would 2:00 p.m. be convenient?" Brooks agreed. If things went well with these two interviews, I would go to Doyle that night, unannounced.

Ted was ushered into Souter's office. Souter was wearing a smart, tailored, gray pinstripe, double-breasted suit. It was clearly expensive. His shirt was crisp white and his red tie was silk. He was clearly enjoying his new-found wealth.

"Mr. Page, good to meet you. I've long been a reader of *The Bugle*, a fine newspaper. Now, what can I tell you about me and my new job?"

"Not much, really, as I don't think you'll hold the job very long."

Souter started to splutter something, but Ted stopped him. "Mr. Souter, tomorrow's *Bugle* is running a story about you. I'm here to ask you if you would care to comment."

"What are you talking about?"

"When you were the State Insurance Commissioner, you were bribed by Michael Doyle and Charles Brooks to agree a settlement of the State Insurance premiums case, a settlement that was very favorable to the insurance syndicate. Our taxpayers, those taxpayers that buy our newspapers, really lost out."

"I did no such thing. I'm calling my lawyers. You should leave immediately."

Ted remained calm. "Are you sure? The story will say that Jerry Pressman formed a corporation for you. You and Pressman are its shareholders. The sum of $95,000 is in the DWS Corporation's bank account."

"So what? I don't have to account to you for private business matters."

"Shortly before that money was deposited, the syndicate members paid $1.8 million to a corporation controlled by Charles Brooks. Those funds were paid to that corporation within two days of the court approving the settlement you recommended. We will publish that if the settlement is not appealed within a year, you will receive a further $100,000. We also know that Brooks received treble the amount you did."

Souter reddened at this, but stayed silent.

"We know that Michael Doyle acted as broker for the deal, bringing the parties together. He was to be paid a total of $3.6 million for his services in two equal tranches. He has already kicked back $400,000 to you and Brooks with a further payment to you both of $400,000 a year later. This means Doyle will receive a total of $2.8 million. He has already got half of this sum. Do you want to deny any of these facts?" Ted was bluffing slightly, but it seemed to do the trick.

Souter said nothing. He looked deflated.

Ted spoke again. "Finally, we will report that you, Brooks and Doyle conspired to defraud the people of this state, the taxpayers and that you have not declared the secret payments for federal income tax purposes. We have it all. Once again, I'll give you an opportunity to respond."

Ted was deliberately harsh. He added for good measure, "Wouldn't it be a pity if you, the smallest cog, paid the biggest price? I have a Treasury agent who is waiting to talk to you." He then spoke softly. "You know, if you confess now and return the money, things may go easier for you. It will certainly be easier for your family."

At this, Souter broke down. There was no purpose in blustering. He knew the game was up. Ted stayed silent as he wept. Souter pulled himself together. He had been a man under enormous pressure, even before Michael Doyle approached him with the deal. The insurance litigation had aged him twenty years, he told Ted. He regretted very much accepting a bribe.

"Before Doyle and Brooks got to me, I had a career and a reputation. Now I have nothing. They made it seem so easy. I've been such a fool. Can I call my wife?"

Ted took Souter to Sheldon White and came back to talk with me. I felt no vindication when I was told what had happened.

James Rosenberg went to meet Charlie Brooks at the latter's offices. Brooks kept James waiting for twenty minutes. Brisk and business-like, Brooks took James into a meeting room. "Now, what does my good friend David Driscoll want? We go back a long way, you know."

"Mr. Brooks, tomorrow *The Bugle* will report that the settlement in the state insurance premiums case was fraudulent and that you were a major conspirator in the fraud. We have evidence that you received $1.8 million from syndicate members and that you paid $1,400,000 in cash to Michael Doyle and $100,000 to De Witt Souter. We know you kept $300,000 for yourself. We also know that if the settlement holds for a year, the three of you will get another set of identical payments."

"Is that it? Big deal. Is appointing a broker a crime in this state? Is sharing part of his fee for the work also a crime? I don't think so. Your boss is off his head. If he goes ahead and prints these slurs, he'll have a defamation action on his hands the likes of which he's never seen."

"Fine, Mr. Brooks. Actually, I didn't say these actions were criminal, although I bet your syndicate members don't know about your kickback. I'd say that was unethical. Where the crime occurs is that you didn't declare your kickback for federal income tax. Also, you conspired with Doyle to bribe Souter, a serious crime. Do you have a comment now?"

"Where's your evidence?"

"A paper trail through Delaware, Cameron and St. Luke and an eyewitness."

"Who?"

"De Witt Souter. He's speaking to a Treasury agent right now."

James hoped the bluff was not called. Brooks was a tough nut. He continued, "Mr. Brooks. I am an attorney. I suggest you call your lawyers and consider carefully with them your limited options. If you fight a criminal case, with the evidence we already have, you're bound to lose and you'll get a custodial sentence. If you confess, return the funds and turn state's evidence, things may go easier for you."

"Mr. Rosenberg, if you are right, and I make no admissions, I'm done for. So I'll be fighting. Some bank accounts and the confession of a criminal don't amount to much."

"As you wish, Mr. Brooks. I can't feel sorry for you. Strictly between you and me, why did you do it? You already have all the money you'd ever need in fifty lifetimes."

"Entirely off the record, and I'll deny I said anything, that's an easy one. Because I can."

James left, not knowing what Brooks would do. He felt uncomfortable.

The team, less Sheldon White, met in my office in the late afternoon to compare notes and brief me for the confrontation with Doyle. I had someone on staff watching Doyle's front door. He called me when he saw Doyle arrive home. I took a five-minute walk to the mansion. A butler opened the door.

"May I help you, sir?"

"I am David Driscoll. I would like to see Mr. Doyle."

"Do you have an appointment?"

"No."

Moments later, Doyle came to the lobby. Clearly, he had been drinking. "I know what you want. You're here to crow. I've had Souter crying down the phone. What a loser he is. Weak, weak."

"Doyle, let's sit somewhere?" He took me into a sitting room.

"Wanna drink?"

"No thanks."

He yelled a name and the butler entered. "Just bring the bottle and leave it."

Doyle glared at me. "So, you've finally got me, have you? I should have let that bully take your little marbles and beat you up all those years ago. I'm always bailing you out and what do I get for it?"

"Doyle, you're drunk. Please listen carefully. I am printing a story tomorrow."

"I know all about your precious story, Mr. *Bugle* man. Yes, I'm Mr. Big and yes, I did the state insurance premium deal. I didn't declare the money to the taxman. I've conspired with others. Blah, blah, blah. Naughty, naughty me! Do you think I'm bothered? I'm done for anyhow."

"What do you mean?"

"Your little stunt in '36 with all those prosecutions pretty well cleaned me out. I bet money I didn't have on the horses to get myself back on top. Well, that worked out nicely. I still owe the mob two million or so, the mob owns me forever, this house is up for sale and the bank has its hooks in and will take every cent the sale raises. I'm broke and I'm a dead man walking."

He slumped where he sat, seeming to shrink visibly. The name, "Mr. Big," was now so inappropriate. I watched the era of Mike Doyle crumple and end in disgrace before my eyes. I had fought this man for years and all I felt now was pity for him. There was nothing more for me here, yet I felt I owed him something.

"Mike, I truly regret what is to come for you."

"As if I give a rat's ass," was the pungent response. "Get out."

Henry Atkins kept his word and I had my scoop. *The Bugle* was the only newspaper to carry the story the next day. There were pictures of Doyle and Souter being taken into custody. Brooks had fled, but was discovered the next day at his estate above the Blue River. He had used a shotgun to take his own life.

Newspapers all over the country syndicated our story. It was quite a day for me. The editors of *The Los Angeles Times, The New York Times, The Washington Post* and *The Chicago Herald Tribune* all telephoned me. Lucas Vine called and we talked for quite a while. I even took a congratulatory call from the President. I should have felt triumphant, but I didn't. Later, Abby told me I had used every ounce of adrenalin to achieve an amazing result. Little wonder I felt spent.

One month later at their arraignments, both Doyle and Souter pleaded guilty to specimen charges of embezzlement, conspiracy to defraud and tax evasion. A week afterwards, Judge Nathan Scott sentenced Souter to four years imprisonment. Scott made it clear that, in his eyes, Souter was as much a victim as perpetrator, but that he must pay his debt to society. Two years of the sentence would be suspended on Souter's good behavior.

What was unexpected was the treatment of Doyle. Judge Scott looked Doyle in the eye as he gave his sentence. "This will not take long, Mr. Doyle. You have pleaded guilty to conspiracy to defraud and federal income tax evasion but you and I know you have done many other things to the detriment of our society. For too many years, Mr. Doyle, you have run this city as your personal fiefdom. You have associated with organized crime when the local Democratic Party should have fought against it. You have bled this city of the funds it needs to help its citizens, justifying your acts by dispensing favors as and when you felt like it. Your corruption of our elections is well known and well documented in the 1936 convictions of many of your people. You have hidden behind those very people and laughed at the good citizens of St. Luke. You have been a dictator.

"Well, this ends today. I cannot sentence you for those crimes I believe you have committed but I can sentence you for those to which you have confessed. Your counsel pleaded in mitigation that your crimes are victimless crimes and individuals were not hurt. His argument is specious. Had you not intervened in the insurance case, I believe that almost $25 million would have been returned to the taxpayers of this state and the several cities who contributed to the premium payments. Even if, individually, the sum involved amounted to just five dollars for each taxpayer, you and your co-conspirators stole it from them. In these terrible days of economic depression, your conduct is all the more appalling.

"I will prepare a brief for the state attorney general to take legal action against the insurance syndicate so that the settlement you brokered is set aside, as well as seeking a restitution of funds order. I will also recommend the attorney general seeks compensation from you, Souter and the estate of the late Charles Brooks to repay the illegal commissions you stole.

"I now send a message to anyone considering taking the same criminal road as you have done. I sentence you to the maximum term, twenty years imprisonment with no remission, the first ten years with

342

hard labor. Had Brooks been before me today, he would have received the same sentence. Take him away."

There were audible gasps in the court. I lip-read Doyle's attorney lips as he told his client, "We'll appeal". The Treasury people grinned their heads off. This was a big, big win.

The state commenced litigation to set the insurance settlement aside. The syndicate didn't fight. A split of 80-20, in favor of the insured parties was quickly agreed. The state recovered all costs. There was an additional settlement provision. Perpetual Insurance, the lead member of the syndicate, agreed to pay extra compensation of $5 million to cover loss of interest and general damages and accepted a five-year ban from writing state business.

I was asked for interviews as, "the crusading journalist," but refused. I was not bigger than the story and anyway, the credit belonged to my team who were happy to celebrate. And why not? They had earned it. They didn't have the history and the Doyle baggage I carried.

The St. Luke Democrats had been badly damaged. Gann and his slate lost in the 1938 election, as a new breed of Democrats emerged, promising to right the wrongs of the machine. The majority of St. Luke people, still loyal to the Democratic Party, voted the new breed in. For their first term in office, there was a lot of housekeeping and the administration seemed clean but I had observed local politics for too long to believe that corruption wouldn't set in.

During the war years, I remained editor-in-chief at *The Bugle* as Abby and I watched the children grow. I concentrated on the national scene and the war effort, leaving day-to-day affairs in the hands of the now very experienced team, headed by Peter Garibaldi. Soon, he would be my successor.

Chapter Thirty-One

The last hour of the drive from Riverton to St. Luke was spent in silence. I think Mike was feigning sleep. I could understand why he didn't want to talk to me. When we reached the outskirts of St. Luke, I nudged him.

"Almost there, Mike."

He grunted as if he was waking from a deep sleep. "Drop me off in The Trench."

"Sure." I drove through downtown and made my way to the poorest part of town. "Anywhere in particular?"

"Yeah. Somewhere I can get a drink."

I parked outside what used to be called The Donegal. It was now called Bart's. "Let me buy you a drink, Mike, for old time's sake."

Doyle shrugged his shoulders, got out of the car and walked into the bar without waiting for me. I followed him and entered in time to hear him say, "Bourbon, the bottle and two glasses."

I paid. We sat at a booth. "Should you be drinking like this in your condition?"

"Oh, Mr. High and Mighty Newspaper Man, what condition is that?"

"Mike, I know why you got an early release. You have a serious heart problem."

"Indeed, I have an infected and damaged heart valve and it's inoperable. The medics have given me three to six months if I'm careful. So I suggest you shut up about it and let me drink."

"Okay, where will you stay?"

"I have a bolt-hole. It's the apartment Joe moved my family into when we arrived in St. Luke. Before I left jail, I arranged with Berman to have the tenants moved out and the place cleaned up. Years ago, I stashed a little cash away as 'fuck you' money for emergencies. Berman has been a good friend. He took care of the details."

Mike raised his glass. "A toast, clogs to clogs in one generation! Drink up."

We sat in silence until I asked, "Penny for them, Mike?"

He laughed. "I was thinking of the women. Those two whores who took my virginity down the hall and Claudine. Do you remember Miss King?"

I looked blank.

"You remember," Mike continued with sadness in his voice, "our teacher in Rawlings. I was nuts about her. Do you ever think what might have happened to us if we hadn't been friends all those years ago?"

We sat in silence again. "Driscoll, you have been the bane of my life. You ruined me. Somehow I'll pay you back."

"Come on Mike, you ruined you, not me. And you know it. Look at you now. You know you shouldn't drink, yet you have a bottle of Jack Daniels you're emptying pretty well on your own. At least be honest with yourself."

Mike Doyle turned his back on me. It was the last time I saw him alive. He died from a heart attack later that week.

Epilogue

For days, I felt empty. Doyle had played such a huge part in my life and now he was gone. There were times in the early days when I distrusted him and for many years I hated his guts, so why did I feel like this, so alone?

It was Abby, of course, who spoke sense to me. "You're not alone. You have the children, Jane, my family and me. All of us love you and rely on you. You have good friends, people at *The Bugle,* editors and politicians all around the country that like and respect what you stand for. Heavens, you can reach the President if you want.

"What you're feeling is remorse for what might have been. Doyle was not all bad. He had good in him, God knows, but he always let his demons get the better of his angels. That's not your fault. You can blame his upbringing, his uncle, all sorts but not you."

Not for the first time, I remembered how was extremely lucky I was that Abby had asked me to marry her all those years ago.

THE END

Smoking Gun

By

J.S. Matlin

Successful journalist, David Driscoll, leaves a comfortable life in New York and Washington D.C. to rescue a North Carolina newspaper, *The Durham Monitor* whose former owner, tobacco baron Jeremiah Burns, purposely drove it into virtual bankruptcy. Driscoll discovers Burns' action was in revenge against a bank which had driven Burns' brother into bankruptcy and suicide.

Shortly after taking charge, Driscoll uncovers a story about fraud by Burns' nephew. *The Monitor* runs the story and the newspaper's circulation improves. Animosity between Driscoll and Burns escalates but Burns sees Driscoll's potential usefulness and tries to lure him into a world of Southern political and industrial cronyism. Driscoll will not be threatened or coerced. He keeps Burns at arm's length.

Driscoll finds himself unpeeling an onion as he uncovers more and more unsavoury events in the Southern way of life. When Driscoll's teenage son is hospitalised with alcohol poisoning, efforts at *The Monitor* to move on Burns are put on hold. Driscoll upsets Burns when *The Monitor* takes the side of the workers in a strike at the Burns factories.

Driscoll discovers a strong link between Burns and the murders of a black family. With the help of a US senator, Driscoll exposes not only the link between Burns and the multiple murders, but also a massive fraud committed by Burns' people over military supply contracts.

Corruption, racism, political favours, murder and the dirty underside of post-World War II Southern wealth and power is exposed. When it comes to the good-ol'-boy network, there are no holds barred.